ONE POLICE PLAZA

ONE
POLICE
PLAZA

WILLIAM J.
CAUNITZ

CROWN PUBLISHERS, INC.
NEW YORK

Copyright © 1984 by William J. Caunitz

All rights reserved. No part of this book may be reproduced

or transmitted in any form or by any means,

electronic or mechanical, including photocopying, recording,

or by any information storage and retrieval system,

without permission in writing from the publisher.

Published by Crown Publishers, Inc.,

One Park Avenue, New York, New York 10016

and simultaneously in Canada by General Publishing Company Limited

Manufactured in the United States of America

Library of Congress Cataloging in Publication Data

Caunitz, William J.

One Police Plaza

I. Title.

PS3553.A94505   1984   813'.54   83-14323

ISBN 0-517-55029-6

Book design by Camilla Filancia

10 9 8 7 6 5 4 3 2 1

First Edition

For my daughters

B E T H   A N N   *and*   T A F F Y

I wish to thank the following people for their editorial help and patience. Without them *One Police Plaza* would have remained an unfulfilled dream. Knox Burger and Kitty Sprague, Marion Wheeler, Martin Cruz Smith, Martin Sanders, Zena Intze-Kostos, Carol Kushner, Bridgette Faul, James O'Shea Wade, Laura Knight, Dr. Patricia Simpson, William E. Farrell.

I acknowledge a special debt to Tony Godwin, who pointed me in the right direction, and to the men and women of New York's finest, who gave these pages life.

O N E   P O L I C E   P L A Z A

1

TUESDAY, *June 9*

His body sprawled over the rumpled sheets, legs sticking over the end of the bed. He opened his eyes, attempting to focus them on the telephone.

"Lieutenant, we got a little problem. Can you come in to the Squad?"

"I'm on the way." Malone grunted, fumbling the receiver back, and sitting up. He glanced down at the vacant pillow next to him and remembered that she had not wanted to stay the night. The shrunken blood vessels inside his head were throbbing from last night's retirement party. He looked over at the digital clock on the wicker night table. It clicked over to nine-sixteen. Only the Job would get a man with a hangover out of bed on his day off. "A little problem," he muttered and got out of bed.

Dan Malone made the turn into Elizabeth Street twenty minutes later. Every time he came on the Job he expected to find something changed. But the usual Chinese women in their black pajamas and straw sandals were still shuffling along, accompanied by their daughters in designer jeans. Eternally bored men leaned against doorways, cigarettes hanging from their mouths. Nat Hymowitz's clothing store on the corner of Elizabeth and Hester was open for the early-morning hondling.

Malone loved the smells of Chinatown best: the confection of fresh ginger and Chinese cabbage and onions never failed to give him a high; each season of the year had its own distinct mixture. It was June and the smells swept gently over the neighborhood. He parked at the fire hydrant in front of the Sun Hong Wu restaurant, grabbed the vehicle identification plate from behind the visor, and tossed it onto the dashboard. Across the street was the hundred-year-old yellow cream stationhouse with the black fire escapes arranged down the center of its four-story façade. Nineteen Elizabeth Street: the Fifth Precinct, the only damn building in New York City with DC current. Radio cars lined the curb, three-wheeled police scooters were parked on the sidewalk, and barriers and A-frames were stockpiled on the side of the stationhouse. The precinct's flag was twisted around the pole, and the green globes by the door burned dimly in the clear morning light.

Malone waved to the desk lieutenant as he entered the stationhouse, walked through the muster room, and went up the stairs; a narrow, winding passage of carved, Neo-Gothic wood; its majestic banister old and weak; its metal steps worn shiny by the feet of thousands of cops.

Dan Malone was a tall, solidly built man with a long, thin nose and a head of sandy hair that was splotched with gray. His clothes were casual: beige trousers, blue blazer, and a white shirt, open. He was proud that he'd never been "made" as a cop.

The detective squad room was standard issue. New green metal desks with antiquated typewriters were placed around the room. The door of the lieutenant's office concealed a two-way mirror. The detention cage, crammed in a corner, contained a huge stuffed teddy bear perched on a stool. Someone had pinned a six-pointed sheriff's badge to its chest and tucked an empty can of Rheingold and a toy machine gun into its folded paws. Steel mesh covered all the windows. Cardboard waste barrels were scattered about, the overflowing garbage topped with empty beer cans and pizza boxes.

Det. Gus Heinemann sat typing reports with two fingers, his three hundred pounds squeezed up to the desk, his small eyes almost lost beneath a heavy, overhanging brow. Gus was known throughout the Job for his insatiable appetite and his addiction to playing dice. He was a familiar figure at precinct club meetings and police conventions, always in the center of the largest game looking to roll his point. Det. Patrick O'Shaughnessy, outfitted in his usual ensemble of polyester gaudiness, stood at the cabinets filing away his case folders.

Heinemann looked up. "Ah, the lieutenant is in bright and early this morning."

"What's so important to drag me in on my day off?" Malone asked, reaching over the carved gate, releasing the catch on the other side.

"Sergeant Brady telephoned from One-four-one Chrystie Street. He said that they had a DOA that could be a problem. He wants you on the scene," Heinemann said.

"Did he say what they had?"

"He only said that a problem had developed," Heinemann said. Malone gave a knowing nod. "Who's catching?"

"I am," Stern said.

Jake Stern was a balding weightlifter who was always squeezing a hand grip. He had a large nose that had been shattered while he was doing bench presses at the Y. On the day in question, Jake had pressed two hundred pounds for the fifth time and was struggling to make the sixth. He was straining his arms upward when a fag ambled over and tickled his balls. The barbell and weights crashed down, tumbling Jake, bloodied and dazed, onto the floor. The other guy never knew what trouble was until that day.

As Stern turned the unmarked police car into Canal Street, the lieutenant asked him if anything heavy had come in while he was on his RDO. Regular day off.

Keeping his eyes fixed on the traffic inching its way toward the Holland Tunnel, Jake answered, "It's been quiet. We caught a few grounders, but nothing heavy. Ya know,

3

Lou, I'm getting tired of catching nothin' but easy ones." He addressed him as Lou, the diminutive of lieutenant that was routinely used in the NYPD.

One of the two policemen standing in front of 141 Chrystie Street waved to the approaching detectives. "It's on the third floor, Lou," he said as they came up to him.

The floor of the studio apartment was covered by grungy chipped linoleum that had been there at least fifty years. A kitchenette ran the length of the room. Next to the open window was a brass bed and a chest of drawers with a homemade paint job. The body of a nude white man stretched flat on his stomach lay on the sagging mattress of the bed. His face was at right angles, with the eyes open. Body fluid seeped from the nose and mouth into a puddle of phlegm next to the jaw. Blood had drained to the lower part of the body, causing dark blue discoloration of the lower torso. The neck and jaw had stiffened from the downward contractions of rigor mortis.

Slumped into one of the chairs, her hand half obscuring her face, sat a woman in a wine-colored bathrobe pulled tightly around her waist. Her clear skin was streaked with mascara. She looked about twenty-four or -five. Stern eyed her as they entered. "Nice tits," he whispered to the lieutenant.

Sergeant Brady was standing over her, a wet, unlit cigar jutting out the side of his mouth. His face was deeply seamed and pitted by the acne of thirty years ago. "Good t' see ya, Lou," Brady said, a visible expression of relief crossing his face. He moved away from the woman to meet the detectives, stepping between the lieutenant and Stern. In a low, apologetic voice he said, "This caper ain't exactly yours, but we weren't sure how to handle it." Brady scratched his head, looked over at the body, and announced, "A certain amount of finesse is needed on this one. . . ."

"What's the wrinkle, Sarge?" Malone said, glancing at the corpse.

4

"He's a priest," Brady whispered.

Malone moved over to the body, placing his palm down on the clammy skin. "How long?"

The woman flicked her eyes to the lieutenant. "About two hours."

Malone grabbed a chair, dragged it to where she was sitting, and sat down facing her. "What's your name?"

"Mary Collins. He was a Monday-morning regular. He arrived around seven each week. . . ."

As she talked he studied her face. High cheekbones that looked chiseled, smooth skin without any trace of hair. His initial suspicion hardened into certainty. Without speaking, he reached out and felt probingly under her chin. The surgeon's thin line was there. He noticed her Adam's apple and then looked down at her hands. They were large and not proportioned to her thin, female body. He slid his hand inside the bathrobe and pushed it aside. The breasts were firm and had perfectly round aureoles that looked as though they had been press-stamped from a sheet of brown rubber and pasted on. He felt one. It was much too firm.

"What was the name you were born with, Mary?"

"Harold."

"Did you have your plumbing fixed?"

She was insulted. "No."

Mary/Harold Collins stood up and bent forward, pulling a limp penis from between her legs. She then tugged the robe closed and sat back down, the perfect lady.

"Did he know that you were a transvestite?"

"Naturally."

"Tell me what happened?"

"He arrived like usual and we went right to bed." She shook her hair back and smoothed it with her hand. "He went down on me. Then he stopped and rolled me over on my stomach. He went into my behind and we were pumping each other when all of a sudden he screams 'Jesus, forgive me,' and collapsed. I thought he came. But I didn't feel his chest

5

heaving . . . hear the breathing." She plastered her hands to her face, rocking from side to side. She was crying.

"What a feeling to have someone die inside of you. God forgive me. I don't know. I don't know . . ."

"Do you live here?"

"No. I use this place for my tricks. My apartment is in Chelsea."

"Get dressed. I want you to leave with us." Malone looked over at the sergeant. "How many people know about this?"

"Nobody outside this room knows anything."

"Let's make damn sure that it stays that way," Malone said flatly. "Has he been I.D.'d?"

Brady waved a brown leather wallet in front of his face. "The Reverend James Gavin of St. Anselm's in Brooklyn."

Malone got up and moved over to the bed. He stared down at the cadaver for a second, then bent downward and picked up the end of the sheet that trailed off the bed. He tossed it over the body and walked back to Mary Collins, who once more had her face hidden. His tone was low, consoling. "Mary? Believe me when I tell you we're just as anxious as you are to resolve this problem as expeditiously and discreetly as possible. Will you do whatever I say is necessary?"

Mary Collins's hands fell to her lap. She looked at the lieutenant. "I'm not going to take a fall. I have no intention of going inside and having to fight for my life. They keep us locked up with the general population."

Malone's lips pursed with satisfaction. He nodded to the others. "You won't have to," he said.

Malone telephoned the medical examiner's office and arranged to have the on-duty M.E. standing by at the morgue to certify the death. Then he put through a call to the archdiocese, confident that the man on the other end would give him no problems. A product of the slums of Philadelphia, an expert on canon law and the head of the ecclesiastical shoofly unit that takes care of problems with rogue priests, Msgr. Terrance McInerney was used to receiving "important" telephone calls from the police. As the personal secretary to His Eminence, it was McInerney's job to handle those unpleasant secular matters that always seemed to crop up.

Malone picked up on the monsignor's calm authority. "What can we do for you, Lieutenant?"

"I am sorry to have to inform you, Monsignor, of the passing of Father James Gavin of St. Anselm's in Brooklyn."

There was a pause on the line. Then, "May God have mercy on his soul. Can you tell me the circumstances of Father's passing? Why are the police involved?"

"Well, Monsignor, it appears that Father was walking down Chrystie Street this morning when he suffered a heart attack. Passers-by carried him into one of the nearby buildings. A young woman was kind enough to let them bring Father into her apartment to await the ambulance. Unfortunately he expired before help arrived. The people who carried him into her apartment left, leaving the poor woman alone with the body. When the police arrived she was hysterical."

"I can well understand the lady's apprehension," McInerney said smoothly.

"I've contacted the medical examiner. Dr. Solomon Epstein is going to perform an immediate autopsy. You'll be able to pick up the remains within a few hours."

The monsignor sighed. "I know Epstein. He's all right. What floor did you say the lady lived on?"

"The third."

"I see. Was Father Gavin wearing his clerical collar?"

"No."

"How was identity ascertained?"

"From the I.D. in his wallet."

"I see. Is there any problem with the press?"

Malone thought he detected the first slight note of tension in the monsignor's voice.

"We've made sure that the incident was not put on the teletype or transmitted over the radio. Only a few people know what happened."

"And how is the young lady holding up?"

7

"Fine. Although it happened at a particularly difficult time for her."

"Oh? Why is that?"

"She wants to leave New York City. She had been promised a job as a cocktail waitress in a Las Vegas hotel, but it fell through at the last moment. Then this unpleasantness . . ."

"Perhaps we can repay her kindness. What's her name?"

"Harold."

A gasp, followed by stunned silence. Malone waited to let what he had said sink in. "He's a transvestite who goes by the name of Mary Collins."

Deep breaths of anger were coming from the other end. "I am going to make arrangements with Sheehan's Funeral Home to pick up Father's body. I am also sending a representative from my staff to get Father Gavin's personal effects. I want to thank you for your consideration in this delicate matter."

"I was happy to help, Monsignor."

"Will the official report have to mention anything about the *lady?*" Malone could feel the tension on the other end now.

Malone paused a moment before he answered. He wanted the Powerhouse to know that they owed him one. "The lady? What lady, Monsignor? Father Gavin expired on the street from natural causes. He was alone."

It was after one and Epstein hadn't called. Malone was at his desk trying to reduce the perpetual mound of paper when a thought crossed his mind: What if Gavin's death was not natural? Would his ass be in a sling! He yanked up the phone and dialed.

Epstein answered. "Don't worry. It was natural. A nice, clean coronary occlusion."

"Thanks, Sol."

"Any time. Can't talk now. I'm in the middle of dissecting a spleen." Epstein hung up.

Malone had one more call to make. He dialed Erica Sommers. When her cheerful voice came on the line he smiled and said, "Thanks for last night. You were wonderful."

"It was nice, wasn't it? I'm sorry I couldn't stay. I just had too much work to do today, and I knew you wouldn't let me escape until the afternoon."

He laughed. "Complaints?"

"On the contrary."

"What about tonight?"

"I'm sorry but I'm busy tonight."

"What are you doing?"

There was a pause. Then . . . "Daniel? I don't question you and I don't expect you to question me. They're your rules."

"I'll call you in a day or two."

"That'll be nice."

Malone returned to his paper. The case folder in front of him read, "Anthony Sardillo M/W/33. Homicide by shotgun . . . February 12, 1938." A department photograph of Sardillo lying on a rain-soaked driveway minus most of his head was stapled to the inside cover. Malone got a kick out of examining old photographs of crime scenes. The detectives in them all looked like Mr. Magoo with straw hats and cheap cigars.

The semiannual "five"—DD5 Supplementary Complaint Report, the workhorse form of the Detective Division used to report all additional phases of an investigation—was stapled on top of the forty-odd-year accumulation of fives. Unsolved homicides were never closed; department regulations required that the assigned detective submit at least two fives a year on each of his open homicide cases. The detective assigned to the Sardillo case had nothing to report, as usual.

Malone knew the Sardillo case by heart; he knew all the

9

open cases. He glanced over the five, signed it, and then tossed the bulging folder into the wire file basket.

Stern and O'Shaughnessy had gone out to pick up lunch, hot heroes, two six-packs, and a pizza for Gus. The detectives were sitting around the squad room eating while Malone was in his office nibbling a strand of melted mozzarella off his eggplant parmigiana hero and reading another case folder.

Stern had his feet up on the desk. He leaned forward and took a can of beer and peeled the top, tossing the tab over his shoulder. He gulped some and looked over at O'Shaughnessy who was sitting across from him.

"You still seeing Foam?" Stern asked O'Shaughnessy.

"Of course. You don't give up a deal like that. Free bed and board and a screw whenever I want," O'Shaughnessy said.

"What's it like to hump a broad who uses foam? Ain't it messy?" Heinemann said.

"No, it ain't messy," O'Shaughnessy snarled.

Stern winked at Heinemann. "Hey, Pat. Does the foam come in different flavors?"

"Yeah, Pat. How does the foam taste?" Heinemann asked.

"How the fuck should I know?" O'Shaughnessy yelled. "You know that I don't go down on women."

"Pity. You really should try it," Stern said.

The telephone rang and Heinemann answered it. He listened for a while, then said, "Right," and hung up. Holding two slices of pizza pressed together, he got up and walked over to Malone's office. He stuck his head inside and announced, "The inspector is on his way over."

Fifteen minutes later Insp. Nicholas Zambrano walked into the Fifth Squad. He was a gravel-voiced, ponderous man with thirty-three years in the department. His body was huge, but still hard and firm, except for his large belly. He had a swarthy face and enormous brown eyes and a warm Mediterranean smile that gave a clue to his inner warmth. But when he had to, Nicholas Zambrano could be a first-class prick.

He walked into Malone's office and plopped his six-foot frame down. "How goes it, Dan?"

"No problems. Want some coffee?"

"Make mine strong," Zambrano said with a sly wink.

Malone got up and walked into the squad room. He returned with two half-filled coffee mugs. He opened the bottom drawer of his desk, removed a bottle of Jack Daniel's, and scowled when he saw that what had been a virgin bottle two days ago was now a third full. He poured a healthy shot into both mugs and slid one over to the inspector.

Zambrano slumped in his seat and held the mug under his nose, sniffing appreciatively. "I was surprised to catch you in. According to your chart, today is your RDO," Zambrano said, his brown eyes moving to meet the lieutenant's.

"Something came up that required my attention. I figured I'd hang around and get rid of some of this paper."

Zambrano frowned mild disapproval. "Don't make the mistake of making the Job your wife. If you do, some day you're going to wake up and discover that you married a whore. Get married, have a family."

"I was married, remember. It sucks."

"Bullshit! They don't all end up on the rocks."

"In this job most of them do."

Resigned, Zambrano sighed and asked, "How many men you got assigned?"

"On paper, twenty-four. I have two men on a steal to the Major Case Squad, one assigned to the borough president's office and one on extended sick, heart attack. That leaves me with twenty men to cover the chart."

Zambrano hesitated. "Dan . . . the mayor wants to borrow one of your guys for a week or so. He has a friend he wants driven around town."

"Inspector! We were stuck the last time driving his girl-friend. Why the hell doesn't he use one of the detectives assigned to guard him?"

"First off, he likes to bounce in Little Italy. He has a lot of friends there. And your squad is the closest. Second, if one of the detectives assigned to Gracie Mansion was spotted in Bloomingdale's carrying packages for some lady, the entire world would know that Handsome Harry has a new girlfriend, that's why. The word is he's stuck on this one. Might even make her a commissioner,'' Zambrano said.

"Cozy. His wife can swear her in."

Zambrano grinned. He drained his mug, then slid it across the desk. "Skip the coffee this time."

Malone poured a respectable shot and handed the mug back.

Zambrano sat for a moment studying the dark, shimmering liquid and then looked up. "Do you know Inspector Bowen?"

"The one in Community Relations?"

"That's the one. He might be stopping by to examine your community-relations parameters."

"My what?"

"It's the latest brainchild of the paper assholes at headquarters. They've convinced the PC that every unit in the department, including precinct detective squads, should become involved in community relations. You're supposed to get in touch with the various community groups operating within the precinct and find out what their needs are and work out a program for your detectives to respond to those needs. It's called Operation Participation. Bowen's been designated to act as liaison between the DCCR and the Detective Division."

"And what do I put on paper? My detectives try to make every halfway decent-looking female complainant who walks into the squad."

"Just throw the usual bullshit on a forty-nine and have it ready to show Bowen when he pops in."

"Look at that basket of paper on my desk. And they're adding more?"

Zambrano shrugged. "I'll drop you an outline of what they're looking for in the department mail. All you'll have to

do is embellish it.'' Zambrano gulped his drink. ''Thanks for
the hospitality,'' he said, getting up. He started to leave, then
turned to face the lieutenant. ''By the way, the man with the
red yarmulka called the PC to say thanks.''

WEDNESDAY, *June 10*

At 7:40 A.M. the following morning Sgt. George Brady stepped behind the Fifth Precinct's massive desk and flipped the pages of the sergeants' clipboard. He glanced down at the desk lieutenant who was making his beginning-of-tour blotter entries and then looked up at the clock. Brady took the cigar from his mouth and laid it in the ashtray. It was time to turn-out the Second Platoon.

Looking down at the desk lieutenant, Brady asked, "Got anything for the boys, Lou?"

The lieutenant looked up. "Tell 'em not to bring in any Puerto Rican mysteries. I'm not in the mood for that bullshit today. And George, tell sector Charlie I want some roast pork lo mein for lunch."

"You got it, Lou."

Brady tucked the clipboard under his arm and stepped out from behind the desk.

"All right, fall in," Brady shouted, walking into the sitting room.

The members of the Second Platoon reluctantly abandoned their coffee and cigarettes and shambled into two uneven ranks.

Brady faced the platoon. "Attention to roll call."

He called the roll, assigning each police officer to his post, sector, calling off their meal hour; he read off post conditions. "Summonses are down for the month. We need movers. Pay attention to your Accident Prone Locations. Sector Adam, watch out for payroll robberies; Sector David, tag the double parkers around the court. The judges are complaining that they can't get into their assigned spaces. The Seventh Squad is looking for a 'seventy-nine green Olds in connection with a homicide. The right front fender is smashed in. The car has Jersey plates and a broken vent window on the driver's side. If found, safeguard for prints. Sector Charlie, the lieutenant wants roast pork lo mein for lunch. You might as well bring him a flute too—he'll be a little parched by then.'' He was referring to a soda bottle filled with whiskey. "You all understand your assignments?"

Two files of policemen stood in indifferent silence, their eyes staring blankly ahead.

"Okay. Open ranks for inspection," Brady growled.

Sgt. George Brady had forty years in the Job. Next year he'd have to throw in his papers. Just as well. It was getting harder and harder for Brady to accept the new breed of cops. He missed the spit and polish of the old days. As he moved down the first file, he glanced with dismay at the short, dumpy female officers with asses as broad as billboards, their flabby waists hanging over their gun belts. The blacks with their damn afros, uniform caps perched on top of a beehive of kinky black hair. Puerto Ricans with their goddamn peach fur on their goddamn wheat-colored chins and their goddamn greasy sideburns. Even the Irish cops had succumbed to the age of permissiveness with their long hair lacquered down with hair spray and their goddamn handlebar mustaches. The locker room smelled like a goddamn French whorehouse. There was only one white cop in the entire precinct with close-cropped hair, spit-shined shoes, tailored uniform that hugged the body, and he was a goddamn fag. Yeah. It was time for George Brady to get out.

The sergeant stopped in front of a female officer who had the contours of a fire hydrant.

"Where's your flashlight?"

15

"In my locker, Sarge," she replied sheepishly.

"In your locker? And what will you do if you have to chase a holdup man into a dark basement? Call time out and run back to your locker? Go upstairs and get your flashlight!"

Brady walked in front of the platoon. "Take your posts."

Blue-and-white radio cars were parked all along Elizabeth Street. Police officers slumped in their cars, waiting. Pairs of policemen loitered near the precinct steps, talking over the night's activities. When the first police officer emerged from the precinct, the cops of the late tour abandoned their radio cars and hurried toward the stationhouse.

Police Off. Joe Velch and his partner, Carmine Rossi, headed for their radio car. Velch moved around to the driver's side. They jabbed their nightsticks between the rear seat, tossed their memo books into the back, dropped their flashlights onto the front seat, and threw their summons pouches onto the dashboard. Velch started to gather up the early-bird edition of the *Daily News* that was scattered over the seat. Rossi stretched his arm under the front seat and scooped out the beer containers and brown bags that had been squirreled away during the late tour.

Velch looked up at the gas gauge. "Ya suppose to gas up on the late tour, you donkey cocksucker!" he shouted after his hastily departing relief.

They drove over to the Sixth Precinct to get gas and then drove to Moshe's on the corner of Canal and Baxter where two containers of regular, one extra sweet, and two bagels with cream cheese were waiting in a bag next to the cash register. The radio car slid to a stop in front of the luncheonette. Velch raised himself out of the car and ambled into the crowded store.

Moshe was busy behind the counter. The store owner saw the policeman enter and started to work his way down the counter to the cash register.

"So how goes it today, Joe? Catch any criminals?" Moshe asked.

"Not yet, Moshe," Velch said, struggling to pull out his wallet.

Velch took a dollar bill out and placed it in Moshe's palm. The store owner handed the policeman the bag, rang up the sale, and gave Velch his four quarters change.

They parked the radio car under the Brooklyn Bridge. Rossi opened the glove compartment and rested the bag on top of the door. He took out a container and a bagel and passed them to his partner. They pried off the tops of the containers and laid them on the dashboard; cops never throw away the tops of containers. They might have to leave fast.

The view was relaxing—a tugboat was shepherding two garbage scows, its stubby bow pushing aside greenish water. The river's day was just starting when a scratchy mutter on the radio broke the silence.

"Five Boy, K."

"Aw shit!" Rossi said, snatching up the radio.

"Five Boy, K," he answered.

"Five Boy, respond to Chatham Towers, One-seven-zero Park Row. See complainant regarding a foul odor."

"Five Boy, ten-four." Rossi put the mike back into its cradle and turned to his partner. "We'll finish our coffee and then take a slow ride over. It's probably nothing."

The Chatham Towers, a twenty-four-story housing complex of naked concrete blocks and jutting terraces, stood in Lower Manhattan in the shadow of the Manhattan Bridge and Columbus Park. Crescent-shaped driveways angled upward to the building. Isolated tiny playgrounds with modular cubes instead of seesaws made the apartment-house setting seem somewhat bizarre in the surrounding area of old buildings.

Tenants were milling in front of the entrance as the radio car rounded the driveway. The policemen got out and walked down the steps leading into the complex. A porter was waiting for them in the vestibule. "The third floor, officers."

When the elevator was between the second and third floor

they got their first whiff of the familiar, awful odor. Velch looked at his partner. "It's ripe."

The elevator stopped on three and they stepped out. Velch made a sudden grab for his handkerchief. The coffee, bagel, and cream cheese exploded from his mouth, splattering his uniform and spewing across the hall. The stench was suffocating. They gagged and their mouths filled with saliva. With every gasp they fought not to swallow their tongues.

"You okay?" Rossi said, pressing his handkerchief over his mouth and nose.

"I'm all right," he choked. "My uniform is shot to hell."

"Chrissake . . . this is one ripe son-of-a-bitch," Rossi said. They reluctantly paused in front of each door in the hall until they got to Apartment 3C.

"Get some ammonia!" Rossi gagged, before he, too, vomited.

Joe Velch ran back along the corridor, banging on doors.

"Police! Open up. We need ammonia."

A door in the middle of the floor finally cracked open and a hand appeared holding a gray plastic bottle.

Velch grabbed the bottle. The door slammed. He ran to Apartment 3C and started to pour ammonia in front of the door. "Carmine, you stay here. I'll call the sergeant and the Squad," Velch said, shaking out the last drippings.

"Tell 'em to bring some crystals with them. We're going to need them!" Rossi shouted after his partner.

Gus Heinemann stuck his massive head in the door of the lieutenant's office. "Lou, they think they've got a DOA in the Chatham Towers. They're calling for the Squad."

"They think?" Malone said.

"They haven't entered the apartment. They're waiting for us to get there," Heinemann said.

"Who's catching?" Malone asked.

"Pat."

18

"Both of you run over and have a look. If it's a mystery get on the horn and call me. If it's just a grounder, clean it up and forget it."

When the detectives arrived they found Sergeant Brady standing among a cluster of anxious tenants. When Brady saw the detectives getting out of their car, he walked away from the people and went to meet them.

"Whaddaya got, Sarge?" O'Shaughnessy asked, walking up to Brady.

Brady answered, "We were waiting for you guys to get here. We poured some DB 45 crystals around the outside of the door. It was pretty bad up there."

"Anything on who lives there?" O'Shaughnessy asked.

"A female, white, by the name of Sara Eisinger. She's about thirty-four or five and lives alone. We questioned some of the neighbors, but none of them know anything about her. According to the building's management, she's lived here for five years," Brady answered.

"The first thing we've got to do is find out *que pasa* inside of that apartment," Heinemann said.

An Emergency Service van careened around the driveway, squealing to a stop behind the unmarked detective car.

"Figured we might need gas masks if the crystals don't work," the sergeant said, looking at the van.

Heinemann looked at his partner. "Think we should call the boss?"

"Naw. All we have so far is a case of bad breath. Let's see what we find," O'Shaughnessy said.

A group of detectives and uniformed officers hovered in the hallway, waiting for the disinfecting crystals to work and turn the stink into a bearable smell faintly like violets.

Heinemann turned to the sergeant. "Sarge, will you start a log? If we got a mystery we'll want a record of everyone on the scene."

"You got it," Brady answered.

The detectives put on gas masks. O'Shaughnessy took the bottle of crystals from the sergeant.

"Here goes," said Heinemann, lifting up his right foot and smashing it into the door, splintering it open.

An unspeakable odor gushed out; all the cops started to gag and choke. Two policemen ran retching down the hallway, while O'Shaughnessy stood in the doorway scattering crystals inside the apartment. There was a large kitchen to the right of the entrance. A black wrought-iron table was on its side, its glass top shattered. The cabinets were open, their contents strewn over the floor. O'Shaughnessy stepped inside and turned to the uniformed cops. "Wait out here."

The detectives entered; O'Shaughnessy spread around more of the crystals. A half-open convertible couch was lying on its side, the cushions slashed and shredded. Tables and lamps were broken. There was no sign of a body. "Nothing," Heinemann said, moving through the living room. "It's got to be someplace."

The masks muffled their voices, giving them a hollow resonance.

Heinemann moved to the window and turned on the air conditioner. He glanced down at the street. His eyes wandered to the duplex pagoda roof of the Manhattan Savings Bank on the corner of Chatham Square and Catherine Street. He liked the way the eaves curled under. A queue of tourist buses were starting to unload their passengers. It was a beautiful day to be looking for death.

The living room led into a small foyer. There were two closets on either side. The floor was littered with linens. A closed door at one end apparently led to the bathroom. Pat looked at Gus. "It's gotta be in there," Pat said, moving to open the door. "Dear Mother of God!"

The bathroom was done in blue. Ceramic tiles covered the floor, blue fluffy scatter rugs on top. The tub was filled to its brim with a dark red liquid. Lying face down was the swollen, nude body of a woman. Her long blond hair fanned out on the surface of the loathsome, hardened mixture of blood and other things. Writhing maggots covered the back of the head, sodden wormlike creatures feasting on human decay. Her hands were handcuffed behind her body, intertwined fingers pointing helplessly upward.

"I ain't never seen nothin' like this," O'Shaughnessy said, his mouth gaping. "Better call the boss and tell him to get his ass here forthwith. We got a homicide on our hands."

They were waiting outside in the hall when the lieutenant and the rest of the squad arrived. Walking up to the gathering, Malone asked, "Who's been inside?"

Heinemann answered, "Only Pat and me."

"Let's keep it that way," Malone said. "I don't want anyone inside unless they've got a specific reason for being there. Has Forensic been notified?"

"They're on the way," O'Shaughnessy answered.

Malone turned to Sergeant Brady. "Sarge, you take care of it out here. If any of the chiefs from headquarters come by, keep them the hell out of the crime scene. I don't want them screwing things up. The last one we had, some chief from Planning held up the murder weapon for the newspaper boys. He got his picture in the centerfold and the perp walked."

Brady asked, "And if some muck-a-muck insists?"

"You call me—I'll handle it," Malone said.

"Ten-four," Brady replied.

"Let's take a look," Malone said, moving to the doorway.

Pat O'Shaughnessy was at the lieutenant's side, a steno pad ready in his hands.

The lieutenant stared into the apartment. "What a shambles."

"Looks like somebody put up a helluva fight," O'Shaughnessy said.

"Or someone was searching for something," Malone said.

Malone started to enter the apartment when Brady called him. The lieutenant turned and the sergeant handed him plastic gloves.

"Thanks," Malone said, putting the gloves on. "I almost forgot them. Make sure that no one enters the scene without them."

Malone stood looking down at the tub, shaking his head in disbelief. He knelt down and, with his forefinger, he carefully wiped the slime off the handcuffs. "Smith and Wesson," he observed, twisting his head, trying to read the serial numbers. "We might be able to trace them."

"How long do you figure?" O'Shaughnessy asked.

"It's hard to tell," Malone said, glancing from the body up to the partially opened window. "From the degree of decomposition and the maggot castings . . . I'd say about a week." Malone stood up and faced his detectives. "I want this apartment field stripped. Overlook nothing. Gather up her telephone book, her checkbook, savings book. I want to know her medical history. Who her friends were. Her enemies. I want to know who she was making it with. If she was a switch hitter. Gay. Where did she work? When Forensic arrives, tell them I want the crime scene sketch done in the coordinate method."

"The Forensic boys ain't going to like that. It's a lot of work," Heinemann said.

"I don't give a fiddler's fuck what the Forensic boys like. I want an imaginary line drawn through every room in this apartment and every piece of broken glass, paper, wood, anything, connected to the line by distances."

"Do you want to call in some extra detectives?" O'Shaughnessy asked.

"When I notify the Borough, I'll ask for a few to help with the initial canvasses. I don't like too many men working on a case. They fall over each other." Malone's face hardened. "Let me reemphasize what I said before. I don't want to see *anyone* inside this apartment unless they've got a reason to be here. No cops using the telephone to call their girlfriends or picking up souvenirs."

"We got the message," O'Shaughnessy said.

"Okay, call in the rest of the Squad and let's get to work. We're going to take this one nice and easy. One step at a time, just like they say you do it at the Academy: Who? What? When? Where? How? and Why?" Malone said, elbowing past the detectives on his way to call Inspector Zambrano.

When Malone returned five minutes later he found a photographer snapping pictures of every room from every angle and a detective measuring distances from the imaginary line and calling them off to his partner, who entered them on the crime scene sketch. Fingerprint technicians were spreading powder and dusting with plumed brushes. Detectives were sticking their noses into every nook and cranny of the apartment, searching for physical evidence. Anything that was considered of value was tagged and placed into plastic evidence bags.

Brady had stationed himself outside the apartment. A rope barrier had been erected in front of the door. There were signs prohibiting entrance into the crime scene area. As detectives arrived from the Borough, the sergeant entered their names and times of arrival into the crime scene log. Malone dispatched teams of detectives to canvass the Chatham Tower complex for witnesses, friends of the victim, anyone who might know something. Additional teams were sent to interview storekeepers, garage attendants, people who worked in the housing complex, bus drivers who had nearby routes.

Bo Davis and Gus Heinemann canvassed the parked cars within a five-block radius of the scene. Every license plate was written down. Later they'd be run through the National Crime Information Center. Perhaps the killer had panicked and run from the scene, leaving his car. The building's underground garage was canvassed for unauthorized vehicles.

Jake Stern was on his knees in the apartment searching the bottom of the linen closet. Malone looked down at him. "Anything?"

Stern crooked his body, straining to look under the bottom shelf. He reached his hand under and ran it along the shelf.

23

"Nothing?"

"Lou, the meat wagon is here," an anonymous voice announced.

"Send them in," Malone said, without turning to look.

Two attendants walked into the apartment lugging a body bag, its wide straps dragging on the floor.

With impersonal detachment the morgue attendants laid the bag alongside the tub and went about their job.

Detectives stopped working and gathered around to watch. Policemen are no different from civilians and firemen when it comes to death. The same thoughts cross their minds: She's dead. I'm alive. Someday I'll be dead. I wonder how long I've got to live. What will it be like, nothingness?

Without hesitation the attendants plunged their bare hands into the red muck. They lifted the body. Slime sloughed off. Maggots rained to the floor. The crust was broken. A new abomination rose from the tub.

The lower part of Sara Eisinger's jaw dangled from one socket. Her battered body was halfway between the tub and body bag when the jaw clattered to the floor.

The body was placed into the canvas bag. One of the attendants bent to scoop up the jaw. He nonchalantly tossed it into the bag.

"Don't close it up," Malone said, kneeling to examine the front of the body. He spread his hands under her neck and slowly ran them down over the body feeling for entrance wounds, something taped to the body. He felt under her deflated breasts. Her armpits. He pushed her legs apart. "Jesus Christ. Look at this."

Protruding from Sara Eisinger's vagina was the curved end of a curtain rod.

Evening of the same day

Malone sat in his office that evening reviewing the fives on the Eisinger homicide. Outside in the squad room a detective was interviewing a female complainant who insisted she had been raped by her common-law husband. As he flipped the pale blue pages of the Supplementary Complaint Reports he was struck, not for the first time, by the impersonal tone of the narratives: time and place of occurrence; physical description of the crime scene; victim's name and pedigree; name and addresses of persons interviewed; name, shield number and command of MOFs on the scene, and notifications made. Malone wondered if there was anyone who would miss Sara Eisinger.

Malone tossed the case folder into the active basket, then arched his back and stretched. He reached down and slid out the bottom drawer and took out the quart bottle of Jack Daniel's and a glass. He blew the glass clean; the booze would sterilize it. Drink in hand, he got up and walked over to the window. He grinned when he saw the black man on the corner of Canal Street hustling tourists in a three-card monte game. Shmucks. They'll never learn.

Malone's office was a sterile cubicle with dirty green-and-gray cinderblock walls, a locker, two filing cabinets, and a glass cabinet-type bookcase that contained the *Patrol Guide, Penal Law, Criminal Procedure Law,* and stacks of unread department orders. His desk was green metal with a gray

Formica top and a glass covering—standard PD issue. Taped to the wall behind the desk was a large piece of cardboard with important telephone numbers.

He moved back to his desk and went to kick in the open bottom drawer when he noticed the ormolu picture frame sticking out from beneath the Manhattan Yellow Pages. It had been a long time since he had stared at her photograph and remembered. He lowered himself into the chair and reached back into the drawer to pull the frame out from under the thick book and set it up on the desk in front of him. He poured more bourbon into his glass and toasted the photograph, staring into her large black eyes. He could still remember the exact date he had snapped it. Sunday, May 4, 1960: over twenty-two years ago. He had caught her preening in front of the seal pit in the Prospect Park zoo, a cheerful nymph with short, coal-black hair and a pixie nose.

She was eighteen. He was twenty.

Dan Malone and Helen Frazer fell in love. Their heads were full of dreams about their future. He was going to earn his B.A. in history from Brooklyn College and become a policeman and go on to become the chief of detectives of the largest police department in the world. Helen Frazer was going to earn her Ph.D. in psychology and become a child psychologist. They were going to marry and live happily ever after.

A marriage that started in bliss and ended in shit, he thought, as he drank. Their union lasted eight years, nine months, and twenty-four days. In the beginning they shared a lot. Each day ended with long, full reports on the day's experiences. By the end of their first year together they had both earned their degrees. She was doing graduate work at Hunter College and was active in both the Literary and Psychology Clubs. In January of their second year of marriage he was appointed to the police department. The metamorphosis from civilian to cop began immediately. His first class at the Academy was a "Don't" class: Don't get involved off duty; Don't

26

discuss the job with civilians; Don't look to be a hero; Don't be a boss fighter; Don't ever trust newspapermen, lawyers, junkies, or hookers.

He enjoyed the structured curriculum at the Academy, learning the law, police procedures, traditions. Twice a week, in the afternoons, policemen from some of the city's busy houses would come to the Academy to conduct informal sessions with the recruits. It was those sessions that would absorb his mind. He would sit wide-eyed and attentive, listening to the experiences of street cops, learning his tradecraft: Never stand in front of a closed door, the person on the other side might fire through it and kill you; When responding to a 10:30 be mindful that the stickup team might have a backup lurking nearby; Remember that a woman or child can kill you just as dead as a man; A woman in a nun's habit is no guarantee that she's a nun; In a crowd stay with your partner, don't get separated; Pull your holster around your front in order to protect your groin and to prevent anyone from coming up from behind and ripping your gun from your holster.

After school, outfitted in recruit grays, he would ride the Lexington Avenue subway uptown to their one-bedroom Yorkville apartment on East Seventy-ninth Street. Usually they would make love and then go out to eat. Luciano's was on Madison Avenue. They both liked Italian food and were too young to worry about calories.

Upon graduation from the Academy he was assigned to the Seven-nine on patrol. The Seven-nine was one of the five precincts that made up the old Thirteenth Division: the Seven-three, Seven-seven, Eight-oh, and Eight-eight. The occupying force of Bed-Stuy, a ghetto ripe with decay and violence. It was during those fledgling years in the Seven-nine that the marriage soured.

There were many cops who were content to do their eight hours and go home. Then there were the active ones, the cops to whom time meant nothing, who doggedly searched out crime and the criminals. Malone was such a cop. As his arrest

27

record soared so did the time he had to spend in court. They were spending less and less time together, the inevitable outcome of a cop's giving more to the Job than to a marriage.

The Seven-nine's watering hole was Leroy's Lounge on Gates Avenue. A smoke-filled room of glittering glass globes, pulsating lights, and soul music. After a four-to-twelve tour, the cops would go to Leroy's to unwind. The session lasted until four in the morning. Policemen's wives have dubbed those tours the "four-to-fours." They despise them. During the four-to-fours Malone was further indoctrinated into the folklore of the department. The rookies went to listen to angry, cynical men recite the epic tales and legends of the Job. Sipping a flat beer, he would listen as ex-detectives told why they had been flopped back into uniform. Someone else was always at fault. Many claimed that a girlfriend or ex-wife in whom he had confided things dropped a dime or wrote an anonymous letter. He heard vice cops tell how girlfriends, the horses, and booze had eaten up all their ill-gotten money. For the first time he heard of the high suicide rate, the divorce rate, even the arrest rate. "I never thought of getting locked up until I came on this fucking job," an old-timer had confided during a four-to-four.

Another old-timer: "Kid, this is the only job in the world where you can go to work hungry, horny, broke, and sober and have all those needs taken care of by the end of your tour."

Helen was alone most of the time now. She kept herself busy with schoolwork and school activities. She told herself that it was the newness of the job that enthralled him. It would wear off in time and they would settle into the normal routine of living. But one morning after a late tour he received a telephone notification at home. He had been transferred into the Detective Division. The sudden promotion was not the result of a blazing gun battle or a spectacular arrest but came about because of the intercession of his Uncle Pat with the then chief of detectives. His uncle and the chief had been

28

radio car partners. That was how men became detectives—contacts.

As a detective third grade he was seldom home. Lovingly prepared dinners went uneaten. Concerts went unheard, shows unseen. He was always busy with investigations or extraditions. Not to mention tails, plants, and testimony before the grand jury and the court. And the paper, the ubiquitous triplicates and quadruplicates. He accepted the long hours and the frustrations. He reveled in it; she came to revile it.

One night after a fifteen-hour tour he came home and undressed quietly. He was bone-weary. He slipped into bed, close to her, caressed her breasts and prodded her warm body with his. She grunted annoyance, slapped him with her hip, and turned away, tugging and tucking the blanket under.

When they awoke in the morning they were silent and tense. She was angry because she was always alone, losing her husband to the damn police department. He was pouting because she had denied him loving. They had their morning coffee and remained in bed reading the Sunday papers, each scrupulously keeping to their own side of the bed.

The awkward silence was broken by the occasional turning of a page.

Finally she said, "I see Westenberg is doing the St. Matthew Passion at the cathedral in April. Want to go?" Her face was hidden behind the Arts and Leisure section of the *New York Times*. He was relieved, the first conciliatory move had been made. "Who is the mezzo-soprano?" He put down the World in Review section and reached across the separating space to push the paper away from her face. He saw that she was crying.

"I love you," he said.

"What's happening to us, Dan? We've become strangers. What is it about that job that consumes you? Tell me; I want to try to understand."

"It's the nature of the Job. Each tour I go to work intending to catch up on my paper, but I can't. The cases keep coming in. Our squad catches five-handed. Every tour each one of us catches an average of twenty-three cases apiece. Some of them we can shitcan. The burglaries and robberies get a fast phone call to jerk off the complainant and then they're filed. But you can't can a homicide or a felonious assault or a rape or a shooting. There are people walking the street that I don't have the time to go out and arrest. I telephone them and try to lure them into the Squad. It's like shoveling shit against the tide. Unending."

Dismayed, she grabbed his shoulders and shook. "But you love it!" He acknowledged her accusation with a nod. She threw herself into his arms. "Resign and go to law school. Teach. Drive a taxi. Anything so that we can live a normal life. I need my husband."

"It's in my blood. I can't quit."

"Will you promise that you will at least try to work fewer hours, be home more?"

"I'll try," he said doubtfully, reaching into her cleavage, playing with her semihard nipple.

The years passed. He had been promoted to sergeant and was the second whip of the Tenth Squad. Dr. Helen Malone was teaching child psychology at St. John's and had a budding practice with the Jewish Family Service. They had become friendly bed partners who had discursive conversations and who engaged in passionless acts of sex. Helen Malone had learned to fake it.

He returned home one summer evening to find his wife sitting dejectedly on their bed, suitcases at her feet. He went and sat next to her, afraid to speak. He knew what she was going to say. She began to cry softly. "Dan, I don't like what's happening to us. I can't live with it anymore. I'm leaving, for my own sanity." He wanted to plead. She stopped him by placing a finger to his lips. "Please don't make it harder. I've made my decision." She took his face in her hands and tenderly kissed his cheek. "I want you to know that I've never been unfaithful to you."

30

His eyes brimmed. "Neither have I."

Tears were stinging her lids. "I know."

He still remembered it clearly, but the pain was less. He poured one more drink, returned the ormolu frame to its place beneath the Manhattan Yellow Pages, and pushed the drawer closed.

"Lieutenant, you got a call on two," a detective in the squad room shouted.

Malone looked over at the blinking plastic button. He gulped his drink and yanked up the receiver.

"This is Captain Madvick from the chief of detectives' office." It was a pleasant enough voice.

"What can I do for you, Captain?" he asked, lowering himself onto the edge of the desk.

"The chief asked me to call. He wants to know if there is anything unusual about the Eisinger case."

Malone stood up. Why was the chief of detectives interested in a run-of-the-mill homicide that was probably going nowhere?

"Nothing," he answered, tucking the receiver under his chin and reaching for the case folder.

"Did you come up with any physical evidence or . . . er . . . property that was unusual?"

Malone pressed the earphone close. "What did you say your name was, Captain?"

"M-A-D-V-I-C-K." He sounded annoyed.

"From the chief of detectives' office?"

"You got it, Lieutenant."

"And you're calling from the office now?"

"Of course."

"I'll call you right back." Malone hung up and looked up at the directory. He picked up the receiver and dialed.

"Chief of detectives."

"Captain Madvick please."

"Ain't no Captain Madvick assigned here, pal."

31

"This is Walter Farrell from the *New York Times*," Malone lied. "I'm trying to get in touch with Captain Madvick. He used to be assigned there. I'm doing a story on the Rosenberg homicide. He was in charge of that case."

"I don't think there is anyone with that name assigned to the Detective Division. Wait a minute and I'll check the ten cards."

There was no active member of the Detective Division with the surname Madvick, he was told by the duty officer. Malone thanked him, hung up, and then dialed Operations. Using the same newspaperman ploy he asked the sergeant on duty to check the uniform force's ten cards and see where Captain Madvick was assigned.

There was no active member of the department with the name Madvick. "Maybe he retired," the sergeant said.

"Yeah, I guess that's it."

Malone sat on his desk idly waving the Eisinger folder. Whoever made that telephone call was on the Job; it was one cop talking to another cop. He opened the case folder and thumbed through to the property vouchers. Physical evidence or property that was unusual, the phony Captain Madvick had asked. He scrutinized the vouchers: a personal checkbook; some keys; a telephone book; thirty-two dollars and sixty-seven cents; a makeup kit; a pocketbook; nail file; emery board; and a lipstick. On a separate voucher—a set of handcuffs and a curtain rod.

Malone could not easily open the door to Sara Eisinger's apartment as it was carefully sealed with an official department seal on which was quoted the pertinent provision of the law prohibiting entry for all those not on official business. He took out his police identity card and sliced down through the seal, and then removed a set of house keys from the plastic evidence bag. As he did he noticed a gold-plated key in the bag. He wondered what it was for. The super had repaired the kicked-in door panel. There were three locks and all the cylinders were protected by steel plates. After struggling through several keys he got the locks open and entered the apartment.

He didn't know why he was surprised to find the place still a shambles, but he was. After all, there was no one to clean it up. The air conditioner was still humming. Fingerprint powder was scattered over the furniture and walls and cigarette butts were crushed into the carpet and floors.

Malone didn't know what he was looking for, but whatever it was, it was making someone in the Job very nervous. He decided to start in the bathroom with its horrifying crusted tub. First he opened jars of creams and lotions inside the medicine cabinet. He poked a finger inside the creams and emptied the lotions down the sink, carefully straining the creamy liquids through his fingers. Finding nothing, he went to the foyer outside the bathroom. He reexamined the closets, getting on his knees in order to run his hands underneath the shelves.

Forty minutes later he was standing in front of the refrigerator searching the freezer. He remembered an old Hitchcock television program where the wife used a frozen leg of lamb to bludgeon her husband to death, but there was nothing there but half of a jar of coffee and a stick of butter. He next searched the cabinets and under the sink and then leaned against the wall trying to think of any place he might have missed. He glanced down at the tiny stove and saw a Pyrex coffee pot on the far burner. His eyes swept the apartment. What had he missed? Perhaps nothing. Maybe he had found whatever it was and didn't know it. That gold-plated key? As he thought, he absent-mindedly picked up the coffee pot and examined it. There was a metal strap around the middle. A screw was fastened through the handle securing both ends of the strap to the pot. He noticed that the screw was loose. He inserted the nail of his forefinger into the screw head and attempted to tighten it. Then he saw it. A strip of negative 16-mm film that appeared to be about three inches long was fitted between the handle and the neck of the pot. Hidden under the metal collar. He looked down at the knife. Eisinger must have unscrewed the handle with the knife, slid the film under the strap and been attempting to tighten it when her killer or killers interrupted her.

Juggling the strip of film up under the light, he attempted to make out what was on it and couldn't. He counted sixteen frames. He put the film into his shirt pocket and went to turn off the air conditioner.

It was a little before nine the following morning when Malone walked into the squad room. O'Shaughnessy was on the telephone promising fidelity to Foam. According to Heinemann, Pat enjoyed walking the tightrope of infidelity with a bottle of nitro stuck up his ass.

Det. Bo Davis, an expatriate from Dixie, lived in East Meadow, Long Island, with his wife and two children. He loved his family, the Job, his ranch-style home with the cyclone fence all around it, and going to bed with women other than his wife. His motto was: Never get involved. And, during sixteen unfaithful years, he hadn't.

Davis was slumped in a swivel chair with his feet stretched up over the desk, admiring his new cowboy boots. He was wearing a white sports jacket with wide blue stripes, white waffle-weave trousers flared at the cuffs, and a blue shirt with a white tie and gold tie clasp with a miniature detective shield emblazoned in the center.

"Getting ready for Halloween?" Malone said, walking past Davis on his way into his office.

"I got a date with a three-way broad with her own mattress," Davis said, leaning forward to buff the point of his boot.

Malone called the detectives into his office. A person who was murdered the way Eisinger was should not end up a faded case folded with years of nothing-to-report fives stapled to it.

"What have we got on the Eisinger thing?" Malone said, glancing down at the sixty sheet, looking over the list of cases that had come in during the night. He was relieved to see that there was nothing heavy. At least he had a clear track for today.

Gus Heinemann spoke first. He had gone through Eisinger's telephone book and found the address of her parents in New Jersey. In line with department procedure he had sent a next-of-kin teletype message to the New Brunswick Police Department requesting them to make the notification. The rest of her book was surprisingly uninformative, except for two numbers, with no names next to them. One had a 703 area code and the other a 212 code. The phone company reported that they had no record of such numbers, so Heinemann contacted the Wagon Board, the department unit that allocated all the department's patrol wagons and as a sideline knew more about telephones than Ma Bell. He had also gone through her scanty collection of personal papers, found her Social Security card, and expected word momentarily from the feds about where she was employed.

Bo Davis was leaning against a file cabinet admiring his manicure and listening to Heinemann's report.

"What about the canvasses?" Malone asked Davis.

"They all came up dry," Davis answered. "We couldn't come up with anyone who knew her. Several of the neighbors said that they'd see her in the elevator or hallway, smile and exchange a few pleasantries, but that was it."

"Did you interview all the people in her building?"

Davis checked the interview sheets. "We missed about a dozen. The apartment numbers are listed on the sheets."

Malone said, "What about the other buildings in the complex."

"Same thing. The broad was a phantom," Davis answered.

"What about Forensic?"

O'Shaughnessy answered. "They came up with a few partial prints. About twelve or fifteen points. More than enough for a positive I.D. if we can come up with a suspect.''

"Were the prints compared with Eisinger's?" Malone asked.

"Yeah. They cut the skin of her fingers off and rolled them at the morgue. They weren't her prints," O'Shaughnessy answered.

"I went back to the scene last night and found this," Malone said, taking out the strip of film and omitting any mention of the phony Captain Madvick's telephone call. "Let's take a look," Malone said, walking out from behind his desk.

O'Shaughnessy went over to the equipment locker and took out the viewing machine. He set it up and then went around the squad room shutting off the lights and pulling down the shades.

Jake Stern slowly maneuvered the film under the machine's glaring light. A conical beam threw a blurred picture onto the wall. Stern reached in front, turning the lens, adjusting the focus. Even in the eerie reversal of the negative, it was clear that the subject matter was a man and a woman in bed, making love.

"That dude can really breathe through his ears," joked O'Shaughnessy.

"I hope he comes up for air so we can get a look at his face," Malone said, watching with interest.

The male star surfaced two frames later.

"Jake, send that film to the lab. Have them blow up each frame and make us some stills," Malone said.

"Ten-four," Stern said, switching off the machine and removing the film.

Malone walked over to the large desk next to the wall. The property that had been removed from the Eisinger apartment was neatly lined up over the desk, each item in plastic evidence bags, tagged with property clerk's evidence tags. Malone picked up the bag containing the keys. "Anything on this?" he asked, holding up the gold-plated key.

"It don't fit any of the locks in her apartment," Stern said.

Malone examined the key. An ordinary house key that had been gold plated. A locksmith's six-digit registration number was stamped across its head. He tossed it to Heinemann. "Check the registration number with Consumer Affairs. Find out who made it and for whom. Anything on the cuffs?"

"Not yet. We're waiting to hear from Smith and Wesson," Stern answered.

Malone walked to the portable blackboard in the corner and wheeled it into the center of the room. He picked up a piece of chalk and started to outline the Eisinger case.

The detectives gathered around.

Across the top of the blackboard Malone blocked out the heading: Eisinger Homicide. Next to it he listed the case's serial numbers: UF 61# 6739; UF 60# 4278; UF 6# 9846; Forensic # 1298-80; Property Vouchers A 456798-812.

The date, time, and place of occurrence were listed below the heading. A diagram of each room was sketched in broken lines, the bathroom done in a larger scale. On the right side of the board each piece of inventoried evidence was listed along with its invoice number. WITNESSES was blocked out on the bottom left side. The space under it was blank.

Malone stepped back, folding his arms, frowning. "Not very much, is it?"

He studied it for a while and then flipped the blackboard to the reverse side.

"Okay! Bo, I want you and Pat to recanvass her apartment building. Get the ones that were missed yesterday. There had to be someone who knew her. Also check with the local storekeepers. She had to eat and brush her teeth. And don't waste time trying to put the make on any women."

Malone listed the assignment on the board. "I want a five on every interview," he added.

The lieutenant turned his attention to Jake Stern.

"Jake, I want you to visit the morgue. Get hold of Epstein. Tell him I want to know when and how."

Malone stared at the blackboard. "The rest of us will hold down the fort. Gus, I want you to stay with the phones and see what you can come up with."

The flower cart standing against the building with the glazed brick façade on the corner of Thirtieth Street and First Avenue had a red umbrella. Its top was terraced with fresh-cut flowers. Roses, gerbera, carnations, irises, tulips, daffodils, a profusion of color that enhanced a beautiful June morning. Medical students in jeans and white jackets, stethoscopes jutting proudly from pockets, crossed from the Bellevue Hospital Center to their dormitories on First Avenue. A group of student nurses were standing next to the cart eying the students, giggling.

Jake Stern glanced at the cart as he hurried up the wide steps into the building. The flowers reminded him of his wife, Marcia. She loved to work in the garden of their Howard Beach home. Whenever he wanted her for something and could not find her in the house he knew that she'd be outside puttering around her plants and flowers. Now that their only son Jeff was away studying business administration at the State University of Binghamton, she was always in the garden. As he pushed through into the lobby, he reflected on how he had almost lost his family. That was three years ago. He had been having an affair with one of his wife's girlfriends.

One night the girlfriend and her husband paid the Sterns a visit. He had a little too much to drink and got stupid. Marcia caught him playing footsy with the girlfriend under the kitchen table. The next day when he told his wife that he was going to take the car in for a tune-up she followed him. When he and his lady friend left the motel on Crossbay Boulevard two hours later Marcia was leaning up against his car tapping her foot. He would always remember that one excruciating moment when his bowels gave way.

Forty minutes later in the living room of their split-level home Marcia Stern gave her husband a choice: wife or girlfriend. There was to be no compromise. Ashen, he began to look around his home: gold wall-to-wall carpet, French provincial furniture wrapped in plastic to keep it clean, bulbous lamp shades with hanging rhinestones, and, also encased in plastic, heavy dining-room furniture with carved cherubs on the breakfront, and in the basement his weights. He begged; she forgave. He never mentioned the incident to any of the guys in the Squad, nor had he ever cheated again.

Stern's cheerfulness vanished as he walked down the stairway leading into the morgue. In the basement were corridors of stainless-steel boxes, their latched doors shining under overhead fluorescent lights. There were bare concrete floors with evenly spaced drains. Gurneys lined the corridors; bodies under white sheets, protruding legs with slanted feet and identification tags looped over big toes. In the corner of the basement there was a huge freezer. Inside, Stern knew, were baby cadavers, waiting their turns to be cut up by medical students. An omnipresent sweet smell lingered in the cold air, tickling the back of the mouth. Stern had often been a visitor to this timeless place and he hated it. He pushed through the double doors with the black rubber apron and turned right, heading for the cutting room.

Six tables were occupied. Four of the bodies had their chest cavities opened by an incision that ran from the neck, down the center of the chest, to the pubic hair. The rib cages were pried open, exposing the inner organs. There was a scale next to each table. An attendant was cutting off a cranium with a high-speed circular saw.

Sol Epstein was studying the inside of a body, whistling "Zippety Doo Dah" and waving his scalpel in a mime of leading a band. A microphone hung over his head recording words and music.

Stern rolled his eyes as he entered the cutting room. "How's my favorite ghoul?"

"Quick, Jose, my saw. We've got a live one to work on," Epstein said, looking up.

"You look right at home, Sol."

39

"What brings you into my world?" Epstein asked, reaching inside the cadaver.

"Sara Eisinger."

Epstein lifted the liver out of the cadaver and held it up to the detective. "Hungry? It's yummy with onions and bacon." He turned away and slapped the organ onto the scale.

"Tell me the results of the post so I can get the hell out of here," Stern said, walking over and looking inside the chest cavity.

Epstein looked up and smiled. "Okay. Person or persons unknown did willfully beat the shit out of her and then shoved a curtain rod up her cunt. Sara Eisinger's skull was crushed. The lower jaw was shattered. A twenty-seven-inch curtain rod was jammed into her. Her intestines were ripped to pieces. The abdominal muscle, the vagina, small intestines, colon, stomach, and abdominal aorta were destroyed. Whoever did it poked the rod around inside of her, like he was fishing. It wasn't a painless death. There was massive hemorrhage and shock, either of which was enough to kill her."

"So what finally did the job?" Stern asked, admiring the skill of the doctor's hands as they probed the various organs of the body.

"She drowned. We found water in the lungs. Evidently she was still breathing when they tossed her into the tub."

"How long was she dead?"

"To be positive, we'll have to wait for the laboratory results of her organs. The castings that we found on the body indicated fourth-generation maggots. From that and the degree of decomposition I'd say about a week."

"Malone would appreciate it if you could rush the lab report."

Epstein removed another part of the body and placed it on the scale. He frowned. "Jake, old buddy, your lieutenant is going to have to learn that the man who made time made plenty of it."

40

Stern shrugged, resigned to waiting. "Did you come up with anything else?"

"We scraped her fingernails and found human flesh. Evidently she put up a fight. The skin was from the face of a male Caucasian with a heavy beard. When I get the lab report I'll send it to you, direct."

"Thanks, Sol." Stern turned to leave.

"Jake?"

"Yeah?"

"I'll walk you out," Epstein said, laying down his scalpel. He stripped off his gloves.

When they were in the corridor outside the cutting room, Epstein draped his arm over Stern's shoulder and shepherded him toward the exit. They stepped aside for an attendant wheeling a loaded gurney.

"I want to thank you and Malone for calling me on the Gavin matter," Epstein said.

"Think nothing of it, Doc."

"Tell Malone that I received a thank-you card from the Powerhouse."

"What was in it? Carving knives?"

"An appointment to the State University of New York Downstate Medical Center in Brooklyn."

"Is that a good deal?"

"The tenderloin, my friend. A dream come true."

"The Powerhouse always does the right thing."

They started on the top floor of Sara Eisinger's apartment building. Today they were lucky. Most of the people were home. But the results were the same: no one knew the victim. After two hours on the recanvass they were only on the sixth floor. One apartment still had to be done, 6B. O'Shaughnessy rang the pushbutton in the center of the brass peephole and stood back as the chime echoed inside the apartment. No answer. He rang again.

"No one at home. We'll have to come back," Davis said, circling the apartment number on the interview sheet.

"May I help you gentlemen?"

The detectives turned and saw an attractive woman in her early thirties stepping off the elevator. She was carrying bundles of groceries.

"I'm Janet Fox and that is my apartment. If you don't tell me who the hell you are and what you want, I'm going to start the loudest scream you've ever heard in your lives."

Davis pulled out his shield and I.D. card and held them up to her. "We're detectives. There was a homicide in this building yesterday and we're investigating it," he said.

"Poor Sara. I just heard about it today. She was such a wonderful human being," she said.

"You knew her?" O'Shaughnessy asked.

"We were friends," she answered.

Janet Fox had a cozy apartment with a terrace overlooking Chinatown. She sat on a cushioned ottoman in front of a recliner. The detectives exchanged glances. Davis arched his brow, indicating that he would do the questioning. O'Shaughnessy picked up the cue, nodded, and moved to the sofa across from where she was sitting.

Janet Fox had first met Eisinger in the building's laundry room. They had become friends; if one of them went on vacation the other would take in the mail and water the plants. Occasionally they had tea together, talked about the latest fashions. Janet Fox wasn't sure where Sara Eisinger had worked. For a travel agency somewhere in Manhattan, she thought. What about her sex life? That was something they never discussed. "Never?" Davis said, not convinced.

The witness stirred uncomfortably. She leaned forward, pulling her knees to her. "I guess there was someone," she said, reluctantly. "But Sara never mentioned him." About a year and a half ago, the witness said, Sara came to her and asked for the name of a gynecologist. "She wanted to get a diaphragm."

"Who were her friends?" Davis asked.

"I don't know."

"What about acquaintances?"

"Sara stayed very much to herself."

"She had no other friends in the building?"

"None that I know of."

Davis said, "You mean to tell me that in the five years that she lived here you never once observed her with anyone?"

"I never thought of it before, but yes. Never," she answered bewildered. "But wait!" she was quick to add. "I did see her with a man. It was about six months ago. It was raining very hard. I had just gotten home from work and was running to get inside when I heard Sara calling to me. She was getting out of a car, opening an umbrella. I ran over to her and we shared her umbrella. A man was driving the car that she was getting out of."

"Did she tell you who he was?" Davis asked, looking at Pat who had his memo pad and pencil ready.

"No, she didn't. I didn't pry and she didn't volunteer any information. I think that's why we got along. Neither of us pried into the other's life."

"Describe the man you saw in the car."

"I was hurrying to get out of the rain. I only caught a glimpse of him."

"Was he white or black?"

"White."

"Was he young or old?"

"Sort of young."

"Was he over twenty?"

"Yes."

"Over thirty?"

"Yes."

"Over forty?"

"Yes."

"Over fifty?"

43

"I'd say somewhere in his early forties."

"Forty-five?"

"I'm not sure."

"Guess!"

"Forty-three, maybe."

"What about his complexion? Dark? Swarthy? Light? Fair?"

"Fair complexioned."

"What color was his hair?"

"Wiry, blond hair."

"What color were his eyes?"

"I don't know."

She also remembered that he was very handsome. With sculptured eyebrows that seemed tweezed. She couldn't recall how tall he was. After all, he was sitting behind the wheel of the car. About six foot, she guessed. And well built. The car? A little red Japanese one. A Honda, she thought. She told her interrogator that there came a time when she picked up mail for Sara Eisinger. He asked her if there was anything out of the ordinary about the mail that the victim received. Just junk mail and an occasional letter from overseas.

"From what countries?"

"Israel."

"Is there anything that you can think of that might help us?"

"I'm sorry, there isn't. I was surprised that I was able to remember what I did."

"You did real good," Davis said, crossing the room to sit next to his partner.

Janet Fox relaxed. She looked down at her palms. They were wet. She had not been aware of the tension before.

"Janet, there is one more question that I would like to ask," Davis said.

Her stomach tightened. "Yes?"

"You told us that you just heard about the murder today.

44

A homicide in your apartment building, and you just found out about it?''

She looked at the detective and said hesitantly, ''I was away for a few days.''

''Where?''

The witness shifted. ''I was at the Concord with my boss. He's married and his name is Joseph Grossman.''

Davis turned to his partner. ''Pat, why don't you continue knocking on doors. I'll stay here and ask Janet a few more questions, get the name of the doctor that Eisinger used. It'll save us time.''

O'Shaughnessy was on the second floor when his partner caught up with him.

''How'd it go?'' O'Shaughnessy asked, making an obscene jabbing gesture with his fist.

''Nothing like that!'' Davis said. ''She's a very nice lady. We sat and talked, that's all. How'd you make out?''

''Zippo. She paid her rent, didn't cause no trouble, and no one knows shit about her.''

''What's with the Curtain Rod Caper?'' Inspector Zambrano bellowed, sweeping into Malone's office.

Malone took the Eisinger case folder out of the file basket and handed it to him.

Zambrano sat down, attentively flipping through the fives. He looked up at Malone. ''Looks to me like you got a winner on your hands. Need any help?''

''I'll yell if I do.''

''Dan, I know that this ain't the right time, but in a few weeks I'm going to do the annual evaluation of your stewardship of the Squad. Try and get your paper in shape and don't forget Operation Participation.''

Malone leaned forward, eyebrows raised. ''Know something, Inspector. Working here is like pissing in a dark suit. You get that warm feeling, but nobody notices.''

''That's a very nice analogy, Dan. But don't forget the fucking paper.''

Heinemann came into the office and closed the door behind him. ''Bwana! I just heard from the Wagon Board. Guess where those telephone numbers belong?''

''Cut the bwana bullshit and tell me,'' Malone said.

Heinemann snapped to attention. ''Both of them are confidential listings of Central Intelligence Agency phones.''

''Aw shit! Not them bastards,'' Malone said, slapping the desk.

Heinemann leaned against the door. ''The out-of-town number is a direct line to their headquarters in McLean. The other is a restricted line to their New York City field office.''

''Did you contact them?'' Malone said.

''What for? They're not about to tell us anything over the telephone.''

Zambrano turned, on his way out, a sardonic grin on his lips. ''Handle this very, very carefully. And I'd watch my ass. They're bigger liars than we are.''

It was after three when O'Shaughnessy and Davis returned from their visit to Eisinger's gynecologist.

''The doctor fitted Eisinger with a catcher's mitt,'' Davis told the lieutenant.

''Did we find a diaphragm in the apartment?'' Malone asked, checking the property sheet.

Jake Stern shook his head.

''I wonder where it is?'' Malone thought aloud. ''That's not something a woman leaves just anywhere.''

Malone sat back and laced his hands behind his head, listening to Davis tell him about their interview with Janet Fox.

Heinemann entered the office and perched on Malone's

desk. "Those cuffs were shipped to Greenblatts. I just telephoned them," Heinemann said, when Davis finished. "Their records show that they sold them to a Philip Alexander back in December. The name is probably as phony as the address that the guy gave."

"What else have you come up with?" Malone asked.

"My source at Social Security informed me that the Eisinger account showed only two employers. The Eastern Shipping Company in Long Island City and Braxton Tours in Manhattan. I contacted another source at Dun and Bradstreet. They have nothing on Eastern Shipping. Braxton Tours is a big travel agency that's run by a brother and sister, Aldridge and Thea Braxton. They work out high-priced trips for special groups. They specialize in Middle East tours."

"Anything else?" asked Malone, snapping forward and getting up.

"The registration numbers on the gold-plated key were traced to a locksmith on Canal Street. They've been making the keys for a joint on the East Side called the Interlude. I called a buddy of mine in the Nineteenth. He told me the Interlude is one of them posh key clubs that cater to the beautiful people. Anything goes, no questions asked," Heinemann said.

Malone walked into the squad room, checking his watch.

"I'm going to pay a visit to Braxton Tours."

"Want me to tag along?" Heinemann asked, following the lieutenant out of his office.

"Pat caught the case. I'll take him. I want you and Jake to stay on the Interlude. Check with the Hall of Records and find out who owns the building. Then get in touch with the Department of State in Albany. Find out who has the charter for the club. Then check with State Liquor and find out who buys the booze."

Braxton Tours occupied a suite of offices on the sixteenth floor of a huge glass-walled office building on Park. Attractive young women padded their way between glass-partitioned offices. The floors were carpeted; the furniture comfortable, expensive. Thea Braxton was waiting for them. She wore a beautifully tailored white, raw silk Chanel suit. Her shoulder-length hair was ash blond, enhancing the mature beauty of her tanned face. Her expression was coldly composed.

"We've been expecting the police ever since we read of Sara's death in the newspapers," Thea said, dismissing her secretary with a wave.

Malone measured her as he entered the office. He already had guessed just what she would say. Sara had been with the company for a year and a half. She stayed to herself and had no close friends within the company. Thea knew nothing of her personal life. What a pity that such a horrible thing should happen to such a beautiful young girl. Who could be responsible for such an act of barbarism? The newspaper accounts were just ghastly.

Thea moved from behind her desk and motioned to a grouping of canvas director chairs in front of a thermopane wall, through which a huge slice of the city could be seen below.

"What can you tell me about Sara Eisinger?" Malone asked, noticing the sunlight reflecting off her head. Her response was exactly what he had suspected it would be.

"She was a conscientious worker," Thea answered.

"She didn't seem to have many friends. Can you tell us why?"

"By choice, I guess. Sara preferred to stay to herself. Everyone isn't gregarious," Thea said, looking at Malone who was standing directly in front of her.

"Hmm. That's true enough," Malone said, walking over to the far wall, examining the paintings.

"There must be big bucks in the travel business," Malone said, loud enough for her to hear. "What was Eisinger's responsibility with your company?"

"She arranged group tours to the Middle East. Israel in particular."

Thea explained that being an Israeli, Sara Eisinger had

access to many Jewish groups. "They love to travel." Eisinger arranged charter tours and received a 5 percent commission on everything over a hundred thousand dollars. When Malone asked her if the travel business was the Braxtons' only business interest, Thea replied that it was their main interest. Lately, they had branched out into social research.

"What's that?" asked Malone, now apparently absorbed by the view of Manhattan.

She explained that before companies do business overseas they want to know all that they can about the country in which they'll do business. A lot of money can be lost if one doesn't know the customs of a host country. What is polite in the United States can be downright insulting in some parts of the world. Malone seemed surprised. "Don't companies have their own research staffs?" he asked.

The large ones do, she told him. But many of the smaller companies that were vying for a piece of the OPEC dollar do not and some of those companies came to Braxton Tours.

"Interesting," Malone said, turning to face her. "Do you know anyone who'd want her dead?"

"Of course not."

"What about her love life?"

Her hands went to her hips. "We do not pry into the personal lives of our employees."

"No office romance?" he asked, sensing her annoyance and deciding to follow it and see where it led him.

"None that I know of."

"Was she straight, gay, or ambidextrous?"

"I don't know what she was. And furthermore I don't care."

"Did she have any close girlfriends?"

"None that I know of."

"How did Eisinger get her job with your company?"

"She answered an ad that we put in the *New York Times* for someone with language abilities. Sara spoke six languages."

"Really? What were they?"

49

"German, Polish, English, Hebrew, Spanish, and Ladino," she replied.

"Eisinger was dead for about a week before her body was discovered. How come you didn't report her missing?"

"Sara took a week off. She went to visit her parents in New Jersey. She wasn't due back until yesterday."

"Can you think of anything that might help us?"

"I wish that I could think of something," she said, reaching for a porcelain jar on the table in front of her. She removed a cigarette and lit it.

"I hope that you catch the people responsible," she said, putting the lid back on the jar.

"We will. We'd like to interview your employees. That is, if you have no objections," Malone said.

"Of course not," Thea Braxton said, taking a drag.

The door opened and a thin man in an impeccably tailored beige suit walked into the room.

"Hello. I'm Aldridge Braxton," he said as he moved toward Malone and offered his hand.

Aldridge Braxton's face was starting to wither. Crows' feet furrowed deep around the eyes; dark circles were terraced in various shades of black. He had styled his unruly black hair into a moderate afro.

"Did you know her well?" Malone asked him after the introductions.

"Not as well as I would have liked to. She was a strange young lady in many ways. She reminded me of a person who was afraid to enjoy life," Aldridge said, moving to the vacant chair next to his sister.

"What can you tell us about her personal life?" Malone asked.

"Nothing, I'm afraid," Aldridge answered.

Malone walked over to Thea's desk. He picked up a figurine that had caught his attention. A gold goddess in a flounced skirt clutching snakes in both outstretched hands. He studied it carefully, then put it back.

"Can either of you think of anything . . . ?" Malone asked them.

The Braxtons looked at each other. They turned in unison and shook their heads.

"In that case, we'd like to interview your employees," Malone said.

Thea Braxton got up, crossed to her desk, and pushed the button on the intercom with her forefinger. Her secretary reappeared. "Arlene, please escort these gentlemen around the office. They're policemen here to interview everyone concerning Sara's death."

As they were walking out of the office, Malone pulled a pad from his pocket and stopped a moment to scratch a note to O'Shaughnessy: *ck.* N.Y. Times *for Braxton ad seeking employee with language ability. Find out when inserted and withdrawn.* He handed the note to O'Shaughnessy and followed Arlene out of the office.

"That Braxton broad has really got her shit all together," O'Shaughnessy whispered.

Malone shot him a look. "Maybe just a little too together." He then whispered to O'Shaughnessy. "Keep Arlene busy while I talk to the operator." He stepped ahead of the woman and entered the telephone cubicle, closing the door behind him.

O'Shaughnessy moved ahead and blocked the door, preventing Arlene from following inside.

The operator was eager to help. "Sara used to receive calls from a man with an accent," she said. "They always talked in a foreign language."

"What language?"

"I don't know."

"Was it Spanish?"

"Oh, no. It was one of the European languages."

"French?"

"No."

"German?"

"It might have been. I'm really lousy on languages."

"What was the man's name?"

"I don't know. He never gave his name. Just asked for Sara Eisinger."

"How old would you say he was?"

"I don't know. How could I tell his age?"

"By the sound of his voice. Take a guess."

"I'd say late thirties early forties."

"When did this man first start to call her?"

"The very first day she started to work here."

"Are you the only operator?"

"Yes. If I'm sick or on vacation, they get a temporary in."

"Did this man call her often?"

"Every day that she was in the office. Sometimes two and three times."

"And he never once mentioned his name?"

"Never."

"Do all calls come through your board?"

"Yes. Only the Braxtons have direct lines."

"Did she ever receive other personal calls?"

"Hmm. I don't think so."

Malone saw a shadow cross her face.

"What happened to Eisinger could happen to every woman who lives alone. It's important that we know who she talked to. Everything that you tell me will be confidential, I promise."

Malone folded his arms over the top of the switchboard, leaning forward, looking down at her. "Please."

She looked up. The board buzzed. She answered the incoming call and routed it.

"You might save another woman's life," Malone said.

"A woman by the name of Andrea used to call her from time to time," she said.

"What can you tell me about this Andrea?"

"Nothing. They used to talk in different languages."

"What languages?"

"I don't know. Sometimes they'd speak in English."

"What did they talk about?" he asked casually.

"Lieutenant! I don't listen in on conversations!"

"I certainly did not mean to imply that you would intentionally listen in. But everyone knows that sometimes operators accidentally press the wrong button."

"Well, actually I did overhear part of a conversation. They were talking in English, Andrea and Sara. It was the Thursday before she left on vacation. Sara was talking very excitedly about a song. She told Andrea to look at the song."

"Did she mention the name of the song?"

"No. She just told her to look at the song. That she would understand when she did."

"Understand what?"

She raised her shoulders and grimaced. "I don't know."

FRIDAY, *June 12*

When Malone walked in he saw an old couple sitting on
the bench outside the squad room. The woman had drawn her
gray hair back into a bun. Her dress was plain and black and
too big for her. Her head was lowered, and her thumb stroked
the clasp of the plastic pocketbook on her lap. The man
slumped and stared at his spotted hands. Malone glanced at
them as he passed. He walked into the squad room and went
directly over to the coffee urn. As he poured, Malone studied
the rolls inside the torn bag next to the urn. He selected one
topped with sugar crumbs, bit into it, and stepped back to
avoid the shower of powdered sugar. "Who are they?" Malone asked, pointing his head toward the door.

Jake Stern looked up from the typewriter. "The Eisingers.
The New Brunswick PD notified them this morning."

"Give me a minute and bring them in," Malone said, taking another bite and heading toward his office.

Malone looked down at the 60 sheet. On the late tour one
Rose Jennings, female, black, age 32, got fed up with her
married boyfriend's broken promises and urinated into a
saucepan. She then went into the kitchen and removed a can
of lye from under the sink. She went back to the bathroom
and poured the lye into the saucepan. Holding the pan carefully with two hands and shaking the mixture as she walked,
Rose Jennings headed for the bedroom. She hovered over the

54

bed, looking down at the sleeping man. "Lying mother-fucker," she screamed just before throwing the contents over his face. He'd never be handsome again. Rose Jennings then went to the telephone and called the police, the wife, and an ambulance. Very accommodating lady, thought Malone, sipping from the mug with the word COP stenciled on the front. Another grounder. His luck was still holding.

"Lieutenant, this is Hanna and Jacob Eisinger," Stern said, steering them into the office and gesturing to the uneven cluster of chairs.

"I want to tell you how sorry we are," Malone began. "I want you to know that we're doing everything possible to apprehend the people responsible."

The Eisingers said nothing. They were frozen in shock and grief; they stared fixedly at the cards and telephone numbers stuffed under the glass top. Gently, Malone probed. Who were their daughter's friends? Did they know of anyone who would want to kill her? Was there anything about their daughter's past that the police should know? Malone's questions were met by silence. He looked over to O'Shaughnessy, Davis, and Stern who were lolling against the wall. Davis drew up his shoulders in a hapless gesture.

"Can't you think of anything that might help us?" Malone pleaded. Cold silence. "Don't you want us to catch the people who killed your daughter?"

Hanna Eisinger started to speak. She told a story that Malone had heard before. She had been persecuted but had survived Nazi Germany. She had emigrated to Palestine and started a new life. She told of the birth of their daughter and the joy of watching her grow into a beautiful woman. When Sara was of age she went into the army and met a boy and fell in love for the first time. When the Eisingers decided to come to the United States their Sara said that she would come with them.

"Do you know any of your daughter's friends?" Malone asked.

Jacob Eisinger stiffened. His shoulders reared up in defiance. "Friends?" he said. "We have learned to live without the luxury of friends. Our Sara was the same way."

Malone started to ask random questions, searching for something that might give him a lead.

"What did your daughter do when she was in the army?" Malone asked.

"She was a clerk at a supply base forty kilometers from Jerusalem," Jacob Eisinger said. Hanna Eisinger leaned across the desk and clutched Malone's arm. A supplicant's grasp. "Why won't they let us have our daughter? We have to bury her. It's the law."

Malone swallowed. He looked over at his detectives in time to see Stern push away from the wall and leave the office.

"I'll see that she is released," Malone said gently.

Jacob Eisinger asked if they might leave. "Just a few more questions," Malone said. "How old was your daughter?"

"Thirty-four," the mother answered.

"And how long had she lived in this country?"

"Six years," answered the father.

"Do you have any photographs of your daughter?" Malone asked, remembering that the only one they had was taken at the morgue. Hanna Eisinger looked to her husband. The old man's face quivered as he reluctantly nodded consent. Hanna Eisinger opened the pocketbook and removed a snapshot. It was a small black and white with a coarse grain. Sara Eisinger was standing on a long pier in front of a file of freighters that stretched along a dock, the ships secured by taut mooring lines. Mounds of crates were stacked on the pier. The girl in the photograph was laughing and waving off the unknown photographer.

"Where was this taken?" Malone asked, studying the photo.

"I don't know," the mother answered.

"When was it taken?" Malone asked.

"It was taken on one of Sara's European vacations before she came to live in this country," replied the father.

"Did Sara take many vacations when she lived in Israel?" asked Malone.

"Yes," the mother said.

Malone laid the snapshot down in front of him, tapping it with his middle finger. "You have no idea where this was taken?"

"No," Hanna Eisinger said. "Is it important?"

"Maybe. May I keep it for a while?" He saw their hesitation. "I promise that I'll return it to you."

Jacob Eisinger lowered his head. Malone took his silence for consent.

"Did your daughter ever mention any of the men in her life?" Malone asked.

"No," Hanna Eisinger said flatly.

"What kind of work did Sara do in this country?" Malone asked, watching them closely.

"She worked for a travel agency arranging tours to Israel," the mother said.

"Will that be all?" Jacob Eisinger said, lifting himself up out of the chair and turning to help his wife.

"Thank you for coming by," Malone said, standing and rounding his desk. "I'll have one of my detectives drive you to the station."

"We'll take a taxi," Jacob Eisinger said.

The department mail arrived at 1400. The blowups Malone had ordered were in a manila folder. He removed the enlargements, thumbed through them quickly, and then examined them a second time, scrutinizing each one. There was a chair next to the bed on which an army officer's uniform was neatly folded. The blouse was draped over the back of the chair and the insignia on the lapels showed that the owner of the uniform was assigned to the Quartermaster Corps. Malone handed the photographs to Davis.

"He's a major," Bo Davis said, flipping through the photographs. "And I'm willing to bet that the ring he's wearing is from the Point. He also likes to eat hair pie."

"She's a pretty lady," Davis added. "Wonder what her name is?"

It was at that moment that Gus Heinemann shambled into the room and lowered his hulk into a chair. "Have I got some bad news," Heinemann said, struggling to lift his left foot onto the edge of the desk. He had just returned from the Hall of Records. The Interlude was owned by the Agamemnon Entertainment Corporation and the building wherein the club was located was owned by the Menelaus Realty Corporation. After that it was a dead end. Finding the real owners could take weeks. "I hope you gentlemen don't have any pressing personal plans for this evening," Malone said firmly. "We're going to be sitting on the Interlude tonight."

Sitting on a "plant"—what cops on TV call a stakeout— is like looking at a small section of a street under a microscope. Few people ever take the time to examine a mailbox or a street lamp. Detectives do. They spend many hours sitting in parked cars or standing in the shelter of doorways waiting for someone to arrive or leave a location; or just waiting for something to happen.

The Interlude was a four-story brownstone on East Fifty-eighth Street. The streets in this part of town were clean and litter free. Each tree had its own well-tended square of dirt. Doormen strolled along the streets holding onto leashes with expensively groomed little dogs. Joggers navigated the sidewalks. Six stone steps led up to a double door with scrolled grillwork. The windows were dark and blank.

O'Shaughnessy and Davis were in the front seat of a department taxi that was parked on the south side of Fifty-eighth Street. Det. Starling Johnson was slumped in the rear. Johnson was a recently divorced black man with a cherubic face, oversize horn-rimmed glasses, flaring sideburns, and plenty of time to kill. The other detectives were on O.T. from the day tour; Johnson was working a night duty. A green Buick Electra that had been confiscated by the Federal Narcotics Task Force in San Francisco, driven cross country by an automobile transporter with a government contract, and traded to the NYPD for a white Eldorado that had been confiscated in Harlem, was parked on Sutton Place a block from the Interlude. Malone and Stern were in the front seat. Gus Heinemann was stretched across the back seat, stuffing Milky Ways into his mouth and discarding the wrappers on the crushed velour seat. An hour passed. The Interlude was in darkness, save for a single light on the top floor. Heinemann felt the gurgling in his stomach. "I'm starving," he bellowed, patting his large belly.

"Any of you ever work with Hy Rothman?" Jake Stern asked, pressing an exercise hand grip in his left hand.

"Suicide Rothman? I had that pleasure," Malone said. "That son-of-a-bitch tried to turn every homicide he caught into a suicide. I was working a late tour one summer on temporary duty in Central Park. I was only out of the Academy a few months. It was around six in the morning and I'd just come out of the heave to make a ring. I was talking to the sergeant over the call box when I noticed a set of legs sticking out of the bushes. It was a stiff with a hole in his left temple and a thirty-eight clutched in his right hand. I called the sergeant, roped off the crime scene as best I could. . . . I did the whole bit. An hour later Rothman comes strolling up to the scene chewing on a five-cent cigar. He looked down at the body, moved the cigar to the other side of his mouth, and said, 'It's definitely a suicide.' I couldn't believe what I was hearing. I told him he was nuts. The stiff would have had to wrap his arm around his head in order to shoot himself in the left temple. Besides, I told him, there weren't any powder burns. Rothman gave that . . . 'Let me take a look, kid' routine and bent to examine the body. He pried the gun out of the DOA's right hand, lets one go up in the air, rubs the barrel against the left temple and plants the gun back in the left hand. He looks up at me and said, 'As I was saying, kid, it's a suicide.' Could you imagine pulling that shit today?''

"No way," Stern said.

Malone ducked his head down and pulled the mike from the cradle of the concealed radio set under the dashboard. He checked to make sure the frequency dial was on two, the frequency which permitted car-to-car communication. He stayed low to make sure that anyone looking in would not see him using the radio. "Bo?''

"Yeah, Lou?''

"See anything?''

"Nothing.''

The detectives waited. No one entered or left the Interlude. Business hours had not yet begun. A light summer rain danced over the cars; uneven rivulets streaked the windshields. Davis and O'Shaughnessy slumped low in their seats. Starling Johnson catnapped.

"How's Foam?'' Davis asked O'Shaughnessy.

Starling Johnson flicked open his right eye. "You still seein' that woman?''

"Yep. It's four years and I haven't gone for a nickel.''

As though a magic button had been pressed, the Interlude sprang to life. The lights blazed on and shortly afterward limousines and taxis began to pull up in front of the club. The beautiful people were gathering.

"On deck,'' Malone said into the mike.

Each license plate number was recorded. A description of each guest was taken down. Johnson kept a record of the times of arrival of each vehicle. It stopped raining; the night turned quiet, the stillness occasionally broken by muted bursts of noise from the Interlude. Just after one, a limousine slid around the corner of Sutton Place and pulled into the curb in front of the Interlude. The windows of the car were over-sized and tinted a smoky black. Aldridge Braxton and two men got out and went up the steps of the club, disappearing into the vestibule.

"What the fuck is he doing here?" Malone said.

The detectives slumped lower. Then a darkened panel truck stopped half a block behind Braxton's limousine. Someone inside the truck lit a cigarette.

"Braxton has a shadow," O'Shaughnessy said over radio.

"Stay low," Malone warned. "We don't want to be made."

More time passed. A stray taxi would occasionally stop in front of the Interlude and discharge its passengers. Davis and Johnson dozed; O'Shaughnessy stood vigil, while Malone kept watching the club and the truck. A cigarette flew out of the truck's window and hit the pavement. Somewhere in the distance a siren wailed. The detectives could tell that it was a radio car on a run; the pitch was right.

Ninety minutes later the door of the Interlude opened and Aldridge Braxton came reeling out followed close behind by his two playmates. There was a woman with them. She was wearing a flowing black-and-white scarf dress and had heavily made-up eyes. Everyone was laughing. One of the men was pulling her by the arm as though playfully forcing her to leave with them. Braxton ran ahead, opening the limousine's door.

"It's now post time," Malone said into the mike.

"Who's the girl?" Heinemann asked Malone.

"Dunno, but she looks vaguely familiar," Malone said.

They piled into the rear and the limousine slid away from the curb. Malone waited. The truck moved off after the limousine with the clouded windows.

"How do you want this to go down," O'Shaughnessy asked Malone over the radio.

"We'll leapfrog them. I'll start," Malone said.

The dead hours of the night were over. Delivery trucks cut their way through the new daylight. Taxis cruised the empty streets. A lone jogger made her way unencumbered by traffic, and the detectives swiveled their heads to watch her bouncing breasts as she passed. The Buick took up position behind the truck for a dozen blocks. A taxi took its place. The limousine sped north on York Avenue. At Eighty-second Street the sleek vehicle cut diagonally across the avenue and came to a stop in front of an expensive co-op. Aldridge Braxton pulled open the door and got out. He stood with his arm draped over the open door, leaning into the car, talking and laughing. After several minutes the woman and two men got out and hurried into the building. Braxton got back inside and the limo sped off. The panel truck parked three blocks away on the east side of York Avenue.

Stern turned to the lieutenant. "What now?"

Malone checked his watch: 4:48. He assumed that Braxton was going home. Anyway, he knew where to find Braxton if he wanted him. Right now he wanted the pedigree on the three people who ran into that building and on whoever was inside that truck. He decided not to follow Braxton. He might need all his cars later. "We sit tight," Malone said, snatching up the mike. Staying low, Malone switched the frequency dial to the number that carried the regular police transmissions. He requested Central to dispatch a marked RMP to 10:85 them at their location and identify the panel truck and its occupants. Within a few minutes, a blue and white rolled to a stop behind the truck. Two hatless old-timers with sagging guts and drooping gun belts struggled out of the radio car. They meandered over, each separating and walking along the opposite side of the truck. "Lemme see ya license and registration, pal. Wadaya doin' parked here this time of the morning?" It wasn't necessary for the detectives to hear the monologue, every cop knows it by heart.

As the policemen waited for the driver to pass out the documents they scrutinized the two occupants. The driver was in his middle twenties. He had black curly hair that danced over a low forehead. A small knitted yarmulka was fastened to his pate. The passenger was shorter; a simian-looking fellow who also wore a yarmulka. Both of them wore rumpled khaki shirts.

The documents were passed out to the policeman. The other officer strolled to the rear of the truck. When he rounded the back, he rested his right foot on the bumper, bending as if to tie a shoelace. He tried the rear door and found it unlocked. He put his foot down and opened the door. When he did this the passenger leaped from the truck and ran to the back. He stood toe-to-toe with the cop, his angry face jutting at the policeman.

"You have no right to open that door!" His challenge of the cop's authority was a serious mistake. They began a shouting match and without warning the policeman kicked the man in the groin. As he doubled over, the policeman grabbed his hair, snapping the head upright. A fist smashed into the man's face, sending him staggering backward. The policeman came after him, ramming his fists into the man's shoulders. The force of the blows slammed him against the truck. He slid to the ground, blood trickling down his shirt front. The driver jumped from the truck and ran back to help his fallen friend. "Take your fuckin' buddy and get the hell out of here," the document taker said, throwing the license and registration inside the truck. The driver helped his friend off the ground, leading him back to the safety of the truck. The detectives watched as the truck bucked several times and then lurched forward and sped off down York Avenue.

"Let me see what that was all about," Malone said, yanking open the door. He walked over to the policemen. "Did they give you a hard time?" he asked.

The policeman who had attacked the passenger had grease stains over the front of his summer shirt. Too many pizzas, thought Malone, looking over the team. The attacker's breath was stale and smelled of alcohol. Both needed a shave.

"A search warrant," the attacker grumbled. "Imagine that fuckin' foreigner asking to see my search warrant."

63

"What were their names?" Malone asked.

The one who accepted the documents read from his memo pad. The driver was Hillel Henkoff and the passenger Isaac Arazi. Both gave an address on Borden Avenue in Long Island City. The truck was registered to the Eastern Shipping Company of the same address.

Malone looked at Heinemann and said thoughtfully: "That is where Sara Eisinger worked before she went to work for the Braxtons." Malone turned to the cop. "Was there anything else inside the truck?"

"A bunch of boxes with funny markings," said the officer who had knocked the passenger around.

"What kind of markings?" Malone said.

"Dunno. But I'll tell you one thing for sure, the inside of that truck stunk from cosmoline."

Malone's left eyebrow arched. "You sure?"

"I spent four years with the First Airborne. I know cosmoline when I smell it. I woulda popped one of them crates open only I didn't figure it a smart move with that guy throwing a shit fit."

"Anything else we can do for you, Lou?" the document taker said. "We're anxious to get back to serving the public."

Bullshit. They probably have a six-pack stashed under the seat of their radio car, Malone thought, but replied, "That's it. Thanks."

As the two uniformed cops sauntered back to their radio car, the document taker half turned and waved over his shoulder.

"What now?" O'Shaughnessy said.

Malone looked over to Gus Heinemann who was leaning against the fender of the Buick, matching the sides of a pair of dice. Seven all around. "You in the mood for one of your performances?" Malone said, lifting his chin toward the building Braxton's friends had entered.

Heinemann nodded, dropped the dice into his shirt pocket, and pushed away from the car. He returned fifteen minutes later, a satisfied smile on his face. "The doorman was a retired cop. He told me that they went to the thirty-first-floor apartment that's owned by Braxton Tours. The corner apartment, facing Eighty-second."

Malone looked up, surveying the canyons of terraced elegance which surrounded them. "That building over there," he said, pointing, "faces the Braxtons' apartment. If we could get onto the roof with a pair of binoculars we just might get a look-see inside that apartment." Malone turned to Davis. "Bo, get the glasses from under the seat. You and I will take a look. The rest of you stand by. If any of them leave before we get back, tail them."

Early-morning haze lingered high above the city streets. Davis looked over the edge, quickly stepping back. His palms were suddenly sweaty. Malone stood with his feet firmly planted on the pebbled roof, trying to get his bearings. Everything looked different so high up. He squandered a minute and took in the view across the river. The red-tipped stacks of the Con Ed plant rose majestically in front of the new sun. He could make out the bubbled tennis courts that dotted the shoreline of Long Island City. The brick-sheathed generator plant of the Midtown Tunnel ascended vertically over the mouth of the tunnel. The gothic crockets of the Queensborough Bridge seemed to be holding up the sky.

Malone looked away and walked over to the edge, staring across at the range of buildings, searching for the target building. He saw acres of glass and silver and steel skyscrapers and medium high-rises and low apartment buildings and terraces and penthouses and duplexes—Manhattan.

He picked out the Braxtons' building and leaned over the edge, starting to count the floors upward from the street. When he reached the thirty-first floor he brought the binoculars up to his eyes and began scanning the floor, adjusting the focus. He moved the glasses right to left. Suddenly he lurched forward, straining, sharpening the focus.

"Wadaya see?" Davis asked.

Malone kept silent. He remained motionless, the glasses fixed to his eyes. After some minutes, he turned abruptly and handed the binoculars to Davis, pointing to the corner apartment on the thirty-first floor.

Davis took the glasses and looked through them, making a slight adjustment on the focus wheel.

"That's one helluva party they're having. It's hard to tell who is doing what to whom," Davis said.

"Recognize the woman?"

"Noooo. But she sure has one beautiful pair of tits."

"You're looking at the female star of the porno film that we found in Eisinger's apartment."

Metal lockers lined one wall of the dormitory, black-faced combination locks hung through the hasps. Four bunk beds were flush against the wall. Large slivers of peeling paint drooped down from the walls and ceilings. Glossy posters of nude women covered the wall next to the beds. Heinemann lay on the bottom bunk, his right leg hanging over the edge. The men snored and the ripe smell of their farts hung in the air. O'Shaughnessy slid off the top bunk and padded to his locker. He pushed it open and took a toilet kit from the shelf. He left the room with his kit under his arm and his right arm thrust into his underpants, scratching his ass.

Starling Johnson was half asleep when O'Shaughnessy returned twenty minutes later, shaved, washed, and smelling like a perfume factory. Johnson shot up. "You mother! Bad enough I've got to listen to all this farting and snoring. I don't need you sashaying in here smelling like a French whore." Johnson leaped off the top bunk, put on his trousers, and walked barefoot out into the squad room. The smell of freshly made coffee filled the air. He walked over to the urn and poured a cup. A lone detective was doing day duty. He was at the far desk with his head buried in the typewriter. He looked up and nodded to Johnson who grunted hello.

Malone was leaning back and resting his shoeless feet on the desk. He had a coffee mug on his knee. He was looking at the blackboard, digesting the growing outline.

"It's beginning to fill out," Johnson said, walking in and draping an arm over the filing cabinet next to the door.

"We've still got a long way to go," Malone said.

Johnson asked, "Are you going to cut them men loose or do we keep going?"

Malone's left hand rose in a gesture of despair. "I hate like hell to lose the momentum, but we can't keep going forever."

One by one the detectives started to file in, sleep-filled eyes glancing at the blackboard. The telephone rang. Without taking his feet down, Malone stretched over and snatched up the receiver. After spending most of the night sitting on the Interlude, he was in no mood for Zambrano's abrasive voice. "Wadaya come up with last night?"

Malone pushed the instrument away from his ear and grimaced. Holding the phone in front of his face, he recounted the night's activities. He told Zambrano that O'Shaughnessy had followed the woman to a row house on Park Place in Brooklyn. The men were tailed to a loft in Soho.

"Did you get a make on them?" Zambrano asked.

"Not yet. O'Brien and Mullens are on the woman. Martinez and Valenti are on the men. They'll I.D. them."

"Why didn't you tail the guys in the truck?"

"Because I didn't have enough vehicles or men and because I wanted to get them the hell out of there so I could find out what was going down inside that apartment."

"How many men you got doing day duty?"

"I've got one detective holding it down. The other two are on the woman. The detectives on the men I pulled off tonight's night duty."

"So you're going to have just one man covering the chart tonight." There was a tinge of annoyed doubt in the inspector's voice.

"That's right."

"And you're holding yesterday's day duty team on O.T."

Malone forced a flat calmness into his voice. "Right again."

"You're stretching it kinda thin."

"Don't you think that I know that."

Zambrano yawned. "Guess it's time for me to get out of bed and get into the salt mine. Seeya later." Zambrano hung up.

Malone stared at his mouthpiece. "Son-of-a-bitch." He looked over at the detectives. Tired men make mistakes. "Go home and get some sleep."

"What are you going to do, Lou?" Starling Johnson asked.

"I'm going to pay a visit to a shipping company in Long Island City."

As Malone was about to leave, O'Shaughnessy called out and told him that he had a telephone call on line three. He went back into the squad room. This time there was no pretense or introduction. The voice that had been attributed to the name Madvick was harsh. "If you know what's good for you, Malone, you'll shitcan this Eisinger thing."

"Go fuck yourself, pal." He slammed down the receiver and left.

A maroon sedan kept a respectable distance behind the taxi as it maneuvered through the morning traffic on Flatbush Avenue. The cab made its way onto the Brooklyn Bridge. At Park Row it exited the bridge and sped east to Chatham Square. At the Bowery it turned north. When the taxi reached the corner of Hester Street it double parked and a woman got out. The chic clothes and fashionable wig of last night were gone. She was dressed quietly, her hair was held tightly in place by a paisley kerchief. She hurried away from the cab, walking up Hester Street. In the middle of the block she ducked into a three-story building. A sign in Hebrew was over the entrance. A plaque in English was bolted to the right of the door: EAST SIDE MIKVAH.

The maroon sedan glided in to the curb in front of a fire hydrant near the corner. "What's a mikvah?" O'Brien asked his partner.

"It's a religious bath that Jewish women go to once a month to get cleansed after their period," Mullens said.

"A hooker like that?"

"It takes all kinds."

Twenty minutes later the woman exited the mikvah and walked north. O'Brien slid out of the car. The woman walked five blocks, occasionally casting a nervous glance over her shoulder. In the middle of the fifth block she entered a restaurant with Hebrew lettering on the window. She went to an empty table next to the window. She was so distraught that she did not notice the man who entered a short time later and sat three tables away.

A stooped waiter with a seamed face shuffled over to O'Brien. "You vant something?"

The woman played with the food the waiter had brought her. She kept looking out the window, casting glances up and down the street, checking her watch. O'Brien had finished his dairy dish and was considering ordering another when a man walked into the restaurant and moved directly to the woman's table.

"Well?" he demanded, lowering himself into the seat across from her. O'Brien could just overhear their conversation.

"It wasn't there," she said.

"Are you sure that was the only mikvah she went to?"

"Yes, I'm sure," she said peevishly.

"We must locate that damned list," the man said.

"What more can I do?"

"I don't know. But I do know that the police are involved." The man leaned across the table, whispering, and

69

O'Brien was unable to hear the rest of the conversation. Suddenly the woman sat back in her chair, agitated. "I don't know where she hid it. She kept mentioning some goddamn song."

5

Van Dam was the last westbound exit on the Long Island Expressway before the Midtown Tunnel. Borden Avenue began on the other side of Van Dam and sliced through the industrial heart of Long Island City. At Borden and Thirtieth the men in hard hats from Tauscher Steel were standing on flatbeds loading shipments of I beams. The sidewalk in front of Alcock and Alcock Box Company was blocked with workmen assembling wooden crates. There was a continuous scampering of hi-lows in front of Capital Provisions as condiments for the city's restaurants and hotels were loaded. Detached trailers were parked everywhere. Railroad sidings crisscrossed the avenue. The normal flow of traffic was constantly blocked by tractor-trailers backing into loading bays. The outdoor vats behind Biddle and Gottesman Pickle and Sauerkraut Company gave the air a sharp, tangy smell.

Starling Johnson had not gone home. He had nothing better to do so he decided to tag along with Malone. He wasn't tired, so why not? Lately he found himself able to get by with less and less sleep.

He had not gotten used to living alone even though he had been divorced for two years and living alone for three. The clock still ticked too loud and the quiet was still too thunderous, and booze was still needed to get to sleep. He hated going into his apartment and turning on the TV or the radio right away. He knew that it was a sign of loneliness; but he just

71

had to hear voices, see people. He had a girlfriend; in fact, he had quite a few girlfriends. He found them boring and found himself counting the minutes until they got up, dressed, and left. He had a standing rule: no women were permitted to stay the night, nor were they allowed to leave any personal things in his apartment. If they left and he found anything of theirs he'd throw it in the garbage. No female was going to stake a claim on him or his apartment.

They had stopped for some eggs and coffee before heading to Queens. After breakfast they drove through the Midtown Tunnel and exited onto Borden Avenue right after the toll booth. It took the toll collector a few extra seconds to copy down the number of their vehicle identification plate before he waved them through the toll. Johnson was annoyed at the delay; perhaps he was tired.

Johnson parked the department auto across the street from the Eastern Shipping Company. After spending thirty minutes watching the place they both decided that there was something definitely off key. The other businesses on Borden Avenue were busy, with trucks pulling in and out of loading bays. The Eastern Shipping Company appeared to be abandoned. The building that they were watching was one and a half stories high and built in the shape of an irregular octagon. There were several banks of loading bays, each bay sealed by a sliding metal door. The windows were high and covered with steel mesh. In the rear of the building there was a railroad siding that was enclosed behind a chain-link fence topped with barbed wire. The filthy water of Newtown Creek flowed past the building's end. Gray crisscross girders of the Long Island Expressway dwarfed the front of the building. All around the outside were high-density lights, as well as TV cameras which surveyed the structure's periphery.

"Somethin' strange going down inside that place," Johnson said, puckering and lifting his eyebrows.

"Why don't we go see what." Malone got out now and led the way to a door with a sign on it that read NO SALESMEN

EXCEPT BY APPOINTMENT. They walked into a tiny drab room paneled in fake pine veneer. Behind a sliding glass panel in the far wall a receptionist who wore astoundingly oversized pink-framed glasses greeted them with total indifference. "May I help you gentlemen?"

"We are here to see the boss," Malone said, reaching into his pocket and pulling out a packet of business cards. He extracted one and glanced at it before handing it to her. "I'm John Grimes of the U.S. Department of Labor and this is my associate Tyrone Washington. We're here on official business."

The woman took the card, swung around in her chair, and pressed a button on the switchboard.

Johnson poked the lieutenant. "Tyrone Washington, man. That be an ethnic name."

Malone winked at him. "Ten-four," he whispered, looking around the reception area. There was only one inner door and it was fitted snugly into the wall. An avocado plant was next to the railing by the entrance. A few leatherette chairs and a coffee-stained table with some out-of-date magazines completed the décor.

A man in his late thirties came out. He had a large, hawk-like nose that dominated his dark features. He wore khaki shorts, a sweaty undershirt, and Roman sandals, no socks. His muscular torso strained against his undershirt.

"I am David Ancorie. What can I do for you gentlemen?" he asked, kicking the door closed and leaning against it. He had a smooth British accent. Malone took the card back from the woman and walked over to Ancorie, handing it to him. Ancorie looked at the card and smiled. "So?"

"We have reports that there are violations of Federal Employment Guidelines within the Eastern Shipping Company," Malone lied. "We're here to discuss the matter with your boss."

"I see." A mocking grin lit up Ancorie's face.

Malone had the uncomfortable feeling that he had not

73

fooled Ancorie with the card. But fuck it. He'd go through the motions and see where the game led.

"If that's the case, I'd better let you talk to Anderman himself," Ancorie said, snapping the door open and motioning the detectives through.

Malone went first. He stepped into a narrow passageway of corrugated sheet metal. There were no windows. Ventilation fans hummed overhead. At three-meter intervals push-bar doors led off the corridor. Centered in each door was a combination box lock with twelve numbered buttons.

David Ancorie stopped before a door numbered 6 and punched in the combination. The door clicked open and the detectives were led through it into another narrow hallway with cinderblock walls. Ancorie walked rapidly ahead of them. At the end of the passage he opened a heavy push-bar door and held it as they walked past.

Ancorie introduced Yachov Anderman. His desk was cluttered with shipping invoices and ICC regulations. He was portly and appeared to be in his late fifties. He had hooded eyes that were cold, weary, and decidedly unwelcoming. His hair was thin on top and thick around the sides with many errant strands looping the ears. An occasional twitch squeezed the right side of his face, and he exuded the strong smell of tobacco and cheap aftershave. He was wearing a white short-sleeve shirt that was spread wide at the collar exposing the matted graying hair on his chest. His blue trousers were strikingly fashionable, cut in a flashy Italian style, and seemed out of key with the rumpled rest of Anderman. He looked balefully at the intruders. "Spare me that nonsense about being from the Department of Labor. You're policemen. So state your business with me and leave," he said harshly.

"What makes you so sure that we're policemen?" Malone said.

"I have lived in many countries during my lifetime. And the one thing that I have discovered is that you and your kind

74

are the same all over the world." Anderman strummed the tip of his nose. "I can smell you."

Malone controlled his rage. He produced his credentials and passed them across the desk to Anderman.

The man behind the desk looked at them and tossed them back to Malone. "So? I'm impressed. Why are you here?"

"Listen, pal! Don't you come on to me with that attitude of yours. We're here on official police business. If you don't want to cooperate here, I'll drag your fat little ass down to the stationhouse and effect an attitudinal change on it. Understand, pal!" Malone said.

David Ancorie made a move toward Malone. Starling Johnson stepped forward, barring Ancorie's path. "Be cool, man, be real cool."

Anderman raised his hand, motioning Ancorie back. He picked up a package of Gauloises, took one out, and lit it. He started to cough. Then he raised his shoulders and smiled. "It has been a difficult week. We all have them, yes. What is it I can do for you?" he asked, dragging on the cigarette.

"We're investigating the murder of Sara Eisinger. She used to work for you," Malone said.

"Yes, I read about her death. But why are you being so devious?"

Malone said, "Because many people are reluctant to speak to policemen. But everyone has time to talk with representatives of Uncle Sam."

"I see," Anderman said, flicking ash into his overflowing ashtray. "I find it difficult to understand why anyone would want to kill Sara. She was such a nice girl." Anderman told him that Eisinger had worked for him for four years. "One day she pranced into the office and announced that she was quitting."

"Did she tell you why she was leaving?"

"Sara had become afflicted by the great American way of life. She told me that she wanted to find herself. Roam the beaches with her tits hanging out, toe the sand, and listen to

75

the cosmic force of the waves breaking over the beach. The usual dribble of the frustrated."

"Why was she frustrated?"

"How should I know?" Anderman said.

"What was her job with you?" Malone asked.

"She maintained running inventories and arranged our shipping schedules. And she was quite good at it," Anderman said, crushing out his cigarette.

"Inventories of what?"

"High-precision industrial machinery."

"I notice that your loading bays are locked. And I don't see any activity in or around the plant. Would you mind telling me why?"

Anderman brought his left elbow up and rested the heel of his hand under his chin, his fingers rubbing the lips, as he decided whether he was going to answer the policeman's question.

"My company is self-insured," Anderman said, deciding it was better to cooperate than fight, at least for now. "I refuse to pay the outrageous premiums that the insurance companies charge. By providing our own security and carefully selecting my own people I am able to eliminate losses due to theft. As a result, our rates are cheaper than our competitors. Those loading bays are open only when trucks are entering or leaving."

"You don't employ union teamsters?" Malone said, surprised.

Anderman was suddenly annoyed. "I employ whomever I want. Gangsters are not going to run my business." Anderman grinned. "Of course every now and then it becomes necessary to grease a few palms. . . . I employ Israeli students who are studying in this country and American students who come recommended by friends. I will hire no one who is not vouched for."

Malone asked Anderman if he ever heard from Eisinger after she left.

Anderman made a sour face. He told Malone that at first there were a few telephone calls, then nothing.

Malone craned his neck and looked at David Ancorie, who was lolling by the door with his arms folded across his chest. "Do you know Aldridge Braxton?" Malone asked, looking back at Anderman.

"No, I have never heard that name before. Have you, Ancorie?"

Ancorie pushed away from the door and moved across the room, glancing at Johnson. He stood next to Anderman. "No, the name means nothing to me," Ancorie said. "Why?"

"Because Hillel Henkoff and Isaac Arazi, both of whom work for you, were following Mr. Braxton last night in a truck that was registered to this company. Harassment is against the law," Malone said.

"Were you responsible for the beating that was inflicted on Arazi?" Anderman was stern. He had removed another Gauloise and was tapping it end over end, staring at Malone through narrowed eyes.

"Beating? I know nothing of any beating," Malone said, turning to Johnson. "Did you hear of any beatings?"

Starling Johnson shook his head.

"Humph. Of course you didn't. Policemen never know of such things," Anderman said. Sunlight poured through the meshed window high on the wall, patterning the cramped office in uneven strips of light.

"Why were they following Braxton and his two friends?" asked Malone.

"You'll have to ask them that," Anderman said.

"Where are they? I have to interview them," Malone said.

"No problem," Anderman said. "I had to send them to Chicago to pick up some merchandise. As soon as they return I'll have them get in touch with you."

"What can you tell me about them?" Malone asked.

"I can tell you that they're both a pain in the ass," Anderman said. "They are our JDL zealots who try to out-Zionist

77

the Zionists. They're both students who spend most of their time mouthing JDL bullshit instead of working. I've been thinking of getting rid of them. I'm in this business to make money, not fight causes. Those two think that by breaking some Arab's balls they're going to be big heroes on campus. Peer-group bullshit. But they're harmless. Together they couldn't fight their way out of a paper bag.''

"When do you expect Henkoff and Arazi to return?'' Malone asked.

"A day, maybe two. Don't worry, policeman. They'll get in touch with you. I promise,'' Anderman said.

"Did you know Sara in Israel?'' Malone said.

"I did.''

"Have you heard from her parents?'' Malone asked casually.

"No,'' Anderman answered.

Malone saw the small shadow that crossed Anderman's eyes when he lied.

Starling Johnson drove the unmarked car into Ericsson Place and parked behind a Sealand truck. He turned to Malone. "Want me to come with you?''

"I'd better go alone. They're funny people.''

Malone cut through a line of traffic that was moving into the Holland Tunnel. He stood on the curb on the south side of Varick Street checking to see if he'd been followed. He turned and entered the gilded lobby of 131 Varick Street. According to the directory, the Funding Development Corporation was on the tenth floor. It was the home base of NYPD's Intelligence Division. Any cop in his right mind stayed well away from it.

Malone stepped off the elevator into an enclosed anteroom that consisted of an old plug-type switchboard and a green metal desk topped with gray Formica, NYPD issue. A well-groomed woman in her late forties looked up.

"I'd like to see Lt. Joe Mannelli," Malone said. "I think he's in Public Relations."

She gave Malone a cold glance, flopped open her palm, and said in a deadpan voice, "Credentials."

Malone handed them to her.

She reached beneath the desk and pulled up a thick file of computer printouts fastened between blue plastic covers. While she was occupied flipping the pages to the *M*'s, Malone's eyes scoured the tiny alcove. Two cameras were bracketed on the walls. Every damn place that he went in connection with this case had cameras.

The woman slapped the identification card down on a line of typed symbols that contained the coded pedigree of Lt. Daniel Malone, NYPD. Her middle finger darted across the line. "What is your tax registry number, sir?"

"Eight three three nine four nine."

"Date of promotion to Sergeant?"

"August, 'sixty-seven."

"Where were you assigned when you left the Academy?"

"Patrol in the Seven-nine."

She handed back his documents and slapped the binder closed. "By the way, sir. What's a forty-nine?"

"Hmm?"

She repeated the question. Her right hand was hidden under the desk. Malone wondered if a .38 was aimed at his stomach.

"A UF forty-nine is the official letterhead of the department."

"A twenty-eight?"

"A UF twenty-eight is a request for time off."

"Thank you, Lou." She grinned.

Malone leaned across the desk. "Did I pass?"

"Sure, lieutenants always pass." She reached under the switchboard and pressed a button. The only door in the alcove sprung open. "Through there, Lou."

Malone stepped through and it closed behind him. There

was another door in front of him. When it popped open, Malone saw the smiling face of Joe Mannelli. He hadn't changed much in three years. There was a little more gray around the edges, but the stomach was still flat. One thing that Malone did notice was that the sparkle was gone from his friend's eyes.

They shook hands and Mannelli led him to his office.

"How's the spy business?" Malone asked, easing himself into a chair.

"Full of trenchcoats falling over each other. What brings you here, Dan?" Mannelli's tone of voice was normal, even casual, but Malone saw wariness around his eyes and mouth.

When Malone finished telling Mannelli about the Eisinger case, Mannelli made a deprecatory shrug. "So? Why come to me?"

Malone uncrossed his legs. "I want to know Eisinger's connections with the CIA. Those two telephone numbers were restricted listings. Which means that she had a direct wire to someone in New York and McLean. I want you to arrange a meet with one of their people. Someone who'll be able to give me some answers."

"Is that all?" Mannelli asked sardonically.

"No. There's more. I also want you to run some names through our intelligence file," Malone took a piece of paper out and slid it across the desk. "Here is a list of everyone connected with this case, including the victim. I'll probably have some more names for you as the case progresses."

Mannelli moved forward, strumming his fingertips on the top of his desk. "Have you any idea what you're asking me to do?"

"According to the department T.O. this unit is still part of the NYPD. Where the hell should I go for help, Nassau County?"

"Danny boy, this department has no, repeat, *no,* connection with the CIA. And we don't, repeat, do not, maintain intelligence files on American citizens. It's against the fucking law, department policy, and the goddamn U.S. Constitution.''

Malone's reply was curt and precise. "Bullshit."

Mannelli watched him for a long minute, a cold smile on his lips.

Malone was first to break the uncomfortable silence. "Joe, we've been friends a lot of years. We came on the job together. Were in the same class in the Academy. I've run into something that I think is in your ballpark. I need a favor. I've done a few for you over the years and now it's my turn to ask. Remember Ann Logan?''

Mannelli looked at him. He had not thought of that name in several years. Ten years ago Mannelli was a married sergeant with a pregnant girlfriend. He went to his friend Malone who arranged a visit to a doctor in Jersey City. Abortions weren't legal then.

"Got a cigarette?'' Mannelli asked, reaching across the desk. "I gave them up two years ago. Now I only smoke O.P.'s . . . other people's. . . .''

Malone lit the cigarette for his friend. Mannelli leaned forward, clasping Malone's hand, watching him over the flame.

"Have you ever stopped to consider how many idioms we use in our job?'' Mannelli said, resting his head back.

"Not really."

"When someone 'wants to buy you a suit' or 'give you a hat' that means that there is a payoff waiting for you if you overlook a violation of law, fail to do your job. And then, Danny boy, there is the biggie, 'he's a standup guy.' That little idiom refers to a man who can be trusted, a man who will deny everything, who will go before the grand jury and commit perjury to protect his friends and the Job. Are you a standup guy, Danny boy?'' Mannelli suddenly looked very old. A knot of concern twisted Malone's stomach. He looked at the solemn face in front of him. "I've always been a standup guy.''

"Okay, old buddy.'' Mannelli slapped his palms over the

Formica. "After Knapp, things got tough in the Job. But the PC and the rest of the shining assholes left the Intelligence Division alone. They were so paranoid with corruption in the street that they forgot we existed. But along came Watergate and that changed fast. This end of the business got tighter than a clam's ass, and that, in case you didn't know, is waterproof. No one trusted anyone. The CIA got their pricks burned because they trained our people in the late fifties and early sixties. One of the Watergate bagmen came from our job and he didn't stand up. Our covert operations were ordered disbanded. We were ordered to destroy our intelligence file, pull out all wires that were not *ex parte,* and stop playing nasty games with subversive groups. Chrissake, we were damn near out of business."

A skeptical grin appeared on Malone's face. "You closed up shop?"

"Not really," Mannelli said, with a little smile. "We blended our records with the records of the Youth Division and subcontracted our subversive business to private detectives who we can trust. Officially, we went into low gear, concentrating only on the wise guys. And you know how goddamn boring they are."

"And now?"

"Things have changed, pal. We get all kinds of foreign spooks and creeps, plenty of them with diplomatic cover, blowing away anybody they get mad at in every single fucking borough. Today we operate on a strictly need-to-know basis. Everything is compartmentalized, every unit has a little piece of the action. We work pretty close with the feds. What they are prohibited from doing under federal law we sometimes do for them. We also run interference for them when things get sticky . . . like now." Mannelli leaned forward, his face somber. "Danny boy, you could not have picked a worse fucking time to come to me with this little drama of yours."

Malone was forced into a corner. "Why is that, Joe?"

"What I'm going to tell you, I never said. Understand?"

Malone nodded.

"Do you remember reading about the hit on the second secretary of the Cuban Mission to the U.N.? His name was Rodriguez and it happened on May twelve of last year on Fifty-eighth Street and Queens Boulevard."

"I remember."

Mannelli continued. "Well, it turned out that Rodriguez was the head of Cuban Intelligence in this country. Castro went bananas over it. He threatened to blow away every CIA station chief in Latin America. The Agency people were able to convince him that we had nothing to do with the hit. They told him that it was some anti-Castro nuts operating on their own. They promised Castro that we'd do everything possible to I.D. the perps and pass their names on to him so that his people could deal with them. But here comes *el rub-o*. Detectives Caulfield and Williams of the One-oh-eight Squad caught the case. Two sharp pieces of bread. A nine-millimeter Deer gun was used to make the hit; it was found at the scene."

"A Deer gun," Malone said, puzzled.

Mannelli explained that during World War Two the OSS manufactured about a million units of the assassination weapon dubbed the Liberator. It was a small handgun that could be concealed in the palm of the hand and chambered a 45-caliber cartridge. The weapon had a simple twist-and-pull breechblock with extra rounds stored in the hollowed-out handgrip. The Liberator was distributed to the OSS clandestine forces in occupied countries. It had a smooth bore and was an excellent weapon for close killing.

During the Vietnam War the design of the Liberator was brought up to date by the CIA. They developed the 9mm Deer gun for use in Southeast Asia. This weapon had an aluminum butt and a steel barrel that screwed in from the front. "I don't know how the hell Caulfield and Williams did it, but they traced the murder weapon to a consignment purchased by the CIA over eight years ago. They also came up with four witnesses who positively I.D.'d the perp. They not only put him on the scene, they have him walking up to the car, raising the gun, and firing.''

"So? What's the problem?''

"The problem, ol' buddy, is that the perp and his accomplices are all CIA contract operatives in Omega Seven, the anti-Castro movement. And if that's not bad enough, the weapon used on Rodriguez was also used in six other homicides around the country . . . all Fidel's people.''

"Christ! What a can of worms.''

"You got it. Caulfield and Williams want arrest warrants issued for homicide and Washington wants the entire case shitcanned.''

"What's going to happen?''

"I don't know.'' He plucked a pencil from a blue mug on his desk and started to doodle, his head lowered in concentration. "The CIA boys aren't going to tell you anything, Danny boy. They're up to their asses in El Salvador and Nicaragua. They'll deny everything. Do yourself a favor and don't get involved in my league. You could get hurt.'' He looked up, studying his effect. Satisfied, he waited for Malone to reply.

"No way, Joe. I don't shitcan cases.''

Mannelli started to doodle again. "Maybe someone'll shitcan *you* if you don't take advice.''

Malone appeared calm; he wasn't.

"Oh yeah? Any idea who?''

"Just rumors,'' Mannelli said, doodling.

Malone snatched the pencil out of his hand, snapped it in two, and threw the pieces over his shoulder. "Tell me about them, Joe.''

"Whispers that you're getting involved in something you don't belong in. Something that's not in your league.''

"Really? Well you listen to me, pal. I'm not going to close the Eisinger case with no results. I'm going to break the fucking thing wide open. And if I can't do it with help from inside the Job, I'll go to some of my newspaper friends who'd just love to do a little investigative reporting on a homicide that is CIA connected.''

Mannelli studied the man sitting in front of him. He crumpled up his artwork into a ball and extended his arm sideways, suspending it in midair. He sprang open his fingers and watched the ball of paper fall into the wastebasket. "Okay, Danny boy. You're over twenty-one. I'll make a phone call for you. But don't come crying back to me when you step on your cock."

Mannelli escorted Malone out to the elevator. They parted without speaking or shaking hands. Mannelli went back to his office, locked the door, and walked slowly across the room, deep in thought. In the corner next to the window was a file cabinet with a metal bar stuck through each handle of the five drawers and secured by a hasp drilled into the top and a thick magnetic lock. He reached behind the cabinet and pried off a magnet. Next he held the magnet over the lock and watched it spring open. The bar was slid out and laid over the cabinet. He pulled out the top drawer and removed a telephone, placing it on top of the cabinet and staring at it for several moments as though deciding whether to use it. He gnawed his lower lip as he picked up the receiver. When it was answered at the other end he simply said, "I need to have a piano tuned."

Ahmad Marku and Iban Yaziji saw the taxi make the right turn off Flatbush Avenue and drive onto Lafayette Avenue. They hurried over to the curb. When the taxi cruised to a stop in front of them, Marku opened the door and both men slid into the rear seat.

The driver checked the oncoming traffic and drove away from the curb. With one eye on the road and the other on the rearview mirror, watching his two passengers, the driver said, "A problem has developed and you two are being detailed to correct it."

The passengers did not answer. They sat, staring into the face in the rearview mirror.

The driver continued. "Andrea St. James was observed

having lunch with Yachov Anderman. One of my men happened to be shopping on the Lower East Side. He saw her walking along Hester Street. He also saw two detectives in a department car tailing her. My man decided to tag along. He saw her enter this restaurant. One of the cops followed her inside. A short time later Anderman showed up and entered the restaurant. He sat at her table and they had what appeared to be a heated discussion."

"Damn!" Iban Yaziji exclaimed, slapping the seat next to him.

"It looks like she was working for Anderman all along," said the driver. "Either way, she has become a liability."

"What do you think she knows?" Marku said.

"I don't see how she could know very much. Working around the Interlude and doing those little odd jobs for us, she might have picked up bits and pieces. But we do not intend to take any chances. We want you to have a nice long talk with her."

"And after we are done talking?" Marku asked.

The taxi pulled into the curb in front of the Brooklyn Public Library and stopped. The driver craned his head over his shoulders and looked at his passengers. "We feel that she should be silenced, permanently."

Ahmad Marku handed the driver a dollar bill. "Keep the change."

"Thanks, sport. You can catch the subway across the street. I'd drive you back into Manhattan, but I don't have the time. There are things that I have to do."

"We understand," Yaziji said, shoving open the door.

The taxi driver watched as the passengers crossed Eastern Parkway, making for the subway station. Suddenly the radio under the dashboard blared. "SOD Seven, what is your location, K?"

The driver snatched the hand mike from its hook. As he did this he glanced out at the massive façade of the Brooklyn Public Library. It would not do to give this location, he thought. "SOD Seven to Central. This unit is at Christopher and Ninth, K."

"SOD Seven—ten-one your command, K."

"SOD Seven—ten-four."

The taxi driver returned the mike to its hook and drove off in search of a telephone to call his police command.

When Malone and Johnson returned to the squad room they found Heinemann typing fives and Davis jerking off an outraged citizen who thought that her apartment should have been dusted for fingerprints. After all, they did steal her television and a pair of earrings.

Malone went over to Davis. "I told you guys to go home and get some sleep."

Davis held up a protesting hand. "We figured we'd hang around till you got back, in case you needed us. But don't worry. It's on the arm. We're not going to put in overtime slips. You can make it up to us when this caper is over. It'll give us some splashin' time."

Malone went into his office, glanced over the 60 sheet, and then looked over to O'Brien who was slumped in a chair, waiting. The detective told Malone that the woman they had followed from the Interlude to Braxton's apartment had been I.D.'d as Andrea St. James. Further investigation revealed that St. James was a hooker who worked at the Interlude. O'Brien reported tailing her to the mikvah and he described her conversation in the restaurant with an unidentified man. He and his partner had followed her back to her apartment when she left the restaurant.

"Describe the man she met in the restaurant," Malone said.

O'Brien flipped open his memo pad and read off the description.

"Anderman!" Malone said, going over to the blackboard. He wrote "St. James" on the board and then blew his hands clean. He concluded that Andrea St. James had to be the same Andrea who had telephoned Eisinger in her office.

Malone reluctantly telephoned Joe Mannelli and gave him the latest additions from central casting. Mannelli promised to do what he could. The exchange was cold and very formal.

The detectives filed into Malone's office. "What next, Lou?" Heinemann asked.

Malone looked at their tired faces. "Go home. We'll pick it up in the morning."

O'Shaughnessy pulled out a timetable and made some quick mental calculations. "I could see her and still catch the eight forty-two to Hicksville. That'll give me time to see Foam."

"What about your marriage vows? Do they mean anything to you?" Davis said jokingly.

"I took them fifteen years ago. The statute of limitations expired."

Malone picked up the receiver and tucked it under his chin as he dialed. With his free hand he started to jot down things he needed. "Inspector, Dan Malone. I'm in the mood to spring for dinner. Interested?"

Gino's was a miraculous little restaurant in the heart of Little Italy, miraculous because it had never been "discovered." Sawdust covered the floor. Antique tables with scrollback chairs were haphazardly scattered about the bar and dining area. A large oil painting hung by the side of the oak bar. It showed Gino surrounded by a group of old Italian men laughing and drinking wine.

"Danny how'r' ya?" Gino said as Malone stepped through the door. Gino's bald egghead seemed as shiny as ever. Only his stomach had changed; it had grown to astonishing proportions. Malone made the introductions. Gino moved the DiNobili to the other side of his mouth. "Pleased to meet you, Inspector. It's good to see one of our own make it in the department."

"We'd like a table in the blue room," Malone said, smiling.

"Why-a sure. Just-a follow me, sir." Gino led them into the dining area, a square room with a miniature balcony running across its length. Several of the neighborhood regulars looked up and made faint signs of recognition and then returned to their pasta. Gino ushered them to a table next to the stairway leading to the overhead balcony. "One minute, sir, while I prepare your table." Gino picked up the grubby ashtray, emptying it on the floor. He snatched off the tablecloth, shaking it clean and reversing it before spreading it back across the table.

Zambrano moved his head next to Malone's. "A class joint," he whispered.

"I always take the boss top drawer," Malone said.

They ordered drinks. Malone told Gino to bring the special of the day.

When their drinks arrived, Zambrano raised his. "Salud, goombah."

They touched glasses.

Gino brought over a bowl of mussels, a platter of pasta shells, a bowl of linguini in white clam sauce, and a large salad. "A feast," he said, putting the food down and turning, walking back into the bar area. He returned with a bottle of Chianti and two water glasses. "All the crystal got broke in the dishwasher," he said, handing each man a glass. Gino leaned across the aisle and took Italian bread from the wall cabinet.

Zambrano broke off the heel of the bread and dunked it into his wine. "What's doing with the Eisinger case?" Zambrano asked, shoving the bread into his mouth.

"If I had some extra men I'd like to plant them on the Eastern Shipping Company and the Interlude." Malone sipped his wine, watching Zambrano over the rim. The next move was Zambrano's.

The inspector dug his fork into the pasta, rolling it onto his spoon. "What else would you do, if you had the men?"

Zambrano shoveled the pasta into his mouth. Permission had been given. Malone could continue.

"Tails. On Anderman, the Braxtons, and Andrea St. James," Malone said, rolling his pasta.

"Anything else?" Zambrano asked.

"Wires on all the locations."

"You're talking about a very expensive operation," Zambrano said, reaching for the salad. "I'd be hard put to justify setting up an operation like that for one insignificant homicide that was yesterday's headline. This is June, and we've had over seven hundred and eighty-three homicides. No one gets excited over one more."

"My instinct tells me that this is a heavy case."

Zambrano sipped his drink. "For instance?"

"Little things," Malone said, picking up a spoon and moving shells around in the bowl. "The fact that she had two CIA telephone numbers in her book and they never heard of her. The fact that a certain member of our Intelligence Division knew about the case, and suggested that I forget about it. The fact that I've been getting threatening telephone calls from someone on the Job. I've got a feeling that there are heavyweights involved in this one."

"Wanna tell me about those telephone calls?"

"No. When I know more, you'll be the first to know."

Zambrano gulped the remains of his drink and looked at him. "From what you've told me, you don't have any grounds to go into court and ask for *ex parte* orders."

Malone shoveled some shells onto his plate. "We could employ extrajudicial methods," he said, raising his glass.

"Black-bag stuff? In this day and age? They'd slice your balls into the lasagna if you got caught. Mine too."

They settled in to enjoying their dinner and ate with gusto. Malone waited; first food, then talk—it was a ritual evolved by wise men, one that both men understood and respected.

Zambrano pushed away from the table, reaching down and taking hold of the roll of fat hanging over his waist, shaking it. "I must have put on five pounds." He reached for the wine. "I can let you have some men on a steal for a week," he said, pouring.

"How many?" Malone asked, scraping a piece of bread around the bowl of mussels.

"Six, maybe seven."

"What about conversion cars for the tails?"

"There aren't enough to go around now."

Malone drank. "I'll manage without then. Any chance of getting a surveillance truck?"

Zambrano waved his hand. "No way. Each borough has one assigned. Ours is being used uptown."

"If I should manage to lay my hands on one would you look the other way?"

"As long as no weight comes down from headquarters, yes."

"I'll need a second whip to help me coordinate the operation."

Zambrano sighed. "I'll let you steal Jack Harrigan from the Tenth. He's one of the best and a solid standup guy."

A consensus had been reached. Malone had gotten what he wanted without asking directly; without putting Zambrano in the uncomfortable position of having to say no. Malone ended the ritual with the ordained, "Thank you, Inspector."

Malone motioned to Gino. "Black coffee and Sambucca, with coffee beans."

Zambrano raised his pony glass and stared at the thick white liqueur.

"Dan, you're a good cop." He sipped the Sambucca and smacked his lips. "This Eisinger thing is a bone stuck in your throat. Spit it out before it chokes both of us. Put it on the back burner."

Malone looked down. "No way, Inspector."

"You're telling me that it's personal."

Malone's head shot up. "You're fucking-A right I am."

"Why do you have such a hard-on for this case?"

Malone swirled the liqueur around in his glass. "So far the Job has cost me my marriage, most of my normal friends, and a lot of sleep. But I still like being a cop. It's what I do best. Most of the homicides I catch are grounders; the rest are either drug related or mob hits and who gives a fuck anyway. But every now and then one comes along that cries to be solved; that's the Eisinger homicide. Besides, I don't like to be pressured into not doing my job. Irishmen are like that; we're ornery and thick-headed."

"I know. But you've just used up a lot of credit. I'm going to give you eight days then I'll let you take an exceptional clearance and file the damn thing."

"You're telling me to dump this case."

"No, I'm not. God help me if I ever gave such an order. But there are other priorities."

TUESDAY, *June 16* . . . **Morning**

Janet Fox was sitting cross-legged on the bed removing the rollers from her hair when the doorbell rang. She looked at her watch and saw that it was only ten minutes after eight. She got off the bed and went to see who was at her door.

"Detective Davis," the voice said. "I was here the other day with my partner."

She remembered. He was the one with the nice shoulders and cute behind. She looked through the peephole to make sure, told him to wait a minute, and then ran back into the bedroom. She put on a pair of slacks and a plain cotton top and quickly brushed out her hair.

"I had a few more people in the building to interview," Davis said, stepping into the apartment.

"You've already questioned me," she said, closing the door.

He faced her. "Janet, this case is going nowhere fast. So far you're the only person we've come up with who called Eisinger a friend. I came by this morning to ask you if you've thought of anything additional that might help us, no matter how insignificant you might think it is."

She smiled. "I'm useless in the morning without that first cup of coffee. Care to join me?"

It was a small kitchen with a lot of sunlight and a round table next to the window. She put a plate of hot croissants down and sat opposite him.

"I've been racking my brain to see if there was anything that I forgot to tell you," she said, reaching for the butter. "There isn't."

"We find it difficult to believe that Eisinger was so closed about her personal life," he said, breaking off a piece of the croissant, his eyes never leaving her face.

"Why? A lot of people are very private types."

"Hmm. Tell me, what kind of person was she?"

"Sometimes she seemed afraid of the world and then there were times she appeared strong and completely in control." She watched him. "Will you catch the people responsible?"

"We're going to give it our best shot," he said, noticing that her eyes were green.

"She was also a kind and considerate woman. I had recently ended a long relationship and was quite distraught. Sara spent time with me and listened and let me cry on her shoulder. That Friday when I was about to leave for the weekend, Sara came to my apartment and gave me her Bible as a gift. She said that it would bring me peace and help me find the right road."

"You just ended a relationship and were upset over it and then you went away for a weekend with your boss?"

"That was nothing. I had to see if I could be with another man after . . ." She looked down into her cup.

He understood. "Why didn't you tell us about the Bible before?"

She lifted her shoulders in a gesture of indifference. "I didn't think of it. It's just a Bible. Would you like to see it?"

"Yes."

Its edges were frayed and brittle. On the inside cover was a colored lithograph of barefoot Arabs loaded down like beasts of burden, walking along the timeless Bethlehem Road below the Citadel of Zion. One of the Arabs reminded Davis of Malone. He smiled. In the background an old man was leading a donkey. A girl was astride the weary animal. She was laughing and waving at the long-forgotten photographer.

Davis felt he had been transported to a day when the earth was barely formed. He felt Sara Eisinger's presence. Her smells clung to the book—perfume . . . lipstick . . . makeup. He haphazardly flipped the pages.

"May I borrow this for a few days?" he asked.

"If you promise to return it."

"Of course. One good turn deserves another," Davis said, picking up his coffee cup. "How about dinner some evening?"

Another one who is married, with a problem, but then, aren't they all, she thought. But she smiled and said, "Why not?"

The squad room was deserted. The rumble of laughter seeped from behind the door of the lieutenant's office. Malone went over and slowly turned the knob. A cluster of detectives were gathered around the blackboard. O'Shaughnessy was standing in the middle. Draped over the board was a poster of a nude woman. She was lying on her back and her legs were spread wide. Jake Stern was standing beside the poster holding a ruler and pointing. Starling Johnson was standing next to Stern.

"This, gentlemen, is the female sex organ. The vagina," Stern instructed. "Our friend and colleague Pat O'Shaughnessy has finally tasted its wondrous fruit."

A polite smattering of applause rose from the group.

"Good show."

"Better late than never."

"Welcome to the club."

"Gentlemen, this slivered erectile structure here that resembles a long boat is the most sensitive part of a woman's body. The clitoris. Kindly observe at the top . . . a small rounded tubercle consisting of spongy erectile tissue. This is the glans clitoris, the most erotic part of this wonderful, sweet-tasting paradise."

"Brilliant dissertation," Heinemann said, clapping from the sideline.

Another burst of applause rose from the detectives.

Stern bowed, acknowledging the acclamation. He held up a quieting hand. "Please observe that the glans clitoris resembles a man standing in a boat. Hence, we receive the nickname . . . the man in the boat. It was here that our friend Pat went astray. Instead of concentrating on the man in the boat he licked the vaginal orifice."

"That's what I did," O'Shaughnessy agreed, crestfallen.

"A common mistake among beginners," Starling Johnson said.

Malone was fuming. He threw the door fully open and stormed in.

"I really hate to interrupt your critique! I went for twenty-five bucks taking Zambrano to dinner . . . telling him how overworked you are . . . how we need help on the Eisinger thing; and what do I find? A bunch of middle-aged whoremasters trying to teach someone how to eat a woman. If he doesn't know now he'll never know!"

"It's never too late to learn," Stern said, ducking out the door.

Malone was unable to suppress a smile.

"How'ya doin', Lou?"

Malone turned. A wiry Irishman was leaning his chair back against the wall cleaning his nails with a silver pocket-knife.

"I'm Jack Harrigan. Understand I'm on lend-lease for a couple of weeks. I got six detectives with me." Det. Sergeant Jack Harrigan had graduated summa cum tough from Stickball U. in Greenpoint. Malone felt that he could be trusted.

"What about the men who came with you. Know them?" Malone's forehead furrowed, eyes clouded.

Harrigan saw the doubt, understood the seemingly innocent question; a query steeped in the subtle nuance of the policeman's language.

"I picked each one myself," Harrigan confided. "If the

96

shit hits the fan each one of them will stand like the Rock of Gibraltar.''

"Do they know how to install wires and video tape?''

"Do Guineas wear undershirts in the summer?'' Harrigan popped the chair forward. "Wadayagot for me, Lou?''

For the next ninety minutes Malone detailed the Eisinger case. When he finished he looked at Harrigan. "I want you to coordinate the operation.''

Harrigan cocked his head, tugging at his right earlobe. "A lot of homicides go down each year. Except for a cop killing or when some heavy dude gets his ass blown away, we don't pull out all the stops. So why have so many men been taken off the chart on the Eisinger case?''

Malone steepled his hands over his nose, massaging the bridge with his forefingers. "Because I want this one, Jack.''

Harrigan pursed his lips, nodding. "I can dig that. Four years ago I caught a case that became *personal*. Almost came in my pants when the perp was sentenced from zip to life.'' A puzzled frown crossed Harrigan's face. "For the kind of operation you want, we don't have enough men or wheels. We need conversion vehicles and men. Ain't no way six or seven detectives are going to keep half a dozen under surveillance round the clock.''

Malone agreed. He told Harrigan that he wanted the Eastern Shipping Company sat on. Two teams of two men each working twelve hour tours should be able to do. Also the Interlude. Any extra detectives were to tail randomly; jumping from one suspect to the other. ". . . We could get lucky.''

"And what do we do for wheels?'' Harrigan asked.

"I've arranged things,'' Malone said. "The telephone company is going to lend us some repair trucks. I got a mail truck from the post office and an ambulance from Gotham Ambulance Service. Con Edison is lending us one of their vans. On Monday I visited a friend in Bed-Stuy. He's letting us use two of his gypsy cabs. I went by the radio shop and signed out eight portables. All set on the same frequency.''

97

"And where do we park this motor pool?" Harrigan asked.

"At the First. You'll use that as headquarters. I've spoken to the C.O. of Narcotics. He is going to let us use a desk and a telephone."

Harrigan grinned. "You've done your homework."

When Bo Davis arrived later that morning he went directly into Malone and told him of his visit to Janet Fox. He handed the lieutenant the Bible and left. Malone hefted the book in his hand, thumbed through a few pages, and dropped it on his desk.

Three hours later Gus Heinemann thrust his head into Malone's office. "Anderman is outside. And he has two beards with him."

"Arazi and Henkoff," Malone said, rounding his desk and hurrying into the squad room.

"See, policeman, I told you I'd bring them around," Anderman said, beaming.

They stood in silent defiance looking up at the ceiling, NEVER AGAIN buttons pinned to their shirts. Both wore patched jeans and had fledgling beards and yarmulkas. Arazi was a skinny kid with bulging china-blue eyes and a large Adam's apple that slid up and down every time he talked. Henkoff was short. He had a barrel chest and rounded shoulders that gave him an appearance of brute strength. A wide bandage ran vertically along the bridge of his nose.

Malone motioned them to sit. They shuffled over, sprawling into the chairs, surveying the walls with do-me-something smirks on their faces.

Malone began. "What were you two doing following Aldridge Braxton and his friends?"

Arazi glared up at the policeman. "We don't have to tell you anything."

Arazi's shrill voice irritated Malone.

"No fascist cop can force us to answer questions," Henkoff said.

Heinemann slipped off the desk and moved between Malone and the two seated men. The heel of his shoe crashed into Arazi's foot—a demolition ball falling down.

Arazi leaped up, dancing on one foot, holding the injured limb. "You did that on purpose," he screamed.

Heinemann's face was wrapped in a blanket of shocked innocence. He clutched at his heart. "Sir. We do not beat people . . . it's unprofessional."

"And counterproductive," Starling Johnson hastened to add.

Anderman moved between the detectives and his employees, his eyes narrowing with displeasure, glaring his warning to behave at Arazi and Henkoff. "Save that undergraduate bullshit for the campus," Anderman said.

"We'll try again," Malone said. "Why were you following Aldridge Braxton?"

Henkoff answered. "We weren't following him. We were interested in his two Arab friends."

"What Arabs?" Malone said.

Arazi looked up at him. "Ahmad Marku and Iban Yaziji —the two men who were with him at the Interlude. Marku is a Saudi and Yaziji is a Libyan. They both belong to the Moslem Brotherhood."

"So what?" Malone said. "That don't give you the right to follow people."

"We belong to the Jewish Defense League at City College. Part of our duties is to follow Arab fanatics and report their movements to our superiors in JDL," Henkoff said.

"Be advised, my young friend, that there are many people who think the JDL is as loony as the Moslem Brotherhood. And be further advised that, according to section 240.25 of the Penal Law, any person who follows another person in or about a public place or places is guilty of harassment. If I find either of you stepping out of line again I promise you a little vacation on Rikers Island. Understand?"

They nodded their heads sullenly.

"Who killed Sara Eisinger?" Malone said.

Arazi shook his head. "I don't know. I heard about Sara's death from Mr. Anderman."

"You said her name like you've said it many times before . . . Sara," Malone said. "Gus, watch the schoolboys. I want a conference with our Mr. Anderman." Malone grabbed Anderman by the elbow and herded him into his office.

Malone held a pencil loosely in his hand, tapping it over the desk, occasionally playing tag with a couple of paper clips. Anderman sat opposite, staring up at the wall.

Malone pushed one paper clip against another. "Mr. Anderman, you and your two schoolboys are full of shit. You don't really expect me to buy that cockamamie story about following Arabs for a JDL fraternity?"

Anderman shrugged. "Policeman, it's the truth."

"You wouldn't know the truth if you fell over it."

"I'm in the importing business—nothing else." Anderman started to get up.

"Plant your ass down there, Anderman. I'm not finished with you yet."

Anderman complied, reluctantly.

"Who killed Eisinger?"

"I . . . don't . . . know!"

"Why was she killed?"

"Same answer, policeman. Those two assholes were only trying to be big men on campus; don't look to make something out of nothing."

"By the way, how was your lunch with Andrea St. James? It's too bad you didn't find the list in the mikvah." Malone leaned back, watching him.

Anderman gasped; his mouth opened, stunned. "How did you know about that?"

"We have our ways. We found the list in her apartment during our initial search," he lied.

"Impossible." Anderman cut the air with a disbelieving hand.

"It was hidden behind the kitchen molding," Malone said, twirling three paper clips around the point of a pencil.

Anderman got up, leaning across the desk. His face was inches from the policeman's. "I want that list."

"Why?"

"If you have it, you know why." Anderman's eyes widened with enlightenment. He knew a good shot at a con job when he saw it. Slowly he retreated back across the desk and sat. "You're good, policeman."

"People do have the habit of underestimating us," Malone said, grinning.

Anderman pushed himself up out of the chair. "Policeman, it has been a pleasure. If you ever want to talk again, just call. I'll be waiting with my lawyer."

"We can do business now, Anderman. Later there will be no deals. Help us and we'll do right by you."

"Shalom, policeman. I have to go and unpack some crates."

After Anderman and the schoolboys had gone, Malone went over to Heinemann and told him to try to scrounge a surveillance truck from somewhere.

"Lou? Those things are worth their weight in gold. It's almost impossible," Heinemann said.

Malone gave him a reassuring pat on the shoulder. "Give it a shot anyway."

Malone went back into his office and picked up the Bible. He flipped through its pages looking for a cutout compartment and found none. Next he rubbed each page to see if they separated. They did not. He held the book up to the light and looked into its spine and saw nothing. He placed it down in front of him and stared at it.

He chucked open the cover with his middle finger and ran his fingertips over the back of the cover. Then he felt it. A thin serration of glue at the bottom. There was something concealed underneath. He pushed back from his desk and opened the top drawer; as he did this he called out to the detectives. "Get in here."

Before he closed the drawer he removed a penknife, opened it, and carefully guided the blade along the bottom of the page. When the incision was complete, he fished his forefinger inside the cut and slid out a sheet of onionskin. Ten addresses typed single space: Trenton, Wilmington, Savannah, San Diego, Eureka, Corpus Christi, Juneau, Texas City, Newark; he recognized the last address. It was on Borden Avenue in Long Island City. He got up and walked over to the filing cabinet. He slid open the bottom drawer and removed a road map of the United States. He then went over to the blackboard and taped the map over the top of the board. Holding the list in front of him, Malone proceeded to circle each of the cities in red pencil. When he finished, he took three steps back and began to study the map.

"Maybe they're cat houses for horny Jews," O'Shaughnessy said.

"Jews don't get horny," Stern said, moving up to the blackboard. He stared at it thoughtfully. "They're all on or near the coast."

Heinemann looked at Malone. "Any ideas?"

"Not really." Malone took out a memo pad and made a copy of the locations. He slid the list into his pocket and handed the original and the Bible to Davis. "Invoice these and put them someplace safe."

"How do you want me to list them on the voucher?" Davis asked.

Malone pondered the question. "A book and one sheet of onionskin."

"Aren't we going to try and find out what's at those locations?" asked Heinemann.

Malone's eyes swept the detectives. "We're going to find out. But not through official channels. They've had a tendency to leak lately. I want none of you to discuss what we've found. No one outside this squad is to know. *Capisce?*"

The detectives nodded.

Starling Johnson meandered over to the blackboard. "That bes a lot of territory to cover. How ya goin' to do it without help?"

Malone winked at him. "It's dues-payin' time, ma man."

It was after lunch when Davis received a telephone call from his friend in Army Intelligence. The male star of the porno film that they had found in Eisinger's apartment had been identified. His name was Maj. James Landsford, and he was stationed at Fort Totten in Queens. "He's waiting to be interviewed," Davis said to Malone.

"Pat and Starling will come with me. The rest of you, hold it down," Malone said.

Fort Totten is squeezed onto a few acres of land that overlooks the western tip of Long Island Sound. The Cross Island Parkway runs past the main gate. Smart-looking M.P.'s with patent-leather holsters and white lanyards are stationed outside the gate's guardhouse. Parked clusters of military trucks with white stars painted on their doors can often be seen from the parkway.

No regular military units were assigned to Fort Totten, as far as Malone knew. Ostensibly it was a place where military dependents waited for transportation overseas. Three barracks with bizarre-shaped antennas that ran hundreds of feet into the sky were located in the center of the fort. An electric fence surrounded the barracks. Dressed in army fatigues, men with automatic weapons strapped across their chests patrolled the perimeter. There was a helicopter pad nearby. There was also a marina where pleasure craft tied up at night —boats with bulkheads crammed with high-frequency radio panels and strange antennas cluttering their masts. But Malone would learn about them in days to come.

A jeep with two armed M.P.'s led the unmarked police car

to a quonset hut where two more M.P.'s waited. The soldiers snapped to attention and saluted. One of them turned smartly and opened the door. A tall, thin man in tailored fatigues and short gray hair was waiting. There was a slight touch of Dixie in his voice. "Welcome, gentlemen. I am Colonel Claymore, the provost marshal of this base."

Claymore's office was functional and strictly government issue. An American flag was on station in the corner; pictures of the president, secretary of the army, the joint chiefs, and a print of Washington crossing the Delaware were on the wall.

"Why do you want to interview Landsford?" Claymore asked, swiveling from side to side in his chair.

"We have reasonable grounds to believe that Landsford is involved in a homicide."

"Well . . . I'm afraid you've arrived a bit too late. He's dead . . . just found a few hours ago. Heart attack."

"I want to see the body," Malone said.

"Want, Lieutenant?" Claymore said, hunching forward.

"Yes, Colonel. Want!"

"I think you're forgetting that this is a military reservation. You have no authority on this land, Lieutenant."

Malone smiled. "That's what I would call a cloudy issue, Colonel. Some people, in fact most, agree with you. But I'll tell you what the NYPD does have. We have access to the little old newspaper and television people. They're our friends. Allies. Why those people in the Fourth Estate would jump on a story about how a Colonel Claymore of the U.S. Army refused to cooperate with the local sheriff in solving the murder of a poor defenseless girl."

Claymore glared and then said, in a deliberate, slow way, "There are matters of national security involved."

"Aren't there always?" Malone said, adding, "Don't worry, we're good Americans."

Resigned to giving ground, Claymore reluctantly replied, "He killed himself."

Malone didn't know why, but he had half expected that

answer. He canceled Claymore's questioning look with one of his own. "We think Landsford was being blackmailed."

"He was," Claymore agreed. "Landsford left a suicide note. In it he mentioned the blackmail."

"May I see it?"

"It's classified."

"What were Landsford's duties at Totten?"

"His work was secret . . . sorry."

"What can you tell me about him?"

"Married. Three children. Graduated from the Point. Picked up a couple of Purple Hearts and other decorations in Nam."

"I'd like to see the body . . . just to satisfy my morbid curiosity."

The provost marshal of Fort Totten shook his head in disgust. "Aw shit. Okay. Let's go."

As they were walking to the jeeps that were waiting to take them to the BOQ, Malone turned to Claymore and asked him if Landsford had always been assigned to the Quartermaster Corps.

"He was an infantry man," Claymore said, stepping into the front of the jeep.

There was very little of Maj. James Landsford's face that wasn't bloody. Brain matter splatted the wall. A small entrance wound in the right temple was covered with heavy powder tattooing. The left side of the head was gone. No weapon was in sight; Malone assumed that the army had grabbed it fast, before the NYPD arrived.

Even in death Landsford possessed a strangely military bearing. His chin was tucked in tight against his neck. Legs together. It was as though he had stood at attention the second he pulled the trigger.

Men in tailored fatigues without any insignia or badges of rank were systematically searching the BOQ with grim concentration. They ignored the detectives.

Malone knelt next to the body. He rubbed his forefinger

around the entrance wound. Charcoal grains stuck in his fingertip. Malone brought his hand down and slid it inside Landsford's shirt. The skin was cold. He looked up at Claymore who was standing over him, watching.

"Where is the weapon he used?" Malone asked, getting up.

"We have it."

"Any chance of getting a look at the suicide note?"

"As I told you before . . . it's classified."

"Appears to me that everything around this fort is secret or classified. Makes one kind of curious. . . . What the hell kind of place you running, Colonel?"

Claymore looked angry. He moved off, without responding, to a group of army personnel who were huddled in the next room. Malone went after him, catching him by the elbow.

"Where is Landsford's family?"

Claymore shook his arm free. "In Texas. Landsford used to fly home on weekends."

"That's a long and expensive flight to take every weekend," Malone said.

"Takes civilians time to understand us simple army folk," Claymore said.

Lt. Joe Mannelli leaned against a jeep smoking a cigarette. When he saw Malone and the detectives leave the BOQ, Mannelli flipped the cigarette away and waved to them.

"Well, I'll be," Malone said, watching Mannelli approach.

"Just happened to be in the neighborhood. When I saw the car, I said to myself, 'Joe, I bet that unmarked department auto belongs to my old friend Malone.' "

"Bullshit, Lieutenant, sir," Johnson said.

Mannelli grabbed Malone's arm and waltzed him away. "Look at that grass. Wish I could get my lawn to look like that."

"Cut the small talk, Joe. What the hell do you want?"

"I'm the liaison between the fort and the city."

"That includes the Job?"

"It does."

"What's on your mind?"

"I'm here to tell you . . ." He stopped midsentence and looked at Malone. "No. Not to tell you. To suggest, that you forget about this base and everything on it. Including Landsford. That's the way they want it on the fourteenth floor."

Malone looked him in the eye, surprised. "This thing reaches up to the PC?"

"The PC has cognizance of and control over everything that happens in the Job."

"Save that bullshit for the rookies in the Academy. Why this case?"

"Because the fucking powers that be don't want the U.S. Army dragged into your fucking little drama. That's why. In case you've forgotten, the banks and the U.S. Government are supporting this town. It just wouldn't do to get either of them mad at us."

"You suggesting that I close the case with negative results?"

"Just leave the goddamn army and Landsford out of it." Mannelli hooked his arm around Malone's shoulder, pulling him close. "There are matters of national security involved." Malone pulled away. He was getting tired of hearing about national security.

They strolled in silence down the winding streets, admiring the willows and manicured lawns.

Malone finally looked at the man walking at his side and said, "What the hell is going on here, Joe?"

"Danny boy, I don't know and I don't want to know. I'm only the guy they call whenever a problem arises with the local gendarmes."

"When am I going to hear from your connection at the CIA?"

"Things like that require careful orchestration. They don't happen overnight."

After several moments, Malone turned to him. "Tell the people on the fourteenth floor that I'll do the right thing."

"Never doubted it for a minute," he said, patting Malone's back.

As the detectives were getting back into their car, Malone turned to Starling Johnson. "Remind me to ask Bo to contact his friend in Army Intelligence. I want a copy of Landsford's military record. I can't help but wonder why a decorated infantry man was working in the Quartermaster Corps."

"Right," Johnson said, starting the engine.

The department auto slowed as it approached the guardhouse. An M.P. stepped outside and bent to scrutinize the occupants of the vehicle. He waved them through. O'Shaughnessy was sitting in the back seat. He suddenly lurched forward, shaking Malone by the shoulders. "Lou, look!"

A panel truck turned off the service road from the Cross Island Parkway and sped into the semicircular driveway to the main gate. David Ancorie was driving. An M.P. leaned out of the guardhouse, looked at the approaching vehicle and its driver, and waved it through.

A gypsy cab with LICENSED BY THE PEOPLE stenciled across its rear doors followed the panel truck into the driveway, then made a U-turn and drove out, parking on the service road. The driver of the gypsy cab adjusted his sunglasses as the department auto drove by. Harrigan's man was sticking close.

Malone was turned in his seat, watching the panel truck disappear inside the base.

"What the hell is Ancorie doing on a U.S. Army base?" O'Shaughnessy said.

"I've got a better question. Why did that M.P. wave him on through without even asking him what his name was?" Malone said.

Malone was examining the equipment in a square, gray, windowless van parked in the no-parking zone in front of the

Fifth Precinct. Large red reflectors had been set into the corners of the van, peepholes through which detectives could film and watch unsuspecting people. A person walking by the rear of the van who glanced inside would see stacks of cartons piled to the roof, a special optical illusion of which the van's creators at Motor Transport were especially proud. Malone had entered the interior of the van through a sliding metal door with a two-way mirror in its center. Immediately on the left was a chemical toilet. When Malone turned from examining the telephones, electronic and movie equipment, he found Heinemann standing in wonder over the toilet. He was fascinated by its compactness. His ass would smother the bowl, he reckoned.

"How'd you ever manage this coup?" Malone said.

" 'Twas nothing, master," Heinemann said gleefully. "A war veteran I was in the Crimea with, Seventh Hussars, works in Motor Transport. To make a long story longer, the van came in from the Bronx for a tuneup. We got it on the Q.T. for a few days."

"I think the time has come for us to take a look inside the Interlude," Malone said. He turned to Bo Davis. "I'd like you to run over to Abe's Army and Navy store on Whitehall Street. It's next to the old draft induction building. Show Abe your shield, tell him you work with me, and ask him to lend us two army officer's uniforms. Starling and Jake are going to make outstanding officers. We'll use the key we found in Eisinger's apartment and try to bluff our way inside."

"What about Andrea St. James?" Davis said. "After your talk with Anderman she's going to know we're on to her. Want us to pick her up?"

"Let's play her a little longer," Malone said. "Anderman might spook her when he tells her that we know about their lunch together. She just might get careless and lead us somewhere." Malone turned and asked Heinemann if the telephones inside the van were working. Heinemann assured him they were. Malone moved to the battery of telephones and picked one up, dialing.

Jack Harrigan answered. "Lou, I was just about to call you."

"What's the story with Ancorie at Fort Totten?" Malone asked.

Harrigan told the lieutenant that Ancorie had left the Eastern Shipping Company and driven directly to the fort. One of Harrigan's men followed in a gypsy cab. Ancorie stayed at the fort for forty-six minutes and then left, going back to Eastern Shipping.

There was a pause on the line. "Lou, there is something else that I have to tell you. Andrea St. James has given us the slip. She went into the Hotel Granada and my men lost her. We figure that she must have ducked out one of the side entrances."

Pat O'Shaughnessy sprawled over the lumpy sofa and lit a cigarette. There had been four hours to kill before they tried to get into the Interlude, so Pat decided to give his old standby Foam a call. The other detectives went on to do their own things. Heinemann went to the Ninth's club meeting; he knew there'd be a big game; Stern went to the precinct's gym in the basement to work out; Malone and Johnson drove to Second Avenue to get some Indian food.

Pat watched her standing in the cramped kitchen off the living room doing the dishes. He wondered what she would say if she knew the nickname the guys in the Squad had given her. When she first told him that she was going to use contraceptive foam, she'd said, "Now you won't have to use those rubber things anymore," watching his face, waiting for his approval.

It was a primitively furnished apartment that in many ways reminded him of her life—empty and dismal. Whenever he called her she was available. He wondered if she spent her life waiting for his infrequent telephone calls. Did she really believe the lies that he told her? Men have been telling women those same lies since the beginning of time. How could she possibly believe me? Single broads who date married men need those lies to maintain their self-respect, he reasoned. There were times when he felt sorry for her and the legions just like her. They spent a few nights a week with their married boyfriends and the weekends alone, usually in a bottle of gin.

Foam was not the usual Manhattan type who had been knocking around the singles' bars for years. She never went to bars. She was a simple woman who Pat knew loved him very much. And that was the part that bothered him. She gave him everything that she had to give and he gave her nothing but lies. But she was over twenty-one, and whatever she did was her decision. He never forced her. She was with him because she wanted to be with him, he reasoned. And there was no way he was going to give up such a good deal. If she wanted to waste her life on him, that was just fine. He watched her drying the dishes and thought, She's a real boat jumper; brogue and all.

When Pat had telephoned her and told her that he was coming over, Karen Murphy hurried from her second-floor walkup on Sixty-first Street and spent her last fifteen dollars on a roast. It did not matter that she only had change left in her pocketbook. She was going to cook dinner for her Pat.

Karen had been a thirty-one-year-old virgin when they met. Many times before that first meeting she had lain in her bed at night and wondered what it would be like to be with a man. Sometimes she would let her hand roam her body, pretending that she was not alone.

They met at one of those large Manhattan parties where few of the people know one another and everyone appears clutching a green bottle of wine in a paper bag. She was taken back by the forcefulness of his warm personality and his beautiful smile. He had a cleft in his chin that she loved almost immediately. He was everything she ever wanted in a man; there was only one problem—he was married. They spent

III

that first evening together, talking. He was so sincere that it never crossed her mind that he might not be telling her the truth. He spoke of his loneliness and of his quest for someone with whom he might share his life; he told her of his wife's unfaithfulness, her drinking, how she mistreated his children. She saw in him a man in need of a woman's love; a troubled man with great inner conflict. Here was a man who put the needs of his children before his own needs and desires. She could love such a man.

Tonight she was taking her time doing the dishes, trying to muster the courage to ask Pat about his plans for their future. Over the years he had often alluded to a life together, but somehow he always avoided being specific. The years were going by, and she felt that he should make a commitment, one way or the other. When the last dish was dried she cleaned off the sink and folded the towel over the faucet. She walked into the living room and sat on the floor next to him. Resting her face over his groin, she asked him how he had enjoyed dinner.

"Terrific. You are some cook."

"I love you so." She was looking up into his eyes.

He tried to reply in kind but was unable to. He had never been able to say those words. Many times he tried to say them, wanted to say them; but they just would not come. "Me too, Karen."

"Pat, will we ever have a life together?" She was aware that she was holding her breath.

Here comes the bullshit, he thought. What do I do? Get up and leave, or stay and feed her some more lies. He felt a pang of guilt for helping her waste so many years of her life; but her face sure felt good resting over him. He felt himself getting hard. I'd sure hate to have to give her up, he thought. I'll string her along for another year, maybe two, and then . . .

"Karen, I always thought that you knew how I felt about us. As soon as my children get a little older I'll leave my wife. We'll have our life together. I promise."

She was happy. Her Pat had reassured her. She touched the swelling in his pants. "Let's go into the bedroom," she said.

Karen Murphy arched her back and slid off her cotton briefs. She was naked. She watched him undress. His boxer shorts were two sizes too big and his undershirt was gray and stretched out of shape. He flipped off his shoes and came into her bed wearing his socks and undershirt.

Karen loved him for himself, not for his lovemaking. He had a small penis and was conscious of it. He required constant assurance and would always ask her if he satisfied her and if he was big enough for her. She had never really enjoyed sex. As her mother had told her, it was something that women have to do, so it was best to get it over with as quickly as possible. She had learned to fake an orgasm to coincide with his.

She sucked him until he was hard and then lay back. He entered her immediately, without benefit of a kiss or foreplay. Karen undulated wildly. She began to say, "Fuck me. Fuck me." He liked to hear her curse when they were doing it. He pumped her in silence, never emitting a sound. She could tell from his breathing that he was almost ready.

"Now! Come with me." She clamped her legs around his hips and rammed her pelvis up into his body. "I'm coming."

His body sagged on top of her.

She continued to vise him to her. "You're so wonderful. I love making love with you."

He did not answer her. He broke her grip on his body and rolled off her. He was asleep within minutes.

She studied his face as he slept. Sex is so unimportant, she thought. She leaned over and kissed his lips.

That night just before nine a gray van rolled to a stop and parked across the street from the Interlude. The spill of street lamps sliced through the darkness, spreading their even circles over the sidewalk.

Starling Johnson and Jake Stern, both of whom were dressed as army officers, turned the corner of Fifty-seventh Street and started walking in the direction of the club. Johnson peeled away from his partner and walked over to a fire hydrant. It was time to test the Kel set that was strapped under his arm.

"Honk if you read me," Johnson said, putting his foot on the fire hydrant and bending to tie his shoelace.

A horn blared.

Johnson took his foot from the hydrant and tugged at his uniform blouse to make sure that it was even all around and then faced his partner. "Come on, brother, let's you and me earn our daily bread."

A heavy mahogany door with large brass door knockers was at the top of the steps. Johnson lifted the knocker, looked at his partner, and rapped four times.

A tall, strikingly thin man with sculptured black hair, glossy fingernails, and an oversized bow tie that complemented large protruding ears, opened the door and motioned them inside.

"Good evening, gentlemen. My name is Paul. Are you members of the Interlude?"

"I am Captain Jefferson," Johnson lied. "And this is Capt. Jake Stern. A buddy of ours, Major Landsford, is a member of the club. He was transferred and he gave us his key. He told us that there'd be no hassle . . . his dues were paid for three years, he told us."

"May I have the key, please," the maître d' said.

Unruffled, Johnson handed it to him.

"Please wait here, gentlemen." The maître d' turned and walked over to a door that was to the right of the hatcheck cubicle. He opened the door and entered, clicking it closed behind him. He went to the filing cabinet by the window and opened it to the L's. He pulled out Landsford's file. Each member's file had statements relating to the member's sexual preference and personal proclivities, and special instructions on how the member was to be treated. Landsford's file told a story of a fun-loving army officer who enjoyed spending an evening with the ladies. Fortunately, the file also gave instructions that Landsford and any of his army friends were to be given the run of the club and extended every consideration. He closed the file, returned it to its place, and slid the drawer closed.

Paul, the maître d', did not know what was going on at the Interlude, nor did he want to know. He followed his instructions, minded his own business, and made a lot of money. That was all he was interested in—the money. If the owners of the Interlude wanted Landsford and his army friends to be shown special consideration, Paul would see to it that they received it.

"You're both friends of Major Landsford?" the maître d' said, leaving the office and walking over to the two detectives.

"Yes we are," Stern said.

"We haven't seen Major Landsford for a while," the maître d' said.

"He was transferred," Johnson said. "Before he left we had a poker game. Landsford ran out of money and called a raise with a watch and this key. He told us that his membership in the club was transferable. Jake won the pot and the key."

"You must have been close friends of Landsford's," the maître d' said.

"We are very good friends," Stern said firmly.

"In that case, gentlemen, I would like to invite you both to be our guests tonight. For the first round of drinks."

The bar was smoky and crowded; its décor tasteful decadence—there were banquettes of red velvet, etched glass partitions, soft lights, and thick carpet. As the maître d' led them into the long bar he explained that there were private dining rooms on the second and third floors where couples, gay and straight, might enjoy the pleasures of cold wine and clean sheets. Waitresses, showing ample amounts of breasts and asses, threaded their way among the guests carrying trays of drinks and canapés.

Two women were sitting at a corner banquette. One was a Valkyrie, a statuesque woman whose long blond hair was braided. She went by the name of Ursula. The other woman was Vietnamese, and she had long black hair that ran down the length of her back. She answered to the name of Iris Lee. Ursula watched the two soldiers being led up to the bar. She gave Starling Johnson the kind of a look that makes a man check to see if his fly is open.

"Who are they?" Johnson asked, catching the look.

"Hostesses. Would you gentlemen like to meet them?" Paul asked, glancing over at the women.

"I think that might be very pleasant," Stern said, adjusting his khaki tie.

The maître d' ordered a round of drinks for his guests, excused himself, and then pushed his way through the crowd over to where the women were sitting.

"Who are they?" Iris Lee asked the maître d' when he came over to them.

"Friends of Landsford's. They are to be treated as special guests of the house," the maître d' said.

Ursula raised her glass and started to dart her tongue over the rim. "And who is going to pay us?"

"You will both be taken care of," he said.

"The nigger looks like he is hung," Ursula said.

"A little change of luck can't hurt," Paul said, moving away from the women and going back to the bar.

The two women slid out of the booth and followed the maître d'.

"How long have you been in the army?" Iris Lee asked Stern.

"I enlisted when I was sixteen," he said, glancing down at the slit that ran along the front of her dress.

Ursula leaned close to Johnson, examining the three rows of campaign ribbons. "You've seen a lot of combat," she said, running a finger over the ribbons.

116

"A little," Johnson said, looking at his partner who was now ensconced against the bar with Iris Lee, whispering and smirking like a prepubescent adolescent.

"Violent people get me off," Ursula said, moving even closer, and sliding her knee between his legs.

"Me too, baby," Johnson said.

"I'm getting a hard-on listening to this crap," O'Shaughnessy said, his ear near the receiver inside the surveillance van.

After they had consumed two rounds of drinks Iris Lee suggested that their little party adjourn to one of the private dining rooms on the second floor.

The detectives cheerfully agreed.

"She doesn't buy their story," Heinemann said.

"She's not sure," Malone said. "When they get them alone upstairs, they'll start to play some parlor games with them to see if they'll go all the way. It's the old hooker game. They figure a cop is not going to play it out until the end."

"Those ladies have the wrong two guys," Davis said, grinning.

"What if she feels the Kel on Starling?" Heinemann said.

"Then we make like the cavalry," Malone said.

Ursula and Johnson were sitting on a cane-backed love-seat that complemented the baroqueness of the second-floor dining room. They had been on the second floor for almost fifty minutes. It was time for the girls to get to work. Iris Lee looked at Ursula and nodded slightly. Ursula picked up the cue and slipped out from under Johnson's arms and went to her knees in front of him. She moved close, rubbing her hand in the crook of his thigh.

Iris Lee and Stern kissed. She reached down and forced his legs apart, then slid out of his embrace and knelt on the floor in front of him. "Does it turn you on to have people watch?" she said, reaching for his zipper.

The receiver inside the van went silent. Detectives

crowded around, each raptly concentrating on the black piece of mesh in the center of the receiver.

"They better not," Malone said, shaking his head incredulously.

"Lou, I think they're going to," Heinemann said.

Slowly, almost inaudibly at first, sounds of carnal pleasure began to seep from the mesh. Detectives snapped to attention, ears pricked.

"I don't fucking believe it," Malone said, turning to O'Shaughnessy and shouting, "Turn off the goddamn tape."

"Can I go in tomorrow night?" O'Shaughnessy asked, laughing as he flipped off the switch on the recording console.

Gus Heinemann leaned against the wall, his head resting on folded arms, laughing.

The sounds of sexual pleasure reached a violent crescendo, and then avalanched into an elongated sigh. . . .

"Lou, I . . . do believe that the cavalry has come!" Heinemann said, wiping his eyes with a handkerchief.

Iris Lee insisted on ordering dinner for her guests. Tanqueray martinis were served in frosted glasses. After two rounds of drinks the door opened and a waiter with a butchboy haircut wheeled in a serving cart. Iris Lee ordered him to put the dinner on the table in the corner of the room.

When they were finished eating, the waiter put a tray of fruit and cheese down on the table. He then reached under the cart and removed an unopened bottle of Courvoisier. He put it down next to a silver humidor.

Blouses open, the detectives sprawled in their chairs sucking on large and deliciously illegal Havanas. "That sure wasn't anything like army chow," Johnson said, blowing a thick ring of smoke.

"You ladies sure know how to treat a soldier," Stern said, raising the snifter to his nose and inhaling the strong bouquet.

In unison the detectives inside the van harmonized, "You fucking humps."

Iris Lee was coiled on the floor next to Detective Johnson, her head resting on his lap, her arms looped around his leg. She glanced up at him. "Can I get you anything else?"

"Nothing, thank you. Everything was perfect," Johnson said, stroking her hair.

"An experienced soldier like you must have a really important job at Totten," Iris Lee cooed, rubbing the tips of her fingers over the back of his thigh.

"Why the hell would you be interested in that?" Johnson asked.

"I'm a taxpayer. I'd like to know that I'm well protected," she said.

"Don't worry," Stern said. "You'd be surprised if you ever knew the stuff we got there."

Johnson shot a warning look at Stern and started to say something when a piercing scream came from the floor above. Both detectives' heads snapped up.

"What the hell was that?" Stern said, getting to his feet, staring up at the ceiling.

"Relax," Ursula said. "That's the Turk. He likes to do it in the rear. The louder the girl screams the more he pays her."

"I think we're going to enjoy being members of the Interlude," Johnson said, sliding his hand inside Iris Lee's silk blouse.

Another scream! Faint. Subdued.

"Sounds like the Turk has finished playing," Stern said, glancing upward.

Iris Lee reached back and unhooked her bra. Her breasts were large, out of proportion to her thin body. "Play with them," she said.

Johnson fingered her nipples.

This time there could be no doubt, a terrifying scream that begged for mercy. The detectives leaped to their feet and ran for the door.

"It's nothing," Iris Lee said, hooking up her bra and going after them.

The detectives ignored her. They stood outside the room

and looked up and down the deserted corridor. Another violent scream forced a decision. The detectives hugged the wall, moving cautiously in the direction of the scream. At the end of the corridor they discovered a darkened staircase partially hidden behind dusty, faded drapes. Stern jumped to the other side of the drapes and pulled them aside. Johnson covered.

The staircase ended in darkness. They stood at the bottom step, straining to see and hear what was going on at the top, where only a faint sliver of light could be discerned. They ascended the steps, one at a time, their backs rubbing the wall, and had almost reached the top when a large, shadowy form stepped out of the darkness and peered down at the two wary cops. "This floor is private," he said in a low, menacing voice.

Johnson moved away from the wall. He braced his right leg behind, slowly moving his left onto the next step, firming his stance. "We're members," Johnson said, sliding his left foot up another step.

The man's hand came out of the blackness gripping a metal bar. He lunged down at the detective. Johnson ducked under the powerful swing. The detective came up hard, slamming his left hand into the man's elbow, at the same time banging down on top of the wrist with his right hand. Johnson pushed in the opposite direction and suddenly the elbow snapped. Then Johnson pivoted, tugging the man forward, tossing him, screaming, down the flight of stairs. The body crashed into the drapes, tearing them off their rod. The man lay whimpering from the agony in his arm.

Johnson and Stern rushed to the top, where they crouched down and let their eyes grow accustomed to the semidarkness. A line of light seeped under a door at the end of the hall. Hearing eerie sounds coming from behind it, they ran toward the door. Johnson moved his mouth to the miniature microphone concealed inside his shirt. "Stay in the van," he shouted. "We'll handle it."

"What should we do?" O'Shaughnessy said, concerned.

"Wait and listen," Malone said. "They know what they're doing, most of the time."

"And if they need help?" Davis asked.

"Then we make like fucking Gang Busters," Malone said.

Stern smashed his foot above the knob. The door splintered and crashed open; the two cops rushed in, crouched defensively to minimize the targets they offered.

The windows were shuttered; street light filtered through the slats. The room was large and bare save for a grotesquely ornate four-poster bed and one heavy wooden armchair. Two swarthy men were standing over a semiconscious, half-naked woman who was tied in it. Her body was swollen, bloody; both breasts were peppered with festering red blotches. Burnt matches were scattered around the chair.

The tormentors whirled as the detectives crashed into the room. One of them pulled a blackjack from his rear pocket and leaped at the detectives. Stern met the attack and pivoted the threatening hand with his outstretched arm, rammed his knee into the man's groin, and smashed his gun's frame into the man's forehead. He crumpled to the floor, blood spurting from the jagged gash on his head.

"Okay, Abdullah, play time's over," Johnson snarled. "Get against the wall before I give you a second asshole!" Johnson cocked his revolver, assumed a combat stance, and leveled the weapon at the man's face.

Andrea St. James tried to get up. She and the chair tumbled to the floor.

"Help me," she pleaded.

Stern stepped back, covering the two men. Johnson removed his blouse and went to her, kneeling at her side. He untied her and gently placed the blouse over her. "Let's get you out of here," Johnson said. "We'll put these two bastards behind bars for a couple of years."

Andrea St. James clutched at his arm. "No police,

please," she said, tears streaming down her swollen cheeks. "Just get me out of here."

"But . . ." Johnson started to protest.

"Please . . . no arrests."

Johnson looked over to Jake Stern who shrugged. "Without a complainant we got nothing," Stern said.

The maître d' and the two hostesses burst into the room.

Stern whipped around. "Against the wall, my lovelies."

"What do you think you're doing?" the maître d' demanded.

"We're leaving and the lady is leaving with us," Johnson announced, cradling Andrea St. James in his arms.

"Who the fuck are you?" Ursula yelled.

"Why, mamma, we're officers and gentlemen," Starling Johnson said, backing out the door.

The emergency room at Bellevue was filled with the night's casualties. Malone peered past the partly drawn curtain at the doctor working over Andrea St. James. It never changes, he thought. She was just another person caught up in mindless carnage; night after night—cuttings, stabbings, shootings. Malone scanned the people patiently waiting their turns to be patched back together. A white man sat pressing a flap of skin from his cheek in place. Malone looked at him. Just your friendly corner knife fight, no doubt, he thought.

A dead-tired intern left the cubicle and shambled over to Malone.

"Are you going to keep her, Doc?" Malone asked.

"Where?" the doctor said. "They're packed in here like sardines. I've patched her up. Her private physician will have to take it from there."

Malone went into a huddle with the detectives. "We need a safe house."

"Do we go the official or unofficial route?" Davis asked.

"Unofficial," Malone said. "We've nothing to hold her on." Malone pondered the situation for a moment. "Bo, call Delamare at the Barton Hotel. He'll give us a room for a few days, no questions asked."

"What about baby-sitters?" O'Shaughnessy asked.

Malone sighed. "We'll have to steal two of Harrigan's men."

The management of the Barton Hotel on Lexington Avenue was glad to cooperate with the NYPD. They knew from experience that small favors reap a large harvest.

Andrea St. James was tucked away in a suite of rooms for which a paying guest would have had to pay three hundred dollars a day. Large windows overlooked the Manhattan landscape. There was a large living room decorated in almost–French Provincial. A rose-pink bedroom and lace-bordered sheets seemed an incongruous setting. She lay in bed, wearing an open-back hospital gown, twisting and turning, her face swathed in bandages.

Malone dragged a chair over to the bed and placed a cassette tape recorder on the marble-topped night stand, thinking of how to question her. He knew only that she was the hooker who had made the porno film with Landsford and that there was a definite connection between her and Anderman. And he assumed that it was she who used to call Eisinger at Braxton Tours, and was the same woman Eisinger told to look at the song.

Frightened, unsure eyes peered up at him from behind an embrasure of gauze. He noticed that her fingernails were broken and chipped. The smooth colored glaze that once covered them had been chewed, leaving atolls of ugly yellowish nail.

Andrea St. James was semiconscious. Her hands worked on the sheets, squeezing and scratching. She let her eyes close. Malone was afraid she would be lost to the sedation they had given her at Bellevue.

123

His knees pressed into the side of the bed. "You took a bad beating. Feeling any better?"

"Who are you?"

"The police."

"Oh. Thank God. Yachov sent you. You're from the Unit."

"Yes. Yachov sent me," he said, playing her.

She clutched his shoulder. "Tell Yachov it was Westy. I saw Westy with them. . . . He gave it up. . . . Yachov was right . . . tell him . . . should have pulled me out . . . no list . . . couldn't find list . . . Sara . . . poor dear Sara . . ."

She was scratching his shoulders as though she was trying to claw her way back to consciousness. Her tongue was heavy in her mouth; her eyes would open, focus, and then close. She tried to get more words out, but could manage only a low mumble.

Malone took her hand in his, soothing it with gentle strokes. His voice was low, calming. "Andrea. Tell me so that I can tell Yachov."

"Yachov . . . the Unit has been breached . . . warn him. Westy . . . I saw him that first time with Sara . . . in the restaurant with the other two . . . one was wearing that stupid shirt . . . it was a beautiful day . . . Fort Surrender . . . Sara . . . remember . . . he waved at her . . . oh, I hurt so much." Her hand slid from his shoulder.

Malone licked at the film of sweat that had formed above his lip. His eyes were wide, fixed in a disbelieving stare. He began to gnaw at the extremity of his lower lip. Had he heard correctly?

He was suddenly conscious of his throbbing temples. He shuffled closer. He now had his direct link. Cops were involved—somewhere, somehow. He bent closer, not speaking, studying her, trying to unscramble her words.

He moved his lips next to her ear and whispered, "Tell me who killed Sara."

Her consciousness was slipping away. "Westy . . . no

. . . don't know . . . yes . . . him . . . Westy . . . warn Yachov . . .''

"Andrea. Tell me about the song."

"Sara tried to warn us . . . she . . . found out . . . about
. . . the Unit within a unit . . .''

"The song," he repeated.

"Song of Asaph . . . Sara's way . . .''

He could feel his heart beating faster. "Andrea. Tell me
about the Unit."

Her eyes opened wide and she struggled up, bracing herself on her elbows. "You're not from Yachov!" she yelled
with surprising energy. Then she collapsed and curled into a
fetal position.

Malone reached out and shut off the recorder. As he
started to get up he noticed the antique telephone next to the
recorder. He picked it up, stretching it as far away from the
bed as the cord permitted. Placing it on the floor, he returned
for the recorder.

When he was by the door he stopped. Without turning to
look at her he said, "You owe it to Sara to help us. Not
to mention the fact that a couple of cops risked their lives to
save your ungrateful ass."

Andrea St. James lay alone, her eyes closed as she listened
to the endless ticking of a clock off somewhere in the distance. *Tick, tick, tick.* It never missed; each tick falling with
monotonous regularity. Her head had begun to clear. She
wasn't sure if it had been a dream; it was so real. She was
being questioned by a man who had said that he came from
Yachov. The pain was still there, a terrible ache throughout
her body. She lifted her head and looked around the room,
ensuring that she was alone. One by one she slid her legs out
from under the sheets and touched the floor. The rug felt soft
and cold against her feet. Light-headed, she collapsed over
the bed, her legs dangling over the side.

She rested, gathering her strength; her chest heaved from shuddering painful breaths. Several minutes passed and she tried again. This time she slid her body over the edge, outstretched hands acting as her guide.

On hands and knees she looked across the room at the telephone. So far away. She crawled over to it, inching painfully over the shaggy surface. When she reached it she stared down at the white circle in the center of the telephone: Barton Hotel, Ext. 345. She knocked the receiver from its cradle and lay on the floor next to it, her face next to the mouthpiece, trying through her blurred eyes to make out the direction over each of the ten circles on the dial. Dial 6 for a local call. A finger moved haltingly toward the sixth circle. She took her time, knowing that she had to get it right the first time. There was no strength left for a second try. The phone on the other end was answered on the first ring. She spoke haltingly in Hebrew.

Andrea St. James felt secure. Friends would be coming for her.

The Golden Kitchen on First Avenue was one of Malone's favorite eating places. He picked his way through the crowd to an unoccupied table by the window. He saw some familiar faces; couples were quietly eating their dinners and sharing a carafe of wine while the singles sat alone reading a book or newspaper and secretly prayed for someone to share their meal. He thought of Father Gavin. Had Monsignor McInerney officiated at the funeral? Was Mary, nee Harold Collins, still turning tricks? Probably. . . . He wondered how many other people in the restaurant were carrying on conversations with themselves. Most, he thought. And then the Eisinger caper swirled into his thoughts. How did they manage to get Andrea St. James into the Interlude without Harrigan's men seeing them? One of the detectives was probably taking a piss someplace and the other was more than likely bullshit-

ting with some broad. And Westy? That was obviously the
name of a man. But who? And the Unit within a unit. What
was it? Was it part of the Job? Anderman was the key. Who
was that son-of-a-bitch anyway? And then there was Fort
Surrender. Only a cop would know about that. He had played
the tape a dozen times; Andrea St. James did not say it was
a T-shirt. But he knew that it was. He had seen them.
Did Westy and his two pals come out of Fort Surrender?
His thoughts quickly returned to the present when an
outrageously attractive woman strode past the restaurant.
Her white gauze skirt fell between her long legs, revealing
the welt of her bikini underpants. He was suddenly aware
of an uncomfortable ache in his balls. His daydreams
changed. He was in bed with a woman, her long legs
wrapped his body, holding him as he pumped relentlessly.
Her head thrashing the pillow; guttural whimpers caught
in her throat. Her black hair was disarrayed and beaded with
sweat. He could feel her spasms, the sliding of her body
against him.

He did not wait for dessert. He got up, paid the bill, and
headed for the old-fashioned telephone booth in the rear of
the restaurant. He slid open the door and dialed, standing. A
self-mocking smile flitted across his face as he tried to remember if he had made the obligatory "it was wonderful" telephone call after the last time.

Erica Sommers chuckled when she heard his voice. "I
figured you would be calling soon."

"If you can tear yourself away from your work I'd sure
like to see you."

"Where are you, Daniel?"

"Four blocks away." He was aware of a sudden burning
sensation in his stomach.

"Give me an hour to finish my work."

"Ten-four," he said, letting the phone fall onto the hook.

●

Erica Sommers read the page in the typewriter.

Jefferson Stranger watched the silky garment slide over his bride's sensuous body. He moved back, casting a lustful eye.

Christina Stranger stepped out of the nightgown, her arms beckoning. This was to be a new beginning; an escape from her secret past. She prayed that Jefferson would never discover her previous life. As he took her into his arms she thought of David and how much stronger his arms were.

Tapping a pencil over her teeth, Erica Sommers reread the page. She took the pencil and struck out an adjective. Enough is enough, she told herself, glancing at the time. Shit! Malone would be here soon. She hurried into the bathroom, pulling her top off as she went.

Erica Sommers wrote Nightingale Romances—two hundred pages of escape that sold at drugstores and supermarkets.

Erica had showered and was standing naked in the bathroom with one leg on the rim of the tub, trimming her pubic hair. She thought of Malone. They had met two years ago at a performance of *Dancin'*. He had arrived late and was trudging down the aisle when he stepped on her foot. During the intermission he came over to her and apologized. She found herself drawn to him from the first. His body excited her and his smile possessed a warmth that caused her to glow inwardly. But during their first date she concluded it would be a mistake to permit herself to become involved with him. He was the kind of man no woman could really be sure of, she decided. A character straight out of one of her Nightingales. But then, perhaps she was wrong. Maybe they could have something together. She went to bed with him on their fourth date and it was nothing like her fantasies, but something better and totally unexpected. He was physically demanding, direct, and at the same time a gentle, considerate lover. Of all the men she had known, he was the first to excite and fully engage her sexuality. They discovered that they were both capable of multiple orgasms and spent hours in bed reveling in each other's body. At times when she was alone she would find herself thinking of his body and would suddenly be consumed by desire for him.

In many ways she found Malone to be a strange and lonely man. A man capable of giving himself totally in bed, yet unable to share any part of himself out of bed. IT was always there, that monolithic secret society of unwritten laws and unspoken nuances that prevented some men from giving of themselves, the NYPD.

She had reached the point where something had to give in the relationship. A commitment or an ending. She had been divorced for five years and was ready to share her life. She demanded only two things of a man: honesty and sharing. To her mind they were simple things. It perplexed her that men found them so difficult.

Erica Sommers was a strikingly handsome woman with a high forehead and an aristocratic nose. Her eyebrows arched sharply and then flowed downward over her brow. Her brown hair was cut in bangs with the back cascading past her shoulders. Deeply tanned skin accentuated her large amber eyes.

Malone had arrived exactly one hour after he telephoned.

She had made them drinks and they were sitting on her minute terrace staring at the inky river.

Malone said, "You get more beautiful each time I see you."

"Why thank you, Lieutenant. I hope you don't tell that to all your lady friends."

He wanted to tell her that there were no others. Instead he said, "I don't."

She was wearing a white caftan and sandals. Getting comfortable, she tucked her legs under her body and looked at him. She then proceeded to tell him everything that she had done since she last saw him. She had gone shopping for a dress and discovered this wonderful delicatessen off Second Avenue that specialized in Greek delicacies. She had cleaned the apartment and done her laundry. Her latest Nightingale was almost completed: *Christina's Fury*. She was giving some thought to writing a serious novel set in the antebellum South. Finished recounting her days, she sat back and looked at him. "Tell me what's new in your life." She sipped at her drink, watching him. "Any interesting cases?"

There's this Eisinger thing, he wanted to say. And these telephone calls from a Captain Madvick who does not exist; and a guy named Mannelli and another guy named Anderman. This and more he wanted to say. But he couldn't. She wasn't on the Job. Wasn't a part of it. His fingers were bobbing the ends of her hair. "Naw," said he, "there's nothing new. The same old stuff day in and day out."

Her face reflected her disappointment. She sipped her drink slowly, thinking. She was in love with a shadow who had built a wall of silence around him. A protective moat. He was a man with no past, no present, and no future. She wanted him on equal terms and would go out of her way to assert her independence with him. She was not a camp follower. Whenever she would ask him about his divorce or ex-wife, or the damn PD, he'd either snap at her or give her an oblique answer. They had been seeing each other for almost two months before he gave her his home telephone number. There were times when she wondered why she bothered, but, then, when she looked into his face and touched his shoulders, she knew. She always knew. "For a lieutenant of detectives you have a decidedly boring job, Daniel."

He flipped his right hand back and forth. "It's just a job, not a calling."

They sat in silence for a while and then he leaned over and kissed her breast through the soft fabric. She moved her head back and pressed him to her body. His hand glided up her smooth leg. "Not here, Daniel."

They walked into the bedroom holding hands.

It was much later. They had made love twice and were lying in bed silently listening to the not-so-muted noise of the City. She decided to try again. She turned toward him. "Tell me about your marriage, Daniel."

"There's nothing to tell," he snapped.

"Please don't be hard with me. I don't like you when you're like that."

"I was soft a few minutes ago," he said, reaching over and running a hand over her thigh. She lifted his hand from her body and carried it out over the bed where she dropped it with a look of exaggerated disdain. "All men are soft then! When they're hard they're soft and when they're soft they're hard. All women know that, Lieutenant."

He looked at her and smiled.

Holding hands, they fell into a peaceful sleep.

The sun rose at 5:12 A.M. Malone was sitting up in the bed staring down at her naked beauty, marveling at the pleasure they were able to give each other. I know what you're trying to do, he thought. You want me to give you what I can't. Would you believe me if I told you that one human being could kill another with a curtain rod, that a father was capable of sodomizing his daughter, that a person's body could be turned into an unrecognizable black mass, that bands of animals roam our city robbing and killing, that the police are the only ones that stand between you and barbarism? Would you believe those things? A cop would. Shall I tell you that there are only a handful of politicians and judges in the city who give a good fuck what happens to you or the rest of the drones? Do you want to know what it's like to work in a concrete sewer; to walk armed through the night constantly watching the shadows, listening for footsteps behind. Perhaps I should tell you of the pervasive corruption. Do you know what a judge has to pay for his black robe? I do. You want to know why policemen don't share. I'll tell you. It's because they see the city being submerged in a sea of stinking shit and because they don't want the excrement of the savages seeping into their private lives. I wish that I could share more with you.

She opened her eyes and saw him looking at her. For a moment she thought she noticed his eyes glistening. She cupped his face with her hands. "Can't you sleep?"

"I want to tell you about my marriage."

She sat up, wide awake.

Squares of light dotted the façade of the Barton Hotel. Frustrated waiters stood grumbling, waiting for the last patrons to leave the darkened nightclub. There was an empty stillness about the near deserted lobby. A cleaning woman dusted the plants, just starting her night's tasks. An occasional couple walked in from the night and went directly to the elevators. Every now and then a Mr. Brown or Smith exited the hotel's piano bar and went to the desk clerk to register while his "wife" fidgeted with her drink at the bar, waiting for him to return with the key.

A man strode briskly into the lobby and hurried to the elevators.

Andrea St. James slept restlessly, waiting.

Two detectives sprawled over a couch outside her bedroom, sipping the last of a six-pack and watching the "Late Late Show." A hard, deliberate knock made their heads jerk toward the door. They put their beers down and looked at each other, concerned. They slid their revolvers out and went to the door, positioning themselves against the wall. "Yeah?"

The reply was sure and crisp. Andrea St. James's attorney. His card was slid under the door:

HANLEY, GREEN, DAYTON, FORBES
12 Wall Street
New York, New York
G. JUSTIN HANLEY, *Attorney-at-Law*

G. Justin Hanley was the senior partner in an impeccable law firm well known both for its discretion in handling delicate matters and its enormous fees. G. Justin Hanley looked like a G. Justin Hanley of Exeter, Yale, Southampton, and Park Avenue should look. Even at 2 A.M. he looked as fresh as he would at the start of any business day. His dark gray suit was sufficiently unfashionable, and his expression the right mixture of amusement at and distance from the company in which he now found himself.

Hanley was polite, firm, and more than a little condescending. He told the detectives that he was aware that his client was being held. She was not under arrest but was being protected by the police from unknown assailants. For this he and his client were grateful. However, it was incumbent upon him to see that his client received proper medical attention. He was therefore taking his client with him, now. The efforts of the NYPD were greatly appreciated. He hoped that the matter might be settled here, now. He would find it distasteful if he had to go into court and lodge a complaint against the NYPD for unlawful detention. He casually asked if the detectives were familiar with the Civil Rights Act. "Its penalties are quite severe," he assured them.

Limping alongside the lawyer with a bed sheet covering her hospital gown, Andrea St. James left the lobby of the Barton Hotel and was guided toward a waiting limousine.

A solitary figure sat in the rear. The lawyer helped her into the back seat. She threw herself crying onto the man's lap.

Anderman stroked her hair. "Everything will be fine now. You're going home."

7

WEDNESDAY, *June 17* . . . Early morning

Yachov Anderman arrived early in order to supervise the loading of the trailer. It was a shipment that required his personal attention. Fork-lifts darted into the belly and dropped their skids; workers inside ensured that the load was secure. When the trailer was full, the doors were closed and sealed. Anderman gave a signal and a button was pressed. The loading-bay door churned upward. The scrunch of wheels jerked Anderman's head toward the street. He saw a car in front of the bay, blocking it. Malone was climbing out of the front. There were other detectives with him. Anderman handed his clipboard to the man standing next to him and jumped from the platform. A glint of victory shone in his eyes. "Still chasing windmills, policeman?"

"Andrea St. James," Malone shot back.

Malone went up to Anderman and looped his arm through the trucker's, turning him and walking him back toward the platform. "That was a very neat operation last night. My compliments."

"I haven't the slightest idea what you're talking about."

They strolled along the side of the tractor-trailer, Malone watching the monstrous wheels. When they reached the cab they turned and headed back toward the door. Stern and Heinemann waited just inside. David Ancorie peered out from the dispatcher's cubicle.

"If they get their hands on her again I might not be around to save her," Malone said.

134

"Save who?" Anderman was enjoying his moment.

"I have a few more questions that I'd like to ask the lady."

Anderman wrenched away from the policeman. "Wait right where you are. I'll go and telephone my lawyer. You can ask him your questions."

Malone's eyes narrowed. He turned abruptly and headed for the platform, motioning the detectives to follow. A short ladder led up. Malone gripped the top and climbed. When he reached the top he straightened, looking around. He moved to the three men who were loading wooden crates onto skids. He asked their names. Each replied in broken English. Malone produced his shield and demanded to see their Alien Registration Cards. The confused workers looked to Anderman and shrugged in gestures of dismay. Malone ordered the detectives to arrest the men. Stern and Heinemann started to handcuff them together.

"What the hell do you think you're doing?" shrieked Anderman, running for the ladder.

David Ancorie came out of the cubicle.

"Every alien is required by federal law to carry and produce on demand his green card. Failure to do so is presumptive evidence of illegal entry into this country," Malone said.

Anderman reached the top. He was out of breath. He bellied up to Malone. "You're city cops, not federal! Their damn cards are in their homes. Each one of them are here legal."

"Too bad." He pushed Anderman aside and prepared to leave. Ancorie was there, blocking his path; his anger evident. The two men stood toe-to-toe, glaring. "If I were you I'd move," Malone whispered.

The pulse in Ancorie's neck pounded. His cheeks were flushed.

"I mean right now, laddie," Malone said, his tone now harder.

"David?" Anderman called.

Ancorie's stare flashed to Anderman. He moved aside. As

Malone was climbing down Anderman shouted to him. "You're persecuting me, policeman."

"Some people might say that," Malone said.

G. Justin Hanley, Andrea St. James's attorney, was waiting impatiently in front of the federal detention center. As the prisoners were being led from the car, the lawyer walked over. "Lieutenant Malone?"

Malone looked at him. "Yes?"

"My card." It was not the plain kind of calling card that he had left at the Barton Hotel. The paper was expensive; the words on it in elegant raised lettering. Lieutenants must rate the expensive ones, Malone thought, handing it back. "Thanks, but I don't need any right now."

Hanley stiffened, his patrician feathers ruffled by the glib reply.

"Those men are not slaves; they're my clients," the lawyer said, pointing to the handcuffed men being led into the detention facility.

Heinemann paused and looked back at Malone. The lieutenant waved him inside. "I told you they're my clients!" Hanley insisted.

"What are their names, Counselor?"

"Their what?"

"Names. Almost everyone has one these days. You should know theirs . . . if they are your clients."

Hanley's face twisted into a grimace. "That makes no difference," he stammered. "I represent those men."

"Oh, but it do make a difference, Counselor." Malone walked away.

Hanley went after him, grabbing him by the shoulder and turning him.

"I demand their immediate release." The lawyer's voice cracked; his lower lip was quivering.

Malone smiled. "Please get your hand off me, Counselor." It was a thin voice, hardly a whisper. Hanley knew that a second request would not be forthcoming. He removed his hand. How he hated the flotsam of the street. In boardrooms among his peers G. Justin Hanley was a champion; but here, at society's lowest rung, he felt outmatched.

"You're stretching the rubber band too far, Malone. It's going to snap and take your head off."

Malone moved close to him. He noticed the beads of sweat bordering the hairline. He ran his fingernails over Hanley's lapel.

"Threats are very unprofessional, Counselor." Malone walked away, leaving the lawyer clenching his fists. Malone craned his head to him. "When you see Anderman tell him that he should have given you all the facts . . . like the names."

A long corridor led to the holding pens where illegal aliens waited inside to be processed. Orientals huddled together, speaking softly in their native languages. Latins talked rapidly in Spanish, casting nervous glances at the immigration officials taking pedigrees through the bars. Some of the aliens were sitting cross-legged on the floor; old habits quickly return. Heinemann was waiting. "What took you so long?"

"It became necessary to give an eminent member of the bar a lesson in street law."

"That eminent member of the bar will have them sprung within the hour," Stern said.

Malone agreed. "I just couldn't let him get away with last night without breaking some balls. Besides, by the time Anderman gets them out the surveillance van is going to be parked on the south side of Borden Avenue. I want to know what's going down inside that place."

It took Anderman and his lawyer the better part of two hours to obtain releases. Malone had laid a professional courtesy requested on the people at Immigration and they complied; stalling and shuffling Anderman and Hanley from office to office. It was almost 4 P.M. when a blue Ford sedan drove into the loading bay of the Eastern Shipping Company. Anderman and his workers left the car cursing the police in four different languages. Anderman hurried off by himself. During the drive back he had reached a decision. Andrea St. James's presence had become a risk. Too many people were looking for her. When he got back to his office he called El Al. There was a flight out in ninety minutes.

A frankfurter man set up his pushcart in front of Tauscher Steel. The peddler snapped the blue-and-yellow umbrella up over the cart, locking it into place. He flipped open the steam tub and stirred the orange-colored water. A log jam of frankfurters concealed the Bren gun wrapped in a waterproof covering. The man's long hair covered the plastic wire that ran up the side of his neck into the miniature receiver plugged into his ear. A steel hat came over and ordered a frank with all the trimmings. The iron man strolled off, gnashing the strands of sauerkraut and onions hanging out of the roll. The peddler waited until the customer was gone. Then he leaned forward, adjusting the stacks of plastic cups. "The gray van that was outside the Interlude last night is across from the plant," he whispered into the cups.

The reply was immediate. "We wait."

The blue sedan bolted from the loading bay and crossed Borden Avenue. Andrea St. James was sitting in the rear next to Isaac Arazi. Hillel Henkoff was behind the wheel. A flatbed of I beams lumbered out of Thirty-first Street. The frankfurter man leaned forward. "A blue Ford sedan just left. Andrea was in the back."

Inside the surveillance van O'Shaughnessy radioed Malone that Andrea St. James had left. "Stay with her," Malone said. "I'll try and catch up with you."

Bo Davis wiggled the transmission into first gear and released the clutch. The van moved from the curb.

Malone and Heinemann hurried from the precinct.

"We're in a hurry," Malone said, sliding into the car. Heinemann reached to the floor and picked up the portable red light. He reached out of the car and slapped it onto the roof.

"We're on our way," Heinemann said, flipping the siren switch.

The blue sedan entered the Long Island Expressway at Greenpoint Avenue. Traffic was backed up over the hump. Andrea St. James stared at the row of A-frame houses that lined the service road. She had never noticed them before. There was a vest-pocket park that she had never seen; the handball court was covered with graffiti. It was funny the things people never take the time to notice, she thought. She was overcome with a sense of sadness at leaving. A delivery truck nosed past the blue sedan blocking her view; a graffito was fingered in the dirt: IRAN SUCKS.

O'Shaughnessy maintained radio contact with Malone. The sedan was fifteen cars ahead of them. "Lou, do you want us to pull them over and grab her?" O'Shaughnessy radioed.

"No," Malone said. "I don't want to blow the van. And besides, I want to see where they're going."

Traffic exiting the Brooklyn-Queens Expressway merged into the Long Island Expressway at the bottom of the hump, creating a bottleneck of inching automobiles and frustrated motorists. O'Shaughnessy was standing by the two-way reflector, looking down into passing cars. A white Cadillac inched parallel with the van. A woman was driving. Her skirt was pulled up over her knees; her legs were apart. O'Shaughnessy gaped down at her but managed to tear his eyes away when he considered what absolute hell he'd catch if something went down while his attention was otherwise engaged.

As the blue sedan made its way on the expressway an unmarked police car screeched into the entrance plaza of the Midtown Tunnel on the Manhattan side. Port Authority police were waiting to guide it through. The left lane of traffic inside the tunnel was stopped, locked bumper to bumper. Motorists felt twinges of excitement at the sight of the speeding police car, its revolving turret light throwing out waves of red. They wondered what was happening. Maybe they would have something new to talk about over dinner, something that broke the monotony of the Long Island Expressway at rush hour.

The blue sedan drove onto the Van Wyck Expressway heading south.

O'Shaughnessy radioed the location. "It looks like they're heading for Kennedy."

Traffic thinned past Liberty Avenue. Motorists pressed down on their accelerators, jerking their vehicles forward, releasing pent-up frustrations.

Bo Davis shifted up to fourth gear.

Heinemann was driving on the shoulder of the Long Island Expressway. When he reached the Van Wyck, the detective forced the police car in ahead of the line of traffic and sped south.

The surveillance van maintained its distance behind the blue sedan. The detectives inside the van did not notice the Hertz truck bearing down on them. The truck cut to the left of the van and continued past, zigzagging the lanes of traffic. When it overtook the blue sedan it swerved in front of it.

"Pat! That Hertz truck!" Davis rammed the accelerator to the floor.

A hand pushed the canvas backing of the truck aside and two rifle barrels were extended. Long, egg-shaped projectiles protruded from both.

Hillel Henkoff saw the puffs of smoke and the vapor trail. He wrenched the wheel sharply, trying to escape. Andrea St. James threw her hands up to her face and screamed.

The car erupted into a ball of orange and yellow flames. The explosion lifted it twenty feet into the air, bending it in half and sending its twisted parts spiraling downward.

One hour later the southbound lanes of the Van Wyck Expressway were still closed, traffic being detoured at Jamaica Avenue. Ambulances and other emergency service vehicles lined the shoulder of the parkway. A Fire Department pumper was watering the smoldering wreck. The steel-basketed bomb squad truck was parked across the highway, blocking it. Detectives sifted the debris. Parts of bodies were being collected and tagged and then put into body bags.

Malone and his detectives were holding a roadside conference with Queens detectives and their commander, Assistant Chief Walter Untermyer, a particularly offensive scumbag who was known throughout the Job for his deep pockets and short arms. The head of Queens detectives wanted no part of this one. Since the place of occurrence was Queens, technically it was a Queens case. But Malone realized that it was part and parcel of the Eisinger thing—so he agreed that it was his. Besides, he wanted to get the hell out of there. There was work to be done. After the mess was cleaned up and the traffic lanes reopened, Malone made a beeline for the Eastern Shipping Company. It was sealed tight. Accordion doors were drawn over the entrance and locked. The loading bays were closed. Only the wall cameras were moving, their little red lights constantly blinking. He rushed back to the surveillance van. Jake Stern stepped out of it and gave him the message he'd just received from Harrigan: Anderman and the Braxtons had disappeared. The detectives had lost them.

Malone kicked the van's tire and turned, leaning against the side, his foot against the hubcap. He lit a cigarette, dragging deep. High above him the constant whine of spinning tires played off the massive underpinnings of the Long Island Expressway. To the west the Empire State Building rose majestically against a backdrop of deep purple. Malone knew that he was in a war zone. Person or persons unknown were turning his city into a battleground.

When they returned to the Squad twenty minutes later they found Zambrano waiting.

"Nice little war ya got goin', Lieutenant," Zambrano said.

"It's not my doing," Malone said, rounding his desk and taking a virgin bottle of Jack Daniel's from the bottom drawer.

"Oh, I know that. But you see . . . it's the mayor. He's suddenly lost his sense of humor. He gets upset when people are blown away by rifle grenades on the parkways of his city. It's bad for the tourist industry. And he wants answers to certain little questions. Like who did it? And why? And more importantly, will they do it again?"

Malone poured.

"Do you have anything? The commissioner has to tell handsome Harry something," Zambrano said.

"Why don't you tell him to take a flying fuck at a rolling doughnut?" Malone said, handing him his drink. "Untermyer decided that it was our baby. So far all we got are some fragments from the grenades"—he raised the cup at Zambrano and drank—"and a description of the truck."

"You were on the scene when it went down. Didn't you give chase?"

"O'Shaughnessy, Davis, and Stern were behind the van. They had to swerve off the road to avoid the flames. It was a goddamn mess. By the time I reached the scene the truck was long gone."

Zambrano stared down into the shimmering liquor. "What's going on, Dan?"

Malone gulped the drink. "I'm not sure."

"But you've got an idea, haven't you?"

Malone shrugged wearily. "When I know for sure, you'll be the first to be told."

Zambrano stood up and measured him. "Be careful. Remember that it's better to be judged by twelve than carried by six."

Malone poured another drink and hoisted the cup. "That, Inspector, is something I never forget."

As soon as Zambrano was gone, Malone called in the detectives. The blackboard was wheeled from the wall and turned to the unused side. Chalk in hand, Malone paced in front of the board, looking at his tired detectives. He started to free associate. "Anderman and the Braxtons have run for cover. We're back to square one and all we have is a body. We don't even have that; it's been buried." He turned and faced the board. "Eisinger worked for the Braxtons after she quit Anderman."

"Lou?" O'Shaughnessy interjected, slapping his leg. "I forgot to tell you. I checked with the *Times*. There was never an ad put in by Braxton Tours. I even checked with their billing department. And there's another thing. My sources in the travel business tell me that the Braxtons don't specialize just in tours to Israel. They handle a lot of travel to the Arab states. Mecca and things like that."

Malone shook a stern finger at the detectives. He turned to the board. "We have Eisinger going to Janet Fox's apartment and giving her her Bible. That was early Friday evening. Epstein's lab report states that she was murdered sometime Friday night going into Saturday morning. I had an Emergency Service crew remove the lock cylinders of her apartment. None of them were raked or picked. Which indicates to me that she let the killer or killers into her apartment, or they had a key"—the finger was again waved at the detectives —"or, the humps were waiting for her when she returned from Janet Fox." He looked at Bo Davis. "You been dancin' with Janet Fox?"

Grinning faces turned to Bo Davis, waiting.

"No, Lou," Davis said. "I interviewed her. That's it. She's real nice, but I haven't had the time to make a play. Exigencies of the service."

"Well make the time. Take the lady out to dinner and get close to her. I want the answer to one important question."

"And where do I get the bread to wine and dine her?" Davis said.

Malone shook his head disbelievingly. He went to the telephone and called Arthur's Cloud Room on Baxter Street. He spoke to Arthur himself. When he was through he replaced the receiver and said to Davis, "It's arranged. Soup to nuts, all on the arm. We owe Arthur one." Next he turned his attention to Gus Heinemann.

"How have you been making out with the ownership of the Interlude?"

"Zilch," Heinemann said. "I traced the ownership from one corporation to another."

Malone folded his arms across his chest, rocking on his heels. "You're using the wrong track. That neighborhood is zoned residential. In order for that place to operate they need a zoning variance from the City Planning Board. You don't use dummy corporations with them. Check it." He looked down, avoiding their faces. "Now comes the unpleasant part. Someone, somewhere in the Job is involved in this caper. I don't know who; and I don't know how. And I don't think it's a corruption matter. It's a question of being involved in a homicide and of fucking around with me personally. If any of you guys are squeamish about working on cops let me know and I'll make adjustments in your charts so you don't get involved."

"Hey, Lou," Pat O'Shaughnessy shouted. "How come Bo gets to get laid in the line of duty and I don't?"

Malone closed his eyes and smiled. "You have Foam."

It was late and the detectives had gone home. Malone remained, drinking and staring at the blackboard. Outside in the squad room two detectives from the night watch were watching "Barney Miller." The din of Chinatown mixed with the scratchy cadence of the police radio and the canned laughter coming from the television set. No matter how much he drank he couldn't drown the stench of burned flesh. It was everywhere. He kept seeing the charred parts of bodies scattered over the grass. Unrecognizable lumps of charcoal fused together. What the hell was it about the Job that he loved, needed? He poured another drink. He didn't want to be alone tonight. A cop never has to be alone. There are plenty of watering holes where he can spend the night with other cops drinking and bullshitting about women and the Job. But not tonight. Not for Malone. He wanted the comfort of a woman's body. To be able to smell her softness, to taste her. To awake in the morning with his hand snug between her legs and to feel her soft ass pressing into him. To press back. To purge himself of the smell of death. He picked up the phone and dialed Erica Sommers.

She sensed his weariness. "Come over, Daniel. I'll fix you something to eat and fill a hot tub."

He was halfway out of the squad room when he remembered something and went back to his office. He picked up the pad, thought a moment, and wrote: "The Song of Asaph"?

8

THURSDAY, *June 18* . . . **Morning**

Bo Davis clasped his hands behind his head and sat up, watching as Janet Fox got out of bed. He cast an anxious glance at the telephone and then focused in on her retreating backside. He had decided last night that she had one helluva perfect ass. Smooth and firm, not one shell crater.

When she reached the bedroom door she turned. "I'll go fix us some breakfast." She pointed her chin at the telephone. "Why don't you make your phone call?"

She returned a short time later carrying a tray with a pot of coffee and a plate of cheeses. There were also two glasses of orange juice. She slid the tray onto the end table and looked at him.

"Everything all right at home?"

"Fine. The kids are going to Jones Beach with their mother."

As she was handing him his coffee, he reached out and caressed her breast. "I like you a lot, Janet."

She fixed him with a distant stare and smiled. Inwardly she was screaming. Why do they all think they have to come on with the tenderness routine? He has a wife and kiddies stashed out in Little Leagueville and I'm here in the big city in bed with him. I understand. Why the hell can't he?

She got back into the bed and propped some pillows behind her. Sipping coffee, she said, "Bo, the last married man I went with told me that he was separated. I didn't know at the time that just meant his wife slept in a separate bed. I've had the moonlight-and-roses bit with married men. It hurts too much and I'm tired of waiting for the phone to ring. You've been honest with me. I know that you're married. So let's keep us light and lively. Okay?"

"I was only trying to tell you . . ."

She placed a quieting finger to his lips. "I know. You'd like to convince me that I mean more to you than just a good screw. Don't."

He raised the cup to his lips and shook his head incredulously. "You're something else."

"I've managed to save a few dollars and have decided to go back and get my degree. I always wanted to go to law school and I'm going to try before it's too late." She leaned over and put the cup on the night table. She then popped onto her side and ran her hand over his chest, dallying with the hair. A cooing lilt came into her voice. "What was it that you told me last night in the restaurant about an eighty-five?"

He brushed an elusive forelock from her forehead and smiled. "Code signal ten-eighty-five—meet a police officer at a certain location. When one cop tells another that he has an eighty-five, he means that he has a date. In the slang of the Job, an eighty-five is a girlfriend."

A silly grin came over her face. She plucked a hair from his chest.

"Ouch!" He feigned a chest wound.

"Well Detective Davis, that is exactly what I am interested in. An eighty-five. A happily married man who does all those wonderful things a man is supposed to do to a woman and who is available one or two nights a week." She began to toy with his penis. "Do you happen to know where I might find such a fellow?" She felt him growing hard.

"I might." He reached over the side of the bed and placed his cup on the floor. Turning back he took her into his arms. They kissed, their embrace growing in intensity. She continued to stroke him, guiding the foreskin up and over the head

147

and then down. He pushed down to her breasts, licking and sucking the erect nipples. She reached down with both her hands and pushed at his head. He obeyed, sliding down between her legs. She cried out sharply as he sucked her wet body up into his mouth, thrashing the man in the boat with his tongue. She vised his head to her, lashing him with her body. Her head mauled the bed, unendurable moans choking in her throat, becoming louder and more painful. And then, as a series of violent convulsions racked her body, she screamed.

He continued to suck her. She could stand it no longer. Clawing, pulling, tugging, she moved him up and pushed him onto his back and mounted him. Legs straddling his hips, she leaned forward and took hold of him, guiding him into her body.

Hearts pounding, they lay holding hands, staring blankly up at the artery of cracks that traversed the ceiling.

"I'd love to be your eighty-five," he said.

She smiled. "I'm so glad."

"Would you mind if I asked you a question concerning Sara Eisinger?"

She turned her head and fixed him with a curious stare. "When you telephoned last night and asked me to have dinner I assumed that your intentions were lustful. Was I wrong?"

"You were right. But there is one question that needs answering."

She was toying with his hair. "What is it?"

"Eisinger came to your apartment on the Friday evening you were going away with your boss."

"Ex-boss," she corrected.

"Sara gave you the Bible and left. It now seems certain that she was murdered sometime later that night." He was watching her. "Think back. When you opened that door and saw her standing there holding that book, what was your first impression of her composure?"

"Scared."

"Why?"

She shrugged. "Fright was written across her face. She kept glancing up and down the hall. She thrust the Bible at me with both hands and practically shouted at me to take it. I asked her what was wrong, and she told me that she had just gotten her period and was edgy."

"Thanks, Janet. You've been a big help."

"Anytime, Detective Davis. Is there any other service that your eighty-five can perform before you leave for work?"

He pulled her close. "Yes."

There were no appointments on the monsignor's calendar. The afternoon was to have been spent reviewing diocesan financial reports. He was deep in thought when the intercom buzzed. He glanced with irritation at the offending machine. His immediate inclination when he heard Malone wanted to see him was to tell his secretary to make an appointment for some time next week. Then he associated the name with Father Gavin. A problem might have developed.

McInerney was a big man with a disarming Irish smile and thick black hair. He was wearing a pair of black trousers, a polo shirt, and down-at-heel moccasins. He had the handshake of a miner. "What can we do for you, Lieutenant?" he asked.

"I need a favor."

McInerney relaxed. It was business as usual. A knowing smile creased his lips. "One good turn deserves another. What is it; a change of assignment?"

Malone took out a sheet of paper and handed it to him. "I want to know exactly what is at each of these locations."

McInerney's eyes narrowed appraisingly. "They're all over the bloomin' country."

"I'm aware of that."

McInerney's face was indecipherable. He studied his visitor. "Why the Church, Malone? You have your own sources."

He lifted his palms helplessly. "Because I need this information fast and because I can't use regular police channels and because you owe me."

The priest scowled. "And what the hell makes you think that I have the resources at my disposal to get you this information?"

"Every archdiocese in the country has specially trained priests who handle delicate matters for the Church. They're able to obtain information fast and discreetly; if the right person presses the right button."

"And you assume that I am the right person."

"You got it, Monsignor."

McInerney looked at the sheet of paper. "You of course realize that under no circumstances can the Church become involved in secular intrigues. We have enough of our own to deal with."

"You have my word. Except for my detectives, no one will ever know."

The monsignor escorted him to the door. "Do you have any idea what we'll find at those locations?"

"Warehouses," he said, walking from the office.

On December 2, 1978, at about 12:40 A.M., an old plumber had left the Bobover Synagogue at 1533 Forty-eighth Street in the Boro Park section of Brooklyn. He bent low and pressed the collar of his coat against his ears to protect them from the howling wind. Even the barren tree branches were straining. As he hurried past the house on Forty-seventh Street, three men had stepped from the shadows and demanded his money. "Don't hurt me," he had pleaded. They had taken the plumber's money and left him sprawled over the sidewalk bleeding from multiple stab wounds in the chest and abdomen. The plumber had died.

At noon that same day there had been four police officers on duty inside the Sixty-sixth Precinct. Three RMPs were on patrol. A sergeant was on the desk and another sergeant was in the stationhouse on meal. A cop was manning the switchboard and one detective was on duty in the Squad.

Suddenly there had been a commotion and within seconds the desk sergeant had been confronted with a mass of bearded, pushing humanity dressed in black coats, fedoras, fur caps, knickers, and white socks. Another two thousand Hasidim had surrounded the stationhouse.

They had come to demand greater police protection. They screamed and pushed and threw chairs and typewriters and pulled apart filing cabinets. Hand-to-hand fighting spilled through the stationhouse. The policeman on the switchboard had managed to get one message off before he was fought to the ground: 10:13, the Six-six was under siege. The three RMPs on patrol raced to the aid of their besieged comrades. RMPs from adjoining precincts responded. The Rapid Mobilization Plan had been activated.

They came with their hats and bats—helmets and nightsticks. Within ten minutes of the initial 10:13 one hundred police reinforcements and a dozen ambulances had been on the scene. The battle to retake the stationhouse had lasted thirty minutes. When it was over the ground floor of the building had been heavily damaged and sixty-two policemen and eight civilians were injured.

On orders from the fourteenth floor, the PC's office, no arrests had been made.

At 6:25 A.M. the same day—almost six hours before the assault on the stationhouse—detectives had arrested three men for the murder of the plumber.

As policemen sifted through the debris of the ground floor a black policeman was heard to remark, "Man, if my people ever pulled this shit there'd be black bodies littering the motherfuckin' streets."

Everyone who had heard him knew that he was right.

From that day the Six-six precinct had been known in the folklore of the NYPD as Fort Surrender.

Malone wasn't sure what he was going to find at the Six-six. He didn't even know what he was looking for or how to garner whatever it was that he was looking for. Three men, one of whom was wearing a Fort Surrender T-shirt, Andrea St. James had told Malone in the Barton Hotel.

It was not a promising lead, but it was worth a shot. Malone was aware of the xenophobic personality of policemen. He knew that there was only one way to obtain unrestricted examination of police records.

He was relieved when he entered the stationhouse and saw a sergeant behind the desk. A lieutenant might know him. He walked up to the desk, flashing his shield. "I'm Lieutenant McDermont from IAD," he lied. "I have to check your rosters for the past two years."

The sergeant looked down at him with an icy disdain that policemen reserve for the humps from IAD and without a word pushed away from the desk and got up.

Malone followed him into the clerical office.

"This lieutenant is from IAD," the sergeant announced in a loud voice, warning all that a Judas was among them.

Malone faced down the cold stare of the lead clerical man. He was an old hairbag with horn-rimmed glasses and smooth face that didn't show its age. He must have had it lifted, Malone thought. He was an essential type in the department; he had mastered the administrative secrets of the Job; he knew how to order toilet paper and towels; how to get plumbers and electricians to come and fix things; what forms had to be prepared; he knew that he was an indispensable necessity to the effective and efficient operations of the precinct. Captains come and go, but clerical men stay, year after year after year, building their empires. Malone had met many of them and knew how to deal with them. For he knew their common nightmare—being forced to do patrol.

The NYPD uses a three-platoon system to divide the day.

The first platoon works midnight to eight; the second platoon eight to four and the third platoon, four to midnight. A certain number of squads are assigned to work each platoon on a rotating basis.

The *Patrol Guide* mandates that each precinct prepare a new roster listing each officer in his assigned squad on the first of each month. This is done because men are constantly being transferred in and out.

As Malone sat at a desk in the corner of the clerical office poring over the old rosters, he could almost feel the furtive glances of the clerical man, who was standing nearby trying to make out in which names IAD was interested. I wonder what he'd say if he knew I don't know what the hell I'm looking for, Malone thought.

When he had completed his examination of the rosters he paused to think out his next move. He had discovered nothing. Perhaps coming to the Six-six had been a mistake. He had exposed himself. Malone hadn't forgotten those telephone calls from Captain Madvick or Mannelli's threats.

Malone turned and looked at the clerical man who was tying last month's roll calls into bundles for storage in the precinct's old record room. "Let me see your In/Out Book," Malone said, his tone harsh and authoritative.

The In/Out Book was a number-seven ledger that contained the names of each policeman transferred in and out of the command, the date and authority of the transfer and the command to which the man was transferred or from which he came.

The clerical man went over to a file cabinet, got the book, and almost pushed it into Malone's face. I'll fix his ass, Malone thought, snatching the book from him.

Malone turned the pages slowly, running his eye down each column, still not knowing what to look for. He smiled inwardly as he spotted the contracts: Patrolman Richard Coyne transferred to the Six-six from the recruit school on March 12, 1979, and transferred out to the Bureau of Management Analysis on June 10, 1979. Another Irishman buried in the bowels of headquarters.

He flipped the pages, his impatience growing. It was a mistake coming here, he thought in a moment of self-criticism. He began to flex his calves and tighten the muscles in his thighs. And then he saw them. Three names, Kelly, Bramson, Stanislaus, all patrolmen, all transferred on the same day, in the same orders, to the same place—the Police Academy. Such multiple transfers were not only very unusual but would have required a very heavy contract. He studied those three names and knew that he had found what he came for.

There were thirty-four patrolmen listed on that particular page and the clerical man knew every damn one of them. He turned to the clerical man. "Come over here a minute. I need your help with something."

He shambled over. "Yes, Lieu-ten-ant?"

"I have to answer out a communication that concerns an unknown member of this command who was assigned here at some time during the past two years. All that we know about this cop is that he's white and short and very thin. I'm going to go over the transfers that took place within the past few years and I want you to tell me what each of the cops looked like and anything else you can think of about them."

A silly smile came over the clerical man's face. "I got a real bad memory, Lieu-ten-ant. Why, I can't even remember what I had for breakfast this morning."

"Is that so? Listen to me real good, pal. You might be the head honcho around here, but that don't cut no shit with me. If you impede this investigation by refusing to cooperate I'll get on the horn to the chief of Inspectional Services and before this day is out you'll be doing a straight eight on a foot post in Harlem. Comes next Christmas you won't be here to collect all them nickels and dimes and bottles of booze that

154

the cops slip into your desk for doing those little favors throughout the year. You'll be freezing your balls off on a school crossing. Understand, pal?"

The clerical man was ashen. A thick belt of moisture had formed across his upper lip. "Whatever you say, Lou," he said, pulling over a chair and sitting down.

Fear was a wonderful interrogator, Malone thought, turning and pointing to the first name.

Malone walked away from the Umberto's trailer nibbling brown onions from his sausage sandwich. Umberto's was one of many of the city's best and most famous ethnic restaurants that had set up trailers along the sides of the cobbled arcade behind One Police Plaza. They brought with them shiny yellow tables and white umbrellas—an urban picnic area in the shadow of the severe government buildings. Malone was trying to let go of the Eisinger case for just a few minutes. He walked around to the front of Police Plaza by the Rosenthal sculpture, a massive piece of metal made of five disks, one for each of the five boroughs that make up the city. He headed toward a walkway lined by files of trees. The question DONDE ESTA ALFREDO MENDEZ? was stenciled on the walkway wall and signed FALN. Still restless, he crossed to St. Andrew's Church. He bit into his sandwich and moved from the front of the church to the small garden on the side. He stuck his foot between the fence and studied the statue leaning on the St. Andrew's Cross.

"He's the patron saint of Scotland," Zambrano said, walking over to Malone.

"The patron saint of bullshit," Malone said, looking at Zambrano.

"I take it you're a nonbeliever," Zambrano said, with a scowl.

"I stopped believing in that mumbo-jumbo about the same time I started to masturbate."

155

"Humph." Zambrano walked away. Malone fell in beside him, taking another bite.

"How did you know where to reach me?" Zambrano asked, staring ahead.

"I telephoned your office and was told that you were at a commanders' conference at headquarters."

"What's on your mind?" Zambrano said.

And now for the moment of truth, Malone thought, taking a deep breath before telling Zambrano of the telephone calls from Captain Madvick, his conversations with Mannelli, his interview of Andrea St. James, and everything that had happened since he opened a file on Sara Eisinger. Now he told Zambrano that after he left the Six-six he went back to the Squad and telephoned the Academy, asking to speak to Kelly, Bramson, or Stanislaus. He was told that no one by any of those names was assigned there. He then went through the Personnel Orders for the last two years and discovered thirty-seven similar transfers. Two and three cops transferred in the same orders from the same command and to the same administrative or support unit. He made a list of the transfers and started telephoning. It was the same at each unit. There was no cop by that name assigned there. He then left the Squad and drove to headquarters. His first stop was the Personnel Bureau. Using the same IAD ploy he had used at the Six-six, he asked to see the personnel folders of each of the forty cops. They were out of file, he was told. Next he went to the Identification Section where he asked an old friend for a favor. The fingerprint cards for each of the forty cops had been pulled and replaced with a charge-out card bearing a confidential file number. Only the chief of Operations knew the significance of the file number, his friend told him.

Malone looked at Zambrano. "Forty cops have been buried in the Job."

Zambrano stopped and faced him. "Dan? How do we put men in deep cover?"

156

"We transfer them to some administrative or support unit and they disappear. All their records are removed and locked up in a safe in the Identification Section. Their names are expunged from the city record and their salaries are paid by other city agencies or deposited in cash directly into blind checking accounts."

"So?" Zambrano demanded, displaying a growing exasperation.

"What do you mean, so? We're talking about forty bodies. I'll bet you there aren't ten cops in the entire department in deep cover. Those telephone calls from Captain Madvick and those three cops walking into that restaurant with Sara Eisinger form a direct link with my murder and the Job. Someone is using cops for something that's not kosher, someone at the top."

Zambrano walked away from him, staring ahead, his cheeks crimson.

Malone remained in place, watching. The inspector went about ten feet and then turned, motioning him to follow.

They strolled through the plaza, each man a prisoner of his own thoughts. When they reached the archway of the Municipal Building, Zambrano veered to his left and walked over to a small monument that had rusted bars set into it. He bent forward, trying to make out the withered plaque: Prison window of the Sugar House, 1765. Used by the British during the Revolutionary War to detain patriots.

Zambrano straightened. "Did you know that I lost my older brother on Guadalcanal?"

"No, I didn't."

"I always fancied retiring from the Job as a chief." He shrugged. "I guess I'm not going to make it. Tell me how I can help."

"I'm going to need some more time. That means keeping Harrigan and his men longer. In addition, I'll need someone upstairs to nose around and at the same time keep the hounds off my ass."

Zambrano put an arm around his shoulder, turning him and leading him away. "Did I ever tell you about my very first tour on the Job?"

Malone walked into his office and called in Davis and O'Shaughnessy. He handed Davis a piece of paper containing the names of the forty cops. "All these guys are on the Job. And they've all been buried somewhere in the department. I want you two to find them."

Davis and O'Shaughnessy looked incredulously at each other.

O'Shaughnessy spoke first. "What's it about?"

Malone lowered himself onto the edge of the desk and told them of the Fort Surrender T-shirt and his visit to the Six-six.

O'Shaughnessy looked over the names on the paper and said, "How are we going to locate these guys?"

"I don't think that the person or persons who buried them also went to the trouble to wipe out their personal lives. My guess is that most of them are married-type people who reside within the City or the nearby suburbs." He popped off the desk and went to the library cabinet where he removed the *Patrol Guide*. After consulting the rear index, he flipped clumps of pages of the massive loose leaf to the front. "Here we are," he said. "Procedure one-oh-four-dash-one; page four of six pages; Residence Requirements. Members of the force will reside within the City of New York or Westchester, Rockland, Orange, Putnam, Nassau, or Suffolk counties."

O'Shaughnessy whistled a sigh. "That's one helluva tall job."

"Not really," Malone said. "I think you should find some of them without too much difficulty. Go over the list and select names that are not common." He took the list from O'Shaughnessy. "Here, Edwin Bramson from the Six-six. Check the telephone directories for each county for that name. You're bound to find some of them. When you do, note the address and then pay a discreet visit to their neighborhood. Ask questions. Once you've established that they're on the Job, it's just a question of sitting on their homes one morning and following them to work. I've got a feeling once you've located one of them, you'll find the rest. Remember one very important thing. They're cops; don't get careless; give them a long leash. I don't want you being made."

Fifteen minutes later the detectives were gathered around a desk in the squad room poring through telephone directories. Jake Stern walked by on his way to the file cabinet to put away a case folder. He bent and whispered to O'Shaughnessy. "How is Foam?"

"Knocked-up," O'Shaughnessy said.

The detectives looked up.

"Oh, that's ducky. Are you and the wife planning a big wedding?" Starling Johnson asked.

"Don't be fucking funny. I got enough problems," O'Shaughnessy snapped.

"What happened?" Davis asked.

"The fucking foam didn't work, that's what happened," O'Shaughnessy said. "She's been calling me for days. I thought that she just needed to be serviced. I went to see her last night. She met me at the door full of love and kisses. I took her into the bedroom, took off her cotton drawers, and threw her a hump. 'Don't leave,' she says after I dropped my load. 'Come out naturally,' she says. I'm on top of her trying to figure what train I got to catch to get home when she starts to ask me if I really meant all them things that I told her"—he waved a hand in front of him—"you know, that bullshit about a lasting relationship in the distant, distant future."

"And?" Jake Stern said.

"And she told me she's late and the rabbit died," O'Shaughnessy said.

"And?" Davis said.

"And I asked her if she was sure," O'Shaughnessy said.

"And?" Johnson said.

159

"And she said she was," O'Shaughnessy answered.

"And?" Stern asked.

"And? What is it with you guys and this *and?* And nothing. She's having a baby. That's what's and!"

"Wadaya tell her?" Johnson asked.

"I told her that I was married, had a house in Hicksville, a mortgage, and six children. I also told her that I'm a Catholic and don't believe in divorce. Then I told her that I'd pay for the abortion."

"Oh, man; real smooth," Johnson said, slapping his forehead.

"And what did she say?" Stern asked.

"She went nuts and threw me out of her apartment. She screamed at me, calling me a male hypocrite and ranted something about not murdering her baby."

Bo Davis looked up from the directory. "Here's a Edwin Bramson, listed at 21 Woodchuck Pond, Northport."

"Where's that?" O'Shaughnessy asked.

"Suffolk County," Davis said.

SATURDAY, *June 20* . . . Morning

McInerney's messenger arrived in the morning. He was a large man with black shoes and a black suit that was too small and made him look like a biped mammal with a crew cut. He was one of the monsignor's shooflys and he did not strike Malone as the type of curate who gave absolution too easily. His message was succinct: McInerney wanted to see Malone, now.

Jake Stern parked the squad car on the west side of Madison Avenue, three blocks away. A nun dressed in the traditional habit of her order admitted them into the cardinal's residence and led them down a sparkling hall, her hand fingering her rosary. Malone wondered what it was about rectories and churches that gave them their peculiar scent. Greenbacks and incense, he decided.

McInerney rounded his ornately carved desk to greet them. He stepped past the detectives and held the door for the nun.

"Thank you, sister," he said, watching her leave. When she had gone he kicked the door closed. "They don't make them like that anymore," he lamented. He went to a table by the window and picked up a folder, flipping it open. He took out a sheet of white bond paper and handed it to Malone.

"Here are your locations. You were right, they're warehouses."

Malone scrutinized the paper. "Were any of your people able to get a look inside?"

McInerney scowled. "We're priests, not burglars."

You're not? Malone thought. He held his own counsel and asked, "Were you able to find out anything else?"

"They are all operated by Israelis." McInerney regarded the lieutenant with the look of a maternal uncle.

"What the hell are you up to, Daniel Malone?"

"I'm not sure," he said, folding the paper and sliding it into his pocket.

McInerney checked his watch. He was not the kind of man who wasted time on nonproductive matters. "If there is nothing else, I'll bid you both good day. Holy Mother Church is a hard taskmistress."

"Thank you, Monsignor," Malone said, walking with him to the door. Malone stopped short and looked at the monsignor. "Do you have any connections in Tin Pan Alley?"

McInerney looked puzzled. "We have friends all over. Why?"

"We're trying to locate a copy of a song. 'The Song of Asaph.' Ever heard of it?"

McInerney slapped his chest and arched his back, laughing.

"It is apparent that your religious training is somewhat wanting, Daniel."

Fuck you, Your Holiness, Malone thought. Aloud: "How's that?"

He removed a Bible from the shelf and opened it, thumbing the pages. "Here is your 'Song of Asaph.' The Seventy-third Psalm." The monsignor read aloud: " 'Truly God is good to Israel, even to such as are a clean heart.' " The psalm told of God's displeasure with his people. Of how the rich are not troubled like other men; neither are they plagued like other men. It told of how pride encompassed the rich like a chair; violence covering them like a garment. McInerney's voice was solemn. He read how God saved the people from

destruction and led them through the wilderness to safety:
" 'And they sinned yet more against Him by provoking the
most High in the wilderness. And they tempted God in their
hearts by asking meat for their lust. In spite of all He did for
them they spoke against God. They said, "Can God furnish a
table in the wilderness?" ' "

The detectives listened intently. The rhapsody of horns on
Madison Avenue was dispelled by the priest's hypnotic voice.
Each man was transported in his thoughts back to the days of
Jacob. McInerney read how they lied unto Him with their
tongues. For their heart was not right with Him, neither were
they steadfast in their covenant. But He, being full of com-
passion, forgave their iniquity and destroyed them not; yes,
many a time turned He His anger away, and did not stir up
His wrath. For He remembered that they were but flesh; a
wind that passes away, and cometh not again.

McInerney closed the book and walked over to the window where he stared down at the bustling avenue. Opening
the book, he repeated, " 'They were but flesh; a wind that
passes away; and cometh not again.' "

Jake Stern was thirteen again. It was Shabbas and his
mother was in the kitchen lighting the Sabbath candles. His
father was saying Kaddish for the dead. The smell of chicken
floated back over the years and filled him with bittersweet
nostalgia.

Malone, too, was thirteen. He was standing inside a
church with his mother. They were in front of the Seventh
Station of the Cross. "Mom, how can God be in every church
in the world at the same time?"

McInerney stopped reading and let the Bible drop to his
side.

An awkward silence filled the room.

Malone broke it by getting up and going to the telephone.
He dialed the Squad. Heinemann answered. Malone told him
to get the Eisinger Bible. The metallic clanging of the receiver
being dropped resounded in Malone's ears.

Heinemann came back onto the line. "Got it."

"Turn to the Seventy-third Psalm," Malone said.

"Here we are," Heinemann said, " 'Truly God is good to Israel . . .' "

"Never mind reading it. See if anything is stuck between the pages or if there are any underlined passages."

Heinemann flipped pages, babbling as he went. " 'God put His trust' . . . nothing . . . 'They are corrupt' . . . blab . . . blab blab . . . 'put my trust' . . . more bullshit . . . 'O my people' . . . bullshit . . . here it is! The Eighty-third Psalm. The first four are underlined in ink."

Malone hung up and unceremoniously took the Bible from McInerney. He turned to the Eighty-third Psalm.

> *Keep not thou silence, O God: hold not thy peace,*
>   *and be not still, O God.*
> *For, lo, thine enemies make a tumult: and they that*
>   *hate thee have lifted up the head.*
> *They have taken crafty counsel against thy people,*
>   *and consulted against the hidden one.*
> *They have said, Come, and let us cut them off from*
>   being *a nation; that the name of Israel may be no*
>   *more in remembrance.*

Malone had been closeted with Jack Harrigan for forty minutes. He had given the sergeant a "forthwith." Malone wanted to know if he had come up with anything on Anderman or the Braxtons.

"Nothing," Harrigan said.

Malone was standing by the window in his office looking out. "What about David Ancorie?" Malone asked, gawking at the tourists flowing through the street in an unending procession.

"Ancorie and three trucks pulled out of Eastern Shipping shortly before Andrea St. James left. Your men were on the

164

scene in the surveillance van, so my men followed him. They went to Kennedy Airport and picked up a load of sealed containers from France. One of my men questioned the customs people and was told that the containers were filled with automotive parts that were consigned to Eastern Shipping. From the airport they drove to Fort Totten. My men waited and waited. Ancorie and the trucks never left Totten. As far as we know they're still there."

"Any idea what's going on at Totten?" Malone said.

Harrigan shook his head. "We can't get too close. If we do, we'll blow the whole thing."

Malone reached into his pocket and handed him a slip of paper. "Here's a list of forty cops that have been transferred and the precincts they've been transferred from. I want one of your men to visit the watering holes of those precincts and start asking questions about those men. Tell him to play it down. You know. 'I was in the Academy with so-and-so. How's he been?' Stuff like that. I want to know what kind of cops these guys are."

Harrigan took the list and put it into his shirt pocket.

Malone turned and looked him in the eye. "I also want wires on the Eastern Shipping Company and the Braxtons. They might return and get stupid."

Harrigan leaned against the wall, bracing himself with his right foot. "We don't have enough probable cause to go into court and ask for *ex parte* orders."

They exchanged wary looks. "This time we make our own probable cause," Malone said.

Harrigan nodded, pushed himself away from the wall, and left the office. Malone continued to look out the window. The sun was against it now, and because it was dirty he couldn't see past the glass. Cigarette butts, burned matches, and dirt covered the sill. Dead flies were snarled in a cobweb between the mesh and jamb. Damn window probably hadn't been cleaned in years, he thought. He suddenly remembered the Grayson case. It had been years since he recalled that one.

Malone was a new detective in those days. Patrolman Joseph Grayson had walked the same beat for twenty-three years. He knew everyone. It was a November four-by-twelve tour when it happened. Grayson strolled into McDade's bar and grill. The unusual occurrence report stated that he entered the license premises for personal necessity. But everyone knew that Grayson liked his ball and beer. Grayson walked into a holdup. Two punks wheeled and put five into the cop's chest. The M.E. said Grayson never knew what hit him. Malone caught the case. It was to be his first murdered cop, not his last. The day after the killing a bird dropped a dime to the Squad. Nicky Giordano, a neighborhood punk, had bragged in a bar that he knew who blew the cop away. Malone could still recall Giordano's swaggering arrogance in front of his friends as Malone dragged him out of the pool hall.

"Lock the door and get his clothes off," the squad commander said, staring at the frightened man as Malone pushed him into the squad room. Giordano was handcuffed spread-eagled to the detention cage, Michelangelo's anatomical drawing of a man. The lieutenant handed Malone a Zippo lighter. "Burn the truth out of the fuck," the lieutenant ordered. Malone's hand shook as he approached him. One pass of the lighter under Giordano's balls was enough. "Esposito and Conti," he screamed. Known punks from Navy Street.

"Take 'im down," the squad commander ordered. Malone released him.

"Get over here, scumbag," the lieutenant barked.

Giordano approached hesitatingly, his hands covering his genitals.

"Bend over and spread your cheeks," the squad commander snapped. Giordano hesitated. The lieutenant slapped his back, forcing the torso down. "Spread 'em!"

Giordano reached back and spread the cheeks of his ass. The barrel of the squad commander's revolver was rammed into Giordano's anus. "This ain't no prick you feel in your ass, Guinea. It's my fuckin' gun. You're going to testify in court against your two friends. You're going to get up on that stand and tell the truth. You're also going to tell the court that we treated you like a fucking gentleman. 'Cause if you don't, one dark night I'm going to meet you in an alley and empty this gun into your asshole.''

Giordano got the message. He testified and Esposito and Conti went to the electric chair.

And now, years later, Malone was a squad commander. The Grayson case was the type of a caper that he understood, knew how to deal with. But this Eisinger thing? He wondered what the common thread was that tied the whole mess together. He found himself searching the cobweb for the spider. But it was nowhere to be seen.

10

TUESDAY, *June 23*

Malone drifted in and out of fitful periods of sleep; his dreams a kaleidoscope of his frustrations. When daylight slid into his bedroom he was propped on pillows staring at dust particles riding the rays of the sun. They reminded him of those damn containers being shipped in and out of those damn warehouses: so visible, yet untouchable. Just for one quick look inside one of them. But how? he asked himself. They'd know how. Of course! He looked at the clock. They'd still be around. He untangled himself from the sheet and sat up, taking the telephone book from inside the night table. Opening it, he slid his finger over the alphabetized tabs until he reached the *Z*'s. Zambrano's number was the only listing on the page.

Zambrano's drugged voice came alive when Malone asked him to meet him right away. "At this time of the morning?" It was a *pro forma* utterance. Inspectors weren't supposed to be called out at five in the morning.

"It's important. I need your help."

"When and where?"

Malone stopped the car for the red light on the corner of the Bowery and Broome Street. He glanced over at the derelicts sleeping in hallways, then directed his stare up to the traffic light. There was no traffic coming so he drove through the light, turning into Broome Street.

He parked on Center Market Place and walked to the corner of Grand Street. He stepped into the opaque doorway of the Dutchman's to wait.

"Hey, Dan," Zambrano shouted, crossing the street.

Malone could see the excitement in his eyes. Zambrano was doing what he loved most in the whole world; playing cop in the streets of New York City. "Whadaya got?" Zambrano asked, stepping into the doorway and taking his place next to him.

"I want you to arrange a meeting with Carlo Fabrizio. I want a favor from him."

Zambrano's face became taut. "And what makes you so sure I can arrange such a meeting?"

"It's an open secret that you have a special relationship with him."

Zambrano spread his hands in front of him and at the same time shrugged an Italian gesture of mercurial agreement. "What do you want from him?"

Malone told him.

Peddlers were setting up their stands along Mulberry Street. Neighborhood women bargained in Italian. Malone noticed one dressed in mourning black bartering with a fish peddler. The man ignored her entreaties and continued to bathe his fish with buckets of ice.

Three-quarters of the way down the block they stepped off the curb and cut across the street. They nudged their way through a crowd and around two stands to four steps leading to a cellar club. The two small windows on the side of the façade were painted black. Brass letters across the door read: NESTOR SOCIAL CLUB, MEMBERS ONLY. They started down the steps. Malone rapped on the door with the hard knocks of a cop demanding entrance. A big man whose muscles were outlined in a dirty T-shirt opened the door. He wore a Byzantine cross on a gold chain around his neck. He raked his fingers through his hair, measuring the strangers. "Wadaya want, cop?"

Malone pushed past him. It was a large room with a padded bar running the length of the far wall. A grossly ornate espresso machine on the end of the bar reminded Malone of an altarpiece. Several card tables were scattered about. In the corner, next to the bar, five men sat playing poker. They looked up at the intruders. The bouncer ran up behind Malone and turned him. "You gotta motherfucking search warrant, cop?"

A distinguished-looking man in a blue business suit lumbered up from his place at the card table and waved the bouncer off. "It's okay, Cheech." His hair was pure white and the nails manicured. Malone noticed that his teeth had been capped and that, despite his smile, his eyes were cold and menacing. He came up to Zambrano and threw his arms around his shoulders. The ritualistic hug and kisses of old friends followed. "How are ya?" Tony Rao asked.

"Good, Tony." Zambrano made the introductions. Rao motioned them to sit, at the same time holding up three fingers to the bouncer to indicate that he wanted three espressos.

"What brings you here?" Rao asked Zambrano.

"I want to see him," Zambrano said.

Cheech brought the espresso and backed off.

Rao fixed his stare on the thin slice of lemon floating in his cup. He picked up his spoon and aimlessly dunked the skin. "Impossible. He don't see nobody outside the Family. That Abscam thing made him leery of all outsiders"—Rao looked Zambrano in the eye—"even old friends."

Zambrano leaned across the table. "You tell Carlo Fabrizio that Nicholas Zambrano wants to see him."

Rao daintily picked up his cup and drank. "I'll see that he gets your message." Rao wrote a telephone number on the back of a matchbook and handed it to Zambrano. "Call this number at eleven o'clock this morning."

When they walked out of the Nestor Social Club twenty minutes later, Mulberry Street was still crowded with vendors and early-morning shoppers.

Malone turned to Zambrano. "Breakfast at Ratner's?"

"Why not? We got four hours to kill."

Carlo Fabrizio's legs dangled over the side of an immense bed. He was a frail man with sunken eyes and a beaked nose. A smile graced his lips when he heard Zambrano's request. He dismissed Rao and lay back in bed, staring out the open doors at a gently swaying tree. He thought back to his first meeting with Zambrano.

Twenty-nine years had passed since the day he first saw the cop trudging through the snow. When Zambrano passed the Hicks Street Social Club he glanced inside. Carlo Fabrizio and another man were standing by the window watching the shifting snowdrifts. Fabrizio nodded to the patrolman. Zambrano nodded back.

"Carlo, watch!" The man standing next to Fabrizio ran to the door. He went outside and scooped up a handful of snow, pressing it into a ball.

Zambrano had a sudden sense of something behind him and wheeled. His face recoiled from the sting of the snowball; his hat flew into the snow. The man turned and ran back into the club, laughing. "Didya see the look on that dumb cop's face?"

The door was flung open. Patrolman Zambrano stood in the frame, hands tucked deep into his winter overcoat. Water dripped down the side of his face. His eyes scoured the club, darting from man to man. He spotted his quarry leaning over the bar. Zambrano moved toward him. Fabrizio watched. The cop had balls, he thought.

"Whatsa matter? Can't ya take a little joke?" the attacker bantered at the approaching cop.

Zambrano answered in Italian. "Me? Sure, I can take a joke. What about you?" Zambrano slid his hands out of his pockets. Thongs of a blackjack were tightly wrapped around his right hand; garbage can handles that had been woven with black tape were gripped in his left hand. The attacker's eyes widened and his hands shot up to his face in a fruitless effort to protect himself. The blackjack smashed into the side of his head. A jagged gash appeared and quickly filled with blood. The man started to sink to the floor. The cop pivoted to his left and lashed forward, smashing the metal knuckles into his face. The scrunching of shattering bone caused men to shiver. The man's eyes rolled up into his head as he splayed to the floor, unconscious. Zambrano tucked the blackjack and knuckles back into his overcoat pocket and turned to leave.

Fabrizio blocked his way. "He's one of my people."

"Then you should teach him some manners."

"And why is that, *paisan?*"

"Because your men are a reflection of you. If they're assholes that automatically makes you one."

Fabrizio nodded. "Makes sense." He moved aside.

Zambrano moved past him then stopped, turning to face him.

"That street out there belongs to me. If any of your people ever give me a hard time again, I'll blow their fucking brains out and plant a throw-away on them. I'll be a hero."

"A capisce."

During the succeeding years their paths continued to cross. Whenever Fabrizio saw the brash cop he'd walk away from his entourage and spend a few minutes talking with him. The seeds of a friendship were sown; a friendship that could never come to fruition. Fabrizio would always end their chance meetings by saying he'd better leave. "Someone might see us together. I wouldn't want you to get into trouble."

When Zambrano married there was a coffee table of Italian marble, a gift from Carlo Fabrizio. When Fabrizio's mother died, the Zambranos attended her wake. As Zambrano knelt at the prie-dieu, Carlo Fabrizio came up behind him. "I hope you didn't park around here. They're taking pictures across the street."

The bond between the cop and the mafioso was sealed forever one sweltering August night. Patrolman Zambrano was standing in the lee of a doorway sneaking a smoke as he waited for the sergeant to come by and give him his "see." The crack of gunfire jolted Zambrano into a tingling state of awareness. He dropped his cigarette and stepped from the doorway. There were two more distinct shots. Zambrano drew his revolver and moved cautiously in the direction they came from. A man staggered from an alley holding his side. He stumbled across the sidewalk and sprawled into the street. It was Carlo Fabrizio.

"I think they've cashed in my chips for me," he said to the familiar face kneeling over him.

"Shut up! I'll get you to a doctor."

Zambrano snapped his head toward the sound of the running feet. Three armed men careened the corner. "Kill them both," one shouted. Zambrano threw himself over the wounded man. He gripped his revolver with both hands. The men were firing at him. Zambrano was scared but he recalled the admonitions of his firearms instructor at the Academy. Don't jerk the trigger; cock and squeeze; aim for the body; keep both eyes open. Zambrano fired; one of the advancing men fell with a bullet in his stomach. A fusillade of gunfire erupted and bullets thudded into the asphalt around the cop. One of the men stopped to take careful aim. Zambrano fired two rounds double action. The man lurched forward, his gun went limp in his hand; he looked with disbelief at the cop then fell dead. The third man looked at his fallen comrades and ran.

Fabrizio clutched the policeman's arm. "I'll never forget what you did tonight . . . never."

At precisely eleven o'clock, Zambrano telephoned the number Rao had written on the matchbook.

"La Terazza at three o'clock," an anonymous voice said.

A Ford station wagon and a Mercedes were parked in front of the restaurant. Well-dressed men loitered on the sidewalk in front of La Terazza. "Are they for us?" Malone asked.

"That's his normal retinue."

The trolling men spotted the policemen and separated, taking up positions along the building line and against parked cars, their surly eyes locked on the cops. Tony Rao was sitting by himself in the outdoor café. "Tony?" one of the bodyguards called. Rao looked up, casting an appraising eye in the direction of the policemen.

La Terazza was a tumult of activity. Waiters in white tailored shirts picked their way from table to table. Tourists gawked at the display cases filled with Italian delicacies.

Carlo Fabrizio was in the rear of the restaurant. He was alone, save for one waiter by his side. He sat erect, his hands clasped in front of him.

"He looks like the little old winemaker," Malone whispered.

Fabrizio rose to greet his friend. The head of the largest crime family in New York City hugged Zambrano and kissed his cheeks. He acknowledged Malone's presence with a nod.

"You look well, Carlo," Zambrano said, choosing a cannoli from the tray of pastries on the table.

"I feel good, Nicholas." He smiled. "Remember that night with the snowball?"

"Whatever happened to that guy?"

"He continued to do stupid things until one night he had an unfortunate accident . . . a permanent one."

Malone felt awkward listening to Zambrano and Fabrizio reminisce. He had done business with *them* in the past and would be the first to admit that they can make impossible things possible. But sitting with Fabrizio was like extending diplomatic recognition to organized crime. You do what you gotta do, Malone rationalized.

"What is it you want?" Fabrizio asked, shifting his eyes from Zambrano to Malone.

Zambrano turned to Malone who took the cue. He removed a folded sheet of paper from his pocket and slid it across the table. Fabrizio looked down at it.

Tapping the paper with one finger, Malone said, "This is a list of warehouses that are located in various cities around the country. It's important that we find out what's stored inside of them."

"Is this important to you, Nicholas?"

"Yes it is," Zambrano said.

"Will there be any . . . problems?" Fabrizio asked, sliding the paper into his pocket.

"They're all guarded," Malone said. "But your people, with their special expertise, should have no trouble getting in and out without being spotted."

Fabrizio looked stern. "I hope not, Lieutenant. That could be very unfortunate. For both of us."

At 2 P.M. that day Yachov Anderman, David Ancorie, and the Braxtons suddenly resurfaced and started to go about their daily routines as though nothing had happened. Malone's first instincts were to drag them into the Squad and have a nice long talk with them. But he knew that that would gain him nothing. By this time they had their stories straight and their lawyers waiting. And they could stall any interrogation for some time, time that Malone instinctively knew he didn't have to spare.

At 3 P.M. Thea and Aldridge Braxton entered the subway station at Fifty-ninth Street and Lexington Avenue. The subway was not the Braxtons' regular method of travel. But today they were forced to tolerate the indignities of public transportation in order to ensure that they were not being followed.

Afternoon shoppers crowded the subway platform, many carrying the Bloomingdale's "brown bag." Aldridge Braxton leaned over and looked into the dark tunnel. He stepped back and checked the time. "Damn trains," he muttered. A businessman stood a few feet away from him meticulously turning the pages of the *New York Times* into another fold. A black man sashayed along the platform. He was wearing jeans and a brightly colored dashiki. His feet were encased in a worn pair of blue-and-red sneakers. A red portable radio in the shape of earphones was stretched over his head. There was a bone necklace hung around his neck and dark sunglasses hid the movements of his eyes. White people gave him a wide berth. Middle-class blacks withered him with their looks while the brothers and sisters smiled. The businessman looked into the tunnel and slapped his newspaper into another fold.

An RR rolled into the station. Passengers stepped back from the edge of the platform. Every car was tattooed with graffiti. One of each double door shuddered open. People lunged out of the train even as new passengers pushed forward. Arguments started and profanity seasoned them. Thea and her brother elbowed and shouldered their way aboard. A finger was thrust into Thea Braxton's crotch. "Did you do that?" she snapped at her brother.

"Do what?"

"Never mind," she muttered.

Every conceivable part of the car was covered with spray paint. People were crushed together and groped for straps that were already crowded with hands.

"Wachder doors," shrilled a barely discernible Latin accent over the loudspeaker. "Denext estacion goinbe Blige Plaza." The train jerked forward, stopped, lurched several times, jerked forward again, then left the station. Aldridge Braxton surveyed the crush of pressing people. He moved his head close to his sister. "God! How do they survive this day after day? They're like fucking cattle."

The businessman stood among the crush, the top part of his paper dropping into his face. He stared out at the naked lightbulbs as they whizzed by the graffiti-covered window. He could see the Braxtons in the glass's reflection.

The black man in the dashiki was in the front of the car,

176

listening to his music and shuffling to its beat. The people around him tried to keep their distance, none looking at him for fear of offending. During his last musical gyration he snapped his head back and adjusted his sunglasses. He could see the Braxtons clearly. They were the straphangers in front of him, to his right.

As the RR train bearing the Braxtons roared through the tunnel approaching the Queensborough Bridge, Ahmad Marku and Iban Yaziji left their Soho loft and hailed a passing taxi. A Con Edison repair crew was at work on the corner. One of the crew slid the manhole cover back while the other member of the crew folded the orange safety stanchion. The taxi bearing Marku and Yaziji turned south onto West Broadway.

Jack Harrigan had just completed the details for the installation of wires on the Braxtons' telephones when the detectives inside the Con Edison truck radioed. They had tailed the two men onto the FDR Drive and were now driving over the Triborough Bridge heading south.

At Bridge Plaza the Braxtons left the train at the elevated station and hurried down the staircase. They stopped in front of the change booth and watched the passengers descend the steps. The businessman had his *Times* neatly folded under his arm when he walked past. Aldridge Braxton went to the exit door that led to the connecting bridge between Bridge Plaza north and south. He pushed through the door and moved to the middle of the bridge. Traffic coming off the lower level of the Queensborough Bridge was heavy. Green Line buses queued the north side of Bridge Plaza. He saw nothing suspicious. They weren't being followed, he was convinced. He motioned to his sister.

The black man with the dashiki danced down the staircase. He hurried over to the exit and peered down into the street. He watched the Braxtons get into a taxi. He made a mental note of the license plate number and pushed the antenna on the right side of his earphone down in front of his mouth.

"Special two to Central, K."

At 3:58 P.M. a citywide alarm was transmitted over the police radio network. All units on patrol were instructed to be on the lookout for the taxi carrying the Braxtons. "Do not intercept. Report location and direction of travel," the dispatcher radioed.

Patrolman Frank Murphy got out of his radio car with the majesty of a true motorcycle cop. His black leather puttees were spit-shined. His breeches bloomed smartly; yellow mohair braid on the outside seam was trimmed of lint. He strutted over to the car he had just pulled over. A woman was driving. Murphy knew the routine by heart. He'd tell her that she was speeding and she would play the coquette. When he asked for her license and registration she'd rummage helplessly through her pocketbook. "Officer, I've never received a ticket before," she would say with feigned innocence. Then she would proceed to confide some personal problem that caused her to forget how fast she was driving. Murphy would smile understandingly, take the license and registration and walk back to his radio car where he would write out her summons. He would then slide out of the car and amble back to her car, summons in hand. It was at this point that the lady would snatch the official paper from him, call him a cocksucker, and plunge her automobile off the shoulder into oncoming traffic.

All part of the J-O-B, Murphy thought, walking toward her, summons in hand. It was by sheer chance that he happened to glance at the parkway traffic and spotted the taxi with the man and woman sitting in the rear. He noted the license plate number and broke into a trot, rushing up to the driver and throwing her documents and the summons onto her lap. As he was running back to his own car he heard her yell after him, "Fascist cocksucker."

At 4:14 P.M. a taxi glided to a stop under the porte-cochere of the International Hotel at Kennedy. The Braxtons inched their way out of the compact cab and hurried into the lobby. A radio car from Highway Two cruised past the hotel and drove onto the shoulder of the Van Wyck. Patrolman Murphy reached under the front seat and removed the portable radar device. He attached the mechanism to the doorpost and then slumped down in his seat to wait.

Thea and Aldridge Braxton walked through the crowded lobby to the bank of elevators. When they stepped from the lift on the sixth floor they walked down a long carpeted hallway, heading for the fire door at the end. Aldridge Braxton looked over his shoulder and, seeing that there were no other guests in the hallway, pushed through the door with his sister following close behind. They hurried down the clanging staircase and exited the stairwell on the third floor.

They stood outside Room 302 listening. Aldridge Braxton held a fist inches above the door and at the same time eyed the second hand of his watch. Exactly fifteen seconds passed and he knocked three times, paused, and then immediately followed with four additional raps.

Ahmad Marku jerked open the door.

They exchanged nods with Marku and entered the room. It looked like any other hotel room: twin beds were covered with a fading gray bedspread; prints of pastoral scenes bolted to the wall; night tables, their edges peppered with black caterpillar-shaped burns.

The drapes were drawn, darkening the room. A file of four chairs had been lined up in front of the window. Iban Yaziji was sitting at the end of the file. He did not acknowledge the Braxtons. Ahmad Marku locked the door and sat next to Yaziji. Aldridge Braxton sat next to Marku, and Thea Braxton next to her brother. Lowering herself slowly into the wooden folding chair, she crossed her legs, revealing the finely shaped topography of her legs, thighs, and hips.

The quartet faced front, watching the shadowy figure standing in front of the drapes, peering out.

Thea Braxton twisted uncomfortably in her seat, tucking the folds of her skirt under her legs.

"Are you all sure that you were not followed?" Police Officer Joseph Stanislaus asked, watching the entrance of the hotel. He noticed a police car parked on the west shoulder of the highway about thirty feet from the entrance. The policeman had just left his patrol car and was approaching a Con Edison truck.

"Yes," the quartet answered in jumbled unison. They were sure they had not been followed.

Westy Stanislaus turned to face them, an automatic held loosely in his hand. He danced it along the file, his eyes studying each face.

Thea Braxton could feel the moisture take hold of her palms. Her brother's mouth was unexpectedly parched. He swallowed the lump in his throat. Ahmad Marku and Iban Yaziji sat perfectly still, their stares fixed on the finger inside the trigger guard.

Stanislaus looked at Marku, his eyes hard and cold, his lips wearing a feigned smile. "I want to congratulate you on the way you handled Andrea St. James. It was a professional job, and a good object lesson for Anderman."

His attention next went to Thea Braxton. He moved close to her, glowering down. "You should have brought in someone from the outside to set up Landsford. It was a mistake using anyone from the Interlude."

"I realize that now," she said.

Stanislaus caressed her cheek with the barrel of his automatic. "Perhaps your taste for women made you call on her services?"

She stared up at him; then, with both her hands, she took hold of his wrist and pushed it away from her face. "St. James was selected because I thought she was the best one to do the job."

Stanislaus stepped back. He tucked the weapon into the small of his back and smiled. He began to pace, deep in thought, and then, suddenly, he whirled to face them, an ugly look on his face, his nostrils flared in anger. "St. James should never have been used! It was a bad mistake." He turned his wrath on the Arabs. "Because of your stupidity she got away and we had to engage in an action that might have exposed all of us."

The four of them waited nervously for his wrath to subside. Thea tasted her tongue.

"No more mistakes will be tolerated. If any of you get stupid again I'll personally see to it that you're made into chopped liver."

There was a fearful silence.

Stanislaus turned from them and moved to the window where he peered out from behind the drapes. "Does Anderman suspect anything?"

"I don't think so," Thea said, running a hand through her hair, trying to appear calm. "After St. James was killed, he sent a messenger to us and told us to go immediately to a safe house in Jersey. We remained there until he sent word to resume our normal activities."

"Did he make any contact while you were in Jersey?" Stanislaus asked, pushing the drape farther aside.

"No. He gave us the name and number of his law firm. We were to call them if the police tried to question us," Thea Braxton said.

"What are we going to do without the list of warehouses? It screws up all our plans," Aldridge Braxton said.

Stanislaus noticed that the highway cop had snared a gypsy cab with its radar device. "There is a new plan," he said, edging himself onto the sill.

The meeting lasted another hour. Business concluded, Stanislaus got up, turned, and looked out the window. A Pan Am 747 was making its final descent. It slid past the cocooned control tower and disappeared. The police car was gone and the Belt Parkway was spilling back. "Aldridge, you and your sister leave first."

The Braxtons were alone in the elevator. Thea was watching the blinking floor indicator. "He was his usual obnoxious self," Aldridge said.

She looked at her brother. Reaching out, she took hold of his hand. "I was just thinking how vulnerable Stanislaus and his friends are. I think, dear brother, that the time has come for us to renegotiate our contract with the police department."

11

All the fives from Harrigan's detectives added up to the same thing: subjects followed to International Hotel. Subjects remained thereat for ninety-six minutes. Subjects left separately. Braxtons first. They went directly back to their office. Marku and Yaziji left together and went back to Soho. They remained in the loft for two hours and then hailed a taxi and went to Atlantic Avenue in Brooklyn, the Arab section. They ate in the Kurdistan restaurant and engaged in conversation with several Middle Eastern types and then left.

Malone sat back, flapping the fives against the edge of the desk and looking up at the chunks of peeling paint. Icicles of decay, he thought. He tried to run through in his mind the reasons the Braxtons and Marku and Yaziji could have for going to the hotel. He snapped forward and moved a spiral-bound pad over to him, tossed it open, and started to list the reasons he could think of for such a meeting: To meet someone? Who? To pick something up? *No.* It doesn't require four bodies to do that. To have an orgy? Why travel to Queens? To receive instructions? To plan something? He continued jotting down ideas. When he had listed his thoughts, he sat studying them.

Heinemann broke Malone's concentration by shoving his head into the doorway. "Ya gotta call on three."

"Wanna meet me for a cup of espresso?"

183

Malone hung up slowly; he thought that he had detected a tinge of hostility in Tony Rao's voice.

Malone walked down the steps leading to the Nestor Social Club and stopped, deciding if he should knock. Screw it. He pulled open the door and entered. The bouncer was at a table playing a game of five-card stud. He was wearing the same russet shirt. He looked at Malone, scowled, and lowered his eyes.

Tony Rao was standing behind the bar pouring Amaretto into a pony glass. When he saw Malone he put the bottle down and came out from behind the bar.

Rao stood in front of him tapping his lips meditatively with his fingertips. He suddenly looped his arm in his and ushered the policeman outside. They walked along Mulberry Street. Rao would pause occasionally to speak a few words of greeting to some peddler or wave at a Mustache Pete sitting on a milk box, or to pat a child on the head while he cast an appraising eye at the mother. When they reached Grand Street, Rao turned in and walked to the middle of the block. He ducked into a cheese store. Malone followed. Customers turned to look, but quickly turned away when they saw who it was.

The mafioso stood behind the row of long cheeses that hung in the window, casting constant glances up and down the street. "Catch." He tossed a small box to Malone.

A label in Hebrew was glued over the face. A blue cord handle stretched from the corners. Malone ripped open one end and spilled out the contents. Several 9mm bullets tumbled out; their tips were painted red. He turned to Rao. "Tracers? This is military hardware."

"Yeah." Rao turned from the window and left the store.

They crossed Grand Street, turning into Center Street.

"Ya wanna know what's inside them joints?" He bent his head to his cupped hands and lit a cigarette. "Military supplies. One of my boys almost got his ass taken off by some punk kid carrying a small machine gun. Those tracers come from the place in New Jersey. That's all my guy could grab. The security was too tight.''

Questions began to whirl through Malone's mind. Rao was still talking . . . ''What's with them joints? Anything in them for us?''

Malone glared at him. ''Forget them, Tony.''

Rao grinned.

''I mean it. You couldn't take the heat.''

''Where do I send the bill?''

Malone looked at him. ''What bill?''

''Hey? I hadda make a lot of phone calls. Ya got any idea what it costs to use the telephone these days?''

''Take it off your taxes; we're a charitable deduction.''

''I want to see your boss,'' Malone bawled.

The receptionist stared at him then hurriedly swung around to the switchboard.

Within minutes David Ancorie was leading him through the corrugated security tunnel that snaked into the interior of Eastern Shipping. Ancorie held the door open and Malone sallied into the cramped, smoky office and plopped himself down in a chair next to Anderman's desk.

Anderman smiled confidently. ''You just won't give up, will you, policeman?''

''We're a persistent bunch,'' he said, placing the cassette recorder he had brought with him onto the desk. He looked his adversary in the eye and snapped down the play button. The slow-moving spindles churned out Andrea St. James's disconsolate voice. Anderman's face twisted with anger. He spun in his chair, showing the policeman his back; his head and shoulders sagged. Words that Malone had listened to dozens of times now filled the office.

When the tape played out, Malone pushed the stop button.

Anderman remained still for a moment then spun around and started to raise himself up, an angry finger stabbing the space in front of him. His breathing was labored and his eyes leered down at the policeman. "You! Take your tape. Recorder. And get out of this building. And don't ever come back. I am going to sue you. The City. And the police department. You're harassing me! Preventing me from conducting my business." His face was inches from Malone. The breath was hot and coated with garlic and cigarettes. Suddenly he slammed his hands over the desk with such force that Malone thought he surely must have broken his wrists.

Malone looked at him, a sarcastic grin on his face. He was savoring his moment. And now for the square knot. He reached into his pocket and removed the box of 9mms which he casually tossed onto the desk.

Anderman stared at the box. He picked up a letter opener and fished the point into the open end. One by one the bullets tumbled out. Anderman gnawed his lower lip, his head shaking with diminishing belief.

Anderman said, "Where did these come from?"

"A warehouse in New Jersey."

"I've been getting reports of strange occurrences." He slapped his knee in frustration. "I really underestimated you, policeman." He looked at him. "Can we still do a little business?"

"Wise men can always do a *little business*." He started to gather up the bullets. "I want to know about Eisinger. The Braxtons. Marku. Yaziji. A cop called Westy. The Unit and a man by the name of Captain Madvick. You can start any place you want."

"How many people know about the warehouses?"

"I know and my detectives. But only me and a friend know what's inside of them." He grinned. "A little life insurance."

"And if I tell you what you want to know, you'll return the list to me personally?"

"I will."

"Where did you find it? We searched everywhere."

"Hidden inside the binding of her Bible."

"Humph." He lit a cigarette. "And if I don't tell you?"

"In that case, your military depots will be page one in the morning editions. And that, Mr. Anderman, is a promise."

"It's difficult for us to trust a *goy*. Especially one who wears a blue uniform."

Malone frowned. "I recall reading about an entire country of *goys* who sewed the Star of David onto their clothing so as to be indistinguishable from the Jews of their country. Denmark? The last war? Perhaps you've heard of it."

Anderman sank into his chair. A long silence passed before he spoke.

"We're a small country without the vast spaces that you have. A surprise attack could deprive us of the spare parts for our machines. So, we store a portion of our spare parts in friendly countries. If we had to, we could airlift them back to Israel within hours. We use Fort Totten as a conduit for our supplies coming into the United States. Someone found out about our operation. They blackmailed Landsford and obtained a copy of the location of the warehouses. Somehow Sara found out about this and recovered the list. She was murdered for her efforts." He leaned back, hands laced behind his head, studying Malone. "That's it. Everything."

"Not quite. I've got a few questions." Malone rested his elbow on the edge of the desk and placed his chin in the palm of his hand. He said, "Tell me about Sara Eisinger. She was one of your people? Right?"

"Yes," he answered reluctantly. "When she was in Israel she helped establish a worldwide computerized inventory of our warehouses. When she came to this country she continued to work for us." He stopped, trying to think of what he was going to say next.

Malone kept up the pressure.

"Tell me what happened," Malone said, watching him.

"She fell in love and went crazy. She started to take days off. Would disappear for long weekends. She became a security risk, so I had to fire her. When she refused to tell us who she was seeing it became intolerable."

"You mean to tell me that you have no idea who she was sleeping with."

"That's exactly what I'm telling you. Sara was a professional. She knew how to avoid being followed. She refused to tell me anything about her personal life. She even accused me of being jealous, of wanting her for myself."

"Was there anything between you?" Malone studied the face.

"No. It was business, nothing more."

"When did she start seeing this person?"

He shrugged. "I'm not sure. Maybe about a year ago."

"Tell me about the Braxtons. How are they connected to this?"

"I don't know. After Sara left me she started to work for them."

"And Marku and Yaziji?"

"They're in the States posing as students. Somehow they're connected with the Braxtons. When we saw that Sara was working for the Braxtons and that there was a connection between the Braxtons and the Interlude and the two Arabs we decided to plant Andrea St. James inside the Interlude."

"Weren't you fearful that Sara would see her in the Interlude?"

"There wasn't much chance of that. Sara never went there and Andrea's *duties* required her presence there at night."

"How did you maintain contact with St. James?"

"We have a safe house on West Seventy-second Street."

"I see. How do you get to use a United States military reservation as a conduit for your spares?"

"With the consent of your government. Some of your people in Washington don't trust us. They think we're erratic. They're fearful that we might hide atomic weapons or some other horrible things within your territory. So as part of the agreement your army gets to inspect everything we bring in."

"And what does Uncle Sam get in return?"

Anderman stabbed a finger upward. "In return, we act as surrogate for your intelligence service in certain"—he pinched the bridge of his nose—"unmentionable parts of the world."

"Why did you go into hiding after St. James was killed?"

"Because I didn't want to get involved and because I wanted time to assess the situation and try to find out what the hell was happening."

"Were the Braxtons with you?"

"Of course not. I know nothing about them."

Malone did not speak right away. He measured his adversary. "You're a very convincing man, Anderman."

"The truth speaks for itself."

"Bullshit. Keep it simple and stick as close to the truth as possible. That's the rule in your business, isn't it?"

"I'm telling you the truth. Everything I know."

"Really? Why would anyone go to the trouble to get the list of warehouses? For what purpose?"

Anderman raised his palms and then let them drop. "I don't know. I guess if their existence in this country became known it could be embarrassing for Washington. The United States is trying to obtain bases in the Middle East for the Rapid Deployment Force; a special relationship has been fostered with Riyadh. Perhaps"—he waved his hand in the air—"there are endless possibilities."

Malone fixed him with a stare as Anderman lit another cigarette. He was ready to ask about cops and Captain Madvick. "Ever hear of a Captain Madvick?"

Anderman exhaled smoke. "No."

"What is the Unit?"

"I don't know, policeman."

"Who is Westy? Is he a cop?"

Anderman was no longer the harried, angry businessman.

After a long pause, Anderman said, "Malone. I know nothing of any policemen, any Unit, or Captain Madvick. I have enough problems of my own without getting involved in any of yours." He arched his shoulders back. "I'm telling you the truth. You are relying on the delirium of a semiconscious woman. That is not a clever move, policeman."

He's good, Malone concluded. Lies with the aplomb of a cop or a politician. Looking directly into the face in front of him, Malone thought, You're giving me a handjob, Anderman. An intelligence agent in the Mossad falling for a guy and you can't find out who this guy is? In a pig's prick.

Malone said, "How did you know that Eisinger had stolen back the list?"

"She telephoned. I told her that I'd come right over to her apartment, but she insisted that I come in the morning. I asked her who was behind it and she refused to tell me over the phone. She said that she would explain in the morning. She was murdered that night."

"Did she sound nervous when she talked to you?"

"No. She sounded relaxed. If I had thought she was in any danger I'd have rushed right to her apartment."

Malone remained with him for another hour. It was not easy distinguishing the truth from the lies. But Malone was patient. He was determined to break this one.

As Malone was getting up to leave, Anderman leaned forward and grabbed his wrist. "I'm sure you'll not repeat anything that we just discussed. I'd find it most unpleasant if I had to . . ."

Malone pulled his arm away. "Top of the day to ya, Anderman."

"Shalom, policeman."

When Malone was gone Anderman went over to the wall and pounded it in a paroxysm of anger and frustration. When he had calmed down he picked up the telephone on his desk.

It rang about fifteen times before being answered. Anderman spoke. "This is an emergency. John Harrison Burke in three hours."

The person on the other end clicked off.

Within the three hours Yachov Anderman was standing on the bow of the Circle Line boat watching the panorama of Manhattan Island unfold. He had made the trip to the Statue of Liberty, trudged up the shoulder-wide spiral to the crown, circled the narrow platform to ensure no one was following, and was now returning to keep his appointment.

The boat was crowded with Chinese tourists dressed in drab clothes and with Japanese cameras slung over their shoulders; Germans, Latins, English, French, and Americans. When the boat docked he waited until most of the passengers had disembarked and then strolled off the gangplank. He walked on the promenade and stared into the choppy waters. When he reached the red buildings of Marine Company 1 he stopped and examined the fire boat, still watching to see if he was followed. He abruptly turned and walked through Battery Park until he came to the West Battery where he slowly made his way around the circular fort.

He moved off, walking along a winding path until he came to a crescent-shaped monument site. Two benches were set against an iron fence. Bags, beer cans, aluminum foil, Big Mac boxes were piled up along the bottom of the fence. Clumps of grass and weeds had sprouted up between the chipped plates in the ground. He strolled around the column reading the plaques: Erected in memory of wireless operators lost at sea at the post of duty: David Staier, SS *Mezada,* 3/2/22, North Atlantic; Jack Phillips, SS *Titanic,* 4/5/12, Atlantic. He moved slowly, taking his time, surveying the surrounding area.

Fifty feet away another monument site had been established to commemorate American heroes of both wars who now sleep in the American coastal waters of the Atlantic Ocean. The site had eight massive steles with thousands of names carved in alphabetical order. Four steles were on each side of the site, and in the center, on a pedestal of black, reigned an American bald eagle, its black talons cocked. Anderman spotted the person whom he was to meet standing in front of the first stele, glancing up at the column. He walked up behind the person. "John Harrison Burke, Seaman First Class, U.S.N., Virginia."

Lt. Joe Mannelli glanced over his shoulder. "What the hell is so goddamn important for you to risk this meeting?"

"Malone knows about the warehouses. He also has an inkling about the Unit."

"Balls!" Mannelli said, toeing the monument.

"My sentiments exactly."

Anderman told him of his meeting with Malone.

"Do you think he's onto us?" Mannelli asked.

"I'm not sure. I told him enough to sound convincing, but I don't know how much of it he believed or what else he knows."

Mannelli rubbed his tired eyes. Anderman moved close to him.

"He has to be eliminated," Anderman whispered.

"Whataya mean eliminated? Fa' Chrissake, he's a cop. We don't kill our own."

"That man is a danger."

"We don't kill him! So he found out about the warehouses. No big deal. Everything is deniable. You hear me, deniable. You do nothing. I'll tell my people what happened and get back to you," Mannelli said, turning and walking away.

A bebopper skated past Anderman. He was a black man and he was wearing a dashiki and had a radio headset on. He adjusted his sunglasses as he danced past.

12

"What time do ya make it?" O'Shaughnessy asked.

Bo Davis was slumped behind the wheel, his hands limp over the inside post. He stretched, looking at his watch. "Five thirty-four."

"Gettin' up at four in the morning in order to plant on some cop's house sucks."

"It's all part of the J-O-B." Davis closed his eyes.

"Ya hear what happened to Crazy Eyes McCormick?"

Davis squint-eyed. "What?"

"The asshole had his load on and turned Saint Pat's into a shooting gallery. Some Rican pickpocket lifted eight bucks from some broad's bag. McCormick opened up on the guy inside the church. He misses the Rican and ended up blowing away sixty grand worth of statues and stained-glass windows. The Powerhouse wanted his balls sautéed and left on the altar as penance."

Davis grunted. "That guy could fuck up a wet dream."

At 7:46 A.M. a man left 21 Woodchuck Pond Lane and opened the garage door. He was a bruiser who stood six-five and had large hands, big feet, and shoulders that looked like a dam. The detectives were parked a block away.

The man backed the car out of the garage and stopped. He got out and went to close the door. As he bent down to close the door his Hawaiian shirt rode up in back. On his right hip was a holster with a thin leather strap securing the gun in

193

place. Equipment Bureau issue. They had found Edwin Bramson, formerly of the Six-six precinct.

He opened his eyes and sensed unfamiliar surroundings. He lay naked in a bed with fresh sheets. He recognized the jade-green wallpaper. He saw his trousers crumpled over a chair. On the floor were a pair of panties and a bra. He remembered their rush into bed. He poked his hand behind and felt her. He turned over.

Last night he had decided that Erica epitomized the perfect woman: beautiful, intelligent, tantalizing. In his own mind he still was not completely sure what he wanted from her. Lately he found himself wanting to be with her, to share with her. And last night, he had talked about his ex-wife again and had found himself beginning to understand his part in the failure of the marriage. It was a beginning.

He kissed her lightly on the temple and got up. Anderman was coming for the list of warehouses sometime this afternoon, and he wanted to be there when he arrived.

The first thing Erica saw when she opened her eyes was Malone dressed only in briefs, balancing on one leg, and tugging a sock up over his calf.

"Good morning," she purred, stretching.

"I tried not to wake you."

She patted the space next to her. He came over and sat on the edge. She pushed herself up. The sheet clung to her body, large aureoles half-moons over the edge.

She said, "I'm glad you came by last night."

He kissed her on the nose. "So am I."

"I enjoyed the things we did. The way you . . ." She felt the flush come to her cheeks.

"You're blushing."

She blocked his view with her hands. "You're not supposed to look."

The sheet plummeted, revealing firm breasts. He bent forward, taking one into his mouth, sucking it. She lay back and touched his lips. "Quickies count, too."

Edwin Bramson drove a battered Ford with a broken left taillight. The snow tires were still on. A bumper sticker read: GUNS DON'T KILL . . . PEOPLE DO.

Motorists stared blankly ahead as they inched through the heavy traffic. Bramson stayed in the middle lane. Not once did he bother to check the rearview. The sign of an overconfident man.

At the Lakeville Road exit of the Northern State Parkway, Bramson drove off onto the feeder road and cruised to a stop alongside a bank of telephone kiosks. He reached over and pushed open the door. A man trotted over and slid into the passenger seat. He was a big man with a large head and a torso that ballooned from the neck and gathered into a tiny waist. No hair was visible on his body. Although he appeared bulky, the man moved with grace and suppleness.

Overhead the WABC traffic helicopter skirted the parkway.

O'Shaughnessy nudged his partner. "Did you see the shape on that guy?"

"I wouldn't wanna have to lock assholes with either one of them," Davis said.

Bramson left the parkway at the westbound Queens Boulevard exit. He drove north. At Yellowstone Boulevard he made a left turn and continued two blocks, stopping in front of an apartment house—the Hamilton.

A man stepped from the lobby and got into the rear seat. He had a ruggedly handsome face and blond wavy hair. Unlike the other passengers, this man was particularly well groomed, wearing a blue summer suit and a quiet patterned tie.

●

The Doric Diner was crowded.

The three men decided on an empty booth next to the long counter.

They talked in whispers, leaning across the table. A waitress came over to take their orders. When she left, the man in the suit took out a handful of change and played the small jukebox that was affixed to the side of the booth.

O'Shaughnessy went directly over to the counter and sat on a stool. His jacket and tie were in the car. The right side of his shirt was bloused, concealing the handle of his .38 S & W. When the counterman looked his way he ordered coffee and a toasted corn muffin. Elbows on counter, he leaned forward, staring at the reflections in the display case, straining to pick up snatches of conversation from the booth to his right. Someone roared with laughter. He thought it was the weirdo with the watermelon head. Was a guy with that shape really on the Job? A cowboy blared from the jukebox; he had met a lady in tight-fittin' jeans. Whenever the music would stop the guy in the suit would feed the box. O'Shaughnessy ordered a second cup and asked for the bill. The three men remained twenty-two minutes and then struggled out of the cramped booth.

Bramson left the tip.

O'Shaughnessy left nothing. He'd never see the hump again.

O'Shaughnessy lingered, examining his check and searching his pocket for change. He ambled up to the cashier. They were ahead of him, each paying a third. Watermelon-head paid his share and turned to Bramson, poking him. "We got the range on Wednesday and then we weed out and we're all set to go."

The man in the suit whirled. "Shut the fuck up."

"Hey, Westy? There ain't no one here . . ."

The man in the suit talked through clenched teeth. "I told you to . . ."

Watermelon-head held up his hands. "Okay. Okay. Don't get your balls in an uproar."

196

The day started officially for Malone when he walked into the squad room and looked up at the clock. That was some quickie, he thought. It was 9:37 A.M. He adjusted his watch as he walked into his office. Davis and O'Shaughnessy were waiting to report the results of their stakeout.

Malone asked, "Are you sure that he called him Westy?"

"Positive," O'Shaughnessy said. "I was standing right behind them."

"What happened after they left the diner?" Malone asked.

Davis looked at his partner who shrugged. Malone caught the exchange. "What happened?"

"We tailed them to the SOD compound in Flushing Meadow," Davis said.

Malone slapped the desk. "Oh Christ!" He leaned back, steepling his fingers.

The silence grew.

The other men watched him, trying to figure out what Malone was thinking. When he finally spoke, his dispirited tone revealed his misgivings. "What about the guy Bramson picked up in Queens?"

O'Shaughnessy said, "After they entered the compound we hightailed it back to Yellowstone Boulevard. He lives in the Hamilton House. His name is Joseph Stanislaus; he's divorced and has lived there for two years."

Malone took out the list of transferred cops. Edwin Bramson, Joseph Stanislaus, Charles Kelly. All from the Six-six; all transferred in the same Personnel Order; friends who went into something big. He assumed the man from Lakeville Road was Charles Kelly. Malone yelled out to Stern to bring him the teletypes for the past twenty-four hours. Stern walked in with the gray posted binder with the thin multiholed pages compressed between the covers. He asked Stern if there were any notifications concerning the range and watched anxiously as the detective slowly turned each page. They at last had three names to work on. But he was bemused because they were cops and concerned because he did not know how or why they were involved.

Stern stabbed a page with his finger. "Here is something. Transmitted 0130 hours yesterday." He read. "The regular outdoor shooting cycle scheduled for this Wednesday is canceled. Members who were scheduled to shoot on that date will be rescheduled by roll call." He looked at the lieutenant. "That's it."

Lacing his hands across his chest, Malone leaned back and recalled Harrigan's earlier visit. The sergeant had been anxious to tell him the results of the canvass of precinct watering holes. O'Brien had spent the better part of a four-to-four drinking with cops from the Six-six and bullshitting about the Job, the lousy contract that the PBA had just negotiated with the City, the injustice of pay parity with firemen, and women.

Fort Surrender's watering hole was Jerry's, a sleazy blue-collar joint that was tucked away under the Brighton line's elevated Utica Avenue station.

O'Brien had latched onto a tipsy Anticrime cop from the Six-six. Every cop in the precinct knew about Stanislaus, Bramson, and Kelly, the Anticrime cop had told O'Brien. "Chrissake, those three guys are legends." He told O'Brien that they were assigned to the precinct's Anticrime Unit. They turned out to be a no-nonsense team who took no shit in the street. Stanislaus was the team's brains. He could con the spots off a leopard. Stanislaus had served in a Special Forces unit in Vietnam that operated behind enemy lines. The others in the unit found out one night when they were drinking that Stanislaus thought General Westmoreland was the greatest thing since Alexander, and tagged him with the nickname Westy. He had been on two sergeants' lists but had never been promoted.

He felt the Supreme Court of the United States, Affirmative Action, and the Department of Personnel were responsible. Blacks, Hispanics, and women who had failed the written

198

test were placed on the lists ahead of Stanislaus because of those damn affirmative-action suits. Both lists ran their normal four-year life and died with his name still on them.

Charles Kelly, the Anticrime cop had told O'Brien, was an ugly brute who enjoyed inflicting pain. He liked to slap nippers around a prisoner's wrist and twist until his victim was groveling in pain. He was also an avid gun collector who was reputed to have a valuable collection of Nazi military small arms.

Bramson was a psycho son-of-a-bitch who drank too much and was ecumenical in his dislikes: he hated just about everything and everybody. When he was in the army, Bramson had been assigned to the military police battalion at Leavenworth. His lumbering walk and chilling brutality sent fear through prisoners and guards alike.

Each of them was morose and brooding. They never mixed with other cops. But when they were together they came alive, each one garnering strength from the other. They drank and carried on outrageously.

They had an incredible arrest record, but it was abnormally full of violence and death. Every cop in Brooklyn South knew of their arrests. Once, two escaping muggers were killed accidentally by falling from a roof. A witness in the adjoining building told the Homicide detectives that she had seen both of the dead men being thrown off. She later denied making that statement. The grapevine had it that Kelly and Bramson had a private little chat with the lady.

During their six years in Anticrime they had been involved in eight shootouts in which nine perps had been blown away. In each case a gun was found next to the body; a weapon which ballistics tests showed had been fired at the pursuing officers. During one of the investigations into these shootings, a witness came forth and stated that he had seen the cops shoot the perp; fire several shots from a gun that one of them had removed from his own pocket, and plant the weapon directly into the dead man's hand. Four days later the witness changed his mind about what he had seen. "Ain't it amazin'!" the cop guffawed, lifting his beer mug at O'Brien. He told O'Brien that the ranking officers who investigated the three men's use of deadly force knew damn well that they were using throw-aways but could never prove it. "You ever hear of a nigger using a Walther PPK? I didn't."

They were being hauled before the Civilian Complaint Review Board on complaints of unnecessary use of force or abuse of authority almost monthly. But they always managed to dance their way out of it. The CCRB could never pin anything on them. Each interrogation was a carefully staged production.

One time, Stanislaus, Bramson, and Kelly wanted to take off one of Frankie the Fish's number banks but did not know the bank's location. They scooped up the head numbers runner and planned to sweat the address out of him. The runner proved most uncooperative. Bramson and Kelly handcuffed him to a chair in the Anticrime office and left the room. Stanislaus remained behind with the prisoner, leaning against the wall, saying nothing, fixing the frightened man with a crazy stare. Ten minutes passed and the door was thrown open. Bramson and Kelly danced naked into the room, whooping Indian war cries. They had on feathered war bonnets, and each one had a long red ribbon tied around his penis. War paint was drawn across their chests and faces and they both were waving cattle prods over their heads as if they were tomahawks.

They danced around the petrified man, whooping.

On a signal from Stanislaus they started to jolt the runner with the cattle prods. Within seconds they had the man scurrying on his back across the floor, desperately trying to escape the war party. A few more jolts and he was begging his tormenters for mercy. He blurted out the address of the numbers bank. Kelly stormed over to him, kicked the chair out of the way, and gave him a final jolt to the testicles.

They then carried him out to the detention cage and locked

him in. Stanislaus stayed behind to guard the "prisoner" while Kelly and Bramson went out and held up the numbers bank. When the runner was released he was warned to keep his mouth shut. He didn't. A week later they were given a "forthwith" to report to the CCRB. When they were informed of the charges against them they looked incredulously at each other and then burst out in uproarious laughter. "Naked? Ribbons on our shlongs? Feathers? You guys gotta be off your rockers. Your complainant sounds like an escapee from a fucking loony pen," Stanislaus was reported to have shouted at his inquisitors.

The charges against them were unsubstantiated.

O'Brien listened, rolling his glass between palms, staring ahead at the rows of terraced bottles. O'Brien turned sideways on his stool and looked stolidly at the bearded cop in threadbare clothes. He raised his right hand, rubbing three fingers together. "They were big money men?"

The Anticrime cop from the Six-six cast a furtive glance around the noisy bar. "Very big," he whispered. "They had everyone on: bookmakers, numbers men, dealers, even the pros. Word was that each pimp had to spring for a dime a night for each hooker that he had out. In return they saw to it that no independents worked the stroll."

O'Brien became wary. Drunk or not the guy on the next barstool was a cop with a cop's predatory instinct. He did not want to appear too interested in these three crazies, so he changed the subject to the latest labor contract and that got him an instant harangue. "The fucking garbage men make more money than we do and not one of them fuckers work more than three hours a day. Drive along Fourth Avenue any weekday and you'll see six or seven garbage trucks parked outside McGill's Bar from eleven in the morning till four in the goddamn afternoon."

When the cop paused to call the bartender over, O'Brien said casually, "I guess their home life must have been shot to shit?"

201

The bearded man glanced at him, not understanding. "Who?"

"Those three cops you've been telling me about."

"Oh, them." He did not know much about their private lives. He did know that Stanislaus was divorced and the word was that he liked the ladies. But he was cool about it and never brought any of them around. Kelly had a family somewhere on the Island but lived alone in a decrepit clapboard house at the end of a dirt road on the outskirts of Great Neck. Kelly had gotten drunk one night and had to be driven home by one of the precinct cops. The cop who drove him home had confided to a friend that it was a creepy place with a couple of wrecked automobiles parked on the lawn, one of which was up on milk boxes. The word around the precinct was that Kelly had an almost sexual fascination with guns and didn't waste time with women. Whatever went on in that lonely house was probably best left unknown.

The only thing the Anticrime cop from the Six-six knew for sure about Edwin Bramson was that he was married. He had heard rumors about the fear and hatred his family had for him. But he knew nothing of the tirades, the beatings, the awful, silent dinners, or the consuming panic that gripped family members whenever Bramson stalked into a room.

Jack Harrigan came away from the meeting with a clear and disturbing picture of three loners who were over the thin line between normality and psychosis. The three of them shared other characteristics with the rest of the forty transferred cops: all had outstanding arrest records and most of them had seen combat in the infantry.

Malone shifted in his seat, a melancholy expression on his face. His gaze took in the photograph of the flag raising on Mt. Suribachi that was taped to the side of his locker. He had put it there years ago. The edge of the tape was frayed, curled, and yellow. He thought of all the marines who had died to plant that flag. He got up slowly from his chair and reached for the keys to the department auto that were on a hook over the filing cabinet. Those three men were not his kind of cops. There were things that needed doing.

Malone loitered across the street from the Hamilton House. When he saw that the doorman was busy he quickly crossed the street, brushed past the doorman, and entered the glittering lobby. The doorman gave him a cursory glance and then returned his attention to the blonde with the capped teeth. A respectable-looking white man was nothing to get alarmed about. The mailboxes and directory were in an alcove in the rear of the lobby.

Joseph Stanislaus lived in apartment 24 J. He counted A through J. The tenth floor.

There was only one cylinder in the door, a rarity in New York City. He slid a thin black pouch from his breast pocket and checked the hallway. A line of round fluorescent lights extended over the ceiling, casting an unnatural chalklike glow over the flower-patterned carpet. The corridor was deserted, closed doors lined both sides. There was an eerie silence. He checked for trip wires and noticed that the mat was flush with the floor jamb. He cautioned himself to leave it that way. He shook out a cluster of thin metal bars and selected two. The tension bar was inserted into the cylinder at twelve o'clock. He pressed it forward until he could feel the first tumbler pin. He looked up and down the corridor, making a final check, and then inserted the raking bar. Applying just the right amount of pressure on the tension bar, he began to rake the lock clockwise. As each tumbler pin was raked open, he pressed the tension bar deeper, past the open pins. One by one the tumbler pins fell and the lock snapped open. He entered quickly and quietly, closing the door behind him, and locking it.

Rows of flowering plants were terraced in front of a casement window. The apartment was clean and neat with everything in place. The furniture was expensive and in good taste. A well-stocked bar was in the corner.

Joseph Stanislaus was a meticulous man.

He moved about, taking his time, studying each piece of furniture before moving it. When he completed a search he made sure that the piece was restored to its original position. On a shelf in the bedroom he found two off-duties: a Colt Cobra and a S & W Chief. Padlocks secured the opened cylinders. Stanislaus was a cautious man.

The bathroom had sparkling gray tiles and silver wallpaper. He poked around the shower curtain. The tub was clean; a face cloth hung limp over the faucet. He flipped open the medicine cabinet, looked at the glass shelves, and then pushed the door closed. Next he bent to check the vanity. Packages of toilet paper. A shoe brush. Stacks of soap. A saucepan. A clump of rags. Standing upright, wedged behind the plumbing, was a bathroom scale. He noted its position and then reached inside, working it out. Behind it he saw a shopping bag. He reached for it but at the last moment snatched his hand back. He ripped off a few sheets of toilet paper and spread them between his thumb and forefinger. He reached inside the bag. A diaphragm. A light coat of powder covered the device. Holding it up to the light and turning, he was able to make out some fingerprints. A triumphant grin crossed his face. Eisinger's diaphragm had never been found. He put the compact back and returned the bag. Next he wedged in the scale. He remembered seeing an electric razor in the medicine cabinet. He took the razor out, opened the top, and began shaking the shavings into the toilet paper. He then folded the paper inward on all sides and slid it into his shirt pocket. When he slipped from the apartment fifteen minutes later he made sure that the mat was flush with the jamb.

When Malone returned to the Squad after lunch he found an impatient Yachov Anderman waiting. There were many things that Malone wanted to accomplish and he certainly did not want Anderman around. He promptly reached into his shirt pocket and withdrew the list of warehouses which he silently handed over. When Anderman asked him if he had made a copy he lied and said that he hadn't. Anderman did not bother to hide his disbelief.

Malone walked into the squad room and saw O'Shaughnessy off in a corner talking on the telephone, trying, without success, to placate Foam's wrath.

Bo Davis was on another line with Janet Fox. He was beginning to like being her eighty-five. Sergeant Harrigan alternately drank beer and cleaned his fingernails. Malone had just finished writing Anderman's name alongside the slash that was behind the word *Interlude*. Bramson, Stanislaus, and Kelly, Charles, were already on the blackboard. An asterisk was next to Stanislaus and in parentheses: "diaphragm." The blackboard was no longer kept in the squad room. Malone wanted it in his office, next to his locker and shrouded in a musty sheet. No one outside the Squad was to see it.

He moved away from the board, tapping his lips with a piece of chalk. After studying it for a few minutes he moved close and bracketed the names of the three cops with the acronym SOD. He turned to Harrigan. "Did you install those wires?"

Harrigan rubbed the side of his face. "N.G. on Eastern Shipping. Their wires don't run in from telephone poles. They're underground. And the terminal boxes are inside. We can't get at them. If you want that place bugged we're going to have to use lasers or conic beams." He leaned back and scratched his testicles. "And we don't have that kind of equipment."

Malone frowned. "What about the Braxtons?"

"A piece of cake. The only problem with them is that they don't talk on the telephone. And when they do, it's strictly business. But there is one little thing"—he scratched his testicles again—"there is a telephone booth on the corner of Aldridge Braxton's residence. A few times we've caught him running out and using it, and then running back inside. He thinks he's being cute. I put a wire on the booth."

Malone said, "I want you to start to concentrate on Stanislaus."

Harrigan nodded, lips pursed. "If we do, we're going to have to shitcan someone. Ain't enough guys to go around."

Malone said, "Have the tails on the Arabs been productive?"

"Zilch. Marku and Yaziji are a couple of creeps. They go to school and hang around their friends on Atlantic Avenue. They don't get laid, that's for sure."

"Take the men off them and cover Stanislaus," Malone said.

O'Shaughnessy slammed the receiver down so hard that it bounced off the hook. "Cunt!"

"Whatsa matter?" Harrigan said.

"Broad's givin' me a hard time."

Harrigan spiraled a finger heavenward. "Hell hath no fury, ma man."

The Fifth's watering hole was Bradley's, a singles' bar on Lafayette Street. It was after 6:00 P.M. and a crowd was starting to pack the place. A little before five each weekday a table with hot and cold hors d'oeuvres was set up. Manhattan's rent poor came to eat and mingle.

Malone was sitting at the end of the long bar making rings with his glass, only dimly conscious of the eddy around him. Heinemann had gone out to Queens to sit in on a card game at an Elks Lodge in Astoria. Stern, Davis, Johnson, and O'Shaughnessy were clustered at the bar nearby. It amused them to watch the maneuvering of older men with dyed hair, gold bracelets and chains, who tried to put the make on anything that moved. Novice cheaters and shy singles fumbled for the right words. Single women wanted desperately to meet a "good" man, tried much too hard.

Malone sipped his drink. He was confused. Was she really making it with Stanislaus? The movie *Laura* came to mind. The detective conjured up a picture of Laura in his mind and fell in love with the murder victim. He was pissed off at Eisinger for going to bed with him. She could have done much better. He glanced toward the entrance. His friend should arrive any minute.

Jake Stern tried to fill the silence. "A woman is like a bus. If you miss one all you gotta do is wait at the bus stop. Another one'll be along in no time."

Erica Sommers was no bus, Malone thought, holding up his glass to the bartender.

A brunette was alone at the other end of the bar. She was a big woman with broad shoulders and a pretty face. The detectives watched as a lawyer-type in a vested suit made his play. She rebuffed him. The rejected suitor slunk back, seeking the anonymity of the crowd. O'Shaughnessy sipped scotch on ice, watching with muted admiration as the brunette foiled the amorous advances of another would-be suitor.

O'Shaughnessy said, "I just might be looking at Foam's replacement."

Jake Stern's face clouded. "Man. I'd love to have her sit on my face. Did you catch them tits? They're magnificent."

Starling Johnson slid his glass onto the bar. "Make your move, ma man. All the lady can say is no."

Stern drank, watching her. He banged his glass on the bar. "Why not?"

She sensed the presence elbowing its way toward her. Another shmuck. Suddenly he was next to her, alternately snapping his fingers and pointing. It was a brawler's face that was dominated by a broken nose and low-set cheekbones. The lips were thick and he was almost completely bald. But he did have a cute smile.

"That's it," Stern blared, with a discovering snap of his fingers.

"What is it?" she said, icily.

"Where I know you from. We were in the navy together. Submarines. Don't you remember?"

"Navy?" Her incredulity turned to a smile that showed her straight white teeth. "That *is* a good opening line."

"I gave it my best shot," he said, careful not to move too close.

They laughed.

She sipped a bloody mary. "You married?"

"Yes. But there's a problem."

She smiled knowingly. "Isn't there always. Do you like cats?"

"Oh. I just love them. They're such adorable creatures."

"I have three."

Your apartment must stink of piss, he thought, motioning to the bartender.

She avoided his eyes. "My name is Helen McGlade."

He saw the red that tinged her earlobe and moved close. "Jake Stern."

Jack Fine was a minor celebrity with a thrice-weekly newspaper column in the *Daily News* and a few beer commercials on television. He was a thin man with a perpetually dour face and a crew cut and always wore a bow tie. His drinking was legendary; his wild parties envied; his tough talk emulated. It was not an unusual occurrence for him to be observed in the wee morning hours pissing on a Third Avenue lamppost.

Fine stood at the entrance. Malone saw him and waved. The newspaperman nodded and started to shoulder the crush, returning the proffered greetings with perfunctory grunts and feeble handshakes. "How'r'ya. Goodtaseeya'gain."

Malone had a very dry martini in his hand. Fine took it and gulped it down in one violent swallow. Malone had another in reserve.

"Got your message. What's up?" Fine said.

Malone leaned close and confided, "I want you to plant something in your next column. 'Usually reliable sources report stuff to the effect that a certain government agency and high-ranking members of the NYPD have colluded to suppress a homicide investigation.' " He sipped his drink, staring at the rows of bottles.

Fine inched close. "You got sunstroke or something. I'd never get a story like that past my editor. He'd want to know my source and I'd damn well have to tell him."

Malone held the glass up to his eyes and looked through it at the distorted face of the newspaperman. "I'm your source."

Fine eyed him warily. "You'd have to come out of the closet."

"Only to you and your editor."

The newspaperman leaned his back against the bar, arms folded tightly into his chest, thinking.

The bartender came over to them. Tony, No Butter, a KG —Known Gambler—wanted to buy them a drink. The bartender put the drinks down and nodded toward Tony, No Butter. They raised their glasses at the gambler. Tony, No Butter acknowledged with a feeble nod of the head. Malone noticed that Stern and the brunette were gone.

Fine said, "This thing has to be big for you to put your head on the chopping block. Want to tell me about it?"

"I'll tell you this much. Play ball and I'll guarantee you an unabridged exclusive. Could get you a Pulitzer."

Fine smacked his lips. He took the olive out of his glass and plopped it into his mouth. "Did I ever tell you about this chick I met in McBain's. She was the best blow job this side of the Mississippi."

They were naked in bed, exploring each other. She was big-boned with strong, firm legs and sagging breasts. Three cats were perched atop a fiberboard wardrobe next to the bed.

An Abyssinian, a Rex, and a Havana brown. Tails coiled, the cats stared down with yellow and green snake eyes at the lovers. The apartment was a scuzz affair with old newspapers and bags filled with clothes scattered about. And the place most definitely reeked of cat piss.

Stern wasted no time. After what he considered an appropriate waiting period, he made his play.

Helen McGlade was receptive.

She was breathing in deep heaves, almost grunts. That consuming passion that caused her to do horrible things was coming. To scream, curse. She loved it when her body was wasted by a ferocity that was beyond her control. She pulled from his embrace and started to kiss him, her tongue moving over his flabby body, gnawing at the folds of skin. She lifted his testicles into her mouth, sucking them ravenously. Then she pushed his penis down and embraced the underside with her lips, moving up and down the hardness, flicking the velvet skin with her tongue. And then she took him deep into her mouth, sucking him.

He was lost in the rapture of the moment. There were no thoughts, no problems, only pleasure. From deep within his body he could feel the beginning eruption. He clamped her head to him. She broke his grip by pushing his arms aside. She leaped up, rolling onto her back. Her legs were up in the air, far apart. "I want you inside of me. Hard. Now."

He hopped between her legs and rammed his erectness into her wet body. She went wild. Her body undulated forcefully, pumping him with hard methodical grinds. And then the horror began. Without warning her powerful legs scissored him at the waist, locking at the feet. He was clamped in a vise grip. She squeezed. The air was forced from his lungs. Her fists sprang for the sides of the bed and began pounding his back. Pain blanketed his shoulders and spread downward. He gagged, gasping for air. "You're crushing me." He frantically tried to extricate himself. He was screaming. The pain was awful. She continued to pound his back. He collapsed on top of her. Prostrated. Helpless. She laced her hands together and beat him. She screamed. Her pelvis rammed him. She screamed once more and then went limp, her body spent by the force of orgasm. "Did you come?" she murmured.

He shot up, choking, gasping. "No . . . I . . . didn't . . . come. . . . How . . . could . . . I? You . . . were . . . beating . . . the . . . shit . . . out . . . of . . . me."

"I love doing it that way. Passionate. Hard." She started to stroke his wet head. "You're quite a man. I've never known anyone like you."

Her adulation inflated his ego, dissipating the pain. "Well, it's just that I've never known a woman as passionate as you."

"Lie back. I'll make it up to you."

She saw the look of concern. "I'll be gentle. I promise." She pushed him down and started to lick his body. When he was hard she took him into her mouth. The cats watched, purring. Any lingering fears were swept away. He reached down, guiding her head. Her pace quickened, sucking him in rapid, hard jerks. "I love it," she screamed.

Oh, my God. She's getting hot again, he thought, glancing down at her.

She glared up at him, her face contorted. "I want you to come in my mouth." She threw herself against his thigh and bit him. At the same time her hand vised his penis, squeezing. He howled in pain. His hands banged her head.

"You're killing me." He pulled her hair in a desperate attempt to drag her away from him. One hand tugged at her thumb. "My cock! You're breaking my cock!" With great effort he was able to free himself from her painful clutches. His penis was limp and very sore. His leg throbbed pain and there were two red crescent marks where she had bitten him. He was almost off the bed when it flew by. For a split second he did not know what it was. Then the Abyssinian's claws furrowed his groin. His screams richocheted off the walls. He grabbed the cat by the neck and heaved it across the room.

Then he ran from the bedroom gathering his clothes and dashing naked out into the seedy hallway.

Never again, he swore, driving home in agony, trying desperately to conjure up a reasonable excuse to account for the teeth marks, bruises, and scratches that marred his body.

18

Malone watched a group of joggers round the track. The man whom he had come to see led the pack, his proud jaw stabbing the space in front of him. He had a high, smooth forehead and deep-set eyes guarded by bushy black eyebrows. His ears had great black tufts sprouting from them. His gray hair was cut military style.

Malone draped his arms over the fence and watched the runner's legs scissor the track with mechanical precision. Though the leader was older than the others, none was able to pass him. Was that due to lack of stamina or fear? Assistant Chief Whitney Zangline was known as a man of iron discipline. He had spent the last ten years molding the Special Operation Division, SOD, into the tactical strike force of the NYPD.

When Zangline assumed command of SOD there were three units under its umbrella. He methodically absorbed the mobile and tactical units within the department. "We're the Job's Rapid Deployment Force," he once told a newspaperwoman who was doing a piece for a Sunday supplement.

Zangline refused to socialize within the Job and never attended department functions. He had managed to circumvent the department's normal chain of command and report directly to the PC.

The SOD compound, in a desolate part of Flushing Meadow Park, and surrounded by high fences and deep underbrush, was patrolled around the clock. The only entrance was manned by motorcycle men. After Malone left the Hamilton House he telephoned the SOD compound and requested an appointment to see the chief. He made the call from Sol Epstein's third-floor office when he dropped off the shavings he had removed from Stanislaus's apartment. He asked the pathologist to compare them with the scrapings that were found under Eisinger's nails and cautioned Epstein not to mention it to anyone. The scrapings had been obtained by black-bag methods and could not be used in court. If they matched, Malone would have to invent some probable cause and apply for a search warrant.

Zangline put on a sudden burst of speed and trotted over to where he was standing. He snapped a towel from the fence and wiped his neck and face, watching him. "Lieutenant Malone?"

"Yes, Chief."

"Come with me," he said authoritatively.

Radio cars and Emergency Service vans were precision parked in front of the headquarters building. Zangline led Malone directly to his spacious office. Trophies won by various SOD units crammed each shelf. Zangline told him to wait while he showered and changed. Malone stood in front of the cabinets. There were framed photographs of Zangline shaking hands with President Carter, the mayor, and the governor. Even one with the cardinal. He studied the man in the flowing silk robe and wide red sash. Pompous prick, he thought, moving off. Four separate piles of reports were on the desk. He started to rummage through them but resisted his impulse and moved away from the desk. The SOD logo emblazoned one wall. Malone had done his homework before he came. Zangline commanded a small army. All Marine, Mounted, Aviation, Tactical Patrol, Emergency Service, and Anticrime units were under the SOD umbrella. Most of the structural changes that had occurred within the Job in the last three years had a direct bearing on SOD functions. Every Emergency Service truck in the city now carried two thousand rounds of 38-caliber ammunition, shotguns and AR-15s with scopes with nighttime capabilities, and tear gas and concussion grenades. SOD was the perfect place to hide forty cops.

Zangline came out of the dressing room in the tailored uniform of an assistant chief of the department. Malone focused on the two gilt stars on his shoulders.

"What can we do for you, Lieutenant?" Zangline said, walking to his desk.

Malone felt uneasy. He had heard that voice before. "I'm endeavoring to locate three officers whom I have reason to believe might be assigned to your command."

Zangline was watching him. "Why do you want these men?"

"It has to do with an investigation my squad is conducting."

Zangline started to roll a pencil over the desk. "I take it then that you're not from IAD."

He nodded.

"If you locate these men are you prepared to give them Miranda or GO 15?"

"No I'm not."

Zangline doodled. "Tell me their names."

"Edwin Bramson, Joseph Stanislaus, and Charles Kelly."

Zangline pointed the pencil at him and said, "None of them are assigned to SOD." He threw the pencil down and leaned back, watching him.

"Isn't it possible that you're . . ."

". . . Lieutenant. I know every man assigned to my command."

"But perhaps?" He raised his palms and let them fall.

"There are no perhapses in SOD. But to put your mind to rest . . ."

He snapped forward, yanking out the top drawer of his desk. "Here is an up-to-date roster of all personnel assigned."

Malone flipped the pages, glancing up and down the neatly typed column of names. There was no Bramson, Stanislaus, or Kelly. His mouth went dry. He looked at the chief and placed the roster on the desk.

He knew where he had heard that authoritative voice. He calmly got up and left.

A door opened and Bramson, Westy Stanislaus, and Kelly entered the room.

Zangline stared at them. "You heard?"

"We heard," Stanislaus said, going over to the window and watching Malone walking toward the SOD parking lot.

Bramson rubbed his chin. "Anderman told Mannelli that he thinks we should hit Malone."

Kelly said, "The problem with that is that neither Anderman nor Mannelli know what is really going down."

Shea Stadium loomed in front of him, a silent colossus with fluttering banners. Malone sped the department auto across the empty parking field, heading for the bank of telephones next to the press gate. He left the motor running and the transmission in park, and got out, fishing in his pocket for a dime.

"Chief Zangline, please," Malone said to the impersonal voice who answered the SOD switchboard.

"The chief is busy on another line."

"I'll hold." The glass panels of the booth were smashed. Names flared in black over the shiny shelf. Empty beer bottles and a used sanitary napkin were on the floor. More urban rococo. He tucked the receiver under his chin and lit a cigarette, his stare wandering the parking field. A few cars were parked next to the press gate. A bumper sticker caught his eye: SAVE A MOUSE, EAT A PUSSY. He laughed.

"I can put you through now."

"This is Chief Zangline."

Malone held the mouthpiece close. "I recognized your voice, *Captain* Madvick." He dropped the receiver onto the hook.

Zangline tore the phone from his ear and stared at it, not wanting to believe what he had just heard. He looked slowly away and stared blankly at Stanislaus. "Do Malone. Use Marku's friends from Atlantic Avenue and make it look like an accident."

"Malone is not the kind of man you catch off guard. He's going to have to be finessed into his grave," Stanislaus said.

"I don't care how you do it. Just do it. And there is something else that needs to be discussed. I got a call from Thea Braxton today. She and her brother think that they're worth more money, a lot more money. She insinuated that we"— he waved his hand at them—"are in a precarious position and should see to it that we don't make enemies, keep our friends."

Stanislaus, Bramson, and Kelly looked at one another and then each broke into smiles. They were going to enjoy the next few days.

14

Malone, Heinemann, Stern, dressed in prison denim, stared out the barred windows of the Department of Corrections bus. The bus threw up a cloud of dust as it lumbered along, and veered to avoid potholes. It jerked to a complete stop inches from the gate of the NYPD's outdoor range, in front of a large red warning sign that read: STOP, POLICE PERSONNEL ONLY, SHOW SHIELD AND I.D. A guardhouse was just inside the gate, and beyond that a parking field that was terraced into three sections by old telephone poles.

A restricted-duty police officer, his face scarred from the ravages of alcoholism, stepped from the guardhouse and ambled over to the gate. Raising himself up on the balls of his feet, he studied the sullen prisoners inside the bus. Shrugging as if to say No one tells me nothing, he unchained the gate and stepped back.

The NYPD's outdoor range was on a secluded tip of Pelham Bay Park. Five ranges built on the water's edge surrounded by high mountains of dirt; barriers to protect boaters in Eastchester Bay from stray shots. Ranges A through D could accommodate fifty shooters at a time; Range E had moving targets and was used for combat and barricade shooting. Alongside E range were the kennels where the department's narcotic- and explosive-sniffing dogs were housed. In the interior of the compound was an explosives range where

218

deadly devices were detonated and a Hollywood-type street where policemen role-played combat situations.

Malone had felt a twinge of guilt lying to his boyhood friend, Tom McCauley. They had grown up together in the old neighborhood, went to the same schools, played on the same teams, screwed the same baby-sitters. McCauley joined Corrections a year after Malone became a cop. McCauley was now the assistant warden of Rikers Island, the city's correctional facility.

Housekeeping duties at the range were done by trusties from Rikers. They arrived each day at 8:00 A.M. and left at 4:00 P.M. This was the one glaring weakness that Malone had discovered when he studied the range's security system. The perimeter was constantly patrolled by men in jeeps. Attack dogs roamed free at night. The bunkers were wired with alarms. Department helicopters flew over at irregular intervals, their powerful searchlights slicing through the night and sweeping the land. But every weekday a busload of prisoners arrived to pick up the garbage and police the brass. With nerve and the right disguise he just might brazen his way inside. He had paid a visit to Tom McCauley. "Need a favor, ol' buddy. A prison bus and some uniforms. For a tail job," he had told McCauley.

Starling Johnson parked the bus in front of A range. The cramped walkways were made of packed dirt; the gutters, uneven files of painted stones. A few skimpy trees shaded the outdoor eating area which had several seldom-used picnic tables. Most men elected to make the four-minute drive to City Island because alcoholic beverages were not permitted on the range. Someone once said that guns and booze don't mix but most cops don't believe it.

A group of range instructors were standing in front of Classroom 3 discussing the latest model Colt. A combat masterpiece, one of them called it.

The detectives left the bus and separated. Each one was to look around on his own. They pulled their denim hats over their eyes. There was a chance one of them might be recognized.

A group of men were lounging in front of Classroom 2. They were dressed in threadbare clothes and had gunbelts strapped around their waists. Goggles hung from their gun handles. Malone had counted thirty-one men when an instructor appeared in the doorway and motioned the class inside. On his haunches, pretending to realign the stones of the gutter, Malone worked his way toward Classroom 2. He moved slowly, not wanting to call attention to himself. Three prisoners were sitting next to a Quonset hut, killing time and sharing a cigarette. He met their eyes, then let his gaze drift slowly away, just another prisoner minding his own business. He moved to the next stone.

The double doors of the classroom were open. His leg muscles were starting to ache. When he reached the doorway he glanced into the classroom and recoiled, looking quickly away. A range instructor was lecturing the class. His khakis were tailored and a .38 Colt, in a quick-draw holster, hugged his right hip. Two men were sitting on a metal folding table behind him. One was a big, blond man with fair skin and wavy hair. The other man was David Ancorie, Yachov Anderman's trusted associate.

While the instructor lectured on the use of deadly physical force, Ancorie and the other man sat patiently, legs swinging over the side of the table.

Malone turned his back to the open door and moved past on his haunches. Pretending to concentrate on work, he made his way around to the side of the Quonset hut. He slumped to the ground with his back against the corrugated shell. He stretched out his legs in front and lit a cigarette. Just another trusty on another self-imposed break. An open window was inches above his head. He could hear clearly. Heinemann and Stern rounded Classroom 3 and saw him. They moseyed over, pausing at discreet distances to police the area.

They sat on either side of him. "Anything?" Heinemann whispered.

"Shhh. Listen," Malone said.

The instructor was lecturing. "Gentlemen, I am now going to read to you Section Thirty-five-point-thirty, paragraph two, of the *Criminal Procedure Law:* 'The fact that a police officer is justified in using deadly physical force under circumstances prescribed in these paragraphs does not constitute justification for reckless conduct by such police officer amounting to an offense against or with respect to innocent persons whom he is not seeking to arrest or retain in custody.' "

The lawbook was slapped closed.

An echo reverberated through the half-empty classroom.

Malone visualized the instructor scanning the faces of his students, getting ready to drive home his point.

"In other words, gentlemen, if you open up at high noon on Madison and Five-three in an attempt to apprehend a perp who just blew away the pope and all the saints and in the process kill a junkie who was nodding by"—a long pause for effect—"your ass, gentlemen, would be in a whooooole lot of trouble."

Another pause for effect.

"Are there any questions, gentlemen?"

A range officer made his way along the footpath heading for the latrine. He glanced at the three goofing-off prisoners and continued to his destination.

A voice bellowed from the rear of the classroom. "Hey, Westy, when are we going to get the scoop?"

For the first time Malone heard Stanislaus's voice: "Okay. Okay. I'll tell you what I can." He sounded poised and confident. "After our good friend, Dave, gets done giving you his spiel, you're going to be divided into two groups. The first group will go out to Easy range and fire the Uzi. Group two will remain here and be tested. Then the process will be reversed. 'Course, the questions we ask the first group will not be the same as those asked the second group."

A chorus of boos went up.

Stanislaus continued. "After you're tested you'll be rated and ranked. When there are openings in the Unit you'll be transferred in. In the meantime you're to be transferred back to commands. Each one of you will get to pick your own house."

A chorus of hoots, whistles, and applause.

"Gentlemen, you are to tell no one about the Unit. Secrecy is vital to our mission. Never discuss what you've learned. Not with your wife. Your girlfriend. Your confessor. Not even with your partner. Are there any questions?"

There was a long silence.

The detectives could hear shuffling from inside the classroom. Westy Stanislaus said, "Good. Now I'll turn you over to our good friend, Dave Ancorie."

Ancorie's now familiar voice announced: "This, gentlemen, is a five-inch gray attaché case that is completely lined with ballistic armor. Every member of the Unit will be issued one. This particular case uses a type-C liner that is one-quarter-inch thick and will defeat, at a distance of four inches, the three-fifty-seven- or one-fifty-eight-grain jacketed cartridge. Keep it close to you. It could save your life." He opened the case and removed a Uzi submachine gun. "You are looking at one of the finest weapons in the world. It was developed in Israel by its namesake Maj. Uzi Gal. This weapon has a cyclical rate of fire of six hundred and fifty rounds per minute. A velocity of thirteen hundred and ten feet per second. It fires nine-millimeter parabellum bullets from a detachable staggered-box magazine with three separate load capacities. Fully loaded the Uzi weighs eight-point-eight pounds. This weapon has a slide selector switch which permits single action or fully automatic bursts." The bolt was slid back, cocking the weapon. "This weapon has almost no recoil." The trigger was pulled and the bolt snapped forward with a clanging thud. "The front sight is a truncated cone with protecting ears. The rear sight is L shaped with sight settings for one hundred and two hundred yards." He placed the Uzi under his right arm. "This weapon is easy to conceal on the person." Malone heard what sounded like the weapon being put down on a table. "Now. If you will all gather around me I will show you how to clean and field strip this weapon."

Malone nudged the detectives. "Let's get out of here."

Dr. Solomon Epstein used a diluted solution of gelatin when he mounted the hairs. He placed the fibers side by side on the slides so that he could study them at full length.

Leaning into the comparison microscope, he adjusted the focus. His white hospital coat was unbuttoned. He glanced up at Malone. "What do you know about hair?"

"It thins in men past twenty."

Epstein smiled and peered into the lenses. Concentrating on the slides, he lapsed into a forensic litany. Head hair was round and curly. Torso hair was oval and kidney shaped. Beard hair was triangular, with concave sides. Hair was generally divided into three parts: the medulla, cortex, and cuticle. The medulla of human hair was narrow; the medulla of animal hair was medium or thick depending on the kind of animal. By checking a hair fiber against the *Medullary Index* a pathologist can determine if the specimen is human or animal and what part of the body it originated from.

Epstein pushed away from the table. "Take a look."

Malone straddled the white adjustable stool and lowered himself. The doctor looked over his shoulder. "Notice that the air network is a fine grain. The network in animal hair is formed in sacs. You are looking at human hair. The fibers on the left slide were taken from Eisinger's fingernails. Notice how the shaft is broken around the root. If you look close you will be able to see the longitudinal splits around the shaft."

Malone had a wry look on his face. "Which all means?"

"It means that Eisinger tore those hairs from someone's face. Most probably her killer's."

"What else can you tell me?"

"Both slides contain beard hair of a male, Caucasian. A man with a heavy beard and blond wavy hair."

223

Malone stood. He plunged his hands into his trouser pockets and strolled around the room. He stopped in front of a specimen case. Epstein's reflection was in the paneled glass. He was staring at him, a smug smile on his hawklike face. Glass shelves were filled with jars containing human organs.

A brain had pins sticking out of it. Little tags were attached to the ends. Right and left cerebral hemisphere. Right and left frontal lobe. The infoldings of the gray mass seemed intertwined in an insoluble puzzle.

"Doc, I have the million-dollar question for you," Malone said.

"You want to know if the hairs on both slides are from the same man," Epstein said, moving to the specimen case.

Malone turned to face him. "Are they?"

"The best I can give you is a definite maybe. The hairs do have the same microscopic characteristics and in my opinion could have come from the same individual."

Malone's disappointment was obvious.

Epstein said, "Hair fibers are not positive like fingerprints. They're circumstantial evidence. You go and bring in your killer. I'll testify. Those fibers might be the nails in his coffin." Epstein smiled impishly. "That is, if the shavings you bring in next time are admissible in evidence."

Wednesday night was cheaters night at Bradley's. The bar and lounge were crowded. Soft music floated from speakers. The telephone calls had been made; the wives had been notified that their husbands would not be home for dinner. An unscheduled meeting or an important buyer were the usual lies.

Malone was squeezed in at the end of the bar, sipping Jack Daniel's on ice. Reasonable Cause does sometimes get in the way, but Malone was fond of saying that a good cop can always make his own. The trick was not to get caught. In order to reenter Stanislaus's apartment legally and dust the compact and diaphragm for her prints and obtain more shavings, he would need a search warrant with a "No Knock" clause. And in order to get one he would have to go before a competent court and show reasonable cause, some evidence, even hearsay, linking Police Officer Joseph Stanislaus to the murder of Sara Eisinger.

Drink finished, he pushed his glass onto the bar's runway and motioned to the bartender for a refill.

Malone hefted the glass without drinking. What was Erica doing at this very moment, he wondered. Probably typing or editing her manuscript. He thought of her shaped triangle of downy hair and sighed. What the hell was he doing in this place? He drank and a euphoric glow began to spread through him. People around him were laughing and the music was louder. He was attuned to the charged atmosphere. His feet tapped to the beat of the music. He spun on his stool to watch the dancers. Small tables with flickering candles stuck inside netted red lanterns ringed the cube-size dance floor. The lights were dim. Swaying dancers pressed close to Malone. A "garmento" held a beautiful black woman in his arms. His knee slid between her legs. She pressed him close, pelvis grinding rhythmically, her head resting on his shoulder. Wifey was probably at home in Jericho playing mah-jongg with the girls. Go to it, ma man. As he spun back, a nagging thought came to mind. The *Patrol Guide* mandated an immediate notification to IAD whenever there was an indication of a MOF's involvement in a crime. He sipped his drink, scoffing. Dear IAD. Forty cops and an assistant chief might be involved in a homicide. Wanna take a case on it? Tell the mothers nothin'. He gulped his drink and ordered another.

Stern, Davis, and Johnson walked in. They hovered around the entrance, looking.

Malone turned and saw them shouldering their way toward him. Business should never be discussed in the presence of civilians, so he looked around and spotted an unoccupied banquette between the service bar and kitchen. He wrapped his glass in the cocktail napkin and motioned to the detectives to follow.

"Heard you had a big day at the range," Starling Johnson said, sliding in next to him.

Malone raised his glass and nodded. "We have to come up with something that links Stanislaus to Eisinger. Any ideas?"

The detectives looked to each other. As their eyes met, they shrugged.

Malone looked at Bo Davis. "You said that Stanislaus was divorced and has been living at the Hamilton House for about two years."

Davis spread his hands expressively and let them drop on the table. "Right."

Malone said, "That is within the time frame that Eisinger started to work for the Braxtons."

Stern wrinkled his brow. "So?"

A waitress came over to take their orders. They stopped talking. Stern leered at her, his eyes taking in her trim body. She wrote down their orders and turned to leave. Stern reached out and snagged her by the hip, turning her. "I'd love to get into your pants."

She glowered at him. "I've got one asshole there now. I don't need a second one." She pulled away from his clutch and left in a huff.

The detectives laughed.

"The broad wants my form," Stern said, watching her swaying backside.

When she was gone, Malone said, "I want to locate Stanislaus's ex."

Davis told him, "Pat and I checked with the phone company."

Malone realized that Pat O'Shaughnessy was among the missing. "Where is Pat?"

"A problem at home," Davis said. "Anyway, according

226

to Ma Bell there are over two hundred Stanislauses in and around the metropolitan area."

The waitress brought their drinks. Stern gave her a big smile. She wrinkled her nose at him and sneered.

Davis said to Malone, "Lou, it'll take a lot of time to check all them subscribers. And the ex coulda moved or remarried, or be living under her maiden name."

Malone toyed with his glass. "Time is one thing we don't have a lot of."

Nobody talked.

Stern watched with growing disbelief as Starling Johnson drank a Galliano with a beer chaser.

Stern grimaced. "How the fuck can you drink that shit?"

Johnson licked his fingers. "Each man to his own poison." Starling Johnson's face harmonized with the darkness, teeth and eyes accentuated by the glow of the flickering candle. "Stanislaus's personnel folder is missing, right?"

"Right," Malone said, wary.

"And we want to find out where he used to live on the assumption that his ex still lives there and might be able to tell us something about hubby and his love life."

Malone held the glass in front of his face and nodded.

Johnson smiled. "This be a very ethnic job. I belong to the Guardians. Limp-dick Stern belongs to the Shomrim. Bo belongs to the St. George. And Stanislaus be a Polish name . . ."

Malone leaned over the table and punched him on the shoulder. "And you be a bloomin' genius."

"Are you sure that you want to use a direct approach?" Johnson said, sipping his cordial.

Malone pondered the question. "No. I don't think I want him to know that we're zeroing in on him. I'm gambling that he's forgotten about those items his girlfriend left in his bathroom." He grabbed a handful of pretzels from the bowl and started to toss them into his mouth one at a time, thinking.

He said to Johnson, "Steal a policewoman from the precinct. Locate the ex and have the policewoman hang around some of the beauty parlors and Laundromats. They're hotbeds of local gossip."

15

When Malone walked into the squad room, Heinemann glanced at him and nodded toward the lieutenant's office.

Bo Davis was perched on Malone's desk, trying to console O'Shaughnessy who was slumped in a chair, hands limp between his legs. Dark folds of skin sagged his eyes.

"Lemme 'lone," O'Shaughnessy was saying.

Malone pushed the door closed and looked at Davis.

"His wife left him," Davis said.

"That cunt!" O'Shaughnessy stormed from the chair and kicked the desk.

Malone was concerned. "What happened?"

O'Shaughnessy lit a cigarette. "The minute I walked in last night I knew somethin' was wrong. 'We have a dinner guest, dear,' " he mimicked, sarcastically. "I just knew. I went into the dining room and there she was, sitting at my table, drinking my tea. That Irish whore."

"Oh shit. Foam," Malone said.

Davis said, "How did she find out where you lived?"

"She works for Sears, Roebuck. She ran a credit check on me. Bam! There I was. A computer printout, address and all. 'Hi. I'm Foam. Your husband has been screwing me for years. I'm in a family way and he's the daddy.' 'Oh?' says my wife. 'Do come in dear. Watch the steps. I'll make us some tea and we'll have a nice long talk.' "

229

"Any chance of patching things up?" Davis said.

"No way. My wife got no sense of humor."

The tour was almost over. O'Shaughnessy had put in a 28 for the remainder of it and was off apartment hunting. Harrigan had telephoned to tell Malone that one of his detectives had taken photographs of three men who fitted the descriptions of Stanislaus, Bramson, and Kelly. They were snapped leaving the SOD compound. Malone had telephoned Erica to ask if she could have dinner with him.

"I'd love to, Daniel."

Her voice caused a stirring in his stomach. He had been contemplating her willing body when a commotion in the squad room shook him from his reverie. Zambrano plunged into the office waving a newspaper in front of him.

"Good afternoon, Inspector. And how has your day been?"

"How has my day been? My fucking telephone hasn't stopped ringing." He shook the paper at Malone. "You better get your fucking circus in the tent. Have you gone mad, planting a story like this?"

"What story?" His expression was deadpan.

Zambrano had read Fine's column. The last paragraph dealt with a usually reliable source within the police department. Zambrano stabbed the column with his finger. "That story!" His eyes were wide and it seemed that every vein and artery in his neck and face were about to burst.

Malone glanced up at the flaking ceiling. "Who said I planted it?"

"Fine's motherfuckin' byline says you planted it! Everyone in the Job knows you two are asshole buddies."

Malone took out two cups and an unopened bottle of Old Grand Dad. He held one of the cups up to his eye and then blew the inside clean. He cracked the bottle and poured. "I needed some answers. Figured a little fire under some ass might make people a wee bit more cooperative."

Zambrano looked at him sharply. "Or desperate."

Malone shrugged indifference and pushed a cup across to him.

Zambrano picked it up and drank. When he put the cup down, he appeared somewhat mollified. "I've just come from the Chief of Op. He wanted to know about you."

Why would the Chief of Operations, the department's highest-ranking uniform member, be interested in him? Malone wondered. Rolling his cup between palms, he asked, "What did you tell him?"

"I said that you were one hundred percent." He moved close to the desk, tapping a fist against his lips. "The Chief of Op is not the kind of man you play grab-ass with. He's where he is because he was the most ruthless and cunning of the palace guard. I strongly suggest that you start looking over your shoulder."

Malone looked up at him. "What can you tell me about Chief Whitney Zangline?"

Zambrano rolled his eyes upward and whistled. "You got a big one. Know anything about the Red Squad?"

"Rumors mostly."

"At one time the Red Squad was a covert subunit of the Intelligence Division. Their mission was the penetration and disruption of subversive groups. Five years ago they were given another mission"—he pulled out a fugitive nose hair, held it up in front of him, examining it—"terrorism."

Malone rubbed his lips in concentration.

Zambrano continued, "Remember the bombing at the World Trade Center five years ago?"

Malone nodded.

"The Red Squad knew about that before it went down. One of their stools sold them the information. Instead of passing it on, they sat on it until every one in their internal chain of command passed on the information's authenticity. When they finally let it out-of-house, it was too late. Twenty-seven lives could have been saved. When the PC found out he went nuts. The C.O. of the squad was reduced to captain and

231

forced to retire. Everyone in the squad who had their time in was told to throw in their papers. The rest of the squad was transferred back into the bag and told to walk with twenty." Zambrano pushed the empty cup across the desk.

Malone broke his concentration and poured.

"About the same time Whitney Zangline had developed SOD into an antiterrorist strike force. That's SOD's real mission. Chrissake, he has more men under arms than some countries. Zangline went to the PC and complained about a lack of communication between Intelligence and SOD. He thought that Intelligence was too compartmentalized. He convinced the PC that SOD needed its own Intelligence arm. The Red Squad was transferred to SOD. Zangline was able to build from the bottom, with his own hand-picked men."

Malone thought of Ancorie training policemen in the use of the Uzi.

"Where does his weight come from?"

Zambrano shook his head. "Dunno. But he is heavy. His budget requests are never trimmed." He toasted him. "And that my brash, young lieutenant, takes powerful connections."

"And who are these connections?"

Zambrano grinned. "Whatya tryna do, make me spread rumors?"

"Yeah!"

"I hear whispers, mind you, not many, or loud, but I hear them all the same. Zangline is supposed to be close with Carter Moorhouse."

"The politician?"

"Yep. When Moorhouse ran for mayor a few years back he asked the PC to let Zangline have charge of his security detail. Since then, they've been spotted having dinner a few times."

"That's not very much."

Zambrano flicked his cup aside with his fingernails. He got up and stretched, his arms reaching for the ceiling. Relaxing, he strolled over to the window. He sat on the sill and leaned forward, hands cupping kneecaps. He realized that his socks did not match. One was black, the other charcoal. "Yesterday I went to the Captain Endowment Association's monthly luncheon. Over the clink of martini glasses, I picked up a few whispers concerning Zangline. Grapevine has it that he's up to his ass in something heavy."

Malone was interested. "Can you find out what?"

"Did you ever stop to think that nothing happens in this job without first passing through some pencil pusher's desk in the Bureau of Audits and Accounts. My brother-in-law is a SPAA there. I've been planning to take him to lunch." Zambrano got up. "What are you doing tomorrow?"

Malone spread his lips and gestured nothing.

"That's good. The Chief of Op wants you in his office at five P.M. He said to be on time."

Photographs of three unsuspecting men walking toward a car were spread over the desk. Malone shuffled them, looking at each one. He recognized Stanislaus from the range. Davis identified Bramson and Kelly. He opened the top drawer of his desk and took out the snapshot of Sara Eisinger that her parents had lent him. He put it with the others and tapped them together into one neat stack. He handed the stack to Jake Stern. "I want you to do a canvass of the joints around the Hamilton House. That part of Queens is a big singles' area. Show these around. See if you can put Eisinger and Stanislaus together."

Jack Harrigan's head was way back, draining a container of beer. He snapped forward and at the same time arched the empty tube into the wastebasket. Malone caught the look that crossed the sergeant's face as he watched Stern walk out. "What's bothering you, Jack?"

Harrigan looked him in the eyes. "Some of my men don't feature working on cops."

233

Malone gave a worried sigh. "None of us do. I think most of the cops involved are either legit or dupes in a caper they know nothing about. Someone out there is using the department, manipulating it."

"I don't want my men branded IAD scumbags."

"They won't be. We won't be. We're doing the right thing."

Harrigan nodded feebly and left.

Malone knew that he had just about used up all his time.

Washing machines rumbled on concrete platforms. Dryers spun. Local announcements tacked on bulletin boards advertised fifteen-year-old girl, available to baby-sit; a two-room mother/daughter was for rent at 7 Plumeding Lane, Pearl River, New York; and there was to be a mammoth garage sale this Saturday at 12 Rosehaven Hollow, Pearl River, New York.

Women waited inside the Laundromat for their clothes to dry. Others pulled items from machines and tossed them into plastic baskets.

Jean O'Day had her hair in rollers. A housecoat with a lavender-and-yellow forget-me-not design concealed her shapely body, hiding the waistband holster.

O'Day was a cop from the Fifth.

She stuffed her laundry into the front-load machine and closed the door. She measured the proper amount of detergent and softener, set the wash cycle, and inserted coins. The machine started to spin, a mass of suds formed behind the porthole. When she turned around, she caught three pairs of eyes leaving her. She gathered up her boxes and walked over to the women. "Hi. I'm Jean O'Day."

Detective Starling Johnson parked the department auto so that he might have an unrestricted view of the Laundromat. He slouched behind the wheel, working the *New York Times* crossword puzzle. One eye was glued on the Laundromat. She was standing among a group of women, gabbing.

The day had begun early for Johnson. He had left one of his girlfriend's bed at 4:13 A.M., dressed, and drove to the stationhouse. In order to steal a policewoman for a day he needed the approval of the precinct commander. Patrol precincts are made up of two separate commands: patrol and detective. A captain is usually in command of the uniform force; a lieutenant commands the detectives.

The precinct captain is charged with the responsibility for the plant and its maintenance. Sometimes the lines of communication between the two commands get twisted and there is friction. But not at the Fifth. Captain Bruno Carini was first, last, and always a street cop. The Fifth was his third command and the word was that he was one of the rising stars. The pressure of running an urban police precinct was taking its toll. There was a time when Carini always wore a smile on his face. No more. He looked tired and drawn. He was finishing up a late tour when Johnson knocked on the door.

After studying the eight-by-four roll call, Carini had said, "I'll let you have O'Day for the day. She's about the only female who knows where it's at." As Johnson was leaving he had said, "Tell your boss he owes me another one."

The first thing Johnson noticed about Police Officer O'Day was that she was flat chested. The second thing was her eyes. They reminded him of gray bottle caps. The third was the smile. It burst over her entire face.

A few minutes alone with her in the sitting room told him that she was intelligent, quick, eager, and had a glowing ambition to get a gold detective shield. As they discussed her assignment, Johnson had fantasized about Police Officer O'Day sprawled naked in bed. White skin blended with black. She only had nipples, brown and hard. He gnawed them and she writhed with ecstasy. She stroked his black hardness. When she could no longer stand it, she demanded that he enter her.

"What I would like you to do is go home and change into

235

something that will make you look like a housewife. I'll meet you back here in one hour."

Johnson had located Stanislaus's neighborhood through the Pulaski Association. He had gone to their suite of rooms in a downtown office building. The grandmother type who worked there looked concerned when she saw him standing there. She was nigger scared. He smiled warmly and showed her his shield and I.D. She relaxed immediately. Her late husband, God rest his soul, worked out of old Traffic B. She went on to berate the inadequateness of the Article I pension system. The cost-of-living escalator clause sucks, she told him.

"Yes'm." He listened to the litany of woe with interest and patience. Twenty minutes later when she paused to catch her breath he leaped into the opening. He told her that he was trying to get the home address of someone he had come on the job with. They were planning a class reunion. Joe Stanislaus was a member of the Pulaski and since he was in the neighborhood he thought that he might save himself a trip to headquarters. Four wooden file boxes were on a clerical cart. She swiveled around and slid open the last one.

"Stanislaus, Joseph," she said, nimbly fingering the cards. She flicked one out. There was a recent address change. What was the old address? "24 Pickwicklan Drive Circle, Pearl River, New York," she read.

"That's the one. I remember Joe always complaining about the damn crabgrass in Pearl River."

A covered carriage carried by poles. Nine letters down. He tapped the pencil against his teeth. O'Day was engaged in animated conversation. He caught her glance in his direction and thought he saw a glimmer of lust. Wishful thinking, he thought.

Palanquin. Nine letters. He filled in the boxes.

Detective Johnson and Police Officer O'Day had a pleasant ride back. They got to know each other, a little. When they drove up in front of the Fifth, the Third Platoon was flowing into the street. O'Day was anxious to make her report to the detective commander. The ladies of the Laundromat had been most helpful, she reported. There was not much that went on in Pearl River they did not know about. Especially when it concerned the carryings-on of husbands. A fat woman with a hairy birthmark on the tip of her nose had been eager to talk. She confided that Joe Stanislaus was having a "thing" with one of the policewomen in his precinct. Pranced home one night and told his dear wife that he was leaving. He was in love for the first time in his life, he told his wife, the woman with the birthmark said. She had moved close to the ladies and murmured, "I suppose *she* did all those disgusting things that men like." Jean O'Day had nodded knowingly. It was at that point that she had glanced in Johnson's direction. Did he always wear tight trousers?

Malone gave her his full attention.

When she finished making her report he got up and went to the blackboard. Next to Stanislaus's name he wrote: Policewoman? Eisinger was not on the Job. If she was Stanislaus's girlfriend then someone was mistaken. He moved back, studying the board. Stanislaus might have had two women on the string, one of whom could have been a policewoman. Eisinger found out. They fought. He killed her. Or? If David Ancorie could train policemen in the use and care of the Uzi, why could not Eisinger train them in computers or warehouse maintenance, or something? They could have met at a training session. Lovers have to meet someplace. It would be a natural mistake for the ex to assume she was on the Job. He liked it. It had the right ring.

Detective Johnson leaned close to Police Officer O'Day.

"How about a bite to eat?"

She looked at him and smiled. "Sounds good to me."

In the window of the restaurant on Austin Street a statue of a boy held a pizza in his outstretched hands. Heinemann and Stern had worn down shoe leather in Stanislaus's Queens neighborhood for the past two hours. The owner of Ricco's was a rotund man with a chunky face and a prairie of shiny skin stretched over his cranium. Heinemann showed him the photographs. "They're not in any kind of trouble, are they?" Stern assured him that they weren't. It was an accident case and they had been witnesses. The owner was relieved. They were such a nice couple. The blond man in the one photo and the woman standing on the pier in the other photo used to eat here all the time. He moved close to the detectives. A man ready to share a secret. "They were very much in love. It made my heart good to see them holding hands and kissing. Like young kids." They questioned him closely. When they finished, Heinemann telephoned Malone and told him what they had discovered. They had a pizza that tasted even better because it was on the arm, and then drove to Hamilton House.

The doorman was a patronizing shit who always had his hand out. The detectives sized him up at once. Stern told him that they were private detectives working on a matrimonial. Their client was a doctor who would do the right thing if someone were to come up with some information on his wife.

"What kinda information you lookin' for?" the doorman asked, squaring his hat to the front.

Heinemann told him the doctor had reason to believe his wife was sleeping around with a resident of Hamilton House. He had followed his wife there on more than one occasion. Stern passed the doorman the photographs. He flipped through them, giving each photo a perfunctory glance. Finished, he flopped the stack into Heinemann's hand and hurried to open the door for a lady and her sheepdog. Returning, he asked slyly, "How much?"

Stern spoke out of the corner of his mouth. "A yard."

"I got a piss-poor memory. Make it five hundred," said the doorman.

"Fuck you, pally," Stern said, walking away.

"Three hundred," the doorman said.

"Two," Stern countered.

"Gimme a break," said the doorman.

"Two fifty," Heinemann said.

"Okay. Apartment 24 J. Name's Stanislaus. She had her own key."

Heinemann looked at him sternly. "You sure she had a key?"

The doorman snapped a thumb in his face and raised his voice. "I'm sure."

The detectives looked at each other. "You wait here. I'll go," Stern said.

"Whaddabout my money?" said the doorman.

"I'm going to see about that right now," said Stern.

It took him forty-eight minutes to drive back to the station-house. He trudged the steps to the squad room, pausing to catch his breath.

Sara Eisinger's property was stacked in plastic evidence bags with property vouchers wrapped around them. Each key that had been identified had a tag attached to it that noted the lock that it opened. Two keys had no tags. He signed them out on the voucher: name, rank, shield number, and date and time. He returned the rest of the evidence and locked the locker.

"Got my money?" said the doorman, walking up to him.

Stern ignored the question. "Does Stanislaus own a car?"

"Yeah. A red Honda. He keeps it in the garage."

Janet Fox had seen Eisinger get out of a red Honda on a rainy night long ago.

"What kind of rent does he pay here?" Heinemann said.

The doorman pulled on his ear. "Five and a quarter for a one bedroom and another seventy-five for the garage. What about my money?"

Stern grabbed him by the gold-trimmed lapels of his uniform. "Three weeks from today at exactly 2 P.M. a guy is going to walk up to you and hand you an envelope. Your bread'll be in it."

"Three weeks!"

Stern tightened his grip. The doorman's lip quivered.

Stern said, "That's the way things work, pally. We gotta check out your story. In the meantime, you button your mouth." He released one hand and pointed at Heinemann. "If you don't, my large friend here will come back and dance the tarantella on your nuts."

"It's over here," Stern said, standing in front of apartment 24 J. The first key unlocked the door. Supressing an urge to enter, Stern locked the door and dropped Eisinger's key into his pocket.

Waiting for the elevator, Heinemann said, "Wait a minute." He ran back and toed the mat square with the jamb.

Stern held the elevator.

Malone spent the rest of the day reading and signing fives. How does a cop pay alimony and still afford six hundred dollars for an apartment and garage? The answer was simple. He doesn't. Not unless he has an unreported source of income or some old ammo boxes stuffed with greenbacks.

It was almost 4 P.M. when a gruff voice piped in from the squad room. "Lou, you gotta call on three." Malone checked the time. Erica would be waiting and he was anxious. He almost yelled out to tell the caller that he was on patrol but the nagging feeling that it might be important caused him to yank up the receiver and press the blinking button.

"Lou, this is Sergeant Vincent from the Nineteenth Squad. Do you know an Erica Sommers?"

"Yes!" he blurted, jerking forward in the chair, aware of a sudden thumping in his chest.

"You better get over to her apartment. There's been a homicide."

Three East End Avenue was on a bluff overlooking the East River. The building had thirty-five stories of reflective glass topped by a penthouse and a huge lobby filled with paintings and sculpture.

With roof light and siren on constant, Malone sped the unmarked car north along the FDR Drive through the blossoming evening traffic. It took him thirty-six minutes to get to Eightieth Street. East End Avenue between Eightieth and Eighty-first was cordoned with police vehicles. Several unmarked cars had been abandoned in the middle of the avenue. Radio cars were parked on the sidewalk. The Crime Scene Unit's blue-and-white station wagon was blocking the entrance to 3 East End's underground garage.

Malone drove the car around the west side of the Eightieth Street cordon and up onto the sidewalk. Halfway down the block he parked, leaving the roof light flashing red. He ran from the car over to the nearest policeman. "Where is it?"

"In the garage, Lou," the startled cop said, staring at the gold lieutenant's shield that Malone thrust at him.

As he ran down the curving two-lane driveway, he was breathless and conscious of a sharp welt of pain across his forehead. He reached the bottom and found himself in an underground garage full of cars, each one in a stall designated by a little yellow number and enclosed within yellow boundary lines. Save for its silent tenants, it was empty. Off in the distance he could hear the echo of voices. He made for them. Walking rapidly, his footfalls added to the hollow sounds. He could smell gasoline fumes and the heavy odor of motor oil. The voices grew louder. He broke into a trot.

When he reached the eastern extremity of the garage he turned the bend and stopped short. Grim-faced detectives, their shields pinned to their sport coats, were gathered around

Erica Sommers's green Oldsmobile Cutlass. A photographer was kneeling on the front seat of the green car flashing pictures of the rear.

He hesitated, afraid of what he was going to see in the rear seat of the Cutlass. And then, with his shield case dangling open in his hand, and the cold knot in his stomach getting tighter, he began pushing past the detectives.

Sprawled over the seat was the body of a man. His hands were tied behind his back and a bloody plastic bag was pulled over his head and garroted around the neck with wire. The cadaver's eyes bulged from their sockets in a wild, dull stare and the tongue protruded limply over the lip.

An overwhelming sense of relief swept over Malone and he felt weak. Sergeant Vincent had told him that she was all right, but he needed to see for himself.

He turned to meet the stares. "Where is she?"

Two policemen were on guard outside Erica's sixteenth-floor apartment. Malone flashed his shield and rushed past them.

She was sitting in a high-backed chair in the sunken living room staring down at the geometric pattern of the carpet. When she heard the sound of the closing door she glanced up and looked disbelievingly at him. She was wearing a pair of white jeans and a blue tunic-top blouse. Before a word could pass between them she sprang up and ran into his waiting arms. He began to say sympathetic things, trying to console her. And then he realized that she was not hysterical. Her face showed no trace of tears. She bore a countenance of resigned bewilderment. "I was going shopping and found that thing in my car. I feel as though I've been personally violated. What kind of animals are there in this world?" For the first time he sensed fear in her voice.

Lt. Jack Weidt, the "whip" or boss of the Nineteenth Squad of detectives, was a trendy dresser. A medium-size man with a throaty voice, he was completely bald and had deep green eyes that had gray spots in both irises. He walked in off the terrace followed close behind by Lt. Joe Mannelli, who looked almost sick with worry. They walked over to the embracing couple and waited for Malone to notice them.

Malone looked at them over her shoulder.

"I saw to it that her name was left out of it, Dan. There'll be no mention of her on any five or to the press hounds," Weidt said.

Malone nodded his thanks.

"Can you give us a few minutes?" Mannelli said in a low voice, motioning toward the terrace.

With a quick movement of his eyes, Malone indicated that they should wait for him out on the terrace and then led Erica into the bedroom and closed the door.

"Lie down and try to get some sleep."

"That was a body, Daniel. In my car. Why? Why me? Does it have something to do with you, with us?"

"Someone probably thought it was a convenient place to dump a body."

"Don't tell me fairy tales, Daniel. I have a right to know what the hell is going on."

"I don't know what's going down. But be assured that you're going to have round-the-clock protection."

"I don't want a bunch of grubby policemen following me every time I go to the bathroom or sit down at the type-writer."

He spent the next thirty minutes soothing her; then he left her to join the anxious men on the terrace of her apartment.

"What the fuck went down in that garage?" Malone said, stepping outside.

Jack Weidt replied, "She discovered the body about three forty-five P.M. A garage attendant heard her screams and came a-runnin'. When we arrived on the scene she dropped your name and we called you. The M.E. hasn't been here yet. He's stuck on a triple homicide in Whitestone. I took a look-

243

see at the body. There's some lividity. Rigor mortis has set in around the head and neck. There are three tightly grouped entrance wounds above the left ear that look as though they were made by twenty-twos. I'd say that he was wasted four to six hours ago, which would make the time of occurrence somewhere between nine and twelve this morning." He paused to light a cigar.

"There were two attendants on duty from eight A.M. The body had to have been planted here during their tour. We've been leaning on them and they know from nothing. And I believe them. We checked both of them out and they're clean. Not so much as a summons for drinking beer in the park." Weidt cast a worried look in Malone's direction. "Somebody went to a lot of trouble to plant that stiff in your girlfriend's car. Any ideas?"

Malone ignored the question. "Has he been I.D.'ed?"

Joe Mannelli had been standing with his back to them, watching the river, seemingly oblivious to the conversation behind him. Now he turned abruptly, a look of alarm etched into his face. "He's from my league, Dan—Ismail al Banna."

Malone was astonished. "Banna!"

"You got it. Banna was wanted in half a dozen countries for terrorist acts. Everything from political kidnappings to murder. We recently received word through the French secret service that he was hiding in New York. SDECE's Bureau Five turned someone around in Morocco. The word within the community is that it was Banna who pulled off the New Year's Eve bombings. It was a contract job for the FALN. Ever since the P.R. freedom fighters blew up their bomb factory in Greenwich Village they've lost their stomach for explosives. They hire out their jobs now, and Banna was one of the best."

Mannelli was frantically rubbing his left thumb. "I don't like it. I tell you, I don't like it. Terrorists are a tightly knit fraternity of nut jobs. They'd only waste one of their own if they thought he had turned. And Banna wasn't—not by us, not by the FBI, and not by the agency."

"Maybe someone in your minor league blew him away," Malone said sarcastically.

"And dumped the body in your girlfriend's car? That ain't how it's done," Mannelli said.

Malone wanted to get back to Erica. "If you don't need me for anything I'm going back into the bedroom."

"I'll clean up in the garage," Weidt said.

The three men walked back into the apartment. Weidt and Mannelli headed for the door, and Malone moved off toward the bedroom. The two lieutenants had climbed the three steps leading into the marble-walled foyer when Mannelli turned suddenly and roared at the back of Malone's head. "Someone is sending you a message in the clear. And it's signed Eisinger."

When they had left the apartment Malone telephoned the Squad and told Stern what had happened. He gave him Erica's telephone number and told him that he was going to stay with her. Then he hung up and went into the bedroom.

Erica was sitting up on the bed with her head resting against the brass-railed headboard and her arms folded tightly across her chest. She was staring unseeingly at a television quiz show. He went over to her and took her hand. Lowering himself he said, "You okay?"

She looked at him wearing a wan smile. "That body had something to do with us. Doesn't it, Daniel?"

He took a deep breath and sighed. "It was a warning. For me. Back off a certain case or . . ."

"They'll kill *me*."

"Nobody is going to kill anybody. I want you to go away for a while. A few days, until I can get to the bottom of this."

She looked away from him. "I think that that might be best." She was crying.

The late tour was coming out of the stationhouse when Malone returned later that night. He walked into the squad

245

room and found one of the desks covered with white containers of Chinese food. He picked up a cold egg roll on his way into his office. Three detectives were present. Two were hunched over typewriters and the third was purring over the telephone to a female who obviously was not his wife. The detective using the telephone saw Malone and clamped his hand over the mouthpiece. "Some guy has been calling you every hour on the hour. Wouldn't give his name."

Not acknowledging the message, Malone walked into his office and slammed the door. He wanted to be alone and think. That body had reinforced his belief that he was dealing with ruthless, brutal men, and he was apprehensive for Erica and himself.

He took out the bottle and poured a stiff drink into a dirty cup. Whoever had done in Banna had done the world a favor, but he knew that that was not the intent behind Ismail al Banna's sudden demise. He was relieved to know that Erica was now safe. He had driven her to her sister's house in Washington Heights and had extracted a promise from her: she would call no one and tell no one where she was.

The liquor had just started to have its relaxing effect when the voice piped from the other side of the door. "That guy is on four."

It was only a frightened whisper. Malone could hear no background noises, but he did pick up on a slight accent.

"I was in the garage. I saw them."

Malone had pad and pencil ready. "How many were there?"

"Three. And I recognized one of them."

"Who was he?"

"Mr. Malone, I'm afraid. I have a family. I live in the same building and know Miss Sommers. She's a lovely lady but I just can't become involved in anything like this. You have to understand."

"How did you know my name and where to contact me?"

"I heard policemen talking in the elevator. They said that

246

her boyfriend was a lieutenant who worked in Chinatown. Malone was his name, they said."

"I can promise you anonymity. No one will ever know we've talked."

A long pause. "If you're willing to meet me I'll tell you what I saw. But you must promise . . ."

"I do. Tell me when and where."

"Tomorrow night at eleven. Drive east on the LIE and get off at Glen Cove Road. I'll be waiting for you on the service road."

"Why so far out of the city?"

"I have a business in Roosevelt Field. We close at nine. By the time I clean up and get ready for the morning it'll be ten. I can't take any chance of us being seen together."

"I'll see you tomorrow night at eleven."

They clicked off.

Across the river in Brooklyn, Achmed Hamed's eyes were fixed on the barrel of dried dates in the rear of his Atlantic Avenue grocery store. He turned slowly away from the wall phone and looked into the face of the man standing next to him, studying the crazed eyes for a signal. "Was it all right?" he asked in an unsure voice.

Stanislaus slapped Hamed's shoulder. "You did real good, my friend. Real good."

On the other side of the street directly in front of the Dime Savings Bank two detectives slouched in the front seat of a taxi. "Wonder what brought him to that place?" a heavy-set detective said to his partner.

"Who the fuck cares," the other detective said, closing his eyes and dozing.

16

It was a black-tie affair.

Crystal chandeliers sparkled over the dining room of the Algonquin Club where judicial dignitaries had gathered to pay honor to retiring Judge Michael X. Brynes. Judge Aristotle Niarxos tapped the sterling-silver bread knife against the linen tablecloth, his stare fixed attentively on the podium, not hearing a word. His mind was consumed with the image of Markell's plump body.

A burst of applause rousted him back.

Judge Brynes was making his way to the speaker's stand. The old man firmed his stance by gripping the edge. He started to speak. Will the senile bastard ever end, Niarxos thought.

Niarxos was a distinguished-looking man in his late fifties. He hated testimonial dinners. Their redeeming feature was that they gave him a solid excuse to get out of the house. The invitation was always left in some convenient place where his wife was sure to see it. Over the years he had learned to employ every weapon at his disposal to further his quest for the perfect woman. His search had ended two years ago when he hired Markell Sphiros as his secretary.

After thirty minutes of dreadfully boring reminiscences, Judge Michael X. Brynes stepped from the podium, tears in his eyes. Niarxos leaped to his feet, applauding. A cue to leave. He backed away from the table and quickly left the room.

"I say, governor, will ya sign a search warrant for an old war veteran?"

Niarxos wrenched, staring at the form looming at him from the shadows.

"Gus? This is one helluva time to ask me to sign a warrant. I'm on my way to see a lady. Catch me in the morning. In my chambers."

Heinemann moved up to him and whispered, "We've always done right by you, your honor. Your name was never mentioned during Knapp. Now we need one."

Niarxos cleared his throat and mimed surrender. He thrust his hand into his tuxedo and removed half glasses.

Heinemann said, "Have all the papers right here. Made them out myself." He proffered the documents with a pleading smile. "How is Markell?"

"She's waiting for me," Niarxos said, scanning the legal papers.

Heinemann said, "She is one helluva woman. Always reminded me of a girl I met when I parachuted into Greece during the big war. OSS. Difficult times."

Niarxos looked at him over his half glasses. "I suppose if my name was Goldberg you would tell me you fought with the Haganah."

Heinemann lifted his shoulders and let them fall slowly.

Niarxos returned to the papers, scanning, picking out main points.

The judge's mouth became a straight line. "Have illegal wires been employed in this case?"

Heinemann feigned shock. "Your honor?"

"Your probable cause is weak."

Heinemann did not answer. He knew how to play the game. Always give the man in the black robe an exit.

"Why the request for the 'No Knock'?"

"We have reasonable cause to believe that the suspect has weapons concealed therein."

Niarxos flipped to the last page, turning the others over and under. He took out a ballpoint pen and snapped the button down, holding it over the line requiring his signature. He read the last paragraph and affixed his name to the order. "This warrant will have to be executed within ten days."

"May Allah grant you ten erections this night."

The judge laughed. "I'll settle for one."

17

FRIDAY, *July 3* . . . **Morning**

Morris Dunbar had gotten four feet inside the reception area when he stopped in his tracks. He blanched. The muscles in his stomach and arms tightened and his eyes grew wide with alarm. He reached up and took the cigar from his mouth, swallowed hard, and then, forcing a smile, rushed to greet his unexpected visitor.

The reason for Morris Dunbar's sudden discomfort was sitting in a canvas-backed chair flipping through the latest issue of *Yachting*.

Lt. Dan Malone, NYPD.

Dunbar had met Malone eighteen years before. A chance encounter in Tompkins Park, Brooklyn.

Patrolman Malone was working a four-to-twelve on Patrol Post 4. The post condition card said to give special attention to park lavatories. Prevent the congregation of sexual perverts. Malone checked the bunker-type bathrooms every hour.

It was September and the leaves were beginning to give hint of yellows, oranges, and umbers. Around 6:45, Patrolman Malone strolled into the foul-smelling bathroom. He saw that all the spaces in front of the urinals were empty. The doors to the toilet cubicles were open, except for the last one. Keeping his distance, he bent dog fashion and peeked under the closed door. He saw a pair of feet, crumpled trousers, and a shopping bag between splayed legs. Grinning knowingly, he got up and padded his way into the next-to-last cubicle. He stood up on the seat and peered over the partition.

Morris Dunbar was seated on the throne. Standing before him with his legs hidden inside the shopping bag, and his naked and erect penis in Morris Dunbar's mouth, was a seventeen-year-old black boy.

"Hi guys," Malone said, waving down.

Morris Dunbar took short deep breaths, trying to shake the panicky feeling that suddenly engulfed his confidence. Right hand extended, he went to greet his old friend.

Malone tossed the magazine on the glass table and got up to accept the proffered hand of the president of Dunbar Research Associates.

Malone saw the same weak smile that always appeared whenever he made one of his infrequent visits. No arrests were made that long-ago night in Tompkins Park. Malone's wife, Helen, had been waiting for him to finish his tour. They had planned to make love, and then go to Luciano's for late night pasta and wine, afterward return home and love again. He had had no intention of giving that up for a bullshit collar that he knew would end up with a hundred-dollar fine, and a "don't do it again boys" reprimand from some liberal judge, so he cut the lovers loose with a warning to keep their private lives out of the public domain.

Morris Dunbar had almost collapsed with relief. Hyperventilating at the thought of not being arrested, he had thrust his business card into the patrolman's hand. "Anytime I can ever be of any assistance, please come by and see me."

Morris Dunbar had always regretted that momentary lapse of discretion. Every few years the cop who knew his secret would appear to collect on his noncancelable marker.

"Morris, ol' friend, need a small favor," Malone said, looking into the man's troubled face.

"Dan? Anytime. You know that," said Morris Dunbar, throwing a welcoming arm around the policeman and steering him into his plushly carpeted office with large tinted windows.

Malone looked into the owllike face with the spirals of smoke rising past the nose. "If I were to give you the names of four men, would you be able to give me a financial profile on them?"

Dunbar drew on his cigar. "Got their Social Security numbers?"

Malone looked puzzled. "Are they necessary?"

Morris Dunbar guffawed. "You kiddin'? They're everything. You can't open a checking account, rent a car, buy a house, or have a telephone installed without listing your Social Security number." Morris Dunbar puckered his lips and blew thick smoke rings. "They're our identification papers and the backbone of my business."

"I'm in a hurry, Morris."

"There are other ways. What are the names?"

Malone handed him a folded sheet of paper. Dunbar read aloud. "Whitney Zangline, Edwin Bramson, Joseph Stanislaus, and Charles Kelly. How do they make their living?"

"They're policemen," breathed Malone.

Morris Dunbar shot him a look and then swiveled his eyes back to the paper. "I think that we will be able to manage without their numbers. They're uncommon names, except for Kelly. Might not have much luck with that one. Our data banks are cross referenced by name, pedigree, occupation, and Social Security number."

Dunbar Research Associates was the seventh largest credit-research company in the country. It occupied the twenty-first, -second, and -third floors of a modern building on Madison Avenue. The twenty-third floor was divided into glass-partitioned spaces that were filled with intricate electronic equipment and tape consoles with constantly spinning and jerking oversized spools.

Morris Dunbar led him into a windowless alcove with four rows of desks with computer consoles mounted on each one. Next to each desk was an electronic printer. Workers were busy typing coded information into data banks.

As they entered the alcove, a thin Oriental man rushed over to them. "Good morning, Mr. Dunbar. May I help you?"

Morris Dunbar shook his head and quickly turned to his visitor. "No thank you, John." He moved to a console and sat down, motioning for Malone to drag a chair over.

Malone looked at the lime-green screen. "How does this thing work?"

Morris Dunbar said, "Each employee who is authorized to extract information has an identification number. The employee types in his I.D. and the computer gives him permission to proceed. When the go-ahead signal is flashed, the employee inputs the access code to the desired data bank. If he is authorized to enter that particular bank the computer will acknowledge his entry by flashing an entry code onto the upper-left-hand corner of the screen. After the access code is displayed, the desired information is then inputted and the input button depressed. And that is all there is to it."

Malone said, "Each data bank has its own access code?"

"That's correct. You must input the right code to enter each bank. Financial, Medical, Sexual, Property, Criminal. Only certain employees are authorized to enter all the banks."

"Do your banks cover the entire country?"

"No. Only the tri-state area. If a client should want information on an individual who at one time lived in California, we have to type in the access code for California. Our computer is then hooked into a California data bank. It's a subscription service. Like Home Box Office."

A grin came over Malone's face. "Do the civil libertarians know you have these capabilities?"

Dunbar replied in a mocking tone of voice. "Fuck 'em where they breathe." He pushed his chair closer to the console. "I'll need as much pedigree information as you have."

The next fifteen minutes were spent listing every scrap of

information that Malone knew about the four policemen. Dunbar listed each trait in a column under the man's name.

"I'll start with Whitney Zangline. I don't think there are too many Zanglines around." Morris Dunbar typed in his I.D. and depressed the input button. The letters RM flashed in the lower-right-hand corner of the screen. He inputted the proper access code. DALL NYSP flashed onto the upper-left-hand corner of the screen. He inputted the pedigree and depressed the PA 1 button. A line of symbols appeared across the top of the screen: RNAM, NYSP, ORI/NY U3U30FI. The PF 3 button was then depressed and a display peeled onto the console, limning the screen with the financial profile of Whitney Zangline, a white male, age 55, assistant chief, NYPD.

Whitney Zangline was a wealthy man.

Morris Dunbar chewed the end of his cigar. Tawny snippets of tobacco splotched his lips and his teeth were coated with a brownish slime. He turned sideways. "Want a copy?"

"Yes," Malone said, thinking that cops will never learn. After the Gross and Knapp investigations into police corruption you'd think that they would hide their money. But they don't. Dishonest men never think that they will be found out.

Morris Dunbar inputted the print code and depressed the PF 3 button. The spoked wheels on the sides of the printer sprang to life, churning out an endless stream of four-ply paper.

Whitney Zangline was a remarkably wealthy man.

Eighteen minutes later Malone was armed with computer printouts on Edwin Bramson and Joseph Stanislaus. They, too, were amazingly well off. The profile on Charles Kelly, patrolman, NYPD, remained a secret. Dunbar said that he needed a DOB or the Social Security number. Nevertheless, Malone assumed that Kelly, too, was a wealthy man.

Tourist buses were disgorging their cargoes on Elizabeth Street when he arrived back at the stationhouse. He paused

255

in front of the steps to watch them. Wide-eyed and country clean they rushed off the buses into the waiting arms of the hawkers. Package tours, the theater, and egg rolls for sixty bucks, he thought, turning and entering the stationhouse.

Malone waved to the desk officer as he made for the stairway. He spotted Starling Johnson in the muster room talking to P.O. O'Day. He smiled and took the stairs two at a time.

Inspector Zambrano was standing by the window with his hands thrust into his pockets, rocking on his heels. He looked troubled. Malone crossed the squad room to him. "What's up?"

"I had lunch yesterday with my brother-in-law, the one in Audits and Accounts."

"And?"

"Whaddaya know about the financial administration of the Job?"

"I get paid every second Friday."

Zambrano turned and gripped the mesh window covering. "That's just about what most cops know." He launched into a long-winded dissertation on police department finances.

Before the end of each fiscal year the PC is required to submit the operating budget for the new year. Most of the lines are mandated expenses like salaries, rents, maintenance of equipment, telephone, electricity, heat, and gasoline. A cash fund is maintained to supply buy money, pay for sting operations, informers, and for travel expenses for members required to leave the city on official business. Whenever cash is needed, proper authorization accompanied with cash vouchers are submitted to Audits and Accounts. No commander is authorized to make purchases on his own. Everything must go through the deputy commissioner in charge of administration.

Malone said, "So? What has that got to do with the Eisinger caper?"

Zambrano faced him. "Zangline is running his own goddamn corporation. My brother-in-law told me that SOD has

256

its own fund which Zangline controls. He is able to buy whatever he wants and he uses the fund to pay. That running track you saw in the SOD compound was built and paid for out of this special fund. He just purchased one hundred Uzi submachine guns and twenty-five silencers."

Malone said, "Where does the money come from?"

"Zangline draws checks on the account of the Simonson Optical Division. A Netherlands Antilles corporation. The checks clear through the Willemsteal Bank of Curaçao."

Malone let out a long, low whistle. "Simonson Optical Division. SOD, the acronym for the Special Operation Division."

"Sounds like that, doesn't it," Zambrano said.

"Any idea where the money comes from?"

"Not an iota."

"If Zangline is into something illegal, why would he have to use the department to make purchases?"

"What better way to hide something. And there is Title Eighteen, the United States Code. Under the Gun Control Act of 1968 corporations and individuals are prohibited from owning machine guns without obtaining federal permits and paying a special tax. Silencers are contraband except for government agencies and the police. And"—he shook a finger at him—"police departments do not pay taxes. A lot of money can be saved by making purchases through the department."

Malone took out the computer printouts and shoved them at him. "Read these."

They told a story of policemen without debts. Of savings accounts far in excess of earnings, of real-estate holdings, private schools, of automobiles without chattel mortgages; policemen with paychecks without any deductions for the Municipal Credit Union. Zambrano handed the printouts back, a scowl of disgust on his face. "What is your next move?"

"I have a command appearance with the chief of Op at five P.M. after which I have to go . . ." His voice trailed off and he moved across the room to where O'Shaughnessy was typing a five.

"Go and what?" Zambrano said, wry.

"Aw, nothing," Malone said lamely, looking over O'Shaughnessy's shoulder.

"Go and what, Lieutenant?"

Malone's eyes narrowed and his face became hard.

Zambrano said, "There ain't no stars in this job, Dan. We're all character actors."

Reluctantly he told him of the telephone call and his 11 P.M. rendezvous at Glen Cove Road.

"And you're going?" Zambrano said.

"Uh-huh."

"Alone?"

"Uh-huh."

"That's real clever. I assume that it just might have crossed your mind that you'll be driving into a setup."

"I thought about it."

"Well to put your mind at ease, I'm going with you."

Malone started to protest. Zambrano shot out a hand in front of him. "Save your breath. That's an order."

Zambrano walked over and looked down at O'Shaughnessy.

The detective wore an angry expression and was typing as though he had a life-long vendetta going with the typewriter. "What got into him?" Zambrano asked Malone.

Malone shrugged his shoulders. "He has a personal problem."

O'Shaughnessy looked up at the inspector. "Did you ever stop to realize that life ain't nothing but a shit sandwich?"

Zambrano folded his arms across his chest and pondered the remark. "Well. I'll tell you somethin' young fellow. You might as well be happy, 'cause no one gives a fuck if you're not."

The tripod of the one-on-one camera straddled the diaphragm on the bathroom floor. O'Shaughnessy peered into the wide lens, centering the crosshairs of the viewfinder on the fingerprint. In the bedroom, Johnson was spreading black powder over the top of a highboy. Knees bent eye level, he carefully spread the adhesive powder with the plumed end of a dusting brush. He could see the powder clinging to the friction ridges, making them visible against the wood background. He returned the brush to its assigned place inside the fingerprint kit and removed three pieces of rubber lifting tape. After he peeled off the celluloid covering from the adhesive side, he carefully placed the tape over the latent fingerprint and pressed it evenly and firmly to the surface, taking care not to shift its position. Snipping one end, he gently peeled the tape away from the surface. Examining the lift, he was able to distinguish three fingers—a forefinger, middle, ring.

He placed the tape inside a plastic envelope and clipped it inside the kit.

A partial palm print and several more fingerprints were lifted off the highboy. After all the lifts were secured in the kit, he reached into the bottom and took out a battery-operated hand vacuum and cleaned all traces of powder from the dresser and floor.

Malone was leaning against the bedroom wall pondering the dimensions of the queen-size bed. He was deeply uncomfortable at the thought of Sara Eisinger making it with Stanislaus on that bed. To his mind, it just did not ring true. A woman reared in the laws of Abraham, a woman who cleansed herself in the prescribed way, would not hop into the feathers with a gentile cop. The more he thought about it, the more it bothered him.

As Malone and his men worked silently inside Stanislaus's apartment, a telephone repair truck was parked outside the SOD compound. Stanislaus, Bramson, and Kelly had been followed into the compound.

If the trio left the compound the detectives inside the repair truck would radio a warning that would be passed over the phone in the apartment to Malone.

The search warrant was in Malone's pocket, officially, unexecuted. He wanted to wait until the fingerprints lifted from the apartment were compared with those lifted from the Eisinger crime scene. If there was a match he would return and execute the warrant officially. The proverbial cat should remain in the bag as long as possible, or nails in the coffin, as Epstein had said.

One Police Plaza is an orange brick mass that resembles a Rubik's cube on stilts. It is a building renowned for its conference rooms. There are small ones with small tables, medium-size ones with medium-size tables, and still larger ones with great tables. There are no executive toilets or dining rooms to differentiate the proletariat and bourgeoisie. There are only the conference rooms.

It was into one of the larger rooms that a female sergeant with a head of thick red hair ushered Malone at five o'clock that afternoon. "The chief will be with you in a minute or two," she said, casting a pitying look at him.

White Formica paneled the walls and red cushioned chairs were arranged around the oval-shaped table. Photographs of former Chiefs of Operations hung on the walls. He moved from frame to frame looking at the dour faces. When he had first come on the Job the Chief of Op was called the Chief Inspector. A lot of changes, a lot of years.

He went over to the window and pushed a vertical blind aside. Far below the evening rush hour was congealing into the usual traffic jam. The FDR Drive was packed bumper-to-bumper, cars spilled off the Brooklyn Bridge blocking Worth Street, and the noise of traffic reached up and penetrated the thermopane. He could see the people rushing into the subway under the archway of the Municipal Building, steeling themselves for the perilous journey home.

The rattle of a doorknob caused him to turn. Joe Mannelli was standing in the doorway, surveying him coldly, his face expressionless, the eyes wide and sullen.

Neither man spoke.

Malone went over to the table and sat down, his gaze riveted on the man in the doorway. Without uttering one word, Mannelli pivoted to the left and slammed the door. So that was how it was to be—a stress interview. Do things to fray his nerves; keep him waiting. Well, two could play at the same game.

At 6:48 P.M. Chief of Operations McQuade entered the room with a manila folder snug under his arm. He glanced at the nodding lieutenant and moved quickly to his place at the head of the table.

Malone opened his eyes, saw him, and eased his back to attention.

The four gilt stars on his shoulders glittered as brightly as the rims of McQuade's gold-rimmed glasses. "So, Lieutenant, we meet at last. I have been hearing your name quite a lot these days."

Malone cleared his throat. "I hope favorably, Chief."

McQuade opened the folder and removed a stack of evaluation reports. He read from them. "Lieutenant Malone is a loyal and competent commander. He is forthright and tenacious in carrying out his responsibilities and is rated above average."

Malone listened with interest.

McQuade read the summaries of eight evaluations. He then tapped them together and returned them to the folder, flipping the cover closed.

McQuade gazed impassively down the length of the table. "It appears that your superiors in the Detective Division consider you a loyal and competent subordinate. Do you agree with their assessment?"

Malone saw the rancor in the tightly pressed lips and was wary. "I've always tried to do my job," he said.

"Have you now? Tell me, Lieutenant. How would you define the adjective *loyal?*"

Malone thought of a response. "Fidelity to the job and its bosses."

McQuade slapped his hands down with such force that his eyeglasses popped off his face. He was on his feet, screaming. "Then why the hell are you trying to destroy this department? Mannelli warned you. Zangline warned you. But no! You persist in blunderbussing through the Job, raking up all kinds of shit. You listen and listen good. Lay off this department or I'll ruin you. I'll flop you out of the Bureau so fast that your eyeballs will dance. You got that, Malone?"

Malone looked him in the eye. "I won't dump the Eisinger case."

McQuade was furious. "Do you really think you're so goddamn perfect? Have you ever made a score? Ate on the arm? Nobody in this job is untouchable. When we want you, your ass is ours." He spilled the contents of the folder and started to shuffle through the pile. He snatched up a sheet of paper and waved it at him. "The statute of limitations for a felony is five years. But we both know that there is no statute in the Trial Room. It's a Kangaroo Court. Everyone on the Job knows that. I have here information that you arranged for an out-of-state abortion ten years ago. You committed a felony."

Mannelli, you dirty son-of-a-bitch, Malone thought.

McQuade continued. "I could serve you with charges and specifications. Conduct unbecoming an officer and prejudicial to the good order and efficiency of the department. And, I can guarantee the outcome. You would be dismissed."

Malone forced a smile. "A stunt like that would never stand under judicial review and you know it."

McQuade leaned forward. "Maybe it would, and maybe it wouldn't. Whenever you go into court it's a crap shoot. And, a legal fight could cost you twenty-five large, out of your own pocket. Line organizations do not pick up the tab for appeals from administrative decisions. Can you afford that kind of money, Lieutenant?''

Malone nodded grimly and got up.

''I will tell you when this meeting is over,'' McQuade shouted.

Malone continued toward the door, sweat trickling under his armpits. He was reaching for the knob when McQuade's hoarse voice caused him to turn.

''You just won't stop, will you?''

''I can't,'' he said quietly.

The expression on McQuade's face became benign. He patted the chair next to him. ''Come here and sit down.''

Malone hesitated, unsure.

''Please.''

The careful tread back was filled with reflections. It ain't easy going up against the system. Many have tried it; few have succeeded.

McQuade was wiping his forehead with a handkerchief when Malone lowered himself next to him. ''You think that all the life-and-death decisions are made in the street,'' he said, heaving to one side and tucking the white cotton cloth into his back pocket. ''Well, let me tell you that they're not. Don't think for one minute that working in this pressure cooker is any bargain. The right wants us to kill the niggers and spicks and arm the cops with bazookas and flame throwers. The left wants us to countenance anarchy, riot, and murder. The politicians see the size of the police budget and salivate. They want lateral entry for their cronies.'' His right hand was chopping the air. ''No more captains and lieutenants. They want civilian managers in charge of police operations. A pork barrel like the Board of Ed. Just take a look at what's happening in the Job today. We have cops with yellow sheets. Cops who cannot communicate in the English language. We're forced to hire females. Some of them don't weigh a hundred pounds soaking wet; they can't reach the accelerators of radio cars; don't have the physical strength to

263

pull the trigger of their service revolvers. We were forced to lower the height requirement to accommodate women and Hispanics. We're becoming a department of goddamn dwarfs. Juggling interest groups and somehow keeping the department in one piece is no easy task." He picked up his eyeglasses and started to tap them against his teeth, his crafty eyes holding him. "Now I am going to tell you why you must drop the Eisinger case." He moved close and confided, "This department is involved in a covert operation that is so sensitive that its exposure would mean the end of the Job as we know it. And that, Lieutenant, is all that I can tell you. You are going to have to trust me."

Malone was cold. He fought a shiver. "Zangline is running this operation?"

"Yes."

"And what do we do about Eisinger, Andrea St. James, and the two kids who died with her on the Van Wyck. Just forget about them?"

McQuade steepled his hands under his chin. "I give you my personal guarantee that no member of this department had anything to do with those deaths."

Malone covered his face with his hands and rubbed tired pupils. "Exactly what do you want me to do?" he said, dropping knuckles to the table.

"Forget any connection this department has to the Eisinger caper. Don't be a party to the destruction of this great department."

A tired man nodded his assent.

McQuade sighed relief. "Good. You don't have the money, do you?"

Malone knew that this particular piece of police argot referred to the designation of a detective supervisor as a commander of detectives and carried with it a five-thousand-dollar yearly increment.

"No, I don't."

"I'm going to put you in for the money."

264

A bribe by any other name is still a bribe, Malone thought. Aloud, "Thank you, Chief."

Two things had caught his attention when he examined the fingerprint card. The first was the biting smell of death impregnated in the fibers of the paper itself. The second was the empty pedigree boxes on the top. Blocked across the head of the form was: HOMICIDE, SARA EISINGER.

The digital impressions looked like a worn parchment of loops and whorls with big uneven spaces where the skin was gone. They had cleaned her fingers with xyline but the flesh was rotten and flabby. So they cut off the tips of her fingers and soaked them in a 15 percent solution of formaldehyde to harden the ridges. Then they took them out and inked and rolled them. Poor Sara. Her only legacy was a filing formula deduced by counting her ridges and tracing her whorls:

$$4 \ 0 \ 5\text{UIOI} \ 12$$
$$\text{I} \ 17\text{WIOO}$$

She no longer had a name. Only a formula. Poor dead Sara.

The Identification Section was on the fifth floor. Before he kept his appointment with McQuade, Malone had delivered the latent prints lifted from Stanislaus's apartment to a friend in the I.D. section. "Need a favor, ol' buddy."

That had been at 4:20 P.M.

Now he left the Chief of Op, pushed through the heavy fire-exit door, and entered the stairwell, a spiral of metal steps that wound down through a vast open shaft. He needed to vent his rage. "The mother is going to get me the money," he said angrily, rushing down the steps.

The DOA fingerprint form, the lifts from the crime scene, and the blowups of the fingerprints from Stanislaus's apartment were clamped together on a comparison board back at his office. Black lines indicated the similar points of compari-

265

son: a dot, a bifurcation, an abrupt ending ridge, a short ridge, a meeting of two ridges, a core, a delta.

The prints off the plastic case and diaphragm matched Eisinger's left thumb and forefinger. There were eighteen points of comparison. The prints taken off the highboy matched up with those lifted at the crime scene. Fourteen points of comparison.

Malone had just hammered some more nails into a coffin.

18

FRIDAY, *July 3* . . . **Evening**

A hooker pushed away from the building on Crescent Street and walked over to the car. She stopped a few feet away and began to scan the interior. She saw no radio under the dashboard; no official forms scattered over the rear seat; no coffee containers with the lids on. Her street-wise eyes went to the driver. Just another john who dashed out for a pack of cigarettes and a quart of milk, she decided. She ambled over and smiled.

"Hi, sugar. You goin' out?"

"How much for a blow job?"

"Twenty, honey."

"Make it ten."

"Fifteen and I'll give you a real good one."

"Okay."

She pranced around the front of the car to the passenger side. She hesitated and shot a look over the top of the car at another strolling prostitute. Her "sister" saw her signal and nodded. The license plate number and a description of the john had been noted. Street insurance against freaks.

She jerked the door open and slid inside.

Det. Patrick O'Shaughnessy handed her fifteen dollars.

"Go down Crescent and turn into Forty-fourth Street," she directed. "Park in front of a truck and then back your car up against it." She put the fifteen dollars in a large pocketbook and removed a handful of tissues. She placed the bag on

267

the floor and locked it between her ankles. Sliding next to him, she draped her left arm around his shoulder and with her right hand started to circle his groin.

"Hmmm. It's nice and big," she said, working the zipper down.

O'Shaughnessy made a quick check. All the buttons were down. The motor was running and the window on the driver's side was cracked inches from the top.

She cupped the tissues in the palm of her right hand and moved her mouth down to meet his body.

Fifteen minutes later her head was still bobbing, the tissues unused. She stopped and looked up.

"You been drinking, honey?"

"No." He felt disgusted.

"Well, sugar. I can't make you come. If you want me to continue, it's going to cost you another ten. Can't spend all night on one trick."

"I'm not in the mood anyway." He pushed her head away, arched upward, and hoisted his zipper.

"Sure, sugar. I understand," she said, returning the tissues to her pocketbook.

He let her out of the car at Hunter and Twenty-seventh. He felt awful. He felt angry, inadequate, lonely, and disgusted. He pounded the steering wheel.

"I can't even get it off with a nigger hooker," he cried.

The traffic light on Twenty-seventh and Bridge Plaza South turned red. Garishly dressed hookers lolled at the corners, beckoning to motorists. Transvestites swaggered up and down Twenty-seventh Street. Standing in the shadows were the pimps, their hard eyes fixed on the hookers they had on the charge.

"I'm right down on their level," he cried, violently shaking the wheel.

The light changed to green.

Suddenly he couldn't breathe. His hands were clammy and he felt nauseated. He tugged at his shirt. He had driven halfway across Bridge Plaza when a bolt of pain struck. He felt a wave of agony in his left arm. He clutched at his chest and gasped for air.

Startled motorists wrenched their wheels to avoid his car as it veered across Bridge Plaza. O'Shaughnessy's automobile jumped the curb, careened along the sidewalk, and plowed through the glass façade of a luncheonette.

The pain was gone. Everything was black and still.

He and Zambrano had just about finished their lasagna when Gino came up to their table and told Malone he had a phone call. It was Bo Davis. "Pat is in the emergency room of Elmhurst General."

"O'Shaughnessy, Patrick," Malone shouted to the woman inside the reception cubicle.

"Down the hall and to your right," she said, leaning out and pointing.

They rushed along the crowded corridor, threading their way past the miseries of the day. Malone banged through a pair of double doors with a thick rubber apron and plunged into the cardiac emergency ward. A black male nurse with muscles pushing against his white nylon uniform blocked his path. "You are not allowed in here, gentlemen."

Malone dug out his shield. "One of my men was brought in here," he said and gave O'Shaughnessy's name.

"They are in with him now," the nurse said. He pointed to a door with a small window in the center.

The two policemen walked over and looked through the glass. The room was divided into private cubicles by curtains. O'Shaughnessy lay on a gurney, his feet over the edge. Tubes ran from his body up to plastic bags. Wires fed from his arm and chest into a series of pulsating monitors. A group of doctors and nurses hovered over him and fought to save his life.

Malone composed himself. For some reason he watched O'Shaughnessy's big toe, expecting it to move. It never did.

"For all his macho bullshit he was a lonely man," Malone said, backing away.

"He shouldn't have lived like he did after hours," Zambrano said.

A voice called to them. "You guys from the Squad?" A hatless police officer had pushed his way inside and was standing behind them. He was in his twenties, with black, curly hair, big bulging brown eyes, and a mouth full of horsy teeth. The three top buttons of his shirt were open. A gold rope chain coiled around his neck and a ball of gold pierced his left ear.

Zambrano showed him his shield. The policeman took hold of the inspector's wrist and pulled him close, examining the shield. "Hey, man. That's cool. I've never seen an inspector's up close before. I really dig the big bird on top."

Malone turned and swallowed a smile. Zambrano snapped back his hand and shook his head with disbelief.

The cop said, "We invoiced his gun and shield in the One-fourteen. We did everything we could for him."

"Thanks," Malone said.

"We were able to get his home telephone number off his ten card. His wife told the desk officer that she didn't give a damn what happened to him."

"They were getting a divorce," Malone said.

"Another one down the tubes," the cop said. "I've been in the batter's box twice."

Zambrano looked at his watch and nudged Malone. "Gotta go. We got an appointment on the LIE."

Malone went back for a final look. A nurse was bending over the gurney adjusting a tube. Her uniform rode up in the back. She had long legs and nice thighs. She was top heavy. Pat would have given her a solid eight.

They sped east on the Long Island Expressway in an unmarked police car. Saplings lined the slopes and grass glistened with dew. A full moon lingered in a star-filled sky.

The next green illuminated sign they saw read DOUGLASTON PARKWAY. Five minutes later they passed another sign: NASSAU COUNTY. The panorama changed. The massive housing complexes of Queens were gone, as well as the constant glow of the city. The night was darker and more ominous.

At Shelter Rock Road there was a stone overpass. A black car hid behind its south base, parked uphill on the sweep of land. Joseph Stanislaus and Edwin Bramson had unwittingly shaken off Harrigan's men by making a precautionary U-turn in the middle of the Queensborough Bridge. They sat in the front seat of the black car and checked each passing automobile with a night-vision handscope. They would recognize a department vehicle, and they both knew Malone. They had seen him at the SOD compound.

Malone glanced sideways. "There was really no need for you to tag along."

"I enjoy playing cop. My time in the Job is almost over and I'd like to get in a few more licks before I leave."

"When do you have to put your papers in?"

"I have three more years," he said.

"You have a lot of friends on the Job. They'll take care of you."

Zambrano roared with laughter. He leaned close to Malone. "When you're in, you're a guest; when you're out, you're a pest. Remember that."

Malone scoffed. "I've heard that one from a lot of old-timers who were getting out."

Zambrano sliced the air with a karate chop. "When your time comes, walk through the door and don't look back. One fast, clean break."

"Any plans?"

"I'll more than likely end up in Florida with the rest of the retirees. Probably spend my days bullshitting about the Job

271

and taking poolside cha-cha lessons in Bermuda shorts, argyle socks, and black-laced shoes.''

''With your background and experience? Private industry will scoop you up.''

They didn't notice when the black car rolled down from behind the base of the overpass and fell in several lengths behind them.

Stanislaus picked up the walkie-talkie and transmitted a description of the unmarked car and its occupants.

Edwin Bramson was driving. ''There is someone in the car with him.''

Stanislaus said, ''That's his tough luck. Get off at the next exit and head back to the City.''

At Willis Avenue an eighteen-wheel tractor-trailer idled on the service road, its chattering diesel emitting a black cloud. Two short, muscled men sat inside the cab. Stanislaus's message had been received. The two men were watchful. Ready.

Zambrano pulled up the headrest and leaned back. ''In a way I'm glad to be getting out. The Job is really going downhill fast.''

''How so?''

''You saw that cop back in the hospital. Shirt open, no tie, a necklace around his neck, and to top it off a fucking earring stuck through his goddamn ear. Can you imagine that, a New York City cop with an earring. Next thing you know they'll be putting on rouge and eye shadow.''

Malone smiled. ''Times change. Cops aren't so uptight about being on the Job.''

''Come on, Dan. Earrings? Where the hell is the discipline?''

''It's still there. Only it's less formal.''

''That is a crock of shit and you know it. Did you hear what happened last week in the One-twelve?''

''No.''

Zambrano sat up and shifted his weight onto one side of his rump and leaned toward him. ''A late tour. Sunday going into Monday. The sergeant on patrol can't locate sector Ida-

Mary. They weren't answering his eighty-fives. The sergeant starts to mosey around the heaves. His RMP cruises into Macy's parking lot on Queens Boulevard. The building is built in the shape of a beehive with circular ramps running top to bottom. Near the roof he spots a turret light sticking up over a ramp. He tells his driver to stop and he gets out and walks over.'' Zambrano punched the dashboard. ''And what do you think the good sergeant found? He found Police Officer Debra Bowden wearing only her open uniform shirt with one leg up on the dashboard and the other hooked over the front seat. And would you like to know where her partner was? Police Officer Frank Watson.''

Malone was grinning broadly. ''Where, Inspector?''

''With his face in her muff, eating her. On duty. In a police car. And do you know what she had the balls to tell the sergeant?''

''That they were on their meal period,'' Malone cackled with laughter.

''That's right. Howd'ya know that?''

''Because that's what I would have said.''

As the two policemen talked, the tractor-trailer behind them resolutely closed the distance. When it drew parallel with the police car the driver wrenched the wheel and turned the massive cab toward the passenger door. It rammed into the police car and plowed it across the parkway, smashing it into the road divider.

''Watch out!'' Zambrano screamed, too late.

As Malone fought the wheel, the unmarked car bounced off the divider, its doors and side panels crumpled inward, and then Malone regained control. The semi continued the pursuit, its bumper homing in on the rear of the automobile.

Zambrano opened his window, thrust his revolver at the approaching beast and fired six rounds double action into the cab. The tractor-trailer backed off. Zambrano opened the cylinder and plunged out the spent rounds. He reloaded from the ammo pouch on his belt.

Every time their pursuers got close enough to ram, Malone

had been able to turn the car in the opposite direction and dart to safety. Now it was on them again, a lizard snapping its forked tongue. Malone swerved the car to the right. It was still with them, its mass casting a deadly shadow over the hood of the police car. It plowed into them. The two rear tires of the police car came off and went spinning across the highway. The car spun helplessly, its undercarriage screeching over the concrete, throwing out a fusillade of sparks. Finally it slammed into the road abutment.

"Get out!" Zambrano cried.

The door on the driver's side was crushed, the windows shattered but still in place. Malone kicked out the front window and started to climb out onto the hood. Zambrano lay back across the seat and kicked the door open. He threw himself out and got to his feet in time to face the charging monster. He turned and saw Malone crawling over the hood on all fours. Assuming a combat stance, Zambrano cocked his revolver, aimed, and fired single action at the driver.

At that precise moment in his life Nicholas Zambrano did not think of issues like life or death. His thoughts were of honor. He could hear his father calling to him. "Nicholas, conduct your life with honor. We are Italians. Ours is an honorable and proud heritage."

Malone was almost off the hood when the tractor smashed into Zambrano, propelling his body off into the night. The semi continued its run, smashing into the car and hurling Malone into the air.

The tractor-trailer backed away from the smoldering wreck and stopped. Although the traffic on the expressway had been very light at the start of the battle, it was now backed up in both directions. Motorists gaped in horror, but none got out to help.

The cab's door swung open on the passenger side and Achmed Hamed, the man who had telephoned Malone at Stanislaus's behest, climbed down. He looked across the highway at the smashed body that was once Zambrano and smiled. They had done their work well. He took out a Heckler & Koch P9S pistol from his waistband and ran for the road divider. Looking over, he saw Malone's body splayed out and motionless. His right arm was bent under his chest and his left was alongside the body with palm up. The head lay in a pool of blood.

Achmed Hamed tucked the pistol back in his waistband and started to climb over the steel divider.

He knew that Stanislaus would ask him if he made sure that Malone was dead. He wanted no problems from him.

Achmed Hamed's right foot had just touched the other side of the divider when Malone whipped up, a .38 Detective Special in his right hand. He shoved the revolver at the frozen man and quick-fired three rounds. In that split second Achmed Hamed knew that he was about to die. He stared down with disbelief at the growing crimson stain. He started to claw at his shirt. He saw the three puffy holes in his stomach and slowly, against his will, corkscrewed to his knees.

Malone approached the kneeling man at the ready. He cocked his right leg and kicked the man in the face, toppling Achmed Hamed into eternal darkness.

Malone was only dimly conscious of what happened after that. He vaguely recalled leaning on the divider and firing his revolver at disappearing taillights. He could recall the warm, thick liquid seeping over his trousers and chilling his thighs as he sat cross-legged on the expressway cradling the body of Nicholas Zambrano. The smells of hot metal and blood made him vomit. He did not hear the excited CBers shouting into their sets. A parhelion of rotating lights came toward him. The taste of tears mixed with blood in his mouth. Most of all he could feel an awful sense of irreplaceable loss.

19

SATURDAY, *July 4* . . . **Morning**

Malone opened his eyes and almost cried out, conscious for the first time of pain, first in his neck and shoulder, then in his rib cage. There was an awful throbbing ache inside his head. He moved his hand out from under the sheet and let his fingertips gingerly probe the gauze. He had landed on his head, causing a long gash in the hairline.

"It took sixty-eight stitches to close you up," Gus Heinemann said in a small voice.

Malone's eyes drifted to the two men looking down at him. Heinemann and Bo Davis. He could see the concern in their faces.

"Where am I?" A dry mutter.

"Nassau Hospital," Davis said. "You're going to be all right."

"Zambrano?" Malone asked, without any hope in his voice.

Bleak expressions gave him an answer. He was seized with a consuming rage to kill, to deal out tough street justice. The detectives pretended not to notice when he brushed his arm across his face to rub his eyes dry. He forced himself up into a sitting position and cleared his throat. "Whattaya got?"

Heinemann slapped open his memo pad and began to read in laconic police prose. "Tractor-trailer found abandoned at Guinea Woods Road. Nassau County PD dusted for prints. Negative results. Vehicle reported stolen yesterday from

276

Hunts Point Market, alarm 14061-52. There were tire tracks next to the vehicle which indicate that an escape car was waiting. Nassau County PD made plaster casts of the tracks. A canvass was conducted of the motorists caught in the spill-back. The police came up with twenty-eight names and twenty-eight different descriptions. The hump you iced was I.D.'d as Achmed Hamed. He entered the country on a tourist visa from Libya on May twelfth, 1976 and pulled a Mandrake. The duty captain from the One-oh-five responded to the scene. Captain McCormick. He prepared the 'Unusual' and the 'Line of Duty Injury Report.' The 'Assault/Firearm Discharge Report' was made out. McCormick found your use of deadly physical force to be within department guidelines. The PC and the Chief of Op were on the scene." Heinemann looked up from his pad. "That's it."

Malone recalled the five that he had read from one of Harrigan's detectives. Stanislaus had visited a grocery store on Atlantic Avenue. Achmed Hamed's store. "How long have I been out?"

Davis said, "About twelve hours."

Malone groaned as he swung his legs out and over the side of the bed. He sat up, doubling over and hugging himself in a futile effort to relieve the pain. "How's Pat?" he grunted.

Davis flinched at the sight of his pain. "They think he'll make it. But the job is finished. He's gonna be surveyed out."

Malone took in a large breath and slowly and painfully hissed it out. "What else?"

Heinemann said, "You have been page one. We gave the press the usual arrests-are-imminent bullshit. You're stashed here under a phony name." He waved his hand in front of him. "No sense giving them another shot at you."

Bo Davis said, "Jake and Starling managed to get inside Stanislaus's garage and plant a beeper under his car. The Braxtons, Kelly, Bramson, and Stanislaus have been very cautious since you got hurt. They seemed to have arranged a signaling schedule at various telephone booths around the city. One of them must have gone around copying down locations and numbers.''

Malone said, ''What about the telephone outside Braxton's apartment?''

Heinemann said, ''None of them have gone near it.''

Malone stared at his feet.

Heinemann said, ''Sergeant Harrigan has taken over in your absence. He detailed us to guard you. He has the rest of the team out following suspects. I checked with him a few minutes ago. He told me that some sort of meet is going down. Aldridge Braxton, Kelly, Stanislaus, and Bramson have all hit the bricks. They're scurrying around town, keeping both eyes over their shoulders.''

''Jack is a good man,'' Malone said, easing himself off the bed.

Davis and Heinemann each took an arm and helped him.

''Where are my clothes?'' Malone said.

''You ought'na leave,'' Davis said. ''The doctor said . . .''

Malone cut him off. ''My clothes.''

Davis shrugged, as if to say You're the boss, and went over to the clothes cabinet. ''I went to your place and got some things. The clothes that you were wearing were ruined.'' Davis took out a pair of brown corduroy trousers, a white pullover, and an Irish poplin sport jacket. He bent down and picked up a pair of penny loafers and underwear.

Untying the loose-fitting hospital gown, Malone said, ''My gun and shield?''

''Vouchered at the One-oh-five,'' Heinemann said.

Stepping into his briefs was painful. He pulled them up slowly. ''Who made the notification to Zambrano's wife?''

Davis said, ''The PC and the Catholic chaplain.''

''How'd she take it?'' Malone asked.

''I hear real bad,'' Heinemann said.

Davis got on one knee and helped him on with his socks. He looked up at Malone's grimacing face. ''Erica Som-

278

mers has been calling the Squad every hour on the hour. She is really concerned about you. Naturally, we didn't tell her where you were.''

Heinemann said, ''Want me to dial her number for you?''

Malone looked at the telephone on top of the white hospital stand. ''I've got more important things to do right now.'' There was a soft, menacing lilt to his voice.

A lash of warm air slapped Aldridge Braxton's face as he stood in the middle of York Avenue waiting for a break in the traffic. He was sure that he was not being followed. When the opening presented itself, he made his way to the other side and stood on the curb checking. Even confident men do not take chances.

A stocky middle-aged man came around the corner on the other side of York Avenue. He had on pilot-type sunglasses and was carrying a yellow sun hat in his left hand. He walked in a slow, unhurried gait, like a shopper searching the window displays.

The man with the yellow sun hat came upon a florist who had taken up half the sidewalk with his wares. He bent to examine them more closely. He picked up a gloxinia and held it up in front of him admiring its luscious purple buds. He shifted his gaze to the impeccably dressed man a block away. He held the clay pot with one hand and with the other de pressed the transmit button on the walkie-talkie that was concealed inside the sun hat. ''He is walking north on York. Just past Sixty-ninth Street.''

A blue Sting Ray pulled up to the corner of Seventy-first Street facing York. The driver was in his middle thirties and had eyebrows that ran a straight line. The passenger was older and completely bald. His taut skin gave him a plastic look. The driver scowled with displeasure. ''Here he comes,'' he said into the walkie-talkie.

Jake Stern was driving the gray van while Johnson, in the

rear of the van, studied the signal motes as they bounced across the direction grid.

"How far ahead is he?" Harrigan said, as they emerged from the Brooklyn Battery Tunnel.

"About a quarter of a mile," Johnson answered.

Joseph Stanislaus came out of the tunnel on the Brooklyn side and wormed his way out of the exact-change line into a toll collector's lane.

The toll plaza was crowded. Stanislaus kept examining the faces of motorists. He had the uncomfortable sensation of being followed. He wished he had been out there on the LIE that night. Why did it have to be Zambrano and not Malone?

When he reached the toll booth he rolled down his window to show the collector his shield. "I'm on the Job. I got into the wrong lane in Manhattan and ended up here. Any chance of turning me around? My wife is waiting for me at the Vista."

The collector leaned out to look at the shield. "No problem." He walked from the booth over to the traffic cones that separated the lanes. He kicked away four cones and then halted the queue entering the tunnel from the Brooklyn side. He turned to Stanislaus and waved him to make a U-turn through the space.

"He's doubling back on us," Starling Johnson shouted, a note of alarm in his voice.

"Stop the van," Harrigan ordered. "If we come out of the tunnel now he is bound to see us. He might recognize the van. We should wait until he is back inside the tunnel."

A sudden cacophony of horns reverberated throughout the white-tiled tunnel as bumpers rear-ended bumpers.

Edwin Bramson drove his car over the George Washington Bridge and onto the Palisades Parkway. Charles Kelly was turned in the passenger seat looking out the rear window for any car that had been with them for too long a period of time.

Bramson said, "Anyone on us?"

"Don't think so," Kelly replied, not taking his eyes from the window. "There was a taxi with us for a while but he turned off at Fort Lee."

Bramson said, "There is a rest area up ahead where we can pull in. We'll take in the view and at the same time watch the road. Then just to make sure we'll drive into Nyack before we turn around. It shouldn't be too hard to spot a tail."

"Them camel humpers really fucked things up. We shoulda handled it ourselves," Kelly said.

"What we shoulda done and what we done are two different things," Bramson said, turning on some music.

A taxi exited the bridge's quickway in Fort Lee. The driver leaned over and opened the glove compartment, pulling out a radio handset. "Bird Two to Nest, K."

Inside the surveillance van Jack Harrigan plucked the microphone from the hook. "Nest. Go ahead, K."

"Subjects drove over the G.W. Bridge into Jersey. They are now proceeding north on the Palisades Parkway. Bird Two continued into Fort Lee. If I had stayed with them much longer they would have made me for sure."

Harrigan toed the metal floor. "Where are Birds One and Two, K?"

"Both waiting on the New York side of the bridge. We figured that whatever was going to go down would go down in New York. It stands to reason that once they feel safe they are going to double back."

"I hope you're right, K." The frequency went quiet. Then Harrigan transmitted. "Bird Two, head back to our side of the bridge and ten-eighty-five Birds One and Three. When you reestablish contact with them I want you to use the leapfrog, but be sure to change the 'close contact car' frequently. I don't want to take any chances on losing these guys, K."

"Ten-four." The detective in the taxi returned the handset and slammed the lid shut.

Harrigan transmitted, "Nest to Birds One and Three. Did you read my last transmission, K?"

From inside the telephone repair truck that was parked on the New York side of the toll plaza came the transmission: "Bird One, ten-four."

Near the entrance of the FDR Drive a gypsy cab was stopped with its hood up. A black man was leaning under checking the carburetor. He picked up the paper bag that was lying on top of the battery and moved it toward his lips, "Bird Two, ten-four."

Starling Johnson did not permit his eyes to stray from the monitor. "Do you really think they'll come back into the City?" he asked Harrigan.

The sergeant's face was grim. With Malone in the hospital and Zambrano dead the whole weight of the case was on his back. The fact that they were going up against other cops was finally beginning to frighten him.

"They'll double back." He tried to sound convinced. Harrigan absent-mindedly depressed the transmit button several times and then snapped the microphone up to his mouth.

"Birds Four and Five, what are your locations, K?"

The detective with the plastic face inside the Sting Ray transmitted. "Bird Four is proceeding north on York. Just passing Seventy-fourth Street. Subject in view."

"Bird Five on foot, going north on York. Subject now turning into Seven-six Street."

An elegantly dressed woman looked with mild curiosity at the pot-bellied man jogging York Avenue and yelling at a yellow sun hat.

"Turn south. West. Lay back. We're too close. The signals are too strong. He is heading over to the East Side."

Starling Johnson sat before the tracking monitors in the van, the bombardier directing the ship, calling out coordinates.

Harrigan shouted out to Jake Stern, "If you can see him, we are too close."

"He's not in view," Stern piped, suddenly filled with a disquieting sense of insecurity at the sight of a bus gridlocking Tenth Avenue and blocking their path.

Harrigan rushed up front. "Why are you stopping?"

"That bus is blocking us," Stern said.

"The signals are getting weak," Johnson warned.

"Go around the cocksucker," Harrigan said.

The van leaped the curb. Stern blared the horn and pedestrians flattened themselves against the building. The van rounded the rear of the bus and plowed back into the roadway.

"Five Detective C.O. to Nest. What is your location, K?"

A momentary silence fell over the radio frequency. Starling Johnson turned away from the monitor and exchanged a quick smile with Harrigan. The sergeant grabbed the microphone.

"Is that you, Lou?"

"Ten-four. What is your location, K?"

"Eight and Five-two, heading east," Harrigan transmitted.

"On the way," Malone radioed without inflection.

"All right!" someone shouted happily over the restricted frequency.

The Pavilion is a luxury apartment complex with massive wood-paneled lobbies and spiring water fountains separated from the East River by the compact John Jay Park. Aldridge Braxton drew parallel with the Volkswagen dealer on Seventy-sixth Street and turned to cross to the other side of the street. A small group of liverymen were standing in front of

283

the Pavilion's garage. Braxton glanced at them as he passed and continued on to his destination.

Braxton walked into the Seventy-sixth Street entrance of John Jay Park, an area of benches and trees that continued through to Seventy-seventh Street. He walked through and exited the park onto Seventy-seventh Street and Cherokee Place. He looked across the street at a building with an unusual façade of white stone and yellow brick. The apartment house had mullioned windows and buff fire escapes. He was interested in the arched ambulatories that led through the building on the corner of Cherokee Place to Seventy-eighth Street. If needed, they could be his escape hatch. He turned and looked around the park. Au pair girls and their wards, chic ladies with their custom jeans and expensive accessories, paddleball players using the handball courts, and a queue outside the bathhouse of people eager to use the Olympic-size pool represented normal activity. The bow of a freighter, its black riveted hull slicing the view, slid past Seventy-seventh Street.

Aldridge Braxton was not a particularly nervous man. But the force of recent events had changed that. He could almost reach out and touch the presence of danger. It was all supposed to have been so easy. Risk free, Stanislaus had told him. He should have known better. Now this meeting and the sudden precautions, the warnings only to use safe telephones. He felt almost physically ill.

Inside the surveillance van Jake Stern turned and glanced into the rear. "Hey, Sarge, will you take the wheel for a minute? I gotta piss so bad I can taste it."

Harrigan made his way out front and exchanged places with him.

Stern steered himself into the back and squeezed himself into the cramped toilet. Urinating into the waterless bowl, he shouted to Johnson. "How you makin' out with P.O. O'Day?"

"We're practically *mispocah*," Johnson said grinning.

284

Stern stepped out of the cubicle pulling up his zipper. "I'm glad that the boss is all right."

"Me too, ma man."

"Nest and Birds, what are your locations, K?" Malone's voice came over the wires.

"Five-two and Madison, heading east," Harrigan transmitted.

"Birds One, Two, and Three on FDR Drive," the detective in the gypsy cab transmitted.

"Bird Four is parked on the corner of York and Seventy-six. Subject has entered John Jay Park, K."

"Bird Five in on foot at Cherokee Place and Seventy-sixth Street. About to enter park. I am going off the air now."

Malone turned to Heinemann. "Looks like the meet is going down in the park."

Heinemann nodded. Bo Davis was in the rear of the car. He leaned forward and tapped Malone on the shoulder. "Braxton or one of the others might recognize the van."

Malone picked up the handset and transmitted. "Five C.O. to Nest, K."

"Go. Nest, K." Harrigan's voice.

"Nest. Bury the van nearby. They might spot it."

"Nest. Ten-four." Harrigan returned the microphone and reached up to the photographic cabinet above the radio set. He flipped the hasp and reached inside, removing two movie cameras. He placed them carefully on the ledge and then selected the correct telescopic lenses.

The van was buried among the jumble of sanitation trucks on Seventy-third Street and the River. Harrigan and Stern got out and walked over to the cavelike entrance of the sanitation garage to wait for Johnson, who was still inside the van securing the equipment. As they stepped out of the way of a lumbering garbage truck, Harrigan walkie-talkied their location to Malone. When Johnson joined them, the three men trotted to the apartment house on the corner of Seventy-seventh Street and Cherokee Place. They entered through the

285

Seventy-eighth Street ambulatory and rushed up to the roof.

Peering down over the edge, the detectives had an unobstructed view of the park. Johnson used a waist-high vent to steady his camera. Stern gripped his camera against the side of the stairwell housing. They were careful not to go near the edge because a sudden movement could attract attention from below. Bird 5 was stretched out on a park bench, his head tilted back to catch the sun's rays.

They sat on a bench near the wading pool and watched Stanislaus pace back and forth in front of them. Stanislaus appeared to be tendering a lecture to backward students. The cameras could only record lip movements, and only when the actors faced them. Stanislaus looked gloomy. Bramson and Kelly would occasionally interrupt to say something. From time to time Braxton would look up and make a comment.

Harrigan transmitted their location to Malone. He cautioned the C.O. not to 10:85 them thereat. The meeting that was going on in the park might adjourn at any moment. One of the conferees might spot him when he was leaving the park.

The meeting inside John Jay Park lasted for another twenty-two minutes and then broke up. Bramson and Kelly were the first to get to their feet and leave. Braxton was next. Stanislaus lingered behind, watching them depart. When they had all gone, Stanislaus walked over to the edge of the park and stared down the precipice at the fast-moving water.

Bird 5 got to his feet and stretched, his arms a V over his head. He turned to his right and walked slowly out of the park.

Malone, Davis, and Heinemann were parked by the sanitation garage, waiting.

Harrigan, Stern, and Johnson were still on the roof watching Stanislaus watch the river.

Stern was the first one to notice the man walking close to

the building line on Cherokee Place. The man crossed Seventy-seventh Street and stopped by the entrance of the park. He turned and let his eyes take in the windows and terraces of the Pavilion. He then turned his attention to the cars and vans that were parked nearby. Apparently satisfied that he was not being watched, the man turned back and made his way over to where Stanislaus was standing.

The man leaning over the fence turned and looked into the stern face of Chief Zangline.

"The piano tuner wants to see us," Zangline said, leaning his back to the fence and examining the park thoroughly.

Stanislaus turned. "When?"

"Now. And we better make damn sure that we're not followed," Zangline said.

The Cloister, an igloo-shaped restaurant with triple lancet windows and a groined ceiling, sits atop the heights of Tudor City. It took Zangline and Stanislaus the better part of three hours to reach the restaurant. Their extended journey took in the Staten Island ferry, a tour of Harlem, and a drink at the long bar of Windows of the World. At 6:20 P.M. Zangline's unmarked car rolled to a stop below the summit of Tudor City. Stanislaus tossed the Vehicle Identification Card on the dashboard and got out. While Stanislaus locked up the car, Zangline read the slogan painted on the stairway wall: HONOR NEW AFRIKAN FREEDOM FIGHTERS!

A Mercedes-Benz limousine was parked in front of the restaurant. A man in a dark suit and wearing a black chauffeur's cap stood nearby. When the man saw Zangline and Stanislaus he waved and walked over to them. There was a round of handshakes. Zangline touched the man on the shoulder and then he and Stanislaus turned and walked into the restaurant.

The surveillance van was parked a block away, its two-way reflectors facing the Cloister.

Malone pressed the transmit button. "Nest to Central, K."

"Go. Nest."

"A ten-fifteen on New York plate Oscar, Union, Charlie, four-eight-six: not holding."

The answer came in seconds. "Oscar, Union, Charlie four-eight-six comes out to a 1949 Mercedes-Benz limousine, color black; Vin number Frank, Oscar, George, eighty-seven David, one, zero, nine, zero, three, zero, Frank. That's a ten-seventeen all around. One minute and I will check NCIC."

Malone waited for Central's computer to check the stolen-vehicle data bank for the United States. His eyes cut to the chauffeur leaning against the fender and lighting a cigarette. The man had the look of a moonlighting cop or a retiree.

"Central to Nest, K."

"Go. Central."

"NCIC is negative, K."

"Registered owner, K?"

"Vehicle registered to Moorehouse International, Eighty-one Wall Street, New York City, K."

"Ten-four." Malone turned to Harrigan. "I want our people inside that restaurant."

Harrigan warned, "They'll be made. Zangline and Stanislaus can smell a cop up close."

Malone said, "Those two went to a lot of trouble to make sure they were not followed. I intend to know why." His head still ached and his eyeballs felt swollen. He could still taste the blood. He swallowed hard, forcing down the heave. He still had not telephoned Erica, but he promised himself that he would as soon as he could. One detective might get inside without being recognized. Who? He looked from man to man and his stare settled on Starling Johnson. "If you removed your jacket and tie and went around to the service entrance you would look like just another black dishwasher showing up for the evening rush."

"I'll give it a shot," said Johnson, tugging off his tie.

"Give 'em a little soul strut," Davis said, snapping his fingers and miming a swagger.

Malone said, "When you get inside tell them that the agency sent you. Most restaurants hire their dishwashers on a per diem basis from employment agencies."

"And then what do I do?" Johnson said.

"You're a detective—improvise," Malone said, taking his jacket.

20

Malone awakened with a start, not sure of where he was. He picked up the sound of a music box, and in the distance, the blare of fire engines. His body throbbed with pain and his eyeballs hurt. His tongue was caked dry. He rubbed his stubble and thought how nice it would be to feel Erica's thighs pressing against his face. He made a small smile and told himself that he must be getting better. Those thoughts were returning. He dabbed fingertips over his wound. He had removed the bandage. Someone had once told him that fresh air was the best thing to heal an injury. The sutures looked like long, black-legged creatures.

Malone checked the time: 8:15 P.M. His brow knitted into deep lines. Had he really slept that long? He had only intended to rest his head on the desk for a minute or two. The movie film was being developed and then rushed to the Concord School for the Deaf in the Bronx where students would read the subject's lips and make transcripts of the conversations. One of the detectives had been dispatched to the telephone booth in front of Aldridge Braxton's house. Returning home directly after the meeting in John Jay Park, Braxton made a fast telephone call from the booth before he hurried into the lobby of his apartment house. The detectives in the Sting Ray had followed him home and seen him make his call.

There had been nothing for Malone to do but wait and think. Sometimes that gets to be the hardest part, waiting, thinking. Police texts discuss the connective-disconnective relationship to the trier of facts. It ain't that way. It's plodding the streets, barrooms, and strolls asking questions, calling in past favors. And then waiting, thinking.

His pupils felt like they were floating on ponds of molten lava. He rested his head in his hands. As he did his gaze went to the notes that he had jotted on the pad.

Carter Moorehouse of Moorehouse International, 81 Wall Street, New York City. He was the man Zangline and Stanislaus met in the restaurant.

Detective Johnson had indeed improvised. The black detective had walked into the kitchen of the restaurant unopposed. The help was too busy to take notice of another nigger who had come to clean dirty dishes for below the minimum wage. He walked through the kitchen and entered the locker room that was next to the meat freezer. He grabbed a service jacket from the hook, shrugged it on, and then pushed his way through the swinging doors into the dining room.

The detective spotted Stanislaus and Zangline sitting at a table within the main dining area. Johnson recognized the third man at the table—Carter Moorehouse. The same Carter Moorehouse who had stood for mayor.

As Malone looked over the notes on Johnson's visit to the restaurant, he became aware of just how much he knew about Moorehouse.

Carter Moorehouse's great grandfather made the family fortune in the China trade. The grandfather doubled it in railroads and the father tripled it in banking. The son, Carter, collected companies and other profitable things.

A Calvinist strain had always stiffened the Moorehouse clan and made them frighteningly rigid and vengeful people. It was said that the present patriarch was no exception.

Carter Moorehouse once made a bid for Gracie Mansion on the Conservative line. His defeat was the first of his lifetime and a humiliating one at that. Calvinism and Conservatism were not the in "isms" in New York City.

291

But if Moorehouse had not won the hearts of the voters, he had become a popular candidate with New York's Finest. He had pushed a very hard line on crime and made many intelligent suggestions about overhauling the entire criminal justice system. Even the *New York Times* had to grant him points for his long, thoughtful proposals on city financial reorganization. But as the campaign wore on, the crime issue seemed to evoke something deeply buried in Moorehouse, something more frightening and savage than the voters wanted to hear, even if a lot of them had similar private fantasies of revenge. Malone couldn't remember exactly when it happened, but the outspoken *Times* editorial against Moorehouse was brought on by his remarks, delivered off the record, at a meeting of the National Associations of Chiefs of Police in Washington. And from that point it had been downhill. Even the *National Review* had dropped him in embarrassment.

Malone tried to remember the specifics, the later speeches and doomed battles with the media that had characterized the last, desperate days of Moorehouse's campaign. But his recollections were too vague; he needed to find out a great deal more about this man, to study him the way he had been trained to study the motives and behavior patterns of criminals. As he sat in the semidarkness of his office, he was filled with a growing conviction that while the public Carter Moorehouse was made inaccessible to him by layers of money, class, and power, the private animal inside Moorehouse was like a lot of the ones he tried to take off the street and put in cages called prisons.

He thought of Zambrano. The wake would be tomorrow night. He had already decided not to attend. He wanted to avoid those curious, secret looks. Besides, he hated wakes. They were barbaric rituals that only served to enrich undertakers. The Jews had the right idea: plant them right away. He knew exactly what Zambrano's would be like. White-gloved policemen milling about whispering. A large room filled with foul-smelling flowers, stands, overflowing with mass cards, chalices, and vestments. An honor guard formed around the coffin. A prie-dieu that was never empty, an immediate member of the family hovering nearby to accept condolences. The body, cold and stiff and regaled in full uniform, the lips sewed into a death smile. Having to endure the endless, stupid asides: Doesn't he look wonderful; he looks just like he went to sleep, so natural.

Malone wanted no part of it. He would attend the mass and remember his friend as he was, not as a broken corpse smelling of formaldehyde and undertaker's cosmetics.

He leaned over and took the bottle of bourbon from the bottom drawer. He poured three fingers into a mug and toasted the empty chair. "Gendarme, my friend."

As soon as he gulped the drink his head started to spin and his stomach churn. All at once his mouth was filled with saliva. He clasped his hand across his mouth and stumbled from his office into the bathroom, a one-cubicle, one-urinal cubbyhole with a faded mirror that was splotched with soap and other substances.

He knelt in front of the bowl, one hand supporting his head, and vomited. Yellow green chunks. His eyes teared. The floor was cold. Brown dots caked the bowl. He heaved and heaved until there was nothing left to come up. His stomach was raw. Sore. He gripped the rim and hoisted himself up.

The basin was laced with dried suds and the one piece of soap was smudged black. He put his head under the faucet and turned on the cold water. Zambrano had been right; he was turning into a bum in a flophouse.

When he got back to his office he started to telephone around town trying to locate Jack Fine. He was not at his desk at the *Daily News*. He started to phone Fine's haunts. Vinny at Dangerfield's told him that he had not seen the reporter in a few days. He called P.J.'s, Dewy's, and Mary Ellen's Room, all with negative results. He located Fine at

Weston's. Bob Dingle, the saloon's major domo, told him to hold while he dug Fine out of the crowd.

The din coming over the line was most definitely that of a saloon. Live music, clinking glasses, loud voices mixed with sudden gales of laughter—he could visualize the smoke raftering the bar.

Fine's choppy voice. "Dan, I was terribly sorry to hear about Zambrano. He is going to be missed. You all right?" Fine was shouting over the clamor.

"Jack, I need one and I need it fast." He realized that he was shouting. His voice drifted downward. "Can you help me?"

Fine said, "If I can, you got it."

"I want you to arrange for me to get into a television film library. I want to know all there is to know about Carter Moorehouse."

Fine made a sound of exasperation. "Wow. Is Moorehouse involved in the Eisinger caper?"

"Maybe."

"I have a lady-type friend who works at CBS. I will give her a call at home. She starts work at seven A.M. Likes to get a jump on the day before the place turns into Willowbrook East. I'll call you right back. Where are you?"

"In the Squad."

He waited for Fine to call back and confirm the appointment on Monday morning before he made the second call. He studied the telephone a long time before he finally picked it up and dialed.

It was answered on the first ring.

"Hello, Erica," he said softly.

Her voice was strained and distant, as though she wanted to detach herself from him. "How are you, Daniel?"

"I'm all right. I miss you." He held his breath, waiting to hear her tone of voice. Listening for the inflection.

"When were you released from whatever hospital you were in?" A cold and reserved tone, one that said, Keep your distance.

"This morning."

"I see." Icicles in June. "Didn't you know how frantic I would be? I have been crying all day. I must have telephoned your rotten office a thousand times. None of your macho detectives knew anything. They never do. It's one big chauvinistic conspiracy. I've broken every one of my nails and to top it off I look like shit. And you, Daniel Malone, could not spare me one lousy minute of your precious time to let me know that you were alive."

"I'm sorry," he said, haltingly.

"Like hell you are. The only thing that you're sorry about is that there are not seventy-two hours in one day so that you can play at your cops-and-robbers games."

"Erica. A cop was killed. There were many things that needed doing. Believe me, I tried to call you several times but the Job always interfered."

"Your job is just too big for both of us. I'm sorry, Daniel. I really wanted us to make it." She began to cry.

"Let me come over. We'll talk."

"No! I'm not the wham-bam-thank-you-ma'am type. I want more out of a relationship. You make me feel like a whore."

He lowered his eyes and shook his head. He was wrong and he knew it. And now he was sorry. "Erica, please let me . . ."

"How could you have done that to me," she cried. "Not one call. I have to feel secure in a relationship. I . . . I . . . Please don't call me again, ever."

A click.

He sat holding the phone and listening to the sound of the dial tone. "If you want security, marry a rent-a-cop," he shouted at the mouthpiece. "Don't bark up this tree."

He pushed himself up out of the chair and went into the squad room. He was on his way to the coffee machine when he turned and went back into his office. He dialed her number and the line was busy. He sat on his desk and dialed over and over again. It was always busy.

295

He went back into the squad room and told the detective who was typing up the arrest reports on a feral youth that he was going to sack out in the dorm. "See that I get a piss call at six A.M."

"Hi. I'm Evelyn Norton. Jack Fine told me that you would be coming my way Monday morning."

She was thirtyish, with scalloped black hair and green eyes. A nice smile and a firm handshake. Her blouse was open just enough to make a man curious. Black skirt with side slits, and dark stockings and a man-tailored jacket. A very attractive lady.

She swept her hand toward a chair. A television set displaying a colorful test pattern was on a table next to her desk. Her fragrance reminded him of Erica.

Evelyn Norton said, "What can I do for you?"

He told her that he wanted background information on Carter Moorehouse. She picked up a pencil and leaned forward in her chair. "Can you be a bit more specific?"

"I'd like to see everything that you have on him."

"Let me explain how our indexes work," she said, a pleasant smile on her face. "Our film library employs several systems. We have a Personality File on the famous and infamous. A Shot Listing Index which lists specific scenes of news footage. An example would be"—she paused a second to think—"Sadat's assassins rushing the grandstand. And we have a Line-up Book which lists the stories carried on CBS news in the sequence that they were aired. We also maintain a card index by subject and story. Everything from 'seventy-five to the present is available on CRT computer terminals, everything before 'seventy-five is still on index cards.

"So you see," she concluded, "it would help if you could be more exact."

"I want," he said, "to get a sense of the man."

She folded her arms across her chest. "I see. S'pose I prepare you a pre-obit on Carter Moorehouse."

"That would be fine."

She got up. He followed her out into a row of secretarial cubicles and down the aisle into a large room filled with movable film racks and card drawers. She pointed to a room with video playback machines and large tape spools on the wall. "This is a shot-listing room."

For the next thirty-two minutes they combed the indexes for material on Carter Moorehouse. She searched and called out reference numbers and he copied them down on gray charge-out cards.

When they were finished, she looked over at him, smiled, and said, "Some of this material is in our basement library."

The library was two stories below ground. Stepping off the elevator, they entered a labyrinth of underground passageways with vaulted ceilings and white stone walls. She saw the surprise register on his face. "At one time this building was a slaughterhouse for one of the big milk companies," she said.

She led the way through passageways crowded with maintenance men. At the end of a long serpentine route she turned right and signaled him to follow. They were in a cloistered area with fourteen-foot ceilings. There were files of portable racks that were crowded with film canisters and storage boxes. The yellow labels on the boxes' spines contained reference codes and content annotations.

It was a cold, damp place.

He noticed the oxygen tanks and masks encased in glass. "What are they for?"

She pointed to a sign on the door—WHEN HELON ALARM SOUNDS LEAVE IMMEDIATELY OR PUT ON OXYGEN MASK.

She said, "We use Helon in our sprinkler system. It removes oxygen from the air and extinguishes fire. That way our film is protected. The difficult part is that anyone trapped in here at the time of a fire would have to put on an oxygen mask or suffocate."

Reference slips in hand, they combed the aisles and removed material. Their quest complete, they retired to a

297

fourth-floor shot-listing room where she spent ten minutes showing him how to work the equipment.

When she was gone he put on the first cassette, sat back, and fixed his attention on the large screen.

Stewart King, the CBS anchorman, appeared in a standup open shot introducing Carter Moorehouse, the candidate. The scene switched to a tracking shot of Moorehouse moving among a cheering constituency. Malone noticed something and depressed the frame-hold button. Although they were much younger, their features lean and hair darker, he recognized Stanislaus and Zangline shouldering a path for the candidate.

It was early in the campaign so the crowds were big and still friendly. Moorehouse had used the occasion, a speech at the old Brooklyn Navy Yard, to present the broad outlines of what came to be known as "Remobilize New York's Industry." As he moved forward in the file tapes, Malone found himself admitting how much sense Moorehouse made when he outlined his program of tax and development incentives for smaller businesses, rebuilding, and restoring the fabric of neighborhoods, creating industrial development zones in dying areas of the city. But then, in a tape made three weeks into the campaign, Moorehouse began discussing rehabilitation of mass-transit services. Business needed workers arriving on time and unharassed by marginal equipment and operations. But they needed, above all, employees who felt they could use subways and buses in reasonable safety. And that took him off on a long tangent about crime. Malone watched with fascination as the tape ran over into outtakes, the unedited footage. Moorehouse left his prepared speech behind; the carefully modulated tones were replaced by the relentless harangue of a religious fanatic. And the crowd loved it, at least for a while. It went on for a long, long time. Moorehouse approved the death penalty and went on to suggest special courts for felony offenders that left no room whatsoever for due process.

In later tapes, Moorehouse's tendency to break into extemporaneous remarks about crime became more pronounced. Toward the end of one such speech a desperate aide had almost pulled Moorehouse away from the podium. The crowds were less and less responsive. There would always be a considerable number of people in each of Moorehouse's different audiences who *would* listen, who seemed locked in a kind of terrible communion with Moorehouse. Malone remembered, now, what the *Times* had said in that damaging editorial: Moorehouse wanted to return to pure retributive justice, the kind of blood-vengeance suited to a savage tribe rather than the measured, constitutional law of a civilized city. As he watched the tapes unroll, Malone saw the animal emerging; it was signaled by the peculiar gleam in Moorehouse's eyes, or the darting of his tongue. Malone also understood the code words. Moorehouse talked about blacks, Hispanics, the welfare poor as the "criminal element," without differentiating them. Malone knew what he meant; and so did the hard knot of true believers in every audience.

Late in the campaign Moorehouse began to address the issue of terrorism. Again, in an outtake that, fortunately, had not aired, Moorehouse gave his thoughts on the subject, even going as far as to warn his somewhat perplexed listeners that New York City would have to look like Beirut before people took the threat seriously. When Moorehouse talked about the horrifying ineffectiveness of our immigration controls, Malone got the clear impression that Moorehouse felt the wrong sort of people had been let in for the last fifty years. That kind of message, in the racial and ethnic stew that constituted the human element of the city, was not likely to be popular. But in the later tapes it was clear that Moorehouse cared little about popularity. He was speaking out of deep conviction and the public be damned.

Malone saw the tapes as a portrait of self-destruction. He was amazed by the kindness of the media to Moorehouse, the same media which Moorehouse perceived as his personal enemies. What had been aired was bad enough; what remained unaired and in the can revealed Moorehouse's pathological disregard of the bare minimum of polite disguise. The code words were there, especially, in his concession speech. When Moorehouse talked about "malign foreign influences" on a free press, he was talking about Jews and Zionists. Perhaps, Malone conceded, Moorehouse had been right in a twisted way. Reporters, producers, and editors had kept many of Carter Moorehouse's less attractive sentiments out of the news, not so much as a means of protecting Moorehouse from himself but to protect a troubled city from the suggestion of remedies that were worse than any disease. The cumulative effect of the footage was overwhelming; Moorehouse was a man who held in contempt much of the law that Malone served. He despised many of the ordinary people who Malone tried to protect. The grinding political process had stripped Moorehouse of his civil veneer and led him to defeat by a humiliating margin.

Malone watched all the tapes and then switched off the machines. He lit a cigarette and remained in his seat, watching the smoke drift upward. He had gotten what he wanted; a sense of the man. He now knew a great and frightening thing about Carter Moorehouse. He knew that Moorehouse was a man who did not know how to forgive or forget.

In the lobby of the CBS building Malone called the precinct. Bo Davis answered. "Are the transcripts ready?" Malone asked.

"Everything is waiting on you. The film, the transcripts, and the wire. You better get back here fast. This shit is dynamite."

"I'm on the way. Who's on deck?"

"The whole crew is here."

Malone looked at his watch: 9:58 A.M. "I want you and Jake to hit Stanislaus's place and execute the warrant, just for the record. Before you go, check with Harrigan and make sure Stanislaus is at the SOD compound. This way he won't know that we were there until he returns home. It'll give us some extra hours. And, Bo, don't forget to leave a receipt for the property."

Malone hung up and dialed Erica Sommers at her sister's house in Washington Heights. The line was busy. He called the special operator and asked her to check it. When she came back on the line the operator told him that the phone was off the hook.

A man with a moon face was waiting on the stationhouse steps. "Lieutenant Malone, I am Deputy Inspector Obergfoll. You have a Forthwith from the Chief of Op." He was a heavy man somewhere in his fifties. A man who had forgotten how to smile.

"What is it about?" Malone said, searching the blank face for a clue.

"The chief will tell you."

"I'll just be a minute. There are a few things I have to tell my men." Malone started to walk around him.

Obergfoll grabbed his arm. "Forthwith, Lieutenant. Your men are waiting for you at One Police Plaza."

While every crime scene has its own special aura, they are essentially all the same.

Policemen loitered in the corridor. Two officers stood guard outside the door leading into Joe Mannelli's official office at One Police Plaza. They had stretched a rope across the doorway and hung a crime-scene sign on it. Deputy Inspector Obergfoll climbed over the rope and then lifted it up so that Malone could duck under.

The cameras in the outer office had been switched off. The Chief of Op was in a corner talking to the first deputy police commissioner. McQuade caught sight of Obergfoll and Malone and excused himself.

301

The top echelon of the department had gathered in the outer office and were talking guardedly. Malone spotted his detectives and started for them. Obergfoll grabbed his arm and told him to remain where he was. The inspector then went over to the detectives and told them to follow him. They were to wait for their boss in McQuade's office. As they filed past Malone each one looked the lieutenant in the face and made a deprecatory little shrug. Malone was relieved to see that Davis and Stern were among the missing. The search warrant was being executed, officially.

McQuade came up to him, and without saying one word looped his arm through his and proceeded to shepherd him across the width of the room to a window.

McQuade said, "Things have changed since we last talked."

"How so?"

"Zambrano. And now this," McQuade said.

Malone looked him in the eye, waiting for an explanation.

McQuade rubbed his palms together. A film of sweat covered his lip. "There has been an accident. Mannelli is dead. Suicide."

Malone was stunned. He slapped his hands over his face and began to press his pupils until he could see shimmering tiles rushing through the blackness. Another dead cop. Sara Eisinger, what hath your grounder wrought? He stared out at the City.

"It's your baby," McQuade said.

"Any direction from the fourteenth floor?" he said, looking up at the golden cupola of the Municipal Building, and envisaging the PC sitting behind Teddy Roosevelt's massive desk pondering what to do with the Mannelli caper.

"The place of occurrence is within your zone. Handle it as you would any other suicide."

Malone glared scorn. "Fuck off with that bullshit."

McQuade bit his lips. "Do what ever you have to, Lieutenant."

302

"What happened?" Malone flared.

"The PC received an envelope with photographs of Mannelli. They were sex pictures of him in bed with a man and woman. The PC called him in and told him that his position in Intelligence had been compromised. He suggested that he vest his pension and get out. Whoever sent the envelope to the PC also sent one to Mannelli's wife. She's a tight-assed Bronx Irish Catholic. She ordered him from their home. I guess something inside him must have snapped." He reached into his pocket and took out a letter. "This is addressed to you."

He took it from McQuade and read it.

Dan. Believe me when I tell you that I did not know what they were doing. They used me. Watch yourself. They are out to kill you. The Braxtons set me up. I'm scared. Stop them before it is too late. I want you to do me one last favor. Please . . .

The letter ended.

Malone folded it and slid it into his pocket. "Where is he?"

"In there," McQuade said, pointing to an inner door.

"Where are my men?" Malone said, with an undercurrent of hostility in his tone.

"Waiting for you in my office."

The apprehension in McQuade's face was apparent. Suicides do not fit the public image. "Let's take a look."

They entered the quiet room. McQuade drew the door closed. The body was slouched in the white plastic chair. The head was back and tilted to the side. The right arm was extended, the weapon clutched in a death grip. His mouth was agape and the eyes half open. A pool of red mud seeped down over the left shoulder.

Malone circled, examining the scene. He placed the back of his hand against Joe's face. The skin was rubbery and cold.

Capilarity cast its spidery hue. There was a heavy accumulation of powder grains around the center of the flame zone.

"Goddamn it!" He kicked the desk. "You could have prevented this."

McQuade shrugged helplessness. "How? I had nothing to do with any of this."

"You are the Chief of Operations. You knew damn well what Zangline and his crew were into." He pointed to the body. "No way you can escape responsibility."

"Lieutenant, not now! We can talk later. At this moment there are more pressing considerations that require our attention."

"How many children did he have?"

"Three. One still in grade school."

"At least they will get his pension."

"They get zilch," McQuade said. "Mannelli did not have his time in the Job, and suicides are not classified line-of-duty deaths. His family will get whatever money he contributed to his pension fund and one year's salary."

Grainy black-and-white photographs were strewn over the floor. Malone bent and harvested them. Mannelli in bed with Aldridge and Thea Braxton. A threesome. Ain't no way, he thought. That was not Mannelli's bag. He remembered Major Landsford and how he died. A suicide by gun with incriminating film as the catalyst. He began to wonder if they *were* suicides.

Malone said, "Is this my investigation?" A purposeful tone.

"Yes."

"Then you better leave. Because I am going to conduct it my way."

McQuade said, "I'll stay. There might come a time when you will need a witness."

They looked into each other's eyes, two policemen understanding a contract. Malone knew what the Chief of Op expected of him.

Standing over the wastebasket that was on the side of the desk, Malone tore up the photographs and rained the pieces into the basket. He shot out a hand. "Gimme a book of matches."

McQuade handed them to him. He squatted and struck a match, turning the contents of the basket ablaze.

He got to his feet and started to rummage the desk. Each drawer was pulled out and searched. Not finding what he wanted, he slowly scoured the room. The coat closet? He went over and jerked the door open. First he checked the floor and then he started to push uniforms aside.

"What the hell are you searching for?" McQuade said.

"Something that every cop keeps nearby," he said, stepping back to check the shelf. Three shoe boxes were stacked one on the other. The corners of the bottom one were stained with oil. "Here it is," he said, sliding out the box.

Mannelli's gun-cleaning kit was placed on the desk. "You don't have to be a party to any of this."

"I am just beginning to appreciate your style, Malone. I will stay. Might learn a thing or two."

Malone assembled the cleaning rod. A patch was removed from the crumpled box and inserted through the rod's eye. The cap was taken off the bottle of cleaning solvent and the patch dipped inside and soaked.

He had to pry the fingers back in order to retrieve the revolver. He opened the chamber and plunged out the rounds, returning the one spent cartridge. He checked the make of the pistol. A Smith & Wesson. The cylinders on S & Ws turn counterclockwise. The cylinder was spun until the spent round fell under the firing pin. It was then closed and the revolver placed on the floor beneath the stiffened hand. He stepped back to check the scene. Realizing that some of the stage props were missing, he then spread the remaining rounds over the desk. He moved away like a director checking the scene before the final shot. Nodding satisfaction, he turned to McQuade. "My investigation leads me to conclude that Lieutenant Mannelli died as the result of an accidental discharge incurred while he was cleaning his service revolver. I shall so testify before the grand jury.''

McQuade said, ''The *Patrol Guide* requires members to maintain their service revolvers in a clean and serviceable condition. Since his death was the direct result of that provision it would be line-of-duty.''

Malone took out the suicide note. He glanced at it briefly and then tossed it into the flickering flame. The center of the paper scorched outward and the ends began to char and curl under. Soon there was nothing left but a smoldering charcoal mass.

McQuade came up to him. ''Obergfoll can clean up here. We had better go to my office and talk.''

21

Some of the men shuffled about the room as though they had no other place to go while others slouched in chairs; each man shared the patina of gloom. Malone stopped short, surprised at the unexpected gathering in the Chief of Op's office.

Yachov Anderman wore a melancholy expression. "Hello, policeman."

David Ancorie's ears were beet red and his face bore a steady, bland expression.

A movie camera and screen had been set up. A tape recorder and a pile of mimeographed transcripts were next to the camera. McQuade saw Malone looking at them. "When Obergfoll went to get you and your men he found the detectives examining this material. He directed that it all be brought here."

Malone nodded to his detectives and crossed the room to Anderman. As he lowered himself into the chair next to Anderman he said, "So? What's new?"

"What could be new, policeman?"

"Well. For starters, the man you met in Battery Park is dead. Mannelli, perhaps you remember him?"

Anderman's face set in a scowl.

Malone continued, "And now I find the man who never associates with policemen in the office of the Chief of Operations with a rabbinical student who instructs policemen on the use and care of the Uzi submachine gun. Don't you find that

307

interesting, Mr. Anderman?'' He spat his words with contempt.

Anderman turned in his seat to say something, then at the last second changed his mind and looked away.

Malone edged close. "You have been pissing on my parade since the beginning. One of these days I am going to shove a cattle prod up your ass and put your balls on trickle.''

Anderman got halfway up and leaned across the table, tapping the stack of transcripts. "I suggest that you wait until you read these.''

McQuade's face reflected his grave concern. "We are facing a crisis.'' He looked to Anderman and Malone. "We must work together, Past differences forgotten.'' He waved a hand at Deputy Inspector Obergfoll, who nodded and went around the room closing blinds. McQuade picked up one of the transcripts and then went over to the light switch and flipped it. He cracked the door so that a sliver of light shone in.

Obergfoll turned on the projector. Holding the transcript in the light from the beam, McQuade watched the screen, ready to deliver the dialogue. A bleak, unsteady picture fluttered onto the screen. Stanislaus was pacing before a park bench. The men sitting were watching him.

McQuade said, "Stanislaus speaking: 'We make our move now. Bramson will contact our Arab. . . . We have enough people to destroy. . . . All the equipment is ready. There is enough Plactic C to do the job and . . .'

"Kelly speaking: 'Some cops are bound to get hurt.' ''

"Stanislaus speaking: 'That can't be helped. We all knew what we were getting into. . . . Mannelli must go. . . .' ''

Malone watched intently, and strained to read their lips.

Aldridge Braxton jumped to his feet.

"Braxton speaking: 'You are all crazy. My sister and I want no part of this. It's madness. We will not go with you. . . .' ''

Stanislaus's back was to the camera. A fist was waved at Braxton. Bramson was on his feet pushing Braxton back down. The camera recorded the tremor in Braxton's legs.

McQuade read aloud, "Kelly speaking: 'All right.'

"Bramson speaking: 'I will see to it.'

"Stanislaus speaking: 'Afterward we go about our business as though nothing has happened.' "

One by one they got up and walked from the park. The film quickened. A jumble of white dots flicked past the upper-right-hand corner of the screen. Smoke floated inside the beam. Zangline appeared walking through the park. He went over to Stanislaus. Both men walked away from the river. The camera recorded their lip movements.

McQuade read aloud, "Zangline speaking: 'The piano tuner wants to see us.'

"Stanislaus speaking: 'When.'

"Zangline speaking: 'Right now. And we better make damn sure that we're not followed.' "

Cameras followed their departure from the park. More dots appeared on the screen, and then Stanislaus and Zangline reappeared walking past a small park in Tudor City. They had a brief conversation with a man in a chauffeur's hat and then walked into the restaurant. McQuade nudged the door closed with his knee and switched on the lights. He walked over to the tape recorder. As he did his eyes met Malone's. He made a tentative movement with his head as if to say, How did we ever get into this mess? He depressed the play button. A hollow sound churned forth followed by a click and then Thea Braxton's voice.

"Hello?"

"It's me." His tone a shrill. "They are all out of their minds."

"Are you nuts calling me here!"

"I have to talk to you now. They are all crazy."

"Aldridge. Calm down and tell me exactly what happened."

"They are going to detonate bombs around the city and then all over the country. That Jew's warehouse in Queens is the first place they're planning to hit. And they expect us to go along with them."

309

"I will leave the office in five minutes. Meet me in my apartment and we will talk. There has to be a way out of this."

"Okay. Do you remember that cop who Stanislaus wanted insurance on?"

"Mannelli. Yes, I remember him. And I also recall that you were particularly wonderful that evening." He ignored her and went on speaking rapidly. "They are going after him. After that cop was killed on the expressway, Mannelli put two and two together and threatened to go to the state prosecutor."

"What are they going to do?"

"I don't know and I don't care. Mannelli is not our concern. What we're going to do is what concerns me."

"And that, brother dear, is what makes life so damnably exciting."

The machine clicked off. Obergfoll went around the room opening the blinds. Malone stood, his fists clenched tightly at his side. "Who is going to tell me how this abortion got started and how the hell this department got itself involved?"

Anderman shot McQuade a look of frustrated helplessness. "Tell him."

McQuade started to pace around the table. He punched his palm, stared upward, and said, "I guess it all started several years ago when an oil executive was kidnapped in Latin America and held for a multi-million-dollar ransom. And then on April third, 1977, the FALN blew up the Mobil Oil building in New York City. One person was killed and seven wounded. After the Mobil thing, we started to get a lot of heat from the top management of major corporations with headquarters in New York City. It got worse when Moorehouse formed a 'citizen's committee' to study the protection that the various law-enforcement agencies afforded to companies with their executive headquarters in the city. To make matters more difficult, Moorehouse brought in Washington. Everyone was seeing terrorists under their beds. Up to that point we had no kind of intelligence picture on Arabs, good or bad. We told that to the Agency people and they admitted that Arab nationals can move in and out of New York just as easy as they do in France. Or fucking Algiers or anywhere. The Agency tells us, Why not try a little quiet infiltration?''

The Chief of Op glared at Anderman. ''I tell them that we haven't got an awful lot of cops who fit the part of Lawrence of Arabia. So they suggest that maybe we can make a deal with people who have a lot of resources in that area. And that was how we got involved with Anderman and his crowd. And I mean *crowd*. You would not believe how many 'assets' the Mossad has got sitting in New York, not to mention God knows how many elsewhere.''

Anderman interrupted angrily. ''We have no more people on the ground here than does any other first-class intelligence operation. From friendly countries. You should be worried about the unfriendly ones. Did you ever take a close look at the Cuban Mission? What do you think such a small island needs with such a big building? You think they store sugarcane there, maybe.''

McQuade continued as if Anderman was not even in the room. ''We believed what the Agency people told us: The Israelis are good at getting their people inside the structure of all the Arab fronts. Trouble is, once we got into bed with Anderman then the whole arms-storage deal was the price tag.''

McQuade turned and looked pleadingly at Malone. ''Look, Lieutenant. This started out being no big deal. We agreed to beef up the department's surveillance capability. Period. But you know, it gets to be like elephants fucking. There's a lot of noise, a small earthquake, and it all goes on at a very high level. The order came down from the PC. We gotta have a counterstrike capability. So I agreed, hell, how could I say no? But it was to be a small unit. Its primary mission was to take out suspected terrorists before they struck. They were to employ extra-judicial methods. Zangline could release the Unit only with the explicit authorization of the PC. Fine. Just fine. Until it snowballed and types like these Braxton people got mixed up in it.''

Anderman stood up, his face flushed with anger. ''The Braxtons were misused by your people, just please remember that. Besides, they were small change. The Libyans used them for minor errands, moving their own assets around, occasionally blackmail. We decided to turn them, and then, the minute we started, Zangline stepped in and insisted that he be allowed to use them for infiltration. It was senseless. They had access to nothing. He wouldn't trust my people. And what your chief failed to tell you was that it was thoroughly agreed that all the policemen in the Unit were to be psychologically screened. We work with professionals, no *meshugas* like Stanislaus and the other two.''

Chief of Op McQuade took an immaculate handkerchief out of his pocket, removed his glasses, and began to polish the lenses thoughtfully. ''Zangline. Goddamn him. I backed him one hundred percent. Until you started making waves, Malone. Well, your fitness reports were right on. I figured you were just what they said, a good cop. A commander of men. So, after I failed to buy you off''—he smiled bitterly at Malone, replaced his glasses, and took a sheet of paper from the drawer of his desk—''I called up Jack Breen, Zangline's exec. It was like Jack was waiting for my call. You know that loyalty comes first on this job, it's got to. We have to trust each other, particularly when we are running this kind of a crazy show. I ordered Jack to tell me what was really going on, and he did, enough to scare the shit out of me. You see, Anderman is right. The three cops in the middle of this didn't belong in the Unit. I think that they should have been thrown off the Job a long time ago. Jack Breen told me they'd all failed to pass the psychological profile screening. But fucking Zangline kept them on. He told Jack they'd be used only for training. Said they had the right kind of killer instincts.'' The chief shook his head as if he could not believe what he was saying. ''Well, at least Zangline was right about that.''

312

Malone walked over to Anderman and stood implacably in front of him. Anderman was staring down at his shoes. Malone waited a long time and then in an ominously quiet voice asked: "Where does Carter Moorehouse fit in all this?"

Anderman continued to stare down. "I don't know, but I can give you a lot of guesses. Zangline had many connections with Moorehouse, because Moorehouse was on the liaison committee of VIPs who formed the Unit's oversight board. We were supposed to coordinate our efforts with the private security forces of many companies in the city." His head shot up and he gave Malone a baffled look. "It's madness, you know. You can't mix outside people up in a clandestine operation like this one." He stopped, thought, and said, "Policeman, I can give you my guess. And I think Joe Mannelli's guess too. We think Moorehouse was . . . is funding something private. A unit inside the Unit."

Malone shook his head in disbelief. "A hit squad for the elite buried in the department."

"What choice did we have? The banks and oil companies hold the first mortgage on this city. They can foreclose any damn time they want," McQuade said.

"And this other unit? Who gave the order for its formation, and what is its mission?" Malone asked.

"I wish that I knew," McQuade said.

"Zangline ordered the formation of the official hit squad," Malone said.

"It was a deniable undertaking. Top secret. Only hand-picked men were brought into it," McQuade said.

Malone glowered at the chief. "It's no longer deniable, is it. There are too many bodies." He walked over to McQuade. "Who picked up the tab?"

McQuade said, "A slush fund of several million dollars was established. Each corporation contributed. They picked one of their own to act as overseer of the money. He was to be the liaison between the department and the business community."

"Carter Moorehouse. The piano tuner," Malone said.

313

"Yes," McQuade said lamely.

"Very nice," Malone said. "They set up the Simonson Optical Division in the Netherlands Antilles to launder the money and pay the bills. And I bet there's another one like it that we don't know about. And presto, Zangline, Stanislaus, Kelly, and Bramson have their own wishing well full of greenbacks. All they had to do was to get Moorehouse to look the other way while they helped themselves."

Malone thought. Why should Moorehouse look the other way? Certainly not for money. And why the bombs? Why risk exposure? Why? Where is the motive? Malone turned and addressed Anderman. "What went wrong? Why was she killed?"

Anderman took out a cigarette and started to tap it end over end. All of a sudden he broke it in half and threw the ends on the floor. "You want it all, policeman? All right, you can have it all. Sara was training your men in the use of simple codes when she met Stanislaus. They started to see each other. When I discovered their relationship I ordered her to stop. I told her that fraternization with policemen would make her position with us untenable. She told me that her life was hers to lead as she saw fit. We fought. She quit and went with Stanislaus. He got her a job with the Braxtons. I tried to get her to come to her senses, but it was no use. She started to socialize with Stanislaus and his friends, and saw that they had unlimited funds to spend. She became suspicious and telephoned me. She started to ask me questions about the Unit's financing. I asked her what was wrong and she told me. By this time she had become bored with Stanislaus and wanted to come back. I told her to stay with him and try to find out what they were doing. It was at this point that I was able to plant Andrea St. James in the Interlude. Sara was told never to contact me directly. She was to communicate through Andrea. They telephoned each other every day. Sara was onto something.

"She started to mention her Bible and the song. She could

never say too much on the phone. One of the Braxtons or the cops were always around. When Andrea informed me about Landsford I never made the connection with the fort. Some army officer, she said.''

Anderman got up and walked over to a filing cabinet. He opened the top drawer, pulled some folders to the front, and then slammed the drawer shut and walked away, aimlessly pacing the room. He appeared to be a man lost within himself, searching for the right turnoff. The City's flag was in the corner. He unfurled it, studying the emblem. He let it drop and returned to his seat. He looked into each man's face and then lowered himself into the chair, ready to continue his narrative.

"The Thursday before she was killed, Sara spent the night in his apartment. She was in the bathroom getting ready for him. She discovered the list and the film hidden under some rags inside the vanity. She recognized the locations on the list. She took them and hid them in her pocketbook and then went into his bed. In the morning he asked her to marry him. She was caught off guard and laughed. She saw the look that crossed his face and quickly regained her composure. She told him that she liked the relationship the way it was. Her parents would never consent to such a marriage.'' He looked up at Malone. ''You see, policeman, in many ways Sara was a troubled woman. She was only able to have intense relationships with gentile men. One short affair after the other. When the man would get serious with her she would end it. A tormentor of gentiles. Unfortunately, the children of the Holocaust did not escape unscathed.

"Stanislaus became enraged. He had left his family for her. He was in love with her. Sara realized that she was in danger and asked him for time. Perhaps she could work out something with her parents, she told him. She left his apartment and rushed home. She phoned me immediately and told me what had happened. I told her to leave and come to me. She was petrified that she might meet him in the street. She

315

was afraid that he could have discovered the list and film missing and might be on his way to her apartment. Of course, she should have come to me instead of going home. But she panicked. I tried to calm her but it was no use. So, I did the next best thing. I told her to lock all her doors and let no one in. I was on my way to her. I should have been there within the hour." He cupped his hands over his face and started to shake his head. "Ancorie and I rushed out. We took the BQE to the Williamsburgh Bridge. A three-car accident happened up ahead of us and we were stuck in the middle of the bridge for over forty minutes." He took his hands away. "When we arrived at her apartment we found the door ajar. Sara was dead in the bathtub. He must have discovered the things missing from his bathroom and rushed over to her apartment. From the look of the place he had help."

Malone unconsciously felt the wound on his head. "And then you locked the door behind you and left."

"What else could we do?" said David Ancorie.

"Was it Stanislaus who used to call Sara at the office?"

"Yes," said Anderman, "he was always calling her. It was his way of checking on her. Making sure she was where she was supposed to be. He would talk to her in Polish and German."

"Who picked Zangline to run the Unit?" Malone asked McQuade.

"The mayor. But I know Moorehouse engineered it. They knew each other from Moorehouse's political days," Mc-Quade said.

Malone rushed over to the telephone on McQuade's desk.

"What are you doing?" McQuade asked.

"I'm going to try to stop this thing before it's too late," Malone said, dialing.

Det. Sergeant Jack Harrigan answered the telephone inside the surveillance van.

"Jack, where are the suspects?" Malone said, an anxious edge to his voice.

"I have been trying to get in touch with you," Harrigan shouted. "Marku and Yaziji showed up at the Braxtons' apartment and took them for a ride in a rented car. They are on the FDR Drive. Stanislaus, Kelly, and Bramson are in another car behind them."

"What is their location?" Malone said.

"Hold on." Malone could hear the Nest communicating with its Birds. Static replies brayed in the background. Then the sergeant's hurried voice. "The drive and Seventy-first Street, heading north."

"Scoop them all up," Malone ordered.

"Ten-four."

Malone said, "I am going to keep this line open. Stay with me and let me know when you have them in custody. I have to call the Squad, but I will get right back to you."

"Okay."

Malone pressed the hold button and then took an outside line.

"We couldn't figure out where everyone went," Bo Davis said.

Malone said, "Never mind that now. Did you execute the warrant?"

"No problem. We got everything we came for and we left a receipt."

"Hang loose in the Squad. I will get back to you," Malone said.

He depressed the open-line button. "Jack, what is happening?"

A high-pitched voice. "We lost them in traffic."

"Get on the air! Have the drive blocked," Malone ordered. All eyes were on the lieutenant. Malone could hear the urgent transmissions. Radio cars would be speeding toward the drive. Would they be in time? Where was Stanislaus going? The frustration of not being there tore at him. Things would be different if he were on the scene. He should have been there. Harrigan was yelling orders, giving directions.

"Harrigan, what the hell is going on?" he shouted. He could hear a great commotion. A short time later Harrigan came on the line.

"We lost them. They sped into the East Side Heliport. Our people were crashing through the gate as their chopper was lifting off the pad."

"Call Aviation and the Coast Guard. I want choppers in the air and . . ."

"No need. I talked to the heliport manager. They had a helicopter waiting to take them to Rabbits Island. A four-minute flight. I have cars from the One-fourteen and One-oh-eight converging on the island."

"I'll hold," Malone said, his gaze darting from face to face. Anderman looked glum, deeply worried. Heinemann and Johnson were anxious to get into the fray, waiting for the word to go. McQuade rubbed the side of his nose, examining contingencies, searching for some way to make it all deniable again. The wait seemed endless. Eight minutes later Harrigan came back onto the line. "They're gone. A car was waiting to pick them up. I've transmitted a description over the citywide band."

Malone said, "Stay on it." He slammed down the phone and quickly redialed. The operator at SOD informed him that Chief Zangline was on vacation for a week.

Anderman said, "What are we going to do?"

"Stop them," Malone said, motioning his detectives to follow as he hurried from the room.

"Where are you going?" McQuade yelled after him.

"To the source," Malone shot back.

22

The Stuyvesant Club was on Park Avenue in the Sixties, one of the last of the great old mansions. It was a quiet, conservative place filled with somber rooms and heavy furniture that glowed from years of polish and care. The first four floors had the clean, slightly sweet and musty smell of old books and older money.

Malone had left One Police Plaza and rushed to the executive offices of Moorehouse International at 81 Wall Street. He presented himself to Moorehouse's secretary and told the blue-haired spinster that it was urgent that he see Moorehouse immediately. He was in possession of confidential information that an attempt was going to be made on Moorehouse's life. The secretary had gasped and clutched her meager breast. He was at his club—the Stuyvesant.

The club's hall porter was an old man who had spent his life serving the rich and powerful. When Malone told him about the threat to Carter Moorehouse he immediately told the policeman that the man he had come to see was in the sauna. He led Malone down to the basement and into the locker room, a place that was full of the faint sourness of sweat and the sharper, more pleasant odor of wintergreen.

The porter left him in the empty locker room. Malone undressed and put his clothes in an empty locker. He took a towel from the pile on the wooden table next to the shower and wrapped it around his waist. He removed another one from the stack and slid his gun inside the fold and carried it with him into the sauna.

A single light glowed down from through the swirling gray mist. He was struck by the tangy aroma of dry, hot wood. He made out the outline of a shadowy figure sitting alone on the top row. "Moorehouse?"

"Who is it?"

Carter Moorehouse appeared to be in his late forties, but he was actually closer to three score. He had an interesting face and a muscular body. His lips were thin and he had a cleft chin. His eyes were black and cold and he used them to intimidate others. The hair was silver gray and formed thick ringlets. He seemed smaller than the man Malone had seen on the TV tapes.

"Police," he said, climbing up onto the first rung.

When Malone reached the uppermost row he sat down next to Moorehouse, who growled, "What do you want?"

Malone looked sideways and made out the eyes peering at him through the steam, searching out his eyes. "I want you to tell me where to locate Zangline, Stanislaus, Kelly, and Bramson."

"I am afraid that I do not know who you are talking about. What made you think that I did?"

"Look, scummer!"—a knifelike tone that caused Moorehouse's face to fill with malice—"I'm telling you right from the giddyap that we know all about your hit team for the rich and the 'Simonson Optical Division of Curaçao.' " He ended his dismal narrative by paraphrasing the transcript of Braxton's telephone call to his sister. Water hissed over hot stones in the claustrophobic wood-lined room. "We traced the ownership of the Interlude."

Moorehouse raised his brow in a look of wary resignation.

"It was clever the way you set up that one. A cop would never have known how to do it."

Moorehouse ignored him, leaning forward, his elbows resting on his knees.

320

"The property was bought by an attorney for a dummy corporation in Delaware and then the shares in the corporation were transferred to another corporation in Delaware. When you applied for the zoning variance you had to produce the principal owner of the property and the attorney of record. So, you just transferred some stock to Aldridge Braxton, making him the principal owner, and you had him sign undated stocks in blank transferring the corporation back to one of your dummy entities. Aldridge Braxton, the perfect stand-in. All you needed was an attorney whom you could trust. And who was that? Preston Welwyn Moorehouse, your nephew and the legal representative in the United States for the Simonson Optical Division. A little nepotism can sometimes screw things up, can't it?"

Moorehouse threw his head back, brushing his hands over his forehead and through his hair as though he were completely at ease. "That is an interesting story. Have you ever considered writing fiction? You have a truly vivid imagination. Too bad that is all you have. There is not one shred of evidence to support that hogwash."

Malone watched him closely. "The department and Anderman are no longer team players. It's down the tubes for you and your friends." Malone brushed the sweat from his chest. "Help us avert disaster and I'll see to it that you are left out of it. Otherwise you'll take the fall with the rest of them."

Moorehouse was unconcerned. "You are serious, aren't you?"

Malone began to wipe his face with the corner of his towel. "Deadly serious."

Moorehouse looked at him and laughed a mocking laugh. "When was the last time you heard of a man of my stature being arrested, tried, and convicted? Not to mention that you would also have to arrest some of the most powerful men in this country." He stretched out over the bench, luxuriating in the heat.

Malone measured him with baffled fury. "Do you really expect people like Zangline and Stanislaus to stand up? Policemen do not like the thought of prison. They are not treated well by the rest of the population. And the Braxtons—they'd turn each other in to stay out of jail."

Moorehouse raised his head. "Didn't you tell me that the Braxtons were brother and sister? Isn't blood thicker than water?"

"So is shit."

Malone realized that he was wasting time. He got up and left the sauna.

Moorehouse glanced at him as he left. He made no comment, but remained on his back, staring upward.

Malone quickly showered and dressed. He was sitting on a bench in front of his locker putting on his socks when Moorehouse came out of the sauna, wrapping a towel tight around his waist. He came up to Malone, who looked up at Moorehouse's wet body and flattened hair.

Moorehouse said, "I confess a mild academic interest in your hypothesis. I assume that you realize that there is a major flaw in your conspiracy theory?"

Malone slipped into his loafers and stood, stamping his feet. His face was inches away from the quarry. "And what would that be?"

"Motive. Why would I permit myself to be a party to such acts?"

Malone became taut. "For the oldest motives of them all. Greed and revenge."

Moorehouse took a step backward. "You must be joking."

"Your election defeat was a little too much for the great Carter Moorehouse to handle. Your first and only rejection in life. You skulked back into your own world and started to brood. Before long all you could think of was getting revenge on the people who had spurned you, the blue-collar slobs who saw through your racist bullshit. And then there was the liberal press, or should I say the Jewish press, who helped sow the seeds of your defeat. You hated them all.''

Moorehouse's eyes widened with anger.

"When you were asked to oversee the money for the Unit you saw your opportunity. Anarchy in the streets, you had warned. You intended to make your prophecy a reality. You knew Zangline and Stanislaus from your election campaign. It was easy for you to have the Unit placed under SOD. Then you made your pact with Zangline and company. They could help themselves to the money, not all of it, but enough to make some middle-class cops happy. All they had to do was gather some Arab types around them and plant a few bombs around the city. The Israeli warehouses were high on your list of things to do. What better way to get even with the Jews than to expose their existence and to force them to remove their arms depots. Violence in the streets. Everything was going according to plan until Stanislaus and Eisinger got the hots for each other.''

"All right! That is quite enough.'' Moorehouse wrapped his towel more firmly around his hips and started to walk away from Malone. "I am going to place a call to the commissioner. Perhaps he can handle this in a compassionate way. You are a sick man, Lieutenant.''

Malone lunged at Moorehouse and threw him against the locker, bloodying his nose.

Moorehouse whipped around, staring with disbelief at the blood on his hands. He became enraged. "I'll see you dead for this, Malone. You hear me! Dead!''

"You will? Let me tell you something wise-ass. The kind of justice that you and your friends are fond of dishing out knows no distinction between rich and poor. It's a fucking two-way street, pally.''

Malone started to leave, hesitated, and spun around, throwing a right cross to Carter Moorehouse's jaw. Arms thrashing at his side, Moorehouse plunged backward into the locker and then slid to the ground.

28

Westy Stanislaus had rented a garage on West Eighty-ninth Street under the name of Frank McMahon as a safe house. From there they would begin the next and crucial move. In the neighborhood surrounding, Latin music blared from tenement windows. The flower boxes on each sill were empty save for soda bottles and cans. On the sidewalk men in T-shirts sat on crates playing checkers while a fire hydrant sprigged a steady stream for children to run through. A patrol car turned in off Columbus Avenue and cruised down West Eighty-ninth Street. One of the players looked up from the board. "*Maricon*," he muttered, glancing back down.

Inside the garage there were two flatbed trucks stacked high with scrapped automobiles, lashed to the beds by steel cables and secured on the sides by long metal slats fitted into the steel edges of the beds. Each of the scrapped cars was full of plastic explosives and the gas tanks had been topped off with gasoline. A pyromaniac's delight. An Econoline van with tinted plexiglass was parked behind the trucks.

Under a line of bare lightbulbs that hung from grimy S-chains, Ahmad Marku and Iban Yaziji were sitting cross-legged on a blanket that had been spread out over the floor. Five other Arabs surrounded them. They were cleaning Uzi submachine guns and talking in low tones, oblivious to the large black flies buzzing around them.

Zangline, Stanislaus, Kelly, and Bramson were sitting around a folding table playing seven-card stud. Aldridge Braxton and his sister were sitting on an army cot between the two groups watching television. Aldridge was busy swatting the flying pests with a folded magazine while Thea reached up to adjust the rabbit ears.

Chief Zangline had the deal. He shuffled the cards meticulously, his pitiless eyes peering through the veil of smoke, studying the face of each of his colleagues. Stanislaus, Kelly, and Bramson reveled in watching the light dim in other men's eyes. Zangline had conducted his own private investigation into their use of deadly physical force when they were assigned to the Six-six's Anticrime Unit. He had located three witnesses who had seen the cops throw the two fleeing muggers off the roof. He was also successful in tracing three of the throw-aways that they had used. All of them had been removed from prisoners at the time of their arrests and never vouchered. The prisoners never complained; it was one less charge. Zangline had decided that if any problems should develop because of the Unit's excesses or because of today's forthcoming action, Stanislaus and his pals were going to take the fall. Whitney Zangline was a survivor.

Each of the players were dealt two hole cards and one facing up. Kelly was high with an ace showing. Zangline anted and began playing by rote, as he contemplated the day's work which lay ahead of them, searching for a flaw in his carefully conceived plan.

They were to leave the garage at four-thirty in the morning and drive by a prearranged route to Anderman's warehouse in Queens. Detonators primed, six of the wrecked autos would be quickly off-loaded by means of the hoist in the rear of each flatbed and placed up against the walls of the arms depot. After a seven-minute time lapse, the explosion and mushrooming fireball would turn the warehouse into a smoldering hole in the ground. They would then leave Queens and drive into Harlem and El Barrio where the rest of the junk would be randomly detonated, precipitating riots. Thing about those people, he thought, was that they can always be counted on to burn and pillage; all you have to do is give them a little incentive. The arms depots would then be exposed and the Israelis would be forced by an outraged public to leave the country. Moorehouse had even suggested to Zangline that one or perhaps two dead Arabs left at the scene of one of the explosions would add authenticity and also lay a false trail of responsibility. Zangline thought that that was an excellent idea. The Moslem Brotherhood and Black September made perfect scapegoats.

The prophecies of Carter Moorehouse's failed campaign were about to come to pass. And, in a certain way, Zangline, too, was about to have his revenge on those who had stymied his drive to become PC. He saw an irony in it all. He was the catalyst for Moorehouse's revenge. And as the commanding officer of SOD he would be called upon to squelch the riots that he was about to start.

Moorehouse had promised each of them a payday of two hundred thousand dollars for today's action. A cop's dream —the big score. He had heard about this small country in Europe—Liechtenstein—where they had numbered accounts and, unlike the Swiss, asked no questions and kept their mouths shut.

The plan called for Bramson and two of the Arabs to ride in one truck, and Kelly and two other Arabs to ride in the other. Zangline, Stanislaus, and the remainder would ride shotgun in the van, ready to take out any interference. He could see no flaws in the plan. But just in case, he had made escape contingencies. Whitney Zangline was indeed a cautious man.

Tossing each player their last card down, Zangline's eyes darted over to the Braxtons and then flashed back to meet Stanislaus's waiting stare. "Now is a good time," Zangline said in a low voice, picking up his hole cards, studying them.

Stanislaus acknowledged his direction with a fitful flicker

326

of his eyes and an evil little smile. He gathered up his hand and tossed it into the center of the pot. "I'm out."

Westy Stanislaus pushed away from the table and got up. Walking over to the van, he slouched against it and lit a cigarette. He had not been home and therefore was not aware that his apartment had been the subject of a search warrant. After leaving the SOD compound the three policemen had driven to Manhattan and waited while Marku and Yaziji gathered up the Braxtons. During the ride to the heliport he kept checking for a tail. He had that feeling that people were onto them. But the traffic was too damn heavy and he could never be sure.

One of Marku's men had been waiting for them on Rabbits Island. He wondered suddenly why the hell it was called an Island. There was no water. Just a large tract of land that was shaped into a pair of rabbit's ears by the railroad tracks of the L.I.R.R. yards in the valley between Skillman Avenue and Northern Boulevard and connected to the outside world by the Honeywell Viaduct in Long Island City.

He thought of Sara and became angry at himself for still missing her. He had never known a woman like Sara. He had been used to the bimbos that he picked up in the singles' bars. Sara was different, so different. She always smelled nice, and her face was always made up to look natural, like she wasn't wearing anything on it. And there was that special way that she had of looking at him, that gleam that told him that she wanted him, that he was her special man. He could never fathom what an elegant lady like her saw in him. One day when they were alone in his apartment he asked her. "Because you're so cute. You're my own big goy," she had teased.

They had been together only three times when she had asked him playfully if he enjoyed doing certain things to women. "No real man does that," he had said. She pushed her naked body close, running her tongue over his lips and a hand through his hair. "I would love if you did it to me," she

327

said, taking his head into her hands and guiding it down her body. "I'll teach you how."

He had given up everything for her and she had betrayed him. He began to vent his sudden rage by heeling the van's tire. She had used him. She had stolen the list, never really left Anderman, and laughed when he asked her to marry him. How could he have been so fucking stupid? He was glad that she was dead, glad that he had done it. It had given him pleasure. He would always remember the horrified look in her eyes, her painful moans as Bramson and Kelly held her and he slowly, methodically pushed the curtain rod into her battered body. And she still didn't talk, he thought, with grudging admiration.

Looking up from the oil-stained floor, Stanislaus noticed the Braxtons sitting on the cot with their heads together, whispering. He pushed away from the van and moved around to the rear where he opened the door and climbed inside. He bent to make his way into the tool chest and flipped open the lid. He reached inside, moved some canvas about, and took out one Ingraham submachine gun. He opened the tubular stock and then reached back into the chest and took out one fully loaded magazine and a stubby, bulbous silencer. He inserted the magazine into the weapon's housing and attached the silencer to the end of the barrel. He then put the gun into a paper bag and climbed out of the van the same way he had entered.

"Just look at those slobs playing cards as though they haven't a care in the world," Aldridge Braxton said to his sister. "And those foul-smelling Semites, picking their noses, impervious to all these goddamn flies."

His sister whispered, "When we leave this place they are going to be too busy to keep constant watch over us. At some point they are going to be distracted, and that is when we will get away from these madmen."

"Thea, I am getting bad vibrations from these people. I wish to hell . . ." He froze as he saw his sister's head explode into gore. Before he was able to utter a sound his body was thrust up off the cot with his outstretched arms flapping through space. For the brief part of a second Aldridge Braxton had the sensation of being spun through a dappling light, and then there was nothing.

24

The locker room in Midtown Precinct North smelled of moldy old sweat. Long benches lined the rows of lockers and old newspapers overflowed from the tops. Empty garment bags hung from hangers that were stuck into the air slots. Bleary-eyed policemen were busy exchanging their street clothes for the bag. Some of them donned their bulletproof vests, most did not; it was too hot to wrap your body in a furnace of Kevlar. The policemen reached into their lockers and took out their gun belts. When fastened around their waists, the hickory batons that were hooked around their revolvers swung freely, striking metal and wood and occasionally a kneecap. It was the same scene in every patrol precinct in the city: policemen suiting-up for another cursed late tour.

Tuesday was about to begin.

At fifteen minutes before the hour the First Platoon was formed into ranks in the muster room of Midtown Precinct North to receive their instructions and assignments for the tour.

The sergeant had called half the roll when the carriage of the teletype machine sprang to life, shattering his monotonous drone.

The urgent-message bell clanged, demanding immediate attention. The lieutenant strode from behind his raised desk to read the orders that were being ejected. He perused them, then tore them off the machine and started to assemble them

330

in consecutive order. He then walked into the muster room to address the platoon. "Gimmeya attention. We got some special orders for this tour."

The lieutenant's gaze slid over the platoon. Fidgeting stopped. He held the teletype sheets out in front and started to read. "Until further orders, routine calls for service are to be canned. We're directed to respond only to emergency calls involving life-threatening situations or to reported crimes in progress. Every member of the patrol force is directed to give continual and sustained attention to the search for the following individuals."

Descriptions were read. They were not read names, nor were they told that the people they were to look for were cops. There was a chance, they were told, that the people they were searching for might be accompanied by three or more Arab extremists. These people were wanted in connection with a breach of national security and were to be considered armed and extremely dangerous. Confidential information revealed that they would be heading toward Queens. Members were therefore directed to give special attention to bridges and tunnels leading into Queens, paying particular attention to two or more vehicles that give the appearance of traveling together. Under no circumstances were any efforts to be made to apprehend these individuals. If observed, their location and direction of travel were to be reported. Aviation would have helicopters standing by to follow them. Borough Task Forces had been mobilized and were standing by. Detective and plainclothes units were patrolling in unmarked cars.

"Look. I don't know what this is all about, but it has got to be a heavy. So protect your ass and follow instructions. If you spot these humps, lay back and report. Do nothing else."

He started to pace the length of the platoon and grinned lightly. "There is one more minor point that I want to cover. We expect sixty minutes to the hour on this one. No eighty-fives with the girlfriends." His eyes moved from face to face.

331

"Anyone got any questions?"

There were none.

"Take your posts."

Patrolmen Andy Jenkins and Juan Rivera walked out of the stationhouse with the rest of the First Platoon.

"Wonder what it's about?" Andy Jenkins said.

Juan Rivera raised his shoulders. "Who the fuck knows?"

They walked over to RMP 2356. Rivera went around to the passenger side and opened the door. He stabbed his nightstick between the seat and started to clean out some of the garbage. Andy Jenkins tossed his summons pouch and memo book on the dashboard and then slid in behind the wheel. "Ya'ever see any Arab extremists?"

"Naw. I useta screw an Arab chick from Fourth Avenue when I worked in the Seven-eight."

"She any good?"

"Her armpits smelled like an asshole."

It was ten minutes past the hour when RMP 2356 pulled away from in front of the stationhouse. Their first stop was Rocco's on Amsterdam Avenue where pizza and a six-pack were waiting for them.

The ramparts were manned. Men were stationed on the roof, at exits and windows. Anderman had fought this kind of war before and knew how to prepare. His office had been converted into the message center for the coming battle. Radios bristled with messages in English and Hebrew. Maps of the city were spread over tables and chairs, every conceivable route to the warehouse outlined in red. Crash cars had been dispatched to prowl the streets with instructions to intercept. He had combined forces with the police force he had been fighting.

Anderman moved about, shouting orders, making sure

that his people had taken up their positions in and around the warehouse.

Det. Gus Heinemann was manning one of the radios, logging every transmission, and between messages munching on Milky Ways. His Israeli counterpart was next to him, monitoring the Hebrew transmissions.

Detectives Davis, Johnson, and Stern were busy studying maps, ensuring that no routes had been overlooked.

Malone, McQuade, and Jack Harrigan were standing around Anderman's desk discussing the disposition of their forces.

"Has Harbor been notified?" Malone said.

"Why Harbor?" McQuade asked. "It would seem to me that we need men, not launches."

Malone held up a map and pointed. "Here is Manhattan Island. To the east, the East River; to the north, the Harlem River; south, the Upper and Lower Bays; the west, the Hudson. We know that their destination is here in Long Island City. Here at Newspoint, Brooklyn and Queens kiss each other. Zangline could load his circus onto a boat or barge in Manhattan and cut across to Brooklyn or Queens.

"Brooklyn is a borough of creeks and canals. The Spring Creek is a few blocks from here. And here is the Maspeth and the Gowanus." He held the map at his side and looked at McQuade. "I really think that we should notify Harbor and the Coast Guard."

McQuade acquiesced. He went over to the radio and made the necessary notifications. Anderman came over to Malone and laid a hand on his shoulder. "I have one of my helicopters standing by at Fort Totten."

"We have our own," Malone said, fixing his gaze on the map.

Anderman grinned, patted him on the shoulder, and walked away shouting something in Hebrew.

"What other precautions have been taken?" Malone asked McQuade when he walked back.

333

The Chief of Op told him that sniper teams had been posted around the depot. The bomb squad had a detail hidden in a building one block away. Temporary headquarters had been established inside the warehouse. The fire department had been notified and a hook-and-ladder company was on alert. St. Johns, Elmhurst, and Doctors Hospital were notified to have their disaster units standing by.

"Looks like everything has been covered," Malone said.

"Do you think there is a chance Moorehouse will call it off? Your visit might have put the fear of God into him," Jack Harrigan said.

Malone flared. "Wishful thinking. Moorehouse is a psycho who really believes that he is above the law. He thinks that he is leading a crusade against the infidels who caused his election defeat. Besides, I doubt that he could stop it even if he wanted to. These things have the habit of taking on their own form, building up their own momentum until there is only one way to stop them—by force."

Time passed and they waited, tensing with each transmission, straining to hear every word. Empty Styrofoam cups littered desks and radio panels, and a thick cloud of smoke wafted over the converted message center.

Malone was weary. It was three-thirty in the morning and the new day gave promise of being even longer than the last one. On an impulse, he picked up the phone and dialed Erica's number. It rang a long time before he heard her sleep-filled voice answer. He hung up.

RMP 2356 was parked in the shadows on Pier 90. Jenkins and Rivera were working on their second six-pack. They had spent most of their tour patrolling their sectors. Rivera had suggested that they pick up some more beer and go into the heave for a little R and R. Jenkins thought that was a good idea. It was going to be a long tour.

Rivera popped open the top and passed the can to his

partner. "I wonder what those guys did to generate so much heat? I can't ever remember the radio being so dead. It's eerie. Central must be shitcanning everything."

Jenkins gulped beer and belched. "Maybe they stole some secrets or something."

"Who gives a shit?" Rivera said, hefting his can.

"Didya hear what them humps in Congress did? They voted a special tax bill for themselves so that they don't have to pay any more taxes."

"So what else is new? Everyone knows that they're a bunch of crooks. Yet they keep gettin' elected. The people of this country are gettin' just what they ask for. A Congress full of pompous, low-life, theftin', scumbag, fag mother-fuckers."

"Yeah!" Jenkins bent his can in half and tossed it out the window.

"Hey? Didya hear why God gave women pussies?"

"No. Tell me."

"So men would talk to them."

Jenkins laughed. His eyes teared and he started to cough. "I like that . . . so we would talk to them . . . that's good." He was reaching for another beer when he noticed the two flatbed trucks speed past. "Hey? Didya see that?"

"What?"

"Them two trucks. One of them guys had on one of them head scarfs you always see them PLO dudes wearing on tele-vision."

"No shit? Let's have a look-see." Rivera gulped the dregs and tossed out the can.

RMP 2356 drove off Pier 90 and fell in behind the trucks, quickly closing the gap.

The radio car crept alongside of the trucks, the policemen feigning early morning doldrums.

Iban Yaziji was driving the last vehicle. Bramson was next to him and Marku was by the window. At the first sight of the police car, Marku tightened his grip around the Uzi which was on his lap. Bramson saw him tense and placed a calming hand over his. "They're just cops on patrol. No problem."

RMP 2356 inched past the trucks and made a right-hand turn into Pier 84. "Get on the horn. It's them."

Everyone in the converted message center was either sleeping, dozing, nodding, or staring at the walls. Malone had been staring for the past hour. He was tormented by the thought of another man possessing Erica. He lived in a world of men; he needed more—he needed her. And he lost her over one lousy phone call that he failed to make. He felt rotten.

He was just starting to nod when the sudden commotion caused him to snap his head up. His countenance was that of a man unsure of where he was, and of what was happening. He saw the men scurrying for the radio sets and plunged up off the floor and made for the map table.

"They've been spotted," Heinemann shouted.

"Where?"

"West Four-four and One-two Avenue, heading south. They're in two flatbed trucks that are loaded down with junked cars and it appears that they are being led by someone driving an Econoline van."

"Have all surveillance teams in the area close in. But tell them to lay back and do nothing," Malone said.

Men gathered around the map table. His gaze went to each one. He could see their excitement blossoming.

Malone bent over, fingering the map. After scrutinizing it for several minutes he began. "As I see it, there are three ways in which they can come at us. First, they take the West Side Highway to the FDR and over the Triborough Bridge and onto the LIE. They go west and exit at Van Dam. They'd be two blocks from here. Two: the West Side Highway to the FDR and then through the Midtown Tunnel," he traced the route. "They exit immediately after the toll and turn onto

Borden Avenue and make a left. They'd be here in less than a minute. Three, the West Side Highway to the FDR and over the Brooklyn Bridge and onto the BQE. They'd exit at Mc-Guinness Boulevard in Brooklyn and take McGuinness over the Pulaski Bridge and into our backyard."

"Before we make any moves against them we'd better make damn sure that they're isolated within a frozen zone," McQuade said.

"But where?" Malone said, studying the map.

"Aviation has them spotted," Heinemann piped. "Still proceeding south, just passing Three-four Street."

Starling Johnson poked the lieutenant. "We're getting real short on time."

Malone glared at him with a look that said, I know, and then returned his attention to the map. "Isolate inside a frozen zone—some area where they'd be boxed," he said as his finger prowled the map.

He jerked his head up and faced the Chief of Op. "We're going to have to have details at three locations. The Midtown Tunnel on both sides. If they come that way, we'll wait until they're inside and then spring both ends closed. The expressway. If they come that route, we wait until they pass the Greenpoint Avenue exit and then spring a blockade across the expressway between Greenpoint and Van Dam. The Pulaski Bridge. If they come through Brooklyn we wait until they're on the bridge and then choke off both ends."

"How many men do you think they have with them?" Anderman said.

"The radio car team that spotted them reported seeing three men in each of the two trucks. If they brought along four or five of Marku's friends plus the Braxtons, that would give them around fifteen people," Malone said.

"Five and fifty at each choke point?" McQuade said.

"Should do it," Malone said.

"I have to talk to the PC," McQuade said, as he walked over to the telephone on the desk and dialed. He cupped his

337

hand around the receiver as he talked. It was a short conversation. When he was finished, he went over to the radio and picked up the handset. "This is the Chief of Operations."

"Go, Chief."

"Signal ten-seventy-seven. Five and fifty at each of the following locations." When he finished his message to Central, McQuade telephoned Deputy Inspector Obergfoll and issued him specific instructions. A captain or above was to be assigned to command each choke point. Personnel to be concealed at least one block on either side of each choke point. When the suspects' route was definitely ascertained the point concerned would be notified. Personnel assigned at other locations were to remain thereat. The suspects might have divided their forces and could be coming at them from different directions. TPU and Borough Task Force Units were to take up positions around the warehouse.

The whirlybirds were now the department's eyes and ears; their assignment, to track the caravan without being spotted and report its direction of travel.

The surveillance vehicles on the ground began to close the gap between the air and ground. Throughout the city policemen responded to the Rapid Mobilization Plan. Vacant patrol sectors were added onto other sectors to provide maximum coverage with a depleted force; desk officers made the necessary adjustments on roll calls.

Inside temporary headquarters, Detective Heinemann manned the radio, calling out the coordinance.

The helicopter pilot's voice was loud and clear despite the static and engine noises: "Passing West Houston . . ." A short time later: "Chambers Street . . . Broad Street. . . . They're turning onto the Battery."

"We'll know soon enough," Jake Stern told the silent men.

Anderman tugged at the lieutenant's arm. He grabbed him by the elbow and walked him across the room to a corner. "Policeman. Listen to what I'm going to tell you. You are not going to be able to talk those men out of what they plan to do. They are fanatics. Greed might have been the catalyst for this whole thing, but the thrill of killing has become the reason. I have seen many such men. You are going to need my help. Police weaponry is no match for military ordinance. Uzi submachine guns can cut your police line to shreds. And who knows what other weapons they might have with them? Your people are going to die without reason unless you let me help.''

"We have shotguns and automatic rifles." A weak retort.

Anderman clutched his arms. "Don't be a fool! Let me call in my men. A precaution, nothing more.''

Malone knew that there was no time to argue. He also knew that Anderman was right. He went over to McQuade and pulled him from a huddle. When he finished whispering to the Chief he looked over to Anderman and shoved his thumb upward.

Anderman went over to the radio operator and spoke a few words of Hebrew. The operator wrote something on a sheet of paper and began to send the message.

Five minutes after Anderman's message was transmitted a twin-engine helicopter lifted off the pad in the center of Fort Totten. This craft had camouflaged markings and showed no identification numbers. Twin lights blinked from the rear. It rose slowly at first but then gathered momentum. When it had risen to a point parallel with the middle span of the Whitestone Bridge, it hovered a short time, and then set off on a compass heading of southwest.

There are many spans in New York City that jut across anonymous creeks and canals. The Pulaski is one. It arches across the Newtown Creek, binding Long Island City to the Greenpoint section of Brooklyn, and to McGuinness Boule-

339

vard, an artery that leads to the industrial heartland of the Borough of Kings. The most noteworthy thing about this bridge is its incredible view of the Manhattan skyline. This morning the outline was sharply defined against a backdrop of a purple sky.

The Econoline van drove off the exit ramp and stopped for the red light on the corner of McGuinness Boulevard and Humboldt Street.

The transmission from the department helicopter that was following the caravan was received simultaneously at Communications and temporary headquarters. "Subjects exiting the BQE at McGuinness Boulevard."

Inside the temporary headquarters, McQuade grabbed the handset. "Close off the Pulaski Bridge on the Queens side."

In Long Island City a line of police cars drove out of the schoolyard on Forty-ninth Avenue and went one block to Jackson Avenue where they snaked into position across the foot of the Pulaski Bridge. When the blockade was established there were three files of radio cars that were backed up by four Emergency Service vans.

On the Brooklyn side of the Pulaski Bridge everything appeared to be normal. Trucks were making early-morning deliveries; bundles of newspapers were stacked on curbs; bags of bread and rolls waited in grocery doorways; rattling milk cases could be heard off in the distance, morning sounds of a city not yet awake.

On cramped streets with names like Clay and Box and Commercial, radio cars idled, their crews lolling about and shooting the breeze, asking one question—What's it all about?

Westy Stanislaus looked into the rearview and saw the trucks struggling with the grade. "Come on. I wanna get this thing over with."

Zangline was in the jump seat. "Patience. We're almost there."

340

Stanislaus looked back at his passengers and saw that they were wearing kaffiyehs and cradling Uzis. Without headgear and guns they'd look like college kids in patched jeans and worn sneakers, he thought.

As the Econoline van peaked the brow of the bridge, Stanislaus's eyes widened with incredulity. He jammed on the brakes and lurched forward, gripping the wheel, leering at the barricade. Suddenly he threw open the door and leaped out, running back to the trucks.

Marku leaned out the window. "What's the trouble?"

"Police! We've been had," he shouted, pointing toward the crest.

The caravan had stopped.

Marku climbed down and ran up to the crest. He stood, defiant, shaking his fist down at the police. He turned back in time to see the police line draw across the Brooklyn side, choking off escape. Suddenly the retiring night was filled with the chilling cry to Jihad—war.

They held an emergency conference behind the Econoline van. Scared men, unsure of what had gone wrong, searching for a way out.

Kelly looked at Stanislaus. "Waddawe do now?"

Stanislaus flashed his eyes to Zangline. "It's up to you, Chief. We're with you all the way."

Zangline was shaken, his face drained. An adage came to mind: If you can't do the time, don't do the crime. He was too old to start over. There were no more chances, no more roads. If he could get himself out of this trap there might be a way out for him. There was no direct evidence linking him to any crime. He was working undercover, trying to ferret out bad cops, protect the security of the country. He had money, enough to last him the rest of his days. He looked at the men around him. "This is the big one. I say we go for broke."

Stanislaus reached out and opened the rear door of the van and climbed inside. He motioned to someone for help. Marku climbed in, and together they dragged up five cases to the edge. Stanislaus opened one and took out an olive-green tube that was about three feet long and cupped on both ends. "These babies are going to get us out of here."

"What are they?" Marku said.

"M-72-A disposable antitank rockets that'll take the treads off a Russian tank at fifty meters. Each one comes loaded with a sixty-six-millimeter shell."

Stanislaus squatted on the edge and held out the tube. He took less than a minute to show them how to use the weapon and then said, "There are six rockets in each case. Each vehicle will take one case with them. I'll lead in the van. I'll blast a hole through their line and we'll plow right through them. The warehouse is near. We'll detonate all the cars up against the depot and make a run for it in the van. We'll stick to the original plan, only now we will use the rockets instead of the cars. It'll have the same effect."

There was a moment when they stood in silence, each man contemplating his own future, and then, they clasped their hands together in the center of the group, and broke, each running to his vehicle, shouldering his weapon. For one fleeting second Edwin Bramson felt the urge to run the other way; to surrender. But he couldn't, not in front of his friends.

Capt. Jeffrey Sefton walked out from behind the police barricade, a megaphone in his right hand. He was a big man with impressive shoulders and a head of untamed hair. He wore no hat; he never did when he thought there was a chance that television cameras might record his heroic deeds for posterity and the promotion board. Peeved that his forthcoming act of bravery was not to be immortalized on film, the captain started his famous strut up the Pulaski Bridge.

"He sure eats this shit up," Police Officer Edmonds said.

"One of these days he's going to get his prick shot off," Police Officer Neale said.

They were slouched up against the side of their Emergency Service van watching the captain. Their shotguns were resting on their hips and their caps were pulled down to their brows. Rows of decoration bars were stacked up over their shields, symbols of their male pride.

Other policemen were gathered around their vehicles, not really caring about what was happening on the bridge. Scuttlebutt had it that this caper was nothing to get excited about. Just another talk-down; some asshole with an ax to grind.

Neale nudged his partner. "I sure hope they get this bullshit over with so I can get home on time. I wanna rap the old lady before the kids get up."

"Boy, do I know that feelin'. Sometimes after a late tour I'm so horny even the crack of dawn ain't safe," Edmonds said, lifting his cap and patting down his pompadour.

They watched as the three vehicles rolled over the crest of the bridge in a wedge formation. The van was on the point, the embrasures were down, the weapons thrust out, crosshairs zeroed in on the center of the barricade.

"Here. Comes. The. Bullshit," Edmonds said, reaching down the front of his pants and scratching his scrotum.

Captain Sefton raised the megaphone to his lips. "I am Captain Sefton of the Hostage Nego-"

The burst of automatic fire lifted the captain up off the ground and spun him completely around. He was dead before he reached the ground.

"Holy shit!" Neale shrilled, diving behind his van.

Two ear-shattering explosions sent policemen running for cover. Submachine-gun fire raked the police line. A radio car blew apart, and then another and another. The van carrying all the automatic rifles exploded. The center of the barricade had turned into an orange fireball. Policemen fled the conflagration. Veterans of the Bulge, Inchon, Tet, remembered their forgotten trades. They popped up from behind their cover to fire at the enemy and then ducked back down. Some fired and rolled away to a new position.

Edmonds and Neale were crouched behind their van.

"Ready?" Neale said.

"Let's do it."

They stepped out from behind their cover, pump-fired two rounds apiece, and ran back. The shotguns had little effect; the distance was too great. A few feet away from them, Sgt. Sam Nelson was crawling on his stomach over to a radio car. He reached up and opened the door and then bellied inside. He glanced up at the radio panel and thought how strange it looked upside down. He pulled down the handset and then tried to figure out which was the right switch. Praying that it was the right one, he pulled one out. "Aim for their tires!" he shouted over the loudspeaker. Bullets riddled the radio car, disgorging chunks of steel and slivers of glass; the fragments tumbled down on him. "Fucking humps can't take a joke," he mumbled, crawling back out.

On the bridge the approaching formation maintained its unrelenting field of fire. It crept down, moving closer and closer. The barricade had been turned into a flaming shambles. Cowering behind their van, Edmonds and Neale reloaded their shotguns. Edmonds pointed to the wire trash barrel on the bridge's walkway. "The garbage cans!"

"What about it?"

"Bottles."

They sprinted from their cover, running low, zigzagging. Slugs slammed into the ground around them. They made a headlong dive, rolling into the can and toppling it, littering the ground with all sorts of disagreeable debris. Lying prone, they rummaged through the garbage. Edmonds found an empty pack of Coke bottles still in its carrying case. They popped up off the ground and made for the van. A radio car behind them exploded in a violent blue flame. A wave of intense heat struck their backs as they ran, scorching their hair. They dived behind the van and fell to their knees, breathless. Edmonds unclipped a knife from his belt and pushed himself under the van. He opened the blade and started to dig it into the gas tank. He punctured the tank and it dripped gasoline. He increased the pressure on the blade, and increased the circumference of his wrist movement, enlarging the hole until the drip was a steady flow. Neale passed him the bottles and he quickly filled them. "Let's get the fuck away from here," Edmonds said, pushing himself out from under the van. As they ran for the radio car about twenty feet away, the van blew apart. Neale tripped over a body, regained his footing, and continued to run. They ran behind the car and Neale immediately ripped off his shirt and started to tear it into strips. He handed them to his partner who stuffed them into the neck of the bottles.

The van and two trucks had stopped in the middle of the downgrade and were spraying the barricade with automatic fire, preparing for the final assault. There was a large hole in the center of the police line. Stanislaus had waited until the flames had died down. Now he gave the signal to move out and the vehicles started the slow, inexorable advance, making for the hole in the barricade.

The police opened fire. Their bullets began to find their mark; miraculously none hit a gas tank. The front tires on the Econoline van blew up and the radiator billowed a thick cloud of steam. The van careened on its rims, thumping to the right and plowing into the side of the bridge, finally tearing out a section of railing.

Neale and Edmonds made their way around to the bridge cutoff on Forty-ninth Avenue. They sprang up from behind the stone balustrade, their arms cocked and the fuses burning. "Now!" Edmonds shouted. They hurled two molotov cocktails, and, then, in quick succession, tossed two more.

An avalanche of flaming gasoline and dense black smoke rolled across the bridge, engulfing the disabled van. The doors flew open and coughing men jumped out and began to run back to the trucks. Marku, Kelly, and Bramson saw them and leaped down from their trucks. They formed a line across the bridge, firing through the smoke to cover their retreat.

Charles Kelly was down on one knee putting a new clip into his weapon when a spray of slugs tore into his body. His Uzi clammered to the ground. The last thing he saw before he slumped over was his right eye dangling out of its socket, held by a twisted white cord.

Two more molotov cocktails exploded.

"Everyone onto the trucks!" Stanislaus shouted. "When the flames die we'll smash through them!"

They threw their weapons on first and then climbed up onto the bed; the first aboard turning and helping the next, extending a hand to a comrade. They squirmed between the flattened heaps of rusting junk, taking up firing positions, in their excitement forgetting the explosive nature of their cargo.

Westy Stanislaus looked out at the body of Charles Kelly and muttered an obscenity.

Edwin Bramson leaned around the skeletonized frame of a '77 Buick and launched a missile.

On the Brooklyn side of the bridge, Capt. George Macklin could not see what was happening in Queens, as the battle was out of sight, beyond the brow. But he could see the smoke, hear the explosions and gunfire. The radio bristled with urgent appeals for help from the Queens choke point.

"I wanna move my men out," Macklin walkie-talkied temporary headquarters.

"You will hold your assigned position, Captain." McQuade's transmission left no room for doubt or maneuver.

"Ten-fucking-four!" Macklin slammed the radio down over the hood of a radio car, venting his frustration. He dented the hood. He looked over his position and saw his men, their weapons at the ready, aimed at the bridge, tensing to go. He wanted to lead them in a valiant charge; to relieve the beleaguered choke point. Should he disobey a direct order

346

from the Chief of Op and give the word to go? He could be a hero. His picture would be on the PBA calendar. But what if he disobeyed and screwed everything up. After all, he did not know the whole picture. No! The smart move was to follow orders. He and his men would have to wait. There was nothing else for him to do but to listen to the din of battle and stare at the flames and smoke and smell the acrid stink of cordite that laced the air—and pray.

The fire on the bridge raged and both sides waited.

"My job is here, coordinating this fiasco," McQuade said to Malone inside the message center.

"And my job is out there," Malone said, leading his men from the room.

Anderman ran up to him. "Policeman, a helicopter is landing in the parking lot. Follow me."

"We don't need a chopper to go a few blocks," he said, tugging away.

"Listen to me, you thickheaded *goy!* Didn't you hear those radio messages? Your side is losing. When those flames die they are going to come at you with everything they have. And! They won't be isolated on any bridge. They'll be in the streets of Queens where there are houses with people in them, women, children, old people. It will be a bloodbath. Do you want that on your conscience?"

A strained silence followed.

Malone was haggard, the shadows on his face were dark, the lines deep. He knew that there was no more time for discussing. It was decision-making time. And that was what it was all about, the rank, the extra pay, department courtesies. To make decisions. Assume responsibility. He knew that Anderman was right. "Let's go."

Anderman led them through the darkened depot, past high mounds of crates and down aisles lined on both sides by phalanxes of oil drums. Anderman ran ahead of the group and rushed up to a metal door that had no knob or hinges. He punched in the combination on the box in the center of the door and it sprang open.

The helicopter had already landed; its propellers were revving down, sending up funnels of dust and papers off the Tarmac. The aircraft's hydraulic system was grinding the nose open.

Malone was aghast when he saw inside the belly of the craft. Five jeeps were lined up single file, each one mounting a GE Minigun M 134 multiple barrel Gatling-type machine gun. Antennas protruded over the rear of the jeeps; each one bore a blue and white pennant with the Star of David. Anderman's students were behind the wheels, manning the guns. A nameless man with an ugly scar was standing in the lead jeep, gripping the vehicle mount. He looked so at home, a warrior readying himself for battle.

"Anderman, you crazy son-of-a-bitch. Someone will have my balls over this!"

"So, we'll lie a little. We'll say that we were on a UJA fund-raising mission and got lost."

"Let's go!" Malone shouted.

They ran up the ramp and into the belly of the helicopter, spreading out and climbing into the jeeps. Anderman straddled into the last one. Malone waited until his detectives were safely aboard the pug-nosed vehicles and then climbed in next to Anderman.

Engines were started. The dull clang of rounds being rammed into chambers reverberated throughout the craft.

The nameless man with the ugly scar craned his head over his shoulder, making sure all hands were aboard the jeeps. When he saw that they were, he made a wide sweep of his arm, motioning the column forward.

The lead vehicle jerked forward and wrenched. The brakes squealed and echoed in the helicopter and then the first jeep surged forward and sped out, followed close behind by the others.

348

The column drove from the parking lot, turned left, and after fifty feet made a sharp right turn onto Borden Avenue, their proud pennants fluttering.

The Queens choke point was in a starfish-shaped plaza; five streets and avenues fed into a central disk—the bridge. A tall triangle-shaped building, a garage and a box-shaped building with orange letters on its side spelling: J & D BRAUNER— THE BUTCHER BLOCK, overlooked the bridge. The Hunters Point Long Island Railroad station was nearby, as was the Bloomingdale's warehouse.

Disaster units were arriving and people rousted from sleep by the explosions and gunfire peered from their windows and ran to safer parts of their homes. The braver residents of the neighborhood appeared on rooftops for a grandstand view of a battle.

Across the width of Jackson Avenue policemen ducked behind anything that would protect them. They tensed for the final onslaught.

Police Officer Edmonds was prone behind a steel chassis that had been blown off a car. His head rested on the stock of his shotgun. His stomach was snarled with cramps and flashes of cold sweat racked his body. His partner, Neale, lay six yards away, his intestines a seeping mass oozing from his stomach. In front of his position lay the body of Sgt. Sam Nelson, his legs still inside the burning radio car.

He thought of his wife and Kenny and Billy and Mary Ann and little Artie and wondered what they would do without him. He had made an Act of Contrition and was now asking God to let him survive. Without warning a warm mass exploded from his body, running between his legs and over his genitals.

A sudden whine filled the air. Two dull thuds were followed by loud explosions. He buried his head in his arms. The rockets hit the center of the police line. Shrapnel splin-

349

tered in the air. A radio car disintegrated in flames while another one leaped up in the air and tumbled down. A body cartwheeled through space. Heavy automatic fire raked the barricade. The carnage had begun again.

Edmonds forced himself to look. The two trucks were rolling down off the bridge, looming through the smoke and shimmering waves of heat. They reminded him of dune buggies from another planet with their flattened pieces of junk stacked one on top of the other. Flames burst from hidden guns; slugs whined incessantly. The men inside might prevent him from seeing his family again; these men had killed his partner. He pushed himself up off the ground into a standing position, his weapon firmly pressed to his shoulder. He leaned forward and pump-fired double action at the advancing enemy.

The trucks were halfway down the bridge. Westy's team was crouched behind piles of junk, firing their weapons at the police. Zangline was in the front seat of one of the trucks. He had smashed out the windshield and was firing his Uzi at the barricade. Not once did he give pause to think that they were policemen he was trying to kill. Ahead lay the enemy. He threw his Uzi down and picked up a rocket launcher. He assembled it and fired at the center of the line.

The men manning the barricade were no match for the combined firepower of the Uzi and the rockets. They started to back away from the barricade, firing as they went. Some ran, to put as much distance between themselves and the trucks as possible. People on the rooftops cheered and catcalled. The first train of the morning pulled into the Hunters Point station from Port Jefferson. The platform was crowded with bewildered passengers, none of them willing to climb the steps up into the street.

Jeeps appeared from nowhere. They were first seen speeding up Jackson Avenue. Men were at the guns, and others knelt beside the weapons and fingered belts of ammunition. Some people on the roof started to cheer. Others booed.

The column sped across the rear of the barricade and made a sharp right-hand turn into Hunters Point Avenue and then pushed its way around the left flank of the police line to take up a position in front of the barricade.

Ahmad Marku and Iban Yaziji were the first to see the fluttering pennants. "Jews!" Marku yelled.

The GE Miniguns laid down a withering field of fire. Tracers found their marks. The tires on both trucks exploded. They were stopped dead in their tracks. A fender flew off one of them and tumbled through the air. A hood was ripped from its chassis and tumbled down. Both radiators exploded. A smoke screen of steam covered the bridge. A loud hissing sound came from the trucks.

Whitney Zangline leaped down and knelt at the side of his truck. He wanted to run, to get away. But how? Where would he go? Perhaps if he could reach the barricade he could find some way to convince them that he was really on their side? Working undercover. A body toppled from the truck and splayed next to him. Run! Get away! Before he was like that lifeless mass with blank eyes. The creek! Dive in and swim away. He leaped up and ran for the railing. He gripped the top and started to push himself over when a hail of bullets cut his body in half. The top part toppled over into the water; the bottom crumpled onto the bridge.

Stanislaus and Edwin Bramson were together, hunched down behind a rusting '69 Ford. Bullets chunked around them. Stanislaus passed his friend a tube. He could see the fear on his face. "We're going to get out of this!" he shouted.

Bramson forced a smile as he readied his launcher.

When their weapons were assembled they looked at each other. Stanislaus nodded and they leaped from their positions and fired.

The jeep bearing the nameless man with the ugly scar blew outward and then collapsed in a fireball. Gus Heinemann was in the next vehicle, kneeling beside the gun mount, feeding the ammo belt up into the action body. The missile hit underneath the jeep causing it to bound up into the air and tumble backward into the barricade. Heinemann was thrown out. His body slammed down over the hood of a radio car and bounced off. Two policemen ran up and dragged him to safety.

The gunner in Starling Johnson's jeep lurched forward, clutching his throat. He knocked into the gun and toppled backward onto the ground. Johnson jumped up and took his place. Another jeep exploded. Missiles were exploding around them. Two jeeps were left. Policemen were running back to the barricade, joining the fight. Jake Stern and Harrigan were fighting on foot from behind a disabled jeep, firing their .38s and cursing at the enemy.

"You better send us help," Malone shouted into the radio. "We're catching hell from those rockets."

"I'll release the Brooklyn choke point," McQuade radioed.

"No! We'd be caught in a crossfire. Our own people would be firing down on us." As he talked, he was watching Anderman feed the ammo belt. He heard his name screamed and turned in time to see Starling Johnson spin in a swirl of blood and fall. He threw down the handset and bounded from the jeep. Slugs chewed up the ground as he ran. He leaped into Johnson's jeep and grabbed the machine gun. "You motherless cocksuckers!" he screamed, firing. Bo Davis was suddenly by his side feeding up the belt. He fired again and again, longer and longer bursts. The Gatling rotated on cue, the ejector spewing out a colony of casings. He sprayed the enemy with a devastating fire. The steel cables that had lashed the junked automobiles to the truck beds were snapped by bullets. No more fire came from the trucks. Clusters of slugs continued to chew up the junk as Malone maintained a relentless field of fire. The cargo started to shift. Then totter. One by one the stacks caved in. And then an enormous explosion shook the earth. Malone was pitched out of the jeep and slapped to the ground. Bo Davis was flung into the front of the jeep, his body smashing into the gear stick. Both Jake

Stern and Harrigan were thrown onto their backs. Anderman landed on his shoulders and rolled about four feet.

A fireball shot hundreds of feet into the air. And then a gush of water frothed down over the bridge, with a waterfall of muddy water that rushed down at the police.

It was quiet. Men began to stir. Malone looked up, slowly pushing himself up off the ground and feeling his body. He was covered with slime and mud and soaked with putrid water. He wiped his palms over his face and body. There was no blood, no holes. He was alive. He looked up at the bridge where the trucks had been. They were gone. In their place was a gaping hole. Girders twisted in the churned-up waters of Newtown Creek.

"It's over, policeman."

The voice came from the rear. He turned his head and saw Anderman lying on his back, looking at him.

"Over? It's far from over. We have our dead and wounded to care for. Notifications to make. And we had better concoct some plausible story to explain this madness. And then there is the matter of Mr. Carter Moorehouse. His ass belongs to me."

25

The first news team arrived at the One-oh-eight, the precinct of occurrence, about twelve minutes after the bridge
blew up. By 5:02 A.M. the front of the stationhouse was
jammed with camera trucks and police vehicles. Inside, the
muster room swarmed with shouting, pushing newspeople demanding information. The desk lieutenant was besieged by
cameras, microphones, and screaming reporters. Tell us what
happened. Who was involved? Is it true that it was the
FALN? What is your name, Lieutenant? Why are you with-
holding information?

"I wasn't there so I don't know what happened. You're
going to have to wait for the official release from the PC." He
had his orders. Direct from the Chief of Op. "Keep your
mouth shut until I tell you what to say," McQuade had told
him when he rushed into the stationhouse.

Policemen stood across the stairway leading to the upper
floors, and the stairs were crowded with more. Their orders
were to prevent unauthorized personnel from gaining access
to the upper stories—newsmen in particular.

In the second-floor detective squad the mayor, PC, first
deputy police commissioner, the chief of detectives and several State Department types were closeted with Malone and
McQuade and Anderman. They searched for a way out. It
was no longer possible to deny; they needed a cover story.
They argued and cajoled each other, while each man at-

354

tempted to protect his vested interest. The Israelis had to be left out of it, one of the men from State said. National interest demands it. The City must be protected from lawsuits, the mayor told them, kicking a chair and glaring at his police commissioner. Every telephone in the squad room was ringing. "Shut off those goddamn phones!" shouted the PC.

A detective scurried to take the receivers off their hooks.

"Our story has to be believable, plausible, and verifiable," McQuade said, looking over at Malone, who sat on the floor with his back against the wall, not paying attention or caring.

Malone was bone tired and his teeth felt numb and cold. His clothes were still wet and he smelled of smoke and cordite. He yearned for a bed, clean sheets, and to awake from this nightmare. But he knew that was impossible. He kept seeing the ambulances pulling up to the bridge; then the doctors and nurses working on the wounded and finally the neatly arranged rows of body bags. He would never be able to find peace until he got Moorehouse. He dwelled on it, searching for a way. He caught himself staring at the tiles, green tiles splotched with gray. Why did every stationhouse have the same ugly tiles and cinderblock walls? Why not oak floors and wallpapered walls? A little class to jazz up the shithouses. Maybe he would kill Moorehouse. Stalk him, learn his routine, and then waylay him. Four in the head with a .22 throwaway. It would mean twenty-five to life if he got caught, and a cop does hard, hard time. Was it worth the chance? He thought so today, but how would he feel tomorrow, or next week, or next year? He could hide in the shadows with a baseball bat. Savor the exhilaration of feeling his skull shatter; watch the blood spurt from his ears and flow from his eyes. Turn him into a living vegetable. Or he could employ all of his investigative skills and gather enough evidence to convict. I could investigate until hell freezes and still come up with zip that would stand in any court, he told himself. He would think of a way. He needed sleep and a clear head. Then the answer would come to him.

Yachov Anderman was sitting on the floor next to him, his knees pulled up into his chest, his chin resting on kneecaps.

"I'm going to miss Ancorie, policeman." A sad tone.

Malone looked sideways. "I'm going to be missing people, too."

The other men in the room were shouting. The PC and McQuade and the mayor wanted to cover up Zangline, Stanislaus, Kelly, and Bramson's complicity. If it were to become known the department would be destroyed, the PC reasoned, and the mayor and McQuade concurred. "But they committed serious crimes," a man from State said.

"So what?" the mayor said.

"I don't believe you people!" Malone shouted. "You want to make heroes out of those humps? Besmirch everything this job stands for? I'd vomit every time I'd walk into headquarters and saw their names up on those scrolls."

"And what choice do we have?" the PC shouted back.

"The truth is available," Malone said.

"Are you for real, Malone?" said the mayor.

"The department would be finished for all time. We would end up with civilians running the show. Every precinct, division, and borough command would have a fucking civilian politician running it. Everyone connected with this case would end up with his head on the chopping block. Including you," McQuade said.

"No way would I make martyrs out of them," Malone said.

"You're overruled, Malone," said the mayor.

"Why don't you fuck off," Malone said, turning and looking at Anderman.

"Shmucks," Anderman muttered.

"What will happen to you?" Malone said.

Anderman twitched his thumbs. "I'm a survivor. I'll be okay. We'll more than likely move the warehouses to different locations."

356

A detective walked into the room and looked around. He saw Malone and went over to him. He bent down and whispered to him. Malone leaped up from the floor and ran from the office. He threaded his way through the gauntlet of policemen on the staircase and plunged into the throng of reporters at the bottom, parrying the microphones with his hands and ignoring their questions.

He saw her standing in the 124 room. She looked beautiful and nervous as she stroked the edge of a desk. "Erica!"

She looked up and waved to him. They ran into each other's arms and began kissing each other with a mixture of affection and relief. The newshounds set upon them, shoving their damnable microphones into their faces and shouldering them with their endless goddamn questions.

He took her by the hand and led her through the crowd, searching for someplace where they might be alone—and talk.

The stationhouse broom—a thirty-year hairbag who in addition to keeping the stationhouse clean was the precinct's gofer—saw his plight and shouted to him. "Lou! Over here!"

Malone heard the unfamiliar voice calling him and looked over the heads of the crowd. He spied the broom standing in front of the door which led into the detention cells.

He pulled Erica through the throng of reporters, slapping their microphones aside, forcing himself to remain calm. He was not going to do what they wanted him to do. Lose his cool before the cameras. Explode at them. Tell them what he thought of them.

When he neared the empty jail cells, the broom pulled the steel cover open and let them slide past him, blocking the reporters with his body and slamming the door closed.

They were alone in a cold, gray hall of empty jail cells. Bare lightbulbs caged in their own tiny cells ran the length of the corridor. Steam pipes were high up on the walls.

For a moment they just stood there, a foot apart, staring

357

at each other, and then, as though on cue, they rushed into an embrace and kissed.

He was holding her again! He felt her press to him. He smelled her scent and felt her hair on his face, caught between their lips. Her tongue caressed his in that special, wonderful way.

He slid a hand over her back, satisfying himself that she was really there, that it was not a dream.

"Erica. I love you. I've been miserable. I know that I was wrong about not telephoning. Forgive me?"

"I've been a shit, Daniel. I'm sorry. I've been unable to sleep. I was sitting up in bed at five this morning watching TV when the news flashed on. My heart stopped. I just knew that you were involved. I prayed that you were alive."

She kissed him lightly on the lips. "I realized then just how much I love you."

He looked around for a place where they might sit down and talk. He took her by the hand and led her into the nearest cell.

The walls, the floor, the ceiling, the bars, the plank that hung down taut from the steel wall and served as the bed; everything was shiny battleship gray—everything except the stainless-steel toilet with a rounded lip and without a flush or a seat. Holding hands they lowered themselves onto the plank. His eyes were on her face, not daring to leave, afraid that he would wake and find her gone. He became conscious of the tumult beyond the door, a muffled din. He told her about the Eisinger caper, all of it, omitting nothing. Except Carter Moorehouse.

They sat in the cell for a time, he talking; she listening, gazing into his eyes, caressing his hands, occasionally bending to kiss them.

"I telephoned you this morning. When you answered, I hung up."

She reached up and touched his cheek. "I. Love. You. Daniel. Malone. You are my Lou."

He kissed her and began caressing her breast. She forced his hand away. She wore a faint smile, one that said, Men! She turned and swept her hand around the cell. "This place is hardly what I would call conducive to lovemaking. Where do you suggest that we do it? On the cold floor? Or shall I lie down on this wonderful slab of wood?"

They looked at each other and burst into laughter.

"Your place or mine, handsome?"

"Yours is closer." He held her face and kissed her. He then broke away and went to the door and cracked it, peering out.

It was 7:50 A.M.

The mayor was standing on the first landing. The PC, McQuade, the Chief of Detectives, the First Deputy Police Commissioner, and the men from State were at his side. Reporters and TV crews pressed against the cordon of police at the foot of the staircase. All cameras and microphones pointed upward. Despite the size of the crowd, there was an unbelievable hush; the only sounds were colliding microphones and shuffling feet.

The mayor put on his glasses and held the prepared text out in front of him. The cover story was ready. The mayor had spoken but five words when Malone was able to imagine the banner headlines around the world—LIBYAN HIT SQUAD FIGHTS TO DEATH ON PULASKI BRIDGE. The mayor told the assemblage that the United States Government had previously announced that it was in possession of irrefutable intelligence that Libya's Muammar al-Qaddafi had dispatched teams of assassins to this country to assassinate the president and other top leaders. He told them how upon receipt of this information the Intelligence Division of the NYPD had launched a massive search for these individuals. Deputy Chief Whitney Zangline had headed up the investigation.

Zangline and an elite unit of SOD trapped the suspects on the Pulaski Bridge as they were on their way with a cache of explosives to blow up the Con Edison generating plant on

Vernon Boulevard in Long Island City. This attack was to have been a diversion for the assassination of the United States Ambassador to the United Nations.

Malone knew that the newspapers would graphically detail the battle and tell how the beleaguered police had to call for help and how a special army unit stationed at Fort Totten was airlifted to their aid. Chief Zangline and three of his bravest men were killed in the final assault. The centerfolds would have photographs of the battle scene and picture spreads of the dead and wounded. Good ole Muammar al-Qaddafi. What would the Job have done without him? He was the perfect fall guy.

He had heard enough. Let them do whatever they think that they have to do. He had a life to live and he wanted to get on with it. He turned and motioned Erica forward. He pushed the door open, and holding hands, they slipped out unnoticed.

They made their way through the army of cars parked on the sidewalk to the Associated Food Store around the corner on Vernon Boulevard. Her car was double parked. She handed him the keys. "You drive. This way your hands will be busy and off of me." She chucked his chin and smiled.

"You don't trust me?"

"I know you, Daniel. You think it's always the right place and the right time."

"A little traffic foreplay can't hurt." He shrugged philosophically and opened the door for her.

"That's what you think," she said, sliding into the car.

He started the engine and was about to slide the transmission into drive when he suddenly remembered to check the time. He looked over at her.

"We don't have much time. There is something that I have to do this morning."

She could feel her stomach begin to knot, and all of a sudden she was scared.

She folded her arms across her breasts, cupping her elbows with her hands. "Oh? At this moment in our lives I thought there was nothing more important than us being together."

"Zambrano is being buried today. I want to be there. That means going to my place and showering and changing clothes. I'd like you to be there, too. He was a special man. A cop's cop."

She felt guilty for her anger and relieved that he had told her. She sighed. Leaning across the seat, she kissed him. "How much time do we have?"

"A couple of hours. It's at eleven forty-five mass."

"We can do a lot of lovin' in a couple of hours." She folded her legs under her and then took his hand from the steering wheel and guided it under her dress.

"I thought you were the one who said no traffic foreplay."

"Did I say that?" She pulled his hand out and slapped it back onto the wheel. "Let's go home, Lou."

The rows of policemen standing at parade rest in front of St. Anthony's Church seemed to stretch into infinity. They had come from as far as Texas to tender the final salute to Nicholas Zambrano.

A thick-set drum major led the cortege. His baton a dead-slow gait. Behind him marched the Pipers, their black-plumed bonnets bobbing above the heads of the onlookers. And behind them crept the hearse, locked between a wedge of motorcycles whose handlebars were aflame with flashing red lights. The limousines bearing the mourning family followed.

A dirge of bagpipes and the timbre of a single drum pealed over the unremarkable Park Slope neighborhood.

As the hearse slid into the curb in front of the church an anonymous voice barked the assemblage to attention. "Present! Arms!" Thousands of white-gloved hands snapped the salute while a lone bugler, standing on the church steps, blew Taps.

The flag-draped coffin was lifted from the hearse and hefted onto the pallbearers' shoulders.

Malone was at attention behind the mayor and other dignitaries. He swallowed hard, but the lump would not stay down. His cheek quivered, and he could feel the sting of tears as his gaze followed the coffin up the steps and into the church. He began to sum up the Eisinger caper. Starling Johnson dead. Gus Heinemann in the hospital with burns and multiple fractures. The Braxtons. Their bodies had been discovered around 8 A.M. when a neighborly wino broke into the garage searching for money to buy his morning bottle of Thunderbird. The nameless man with the ugly scar and David Ancorie both dead. And the others. Twelve policemen, not counting Zangline and his humps. There were going to be a lot of inspector's funerals during the next week.

The Eisinger case had proven to be a deadly little grounder.

When the coffin had disappeared inside the church the voice barked, "Order! Arms!"

The family was the first to start up the steps, assisted by policemen who had been assigned to aid them. After the family came the police brass, followed close behind by the men who had worked with Zambrano.

The little church filled quickly. Most of the mourners remained outside, with no chance but to hear the mass over loudspeakers.

The cardinal and Monsignor McInerney were waiting on the altar, police chaplains at their sides, their hands clasped in prayer.

A Mass of the Resurrection began. Mourners knelt in prayer. Malone remained seated, staring at the coffin, and recalled the moments that he had shared with Zambrano. But still he dwelled on how he was going to get Carter Moorehouse.

High in the choir loft, above the organist and the tenor, an old man sat alone, leaning over the pew. His eyes bored through the coffin. Carlo Fabrizio remembered a summer night long past. He could still feel the policeman's strong body covering his, protecting and saving him. "I don't forget, Nicholas. Your family will be taken care of; your death avenged," he prayed.

363

The cardinal walked down off the altar and circled the bier, sprinkling it with holy water. He intoned, "Eternal rest grant to him, O Lord." To which the mourners chanted, "And may perpetual light shine upon him."

Malone was leaning forward, his arms folded over the top of the next pew, his forehead resting on top of his arms. But he was not in prayer or mournful contemplation. He had finally thought of a way to get Moorehouse and was thinking out the best way to set his plan in motion.

Mass over, the ranks reassembled.

The pallbearers halted at the top of the church steps and the honor guard presented arms, while the bugler played the final Taps.

Malone was at attention, tendering a breast salute. His eyes fell on the faces of the onlookers—most of them strangers who happened to be passing by, the curious who always come to police funerals. They were neighborhood people who had never seen such a spectacle and most of them had tears in their eyes. It was a sight that they would never forget.

When Taps finished, the coffin was carried down and slid into the hearse. The cortege pulled away from the curb. When it had driven a block away from the church, the anonymous voice barked its last command. "Company! Dismissed!"

The ranks broke.

Policemen looked around at each other and renewed acquaintances. Many of them headed for the local gin mills where they would spend the rest of the day and most of the night drinking and talking about the Job and broads.

Malone moved among the thinning crowd looking for Erica. He had caught a glimpse of her in church, but then was unable to locate her when he was filing out into the street. He saw many faces that he recognized; nameless men who had crossed his path somewhere in the Job; some of them required a nod, some a meaningless How'r'ya, and some were to be ignored. He saw her standing in front of the church talking with Bo Davis and Janet Fox. The detective and his girlfriend were holding hands. He wondered if they were coming out of the closet. Sometimes 85s have a way of becoming more. He started to make his way over to them when he spied the man he was looking for. The man who was going to be his agent for revenge.

Carlo Fabrizio was being ushered toward his limousine by a phalanx of bodyguards. Up until that moment Malone was not sure how he was going to handle things when he saw Fabrizio, but as he watched his people make a path through the crowd, he knew exactly what he was going to do and say. He made his way over to the bodyguards and intercepted them in front of the open door of the limousine. Tony Rao nodded to him. He made a move to enter into the phalanx but was blocked by four mean-looking men, one of whom he recognized as the bouncer from the Nestor Social Club. Fabrizio grunted to let him pass.

"I want to talk."

"About what?"

"Our dead friend."

Fabrizio made a guttural sound which Malone took to mean assent. They walked away from his men and strolled along the curb, Tony Rao and three of the bodyguards close behind. Fabrizio clasped his hands behind him and looked downward at the street. "What's on your mind?"

"Carter Moorehouse had Zambrano killed and he is going to walk."

"You telling me the truth?"

"I wouldn't bullshit you about something like that."

"Why is he going to walk?"

Malone raised his shoulders and arms in a gesture of helpless frustration. "Because he is rich and because the people who might have testified against him are dead."

"Why you telling me your problem?"

"Because the grapevine has it that you owed Zambrano."

"That was a long time ago."

"Some debts can never be canceled."

Fabrizio made a jeering hiss through the nose. "You're beginning to sound Sicilian."

"Moorehouse entered our world uninvited. Your world and mine, a world where we got our own set of rules. Rules that civilians could never understand; but rules that you and I understand. They keep us from becoming complete animals. He came and killed our friends, yours and mine, and now he thinks he is going to prance back into the good life unharmed. It shouldn't be allowed to happen."

Fabrizio regarded him slowly. "You asking me to have Moorehouse whacked?"

"Don Carlo? I'm a cop! I would never ask anyone to take a human life. You should know that. It would be a violation of the *Patrol Guide*."

"Of course you wouldn't."

Malone started to walk back toward the church.

"Seeya 'round, Don Carlo."

Carlo Fabrizio's lips came together in a thin line. "*Ciao, Malone.*"

Malone and Erica stood in front of the church watching the last mourners leave. He felt an obligation to be the last. Bo Davis and Janet Fox had left some fifteen minutes earlier. They had gone back to her apartment to spend some time together before he left to catch the 5:18 to East Meadow.

"Who was that man I saw you talking to?"

"Just an old friend of Zambrano's. I hadn't seen him in a long time and wanted to say hello."

The crowd was gone, and the Brooklyn street had retreated back into its normal state of oblivion. A sanitation sweeper was roaming the gutters for litter. He saw an ice-cream parlor on the other side of the street, a block away. "May I buy you an ice-cream soda?"

Her eyes were wide. "Oh yes! A black-and-white with loads of whipped cream and sprinkles and a cherry. And then I want to take you home and work off all those wonderful calories."

They wrapped their arms around each other's waist and started to cross the street, leaning into each other, laughing and kissing. A radio car cruised past them. The recorder recognized Malone and tossed him a two-fingered salute. "Howyadoin' Lou?"

"Great. Just great."

EPILOGUE

An August sun beat down on the boats leaving their slips in Sheepshead Bay. Charter boats crowded with fishermen anxious to test their skills and pleasure boats manned by weekend sailors rushed headlong to meet the open sea.

Burly men cast off the lines on the *Anthony Joy*. The thirty-foot cruiser inched her way out of her slip. Once free, she followed in the wake of the miniature armada, careful to stay far behind. In the Lower Bay she changed her course and headed out into the Atlantic, her bow slicing the blue green water.

Men were stationed fore and aft, searching the horizon for signs of another ship as the shoreline sank to nothing.

Tony Rao was at the helm. He called to one of the deck-hands to take over and then made his way below deck, followed close behind by four sullen men.

Carter Moorehouse lay on the floor of the cabin. Heavy chains curled his body and his mouth was filled with a mound of gauze. His panic-stricken eyes begged for mercy and his desperate grunts went unanswered.

"Bring 'im topside," Rao ordered.

Kicking and struggling against his bonds, Carter Moore-house was carried topside and unceremoniously dumped on the deck.

Tony Rao stood by and watched as weights were attached to the chains.

368

Moorehouse continued to struggle.

"Make sure those things don't come off. He's gotta disappear without any trace."

"This guy ain't never comin' up," said a deckhand.

Rao bent to examine each weight, checking that it was secure to the chains. Satisfied, he stood up. "Toss him in."

Carter Moorehouse's fight continued unabated as he was lifted up off the deck. His twisting body crashed into the water and sank into the cold darkness.

Rao stood watching as the relentless sea covered all traces of his turbulent entry. He walked over to the deck freezer and took out a can of beer. He popped the tab and tossed the sliver of aluminum over the side. From far below, the last batch of air bubbles rushed upward to meet the boat's wake. Only the cries of sea gulls filled the heavy summer air.